George Cruikshank, George Mills, Colin Rae Brown

The Beggar's Benison

A hero without a name but with an aim - a Clydesdale story - Vol. 2

George Cruikshank, George Mills, Colin Rae Brown

The Beggar's Benison
A hero without a name but with an aim - a Clydesdale story - Vol. 2

ISBN/EAN: 9783337195373

Printed in Europe, USA, Canada, Australia, Japan

Cover: Foto ©Andreas Hilbeck / pixelio.de

More available books at **www.hansebooks.com**

THE

BEGGAR'S BENISON.

THE

BEGGAR'S BENISON:

or,

A HERO, WITHOUT A NAME; BUT, WITH AN AIM.

A CLYDESDALE STORY.

ILLUSTRATED BY UPWARDS OF 300 AMATEUR PEN AND INK
SKETCHES.

IN TWO VOLUMES.

VOL. II.

CASSELL, PETTER, & GALPIN,
LONDON AND NEW YORK.
1866.

GLASGOW
PRINTED BY ROBERT ANDERSON,
85 QUEEN STREET.

LIST OF ILLUSTRATIONS

IN VOL. II.

THE BEGGAR'S BENISON.

CHAPTER XXXI.

INTRODUCTORY DOGGERELS.

Great London!—now thy spires I view,
    Thy streets, thy slums, thy squares;
Where Christian Plutus leads the throng,
    And none for others cares!

Here, Dives feasts with Lazarus,—
    Here, Beauty hugs the Beast,—
Here, Wisdom and Philosophy
    Join Folly at the feast!

Huge changeable Kaleidoscope!
    Vast world within a town!
Yet, after all, thou art at best,
    A world turned upside down!

                  The Goosedubbs Poet.

"HOME again!" I exclaimed to myself, as the North Foreland, on our "port," and Margate Sands on our "starboard," received us into their embraces, and the colour of the water became yellow instead of blue, and passengers began to have their "traps" brought on deck, and to assume hats instead of caps, and to dress more dandily than they had done for many a day, while rewarding stewards with gratuities for having been attentive to them during the dreary days and nights they had been "cabined, cribbed, confined" in close berths, suffering sea-sickness and nausea.

"Home again!—but not the youth I was, when, some fifteen years ago, or more, I left the Clyde, full of hope, and vigour, and activity; but still hale and hearty, and as keen and determined as ever to go a-head!"

A 2

As I sailed up the Thames, and viewed its cultivated banks on either side, I thought I had never seen a happy land till now. It was on an autumn forenoon; the tide was flowing, and it was nearly high water; all which circumstances added to the beauties of a locality which, of itself, possessed wondrously delightful and changing scenes.

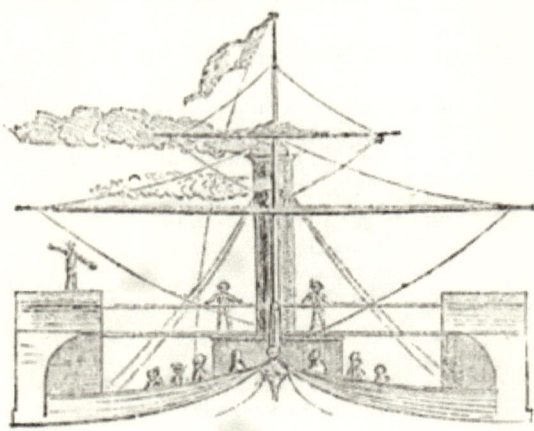

It was altogether different, too, from anything I had seen before. Even the Clyde, with its mountains and loughs, dwindled in my recollection. There, nature still asserted her ascendency; but here everything appeared to be formed by cultivation, and accumulated riches. "There were nae hills and nae heather," to be sure, as the Highland laird complained to the captain of the Leith steamboat; but the absence of these was compensated by the numerous elegant villas that dotted the undulating banks, with their beautiful variety of umbrageous luxuriance, the latter again dividing agriultural fields from pastoral meadows, and mansion houses from hamlets.

At last our moorings were reached, where the steamer was made fast to them, and her "biler" blown off, when everything became calm, with the exception of some little stir that was made by the custom-house officers, whilst examining baggage, in the performance of their duty.

This scrutiny was, however, soon got over, and in a short time, with my baggage, I was being trotted along the rattling lanes and streets of London, while reading all the names above the shop doors, and amusing myself with their variety and peculiarity. These shops seemed to contain everything, and in profusion. Here were rich suits of clothing for gentlemen, and gaudy dresses for ladies, displayed on lay figures, according to the respective sexes they represented, inviting with their painted faces, and unmeaning staring eyes, the passers-by. There, were beautiful articles of furniture that would have stocked a palace, instead of an ordinary house; while, everywhere, there were articles of jewellery and plate that one could have supposed to have exhausted the mines of Potosi, or the Ural Mountains, to produce them.

Such a city, to be sure, and such a throng!—what a stream of human beings all hurrying to and fro, as if each had a last undertaking to perform, and a last five minutes to perform it in. Here every one was something, and yet nothing—an atom that cared for himself, and yet was uncared for by the other atoms around. Had twenty of these atoms dropped down dead, the circumstance, for a moment, would have made a ripple in the stream, but in another moment, that stream would have been flowing uninterruptedly as before. I never felt myself to have previously been so much in a position that proved my own littleness. Including my baggage, the hackney coach, the Jehu, and the "hosses," I was literally a mere fact, and that was all!

On arriving at St. Paul's Coffee-House, to which hostelry I had been recommended by a fellow-passenger, I engaged a bed-room, where, having deposited my traps, and refreshed myself with a "scrub," I descended to the coffee-room—a large hall on the street level, from which it was entered, with two large bay windows, where I found numerous individuals sitting around, enjoying their solitary dinners, seemingly to their satisfaction.

This description of domesticity was quite different from what I had been accustomed to; it looked so mean, and yet so independent. Here, one was devouring his soup, while another, quite opposite, and at the same table, was sipping his wine. There another was gobbling his chops, while his neighbour was picking his teeth. And yet not a word passed betwixt them: the waiter, with stereotyped mannerism, being the only medium of communication, when it was necessary that intimations should be made, such as "gentleman opposite, Sir, will take *Times* when you are done," or "*Globe*, Sir, when you are finished, for gent at window," &c., &c.

Being uncertain what to do, I sat down at one of the tables, which, being re-

marked by one of the waiters, he slipped over to me, and probably, assuming from my looks that I was hungry, addressed me as follows:—"Dinner, Sir?—soles, eels, cod's-head-and-shoulders, salmon, roast-beef, roast-mutton, boiled beef, boiled mutton, jugged hare, roast fowl, and beef-steak pie!"

Having uttered this catalogue of good things, he stopped short, and looked me imperturbably in the face, whilst I, not knowing what he meant, merely replied, "Well, what about it?"

"About it?—yes, Sir!" said the waiter.

"What's your meaning?" I retorted imploringly, while all the munching and sipping gentlemen cast their eyes on me and the waiter.

"Meaning, Sir; yes, Sir!" continued the latter, "Oh! I beg your pardon, Sir—I mean, will you please to dine?"

"Dine?" said I, while the waiter's kind intentions at last dawned upon me, "Well, I don't care though I do—what would you recommend?"

"Recommend, Sir; yes, Sir!" answered the waiter, "soles, very fine; cod's-head-and-shoulders, very fine; salmon, very fine."

"Salmon from Scotland?" I inquired.

"Scotland?—yes, Sir!"

"Then bring me salmon."

"Salmon; yes, Sir!—roast-mutton, very fine—from Scotland too!"

"Well, bring me mutton likewise," I replied rather impatiently, while hoping that the waiter would now relieve me of his presence, for no other reason than that the eyes of the company should be averted from me, some of the gentlemen, as I thought, being rather inclined to titter.

In this expectation, however, I was mistaken, for the waiter continued in his old sing-song style—"Sweets, Sir? —apple-pie, cranberry-tart, rice-pudding, plum-pudding!"

"Oh! any of them you like," I cried in desperation, while my cheeks were like fire.

"Like, Sir; yes, Sir," answered the waiter, and at last relieved me of his presence; while, shortly after, I heard him bawling at the door which led to the kitchen, as I supposed, "Biled salmon, to be followed by roast mutton, and cranberry tart, for bed-room number *heighteen!*"

At this moment a gentlemanly looking man entered the appartment, and taking his seat at the same table, and right opposite to me, was immediately addressed by the waiter, and in the same monotonous tone as before, while recapitulating his bill of fare.

The stranger heard him patiently to an end, and then quietly naming a plain dish from the catalogue, laid his hand upon a newspaper that was on the table, and proceeded to read, but only after having said to me, with an accent that proclaimed him to be a Scotsman, accompanied by rather a winning smile, "I hope I am not depriving you of this?"

"Not at all," I replied, and then I went on to say to myself, "well, here is something like manners at last!"—for up till this moment nothing approaching to this little act of civility had passed betwixt any of the other guests, everything being on so very cold, frigid, stiff, and selfish a style, as seemingly to forbid even the idea of such an extent of sociality.

Nor did anything that I observed that afternoon go to improve my ideas of English tavern manners; for after my courteous neighbour opposite, who formed the small exception to my remarks, had partaken of his dinner, which he washed down with a simple draught of pure water—that is, if London water be pure—and had taken his departure, with a slight bow that was quite winning, I had cause to observe an instance of striking eccentric sensualness, that I expect is alone peculiar to a London atmosphere.

It was illustrated by the proceedings of an elderly, fat gentleman, who drove up to the door of the tavern in a splendid cabriolet drawn by a magnificent long-tailed horse, and attended by a gold-laced tiger.

Having descended from his vehicle, which then drove off, he entered the coffee-room, and took his seat at a table placed in a snug corner of one of the bay windows, and which had been kept sacred by the waiter, by means of a plate turned downwards. There, without requiring to speak a word— silence seemingly being a privilege that he duly estimated —he got a table-napkin arranged round his neck and over his breast, by said waiter, but during which process not even a grunt escaped from him. A pint of bright sherry, evidently of a superior vintage, was next placed at his right hand, and an unused copy of the evening paper at his left one—both of which vinous and literary supplies he proceeded to address himself to, only to be interrupted by his soup, and his fish, and his joint, as they were successively placed before him, and which, consequently, only allowed him to sip and to read by snatches, but which variety of good things he seemed to enjoy amazingly.

The old gentleman then had his sweets, followed by some preparation of cheese, to restore his palate for a bottle of ruby

bright port that was now placed before him, along with fruits and filberts, and then, oh! what a sloppering, and cracking of shells, and gulping of port—through the glass containing which, he ever and anon preliminarily peeped with knowing eye, so as to observe the beeswing.

At last the smacking and cracking, and also the bottle of port, came to an end, when over he toppled into a pleasant snooze, which was only broken by the great bell of St. Paul's chiming five o'clock, and his cabriolet with the gilded tiger again driving up to the door, into which he now scrambled, and so vanished.

As for myself, after moralising on the event, which convinced me that there were various descriptions of selfishness in this world, and displayed in various ways, I finished my pint of sherry, and walked out, to be guided in a ramble by a small map of London which I carried in my hand, and a good Scots tongue, in case of necessity.

With these I managed my way pretty well, although London was a thoroughly strange place to me. I wandered along Fleet Street, admiring the shop windows and other gratuitious exhibitions of a like nature, so profuse in the great metropolis. I passed along the Strand to Charing Cross; thence down by the Admiralty, the Horse Guards, the Treasury, and so on, to Westminster Hall and the Abbey, till I reached an entrance hall door, where something like a well-bred crowd was standing, to see a number of gentlemen enter, some of whom arrived by means of walking and some by carriages, in which occasionally were elegantly dressed ladies, who did not alight like the gentlemen, but drove off again in the vehicles.

Amongst the arrivals, I was struck with the appearance of my elderly fat friend who had dined, so gratifyingly to himself, at the bay window of the hotel, and who was now all alive and active, as he dropped from his cabriolet and toddled along the passage that led inwards.

I now inquired at a bystander what important gathering this was, when he informed me it was that of the House of Commons, and that the gentlemen I had observed were honourable members pouring in— a rather interesting debate, on an important subject to the nation, being expected to take place that evening.

Unless I had been told that the gentlemen walking into this lobby were Members of Parliament, I confess I would never have guessed them to have been such, for although a few were decidedly good looking, and gentlemanly in their appearance, the generalty of them more resembled decent clerks, or honest shopmen, or respectable schoolmasters, than what they were: some having under their arms rolls of paper, or in their hands parcels of books, or sticking out of their pockets, petitions; all of which had a considerable resemblance to the commodities that pertain to the worthy professionals I have named. There were likewise a number of totter-

ing and seemingly doted old gentlemen, who I thought
would have been better at their firesides than where they
were; and not a few mere youths, or, as we would denomi-
nate them in Scotland, "laddies," who apparently looked upon
the House of Commons as a very good sort of lounge, or club.

I felt a desire to witness the debate, and having learned
from my informant that I might obtain this gratification by
the exercise of a little patience and the payment of half-a-
crown, I pressed my way along a passage that was pointed out

to me, and up a dark, narrow,
and crowded staircase, till
I arrived at a door, through
which I was admitted, after
a lapse of about half-an-hour,
to a gallery, where I found
myself in the presence of the
assembled Commons of Eng-
land, in full debate, the
scene being something like
that of a bear-garden, for
many vociferous and angry
members were on their feet
at once, and the Speaker, with
stentorian voice, was calling
out "order, order;" while
not a few honourable gentlemen, by way of supporting
the Speaker, were bawling
"chair, chair," and "hear, hear," thereby adding, as I thought,
more to the disorder than otherwise.

During this period, we in the gallery were under the strict
surveillance of the half-crown recipients, who, the moment
any one of us, carried away by the excitement of the members,
smiled, or made a remark to his neighbour, or stood up, to
see to more advantage the *melée*, would order him at once
to be quiet, or to be seated, as the case might be, so that we
looked more like a parcel of quakers, staring a company of
comedians, while enacting a farce, out of countenance, than
an audience of free born Britons, witnessing unrestrainedly
the proceedings of their representatives, and for which they
had paid full admittance money.

This sort of drama, although new to me, was somehow or other not strange, and on inquiring the reason why, in my own mind, I found it was because the squabbling had a resemblance to what used to go on, in my infantile days, in the Goosedubbs, on the occasion of some of the crowded social meetings pertaining to the locality, with this difference, that while the members of either regarded each other with equal malignity—so far as expression of countenance could reveal—there was a modification here in the expression of speech. For instance, in the Goosedubbs, we called a spade, a spade; but in the House of Commons, they gave it a very round-about name, so that when one Member wished to insinuate that another was bouncing, he did it in such a way as follows:—"The honourable Member has made an allegation; well, all I have to say is, that any alligator may do so!" while shouts of laughter, and cries of "hear, hear;" or "oh! oh!" saluted the vile attempt at a pun.

The scene which had continued fully five minutes, at last moderated down, and the debate then flowed on monotonously and drowsily, so much so, that most of the Members composed themselves to sleep, and, conspiciously so, amongst them my elderly friend, who had dined at St. Paul's Coffee-House.

I now saw there was to be no further excitement that evening, so, after giving two or three yawns, I left, heartily tired of the House of Commons, and made my way to the House of Lords, where I found a very different description of discussion being carried on, and though, perhaps, a little dull, still not devoid of interest.

What the debate was about, I do not at this distant period remember; indeed, I did not pay any particular attention to it, what interested me being more the manners and conduct of the peers towards each other than their eloquence. I was deeply impressed by this fact, however, that there was a wide difference betwixt the characteristics of the House of Lords and those of the House of Commons, as well as the Houses of the Goosedubbs!

On the adjournment of the Lords taking place, I left the precincts of St. Stephens, after amusing myself by observing the Members of the Upper House drive off in their carriages —the most splendid of which, I thought, belonged to the burly, shovel-hatted gentlemen, who wore black silk aprons, and rejoiced in the title of Spiritual Peers.

All these prelatical magnates, I observed, had each two flunkies, who stood with long staffs at each side of their carriage doors, and as the respective equipages drove off with these tall gentlemen standing abreast of each other on the rumbles, I wondered if the fashion was followed by the bishops who lolled within, in imitation of their meek and lowly Master, who, while on earth, had not whereon to lay His head. Regarding this, however, I give no opinion.

Amongst those who left the house, and by the principal door, I observed one gentleman whose face was familiar to me. It was that of the well-bred stranger who had dined at the same table so moderately alongside of me, and who had bowed so politely to me as he left. Whether or not he was a peer, however, I could only conjecture, as he had no carriage, nor did he converse or go arm in arm with any one, but simply walked off solitary and alone. He might have been a Clerk of the House, or a door-keeper, or a mere stranger, that had got into the body of the House, but I was more inclined to believe he was some official, as I learned from a by-stander that none was privileged to leave by that door but peers and office-bearers.

I now returned to my hotel considerably impressed with what I had seen, and feeling convinced that, from scenes such as I had witnessed, much was to be learned that was useful and instructive in life. I felt, at the same time, my own ambition whetted thereby, although, as I have repeatedly explained, it was sharp enough already—perhaps sharper than was even requisite—still it had got another rub on the grinding stone.

"Ah!" I exclaimed to myself, as I passed along the Strand, "the foundation of all this is wealth—patriotism, indeed, is represented by money, justice by money, Christianity by money!" "How," I continued, "could all these disputers, and orators, and reasoners, and bishops be there, but for money—their seats have even a money value—and every idea or sentiment they give utterance to, is some way or other connected with money. They patriotically call to account the Ministry for this act of injustice to the country, or that act of tyranny to the people; but it is not that the abuses they point out should be rectified, but that their opponents in power should be embarrassed, and they themselves get their offices—their salaries—and their chances of acquiring money! Therefore," I said resolutely, "I shall go ahead, and make money!"

Pursuing these ideas, I reached my hotel, had a moderate supper, a good night's rest afterwards, and arose next morning more resolved than ever to go ahead in the acquirement of wealth; towards which determination, I duly presented myself at the office of Messrs. Pull & Hawl, as the Royal Exchange clock chimed the hour of ten.

I was received by Mr. Hawl with extreme commercial civility, and immediately instructed as to how accounts stood betwixt us—the balance in my favour being considerable, and quite sufficient to meet the bills that were drawn against the cotton which was now on its way from Bombay, even should it not be sold before said bills were due. As to the cotton market, according to Liverpool advices, it was in an animated state, and the quotations, such as to leave me, if I chose to sell what I had, "subject to arrival," a very handsome profit.

Altogether, I had a most satisfactory interview with Mr. Hawl. He communicated to me the state of the foreign exchanges, the rates of freights to and from different parts; the price Consols had left off at the day previously; the charge for discount at the Bank of England, and what was likely to be

the alteration thereon at the next parlour meeting of its
directors; the quantity of bullion in its coffers, the amount
of the "Rest," and so on, to all of which I nodded my head
knowingly, although the latter portions of his information
to me were rather incomprehensible, as I had never before

paid attention to what are
called monetary matters,
although I have since—as
perhaps will be shown—
to no small extent.

I then parted with Mr.
Hawl, who shook me very
warmly by the hand,
while stating that he
would no doubt meet me
on 'change. He at the
same time hospitably in-
viting me to look in upon
him occasionally at his
office, where I would always find him betwixt ten and the
hour of 'change.

I thought, I must confess, that there was something rather
cool, if not coldish in this reception of Mr. Hawl, considering
it was my first visit to the firm, and I could not help contrasting it with what generally had taken place with Gunter,
Slide, & Company on like occasions, when visited by their
correspondents. Then, invariably, these strangers had been
introduced to the several members of the firm, by whom
they were entertained, at their own houses at dinner, and
that, too, whether it was likely to lead to business or not.
Mr. Hawl, however, said not a word regarding his partner,
and as to inviting me to dinner, that seemingly never entered
his noddle at all.

To do Mr. Hawl justice, however, I found he only acted
similarly to his neighbours, for, having occasion to call on
several firms to whom I had letters of introduction, I found
invariably they were all "tarred with one stick," and that
although some of them accepted considerable orders from me
with cash down, or the most satisfactory references, (of course
to Pull & Hawl, and that too with quite a talismanic effect)
they only requited these orders with a long list of commercial

quotations, ending with the never failing information as to the price of Consols up to within the last quarter of an hour.

I accordingly, after 'change hours, had always a free afternoon to myself, which I generally spent in dining at St. Paul's Coffee-House, though a little later than on the former occasion that I have alluded to, and, consequently, I had invariably the satisfaction of seeing my fat Parliamentary friend, with his eternal table-napkin girded around his chops, and surrounded with the *debris* of filberts and peaches, finishing his bottle of port, composing himself to sleep, and then riding off in his cabriolet to the House, to attend to his public duties, which consisted, I have no doubt, in finishing off the balance of his nap there, and voting faithfully in favour of his own party, whoever that might be, and whatever the measures they brought forward, or opposed.

CHAPTER XXXII.

INTRODUCTORY DOGGERELS.

To study the barbarian,
  Go search the wood and cavern;
But for the class called civilized,
  There's no place like the tavern!

The Goosedubbs Poet.

At the St. Paul's Coffee-House, I occasionally saw the well-bred Scotch gentleman; as he now and then dined there about the same time of the day as I did, and always in a like moderate manner as before, never drinking wine, nor, indeed, anything stronger than water.

I myself liked a glass of wine; indeed, now that I had got back to the cool latitudes again, I felt that I could have indulged even in something more potent—in my old pleasant mixture of whisky-toddy, to wit—had I had my ancient friend Tom Throstle to join me therein, for it was said that one could get anything in London by paying for it, not even excepting the best of Scotch whisky.

Alas! however, I had not my friend Tom by me; nor was it possible that I could again see him, even when I got to Glasgow, for, some years previously to leaving South America, I had received a letter from him saying, that despairing of getting on any further as a man of business, in the western metropolis, and, therefore, likely to stick on hand as a mere clerk, he had resolved to emigrate to the promising and rising colony of New South Wales, where he hoped to make a fortune, or perish in the attempt. At all events, I judged the latter to be honest Tom's intention, or apprehension, from the perusal of a poem he enclosed to me on the subject of his proposed exodus to the antipodes, and which ended with the following touching lines :—

> "There, I will leave my bones to bleach,
>   'Mongst the *Caffir* and *Yahoo*,
>   Where the *Ostrich* stalks, and the *Tiger* roars,
>   And bounds the Kangaroo !"

This distich, although it revealed that Tom's reading had been limited, or perhaps, rather, that it had been so extensive as to become jumbled, demonstrated at the same time that he was still given to the cultivation of the muses. It was, however, particularly interesting to me, in respect that I was assured thereby that Tom, being removed from Glasgow, there would be the fewer witnesses left of my former connection with its less aristocratic denizens—my aim being now to take my position with the best society in that quarter, when I arrived there, and to get on, not only as a private, but as a public citizen. "Who knows," I thought to myself, " but that I may yet be a provost, or at least a bailie, and stalk to the church, with a cocked hat on my head, and a gold chain of office around my neck !"

I, therefore, longed to leave London, and get to the north, being now heartily tired of visiting counting houses in the forenoon, and dining in the afternoon in the St. Paul's Coffee-House, where my only regular companions were the silent strangers around, not forgetting my quiet fellow-countryman, and the luxurious M.P., with his never failing superior dinner, desert, bottle of port, and constitutional nap.

I tried hard and vainly, to find out who this latter gentleman was, as the following conversation that I had with the waiter will show :—

"Pray," said I, one day, before the throng of the diners had arrived, to that staid official, as he was placing knives and forks, glasses, &c., on the tables around, "who is the elderly stout gentleman that dines here every day at three o'clock in the bay window, there?"

"Elderly gentleman, Sir!—yes Sir!"

"Aye," continued I, taking no notice of the waiter's vacant stare, "what is his standing?"

"Standing, Sir?—never stands, Sir—gentleman always sits, Sir!"

"Well, I don't dispute that," I continued, "but I mean, what's his name?"

"Name, Sir—don't know gentleman's name, Sir."

"Do you know his occupation or business, then?"

"Occupation, Sir—no, Sir—don't know gentleman's occupation, Sir."

"Where does he live?"

"Live, Sir—don't know where the gentleman lives—only know where he dines, Sir."

"And where does he dine?" said I, losing patience, and putting a cross question to the waiter, which perhaps was not altogether in order.

"Dine, Sir!—ha! ha!—gentleman always dines here, Sir!" answered the waiter, relaxing into a grin that I had never seen on his face before, and which seemed to thaw him into a more communicative disposition; for, without requiring much further pumping, he went on as follows:— " Fact is, Sir, gentleman as dines here every day, is a wery peculiar gentleman. Always makes a good dinner, Sir, and never speaks, nor allows himself to be spoken to. It's his way, and his humour, Sir, and we respects it. Consequently, as he never speaks, how are we to know anything about him, Sir?"

" Well, but if he never speaks," said I, " how are you to know what he wants for dinner? I notice that he has variety."

" Variety, Sir?" answered the waiter, " no great variety, Sir. Always dines on haddocks and roast mutton, on Mondays—cod's-head and stewed veal on Tuesdays—salmon and biled beef on Wednesdays—fowl and bacon on Thursdays— oyster patties and roast beef on Fridays—and biled mutton and capers on Saturdays—does'nt dine here on Sundays, Sir!"

" And how do you know about that variety?" said I. " That is to say, how does he make his wants known, if he never speaks ?"

" Writes them on the back of his bill, Sir," answered the waiter, " if he wants any change ; but he really never wants any change, for its always haddocks and roast-mutton on Mondays, cod's-head and stewed veal on Tuesdays, and so on."

" Did he ever speak, that you are aware of?"

" Speak, Sir?—no, Sir—never spoke that I am aware of."

" Then how did you know how to commence to serve him so much to his satisfaction?" said I, thinking that I had now posed the waiter.

" Vy, I will easily explain that, Sir," replied the waiter, who was now quite communicative, " it was in this way :— One day, about five years ago, as I was a-serving master's customers as usual, gentleman comes in, and sits down on that chair in the bay window there, and, as it was 'xactly three, I knew at once he had come to dine, having served him before in the same way, in the Goose and Gridiron, near the Mansion-House, where I was under-waiter for some time. Well, he sits down, and says nothing ; but, as it was a Wednesday, I immediately orders salmon and biled beef, which I sets before him ; and next day, being Thursday, when he comes again, I sets down fowl and bacon, and so on, consequently he has continued to dine with us ever since."

" But why did he leave the Goose and Gridiron?"

" Goose and Gridiron, Sir?—yes, Sir—way was this, Sir, as I ascertained :—One day he came in, and a new waiter as had come, asked him what he would have for dinner, although his plate was turned down, as usual. This was aggravated by a gentleman, who had unfortunately come in and sat down right opposite to him—the chair not being removed— and asking him for the paper when he was done, which so annoyed elderly gentleman, Sir, that he never came back again to the Goose and Gridiron, Sir!"

" Well," said I, " he must be very easily offended. Pray, would he leave this, if he were spoken to?"

" Leave, Sir?—yes, Sir," replied the waiter, " for sartin he would, Sir ; only we always takes precautions against any one speaking to him, as you may observe; besides, nobody almost speaks, that dines here."

As to the philosophy of this additional fact, I was prevented from making further inquiry, for at the moment, the fat M.P. entered, and the waiter returned to his duties.

As I contemplated the elderly gentlemen, however, I could not help thinking that there was something extremely mean, selfish, and unsocial in his thus, day after day, indulging in his voluptuous whim, while ignoring, as it were, the entire world that existed beyond his favourite nook in the bay window.

Still, I found that he was not the only one visiting the St. Paul's Coffee-House that indulged in eccentricities; for, one day, my affable fellow-countryman, having dined there, and, as usual, favoured me with a polite smile and bow—though we never conversed—he, on taking his leave, apologised to the waiter for being short of money, and not able to pay him till next day. This, I—vulgarly, I confess—thought too good an opportunity for showing my munificence to be lost, and so I offered to advance what he required.

The offer seemed to take my countryman quite aback. He stared at me as if I had given him a blow, and he blushed at the same time like a maiden; while I felt awkward, and began to think I had made a heinous mistake.

And so I no doubt had, as my subsequent experience in upper society has revealed to me. Still, it was meant for kindness, although I must acknowledge that it was the kindness of sycophancy. Who knew but I might have been obliging a great man, and what might be the consequences?

The consequences simply were, that the gentleman, after collecting his equanimity, thanked me very much; but I never saw him dine there again. He no doubt called next day and paid the small sum owing—as I by chance heard from the waiter—but the St. Paul's Coffee-House eventually lost his custom—an injury to it, for which I was never punished, excepting when I used to recall the circumstance to my recollection, while feeling that I had done a thing worthy of my extraction from the Goosedubbs of Glasgow, and, consequently, I felt much mental annoyance.

But the time drew near when at last I was myself to bid adieu to the St. Paul's Coffee-House, with all its guzzling, and silent and eccentric customers, and with London counting houses, and London as well, I having made all my business arrangements, for which it had been necessary that I should stay so long in the great Metropolis, before proceeding to my native city in the north.

I had, therefore, little else to do than to make a few farewell calls at certain houses, and amongst these, at that of Messrs. Pull and Hawl, where, as usual, I found the last-named gentleman at his post, quoting the prices of the day, and in particular, that of Consols.

" Dear me," he exclaimed, as I communicated to him my determination to leave, " you are about to go from London, and yet you have never dined with me!"

" Neither have I ever been introduced to, nor seen Mr. Pull," I replied, "although I have heard his voice when his door happened to be opened on any occasion when I was waiting in the ante-room till you should be disengaged."

Mr. Hawl smiled at this remark, for the fact was that Mr. Pull must have been a great talker, if I was allowed to judge from the monotonous and continuous clack, clack, clack, that came from the jaws of the occupant of that room, when the door chanced to be opened, and which I took to be that of the said Mr. Pull.

" Ah! yes, indeed," replied Mr. Hawl, "Mr. Pull can talk a little, but he only indulges in that way on things in general, for you see, he is our senior and moneyed partner, and doesn't go into the details of business, so that he may be enabled to devote his entire time to his public duties as one of the members for the city. This, in short, is the reason I have not introduced you to him ; but I will do so now, if you will step this way!"

" But, before doing so," continued Mr. Hawl, as we rose to

proceed to Mr. Pull's apartment, "will you engage to dine
with me on Thursday, at the annual dinner of the St. Lloyd's
Welsh Association, of which I am a member, and, indeed, one
of the Council? It is a charitable institution, and we have
always a delightful social white-bait feast in the London
Tavern on the day of its anniversary. Lord Cwm Slanlaggan
will be in the chair, and we will have capital speaking. Of
course, you will be my guest, and we will get to the cross
table at the top, as you will see from this ticket which I now
present to you, while begging your acceptance of it."

I readily accepted Mr. Hawl's engagement and ticket,
although I thought an invitation to a public dinner a queer
way of displaying private hospitality to a stranger. However, I reflected that in the eyes of a London man, the dinner
is the thing, and not the manner and style of giving it, and
as this occasion held out the prospect of the feast being a
"*good un*," I concluded that Mr. Hawl considered he was
acting the part of a very munificent host in inviting me to it.

We now proceeded to Mr. Pull's room, on entering which,
what was my surprise to behold, sitting on an easy chair at a
low desk, no other than the identical stout elderly gentleman
who dined at the St. Paul's Coffee-House, and never spoke
there, although here the recreation of chattering seemed to
be his principal luxury.

He was wide-awake, however, and the table at which he

sat presented a great contrast
to that of the St. Paul's Coffee-
House, there being upon it,
instead of wine and filberts,
abundance of business letters,
price currents, and the morning
papers of the day, while the
only liquids were red and
black inks, and the only glasses,
the glasses on his nose.

Of course, I never indicated
by my manner that I recognised him as an old acquaintance, nor did Mr. Pull appear
to recognise me; for, after giving me a warm and hearty shake
of the hand, on Mr. Hawl introducing me, he beckoned upon

me to be seated, and after that gentleman had retired, commenced a long talk, asking me never so many questions, and answering them himself, much in the style of Mr. Charles Matthews, while enacting his inimitable verbose character of Patter, in "Patter *versus* Clatter."

Mr. Pull, indeed, made up for his taciturnity at the St. Paul's Coffee-House, for he talked incessantly for fully half an hour, as I remarked by the timepiece that ticked on his mantlepiece, and whose pendulum did not vibrate more regularly, and equably, and monotonously, than did the honourable gentleman's tongue. As for myself, I never spoke a word, but hearkened to what I would call a very good recapitulation of the articles and leaders in the morning newspapers, comprising as it did a summary of all the foreign and local news, a critical report of the Parliamentary debates of the night previous, a touch at the law courts, a gossip about the Common Council proceedings, ending with the never-failing last price of Consols, which I took to be the amen of the worthy gentleman's discourse, and, therefore, a hint to be off, which, indeed, I was not reluctant to do, as I observed that Mr. Pull, rather than allow the one-sided conversation to flag, was beginning to go over the same subjects again, and this I could not stand.

I accordingly rose, and, after receiving once more his warm and hearty shake of the hand, bid him adieu, while reflecting on the singular satisfaction that this rich merchant, worth, as I had learned, fully a quarter of a million, could have, in being all tongue in the forenoon, and all stomach in the afternoon, for I was told by the waiter, on getting home in the evening, having dined elsewhere, that " the gentleman as never speaks" had dined as usual in the bay window, and with no change in his habits.

I could not resist the temptation, however, of telling Mr. Hawl next day, as we walked from his office—where I had met him by appointment—to the anniversary dinner of the St. Lloyd's Welsh Association, that, although I never had the pleasure of hearing Mr. Pull speak before, his person was perfectly familiar to me, as a frequenter of the tavern at which I staid.

This was quite a piece of news to Mr. Hawl, whose partner seemed to have kept him as much as possible in the dark regarding his private habits. "I did not know," he said, "that the St. Paul's Coffee-House was his favourite haunt now, although I knew he had given up the Goose and Gridiron many years ago."

Mr. Hawl went on, however, to explain the eccentricity of his colleague, and begged that I would not be prejudiced against him, for his indulgence therein. "It's Mr. Pull's pleasure and way," he said, "and nobody knows the reason why, but himself. He has a very nice family of grown-up sons and daughters," he continued, "that live in a magnificent villa of their father at Tooting Common, where they have every luxury and indulgence they can think of, and where, I need scarcely tell you, far more sumptuous fare and entertainment are prepared, than can be got at the St. Paul's Coffee-House, or indeed any coffee-house in London. Mr. Pull, however, prefers his own way of living to all the grandeur and sociality of Tooting Hall, where, it may be said, he only sleeps and breakfasts, although he is the most affectionate of husbands, and the most indulgent of parents, when he is amidst his family circle."

Mr. Hawl then went on to tell me about the many bene-

volent actions his partner did, and of the numerous charities he subscribed to—the sum expended thereon, being, annually, the amount of a little fortune.

Mr. Hawl, however, might have spared me the recital of the latter circumstance, as I had been a witness to the fact myself; having repeatedly seen long, sombre gentlemen, dressed in black, with white chokers, and book and pencil in hand, call at the office in Lombard Street, while I was waiting for Mr. Hawl, and receive vast sums of money from the cashier towards this and that charity. There was something, however, cold and stereotyped connected with the dispensation of these benevolences; for, on such occasions, that official, after hearing the name of the institution, would call for what he denominated the "Charity Book," on consulting which he would say, "Aye, Decayed Merchants' Hospital—Mr. Pull gives £50," or, "Paddington Deaf and Dumb Institution, he gives £30"—or according as the name of the charity was stated in the Charity Book, so the amount. He would then demand a receipt for the sum given, and the transaction ended.

I could not help coming to the conclusion after considering all this, notwithstanding the immense sums given by Mr. Pull, that, compared with these, the widow's mite was the true charity, and what, perhaps, would carry along with it the greatest benefit and the most lasting blessing.

Ere my contemplations had come to an end, Mr. Hawl and I had arrived at the London Tavern, in the large banqueting hall of which we found a brilliant assembly of gentlemen, with a galaxy of ladies in the gallery, and a most sumptuous dinner, which all parties did justice to. There were real turtle and iced punch, white-bait fried, plain, and devilled; every other description of fish, venison, turkeys, and game; indeed, what would require the eloquence of the waiter of the St. Paul's Coffee-House to describe.

These, washed down by the choicest Champagne and Rhine wines, and followed by sweets, and an exquisite dessert, consisting of the most luscious home-grown fruits, such as grapes, melons, peaches, pine-apples, and others, too numerous to mention—but which nothing, in respect to quality and superiority, can produce excepting a British climate, properly qualified by heat, manure, and scientific superintendence, under a chrystal covering—soon put us into the best of humour, accompanied, as the latter were, by the loving cup —a symbol of London affection—which makes the company present feel like a band of brothers, although, more than likely, they will cut each other next forenoon on the streets, if it suits their whims, or their convenience!

The Welsh lord in the chair with the unpronouncible name, then gave the usual loyal and patriotic toasts, includ-

ing the Army and Navy, to the former of which an old tottering General, with a military stock and his red coat buttoned to the throat, made a mumbling reply, the gist of which was that the British army when call-ed upon, would do its *dooty*; while to the latter, another old gentleman, in blue uniform—evidently an Admiral—who rolled a quid of tobacco from one cheek to another, likewise replied, his speech being to the effect that the British navy also would do its *dooty*, after which we had from the Band, the British Grenadiers, and Rule Britannia, played in very good style.

I really was beginning to enjoy the thing, and to consider, that after all, such occasions as this, afforded capital oppor-tunities for discharging hospitality on the part of London

gentlemen, for the wines were superb and most profuse, and every one in the most hilarious temperament, which extended it-self even to the ladies in the gallery, who waved their white handkerchiefs in token of approval of the speeches, when a damper was rather thrown upon us, by the ap-pearance of a sedate gentleman, who rose near the chairman, with an ominous manuscript in his hand, which he commenced to read, after placing across his nose a pair of very business-like golden spectacles.

This document proved to be the Annual Report of the Council of the St. Lloyd's Welsh Association, and it gave a very feeling account of the object of the society, which did much good, it being the means of assisting decayed Taffies who had been unsuccessful in business in London; or, in other words, who could not make as much money as would maintain them comfortably, in the great metropolis, in leeks and toasted cheese!

The report went on to give a statement of the revenue and disbursements of the St. Lloyd's Association, both of which were considerable, large sums of money being collected and expended, and it then concluded by an appeal to the public, and particularly to the members of the Association, to be liberal with their subscriptions for the forthcoming year.

This satisfactory report was received with great joy and cheering, in which I joined heartily, as much to please Mr. Hawl, who had paid due attention to it, as to testify my gratification that it was ended, and the speeches again commenced : for now the noble chairman was once more on his legs, and recapitulating certain portions of the report in more eloquent and pleasing phrases than the secretary's matter-of-fact phraseology had clothed them in.

A new and unexpected proceeding, however, was about to commence, to vary the entertainment of the evening; for the secretary, at the end of the chairman's address, produced an elegant mahogany box, studded with silver clasps and bindings, and having a yawning parallelogramic opening on its top, like that of a post office. This box was placed on the table opposite the chairman, who immediately wrote something on a paper which he wrapped around a Bank of England note, and placed it in the box. He then passed the box to his neighbour, who likewise wrote something, and made a similar deposit, and then it came on slowly, tacking from one side of the table to the other, like a coasting lug-

ger or steamer, while collecting parcels of goods on freight.

I rather disliked the appearance of this approaching vessel or box, at the very first, probably on Tom Campbell's principle that "coming events cast their shadows before," but I liked it still less as it neared the quarter where Mr. Hawl and I sat. I looked, however, to Mr. Hawl for counsel in the matter, and was horrified on observing that he held in his hand a Bank of England note for £50, with his name, on a separate piece of paper, attached to it. A like sum to that, however, I could not give, for I had only a ten-pound note upon me, else I have no doubt that my snobbishness would have induced me to lavish it upon the box. I, accordingly, timidly wrote my name, and, with the paper that contained it, committed the ten-pound note to the hole, which relentlessly and ruthlessly swallowed it, the only return for the sacrifice being, that the names of the donors and their subscriptions were all read out by the chairman, when cheers, according to graduation in amount, met the announcement.. A hundred pounds received, for instance, vociferous applause; fifty pounds, great applause; but thirty and twenty pounds, only received a "hear, hear!" or Paliamentary cheer. Alas! for my ten-pound note, it was announced amidst solemn silence; but Mr. Hawl gave me a bow, which was, no doubt, intended to compensate me for the disappointment.

Whether or not I felt compensated, however, I will not say. The company soon after broke up, when each took off his several way; while I felt resolved that I never should meet them on any other day!

CHAPTER XXXIII.

INTRODUCTORY DOGGERELS.

A gloomy morning after a fuddle,
    When one's roused early from his cuddle,
And scarcely can the rain descry,
    For smoky air and bleary eye;
Is not the choicest time of day,
    To think of plodding on one's way.

The Goosedubbs Poet.

I HAD intended to leave London next morning for the north, by the celebrated fast stage-coach called the Red Rover, which ran betwixt the Bull and Mouth, St. Martin's-le-Grand, and Manchester, in seventeen hours, her speed being at something like the rate of thirteen miles an hour, and for securing the box seat of which I paid a deposit of half a sovereign; but, although I had made every preparation for my journey, having packed up my baggage, and shaved myself the night before, in which process I cut myself bitterly in two or three places, in consequence of the unsteadiness of my hand, from the effects of Mr. Hawl's hospitality, I found it impossible to rise with any degree of satisfaction, far less pleasure, on being called by the "boots" of the hotel, shortly after four o'clock, and, therefore, lay still, with a sulky determination to sacrifice my half sovereign rather than rise,—thereby making the cost of the splendid treat at the St. Lloyd's banquet fully ten guineas,—and at the same time endure another day of London, a city which now had become unbearable to me, on account of the dirtiness of its streets, the mugginess of its atmosphere, and the cool friendliness of its commercial denizens whom I had had the pleasure of meeting with.

Ugh! I remember with pain to this very day that dismal occasion—when, after "boots"

had placed on my dressing table a mutton dip, with a long charred wick sticking out of its gloomy flame, and a jugful of tepid water, pronounced by the said boots as being *hot* —the abominable sensation I felt, as with a racking headache and bleary eyes, not to mention the stiffened gashes of the razor on my chin, I turned aside the window blind and gazed, in the gray of a wet and bleak autumnal morning, upon the brick walls and black chimney-cans of the neighbouring houses, while scarcely able to descry the rain-drops, but which I heard plainly pattering, on the glass panes of the window.

My resolution was formed in a moment. "Perish the half sovereign!" I said to myself, and immediately I was enveloped in the blankets again, after blowing out the candle, the perfume from the smouldering wick of which added to the delights of the London atmosphere.

To sleep, however, I found to be impossible, for "boots" was again knocking at my bed-room door, with the intention of carrying down my luggage, and after his dismissal, with the announcement that my journey was adjourned for twenty-four hours, came the chamber-maid to put the room in order for new customers: and subsequently came the morning waiter, with one of said new customers, who had arrived by an early coach, and who went growling away, it having apparently been taken for granted by all parties concerned, that if I had not gone, I ought to have gone.

I suffered, indeed, from all causes conjoined, very much, and it was not till I had sent out for, and partaken of a rather bitter and nauseous febrifugal draught, the recipe of which I luckily carried in my pocket-book, that I got a few hours of undisturbed slumber, and was enabled to get up for the day, about twelve o'clock, when I proceeded to the City, wondering if what I had been treating as a misfortune— namely, the expensive dinner, the loss of a day, and the bodily suffering I had endured—would not turn out, after all, as usual, a bit of good-luck to me.

And, indeed, it did so, for on getting to Pull & Hawl's I there found lying for me, and luckily not forwarded, a foreign letter, containing a price current, in which I found favourable quotations of a description of goods, a considerable parcel of which I had been offered, at a cheap rate, only a few days previously. These I was fortunate enough to find still on hand, and to purchase, even at a still more reduced price, and they, on arrival at their destination, left fully fifty per cent. of profit. Next, the weather that same afternoon became bright, balmy, and settled, after a long course of wetness and cold; and this brought me comfortably to the Red Rover betimes next morning, on the box-seat of which I placed myself, in the best of spirits, with a clear head, a settled stomach, and a cigar in my mouth.

Nor had my good-luck finished here, for, after we had trotted along the streets, cantered through the suburbs, and got into a smart gallop, on attaining the country, I learned a piece of news that, with good cause, interested me much.

"Fortunate thing, sir," said Jehu, as his *prads* pranced along the Macadam, "that you did not occupy that ere box-seat yesterday morning!"

"How?" said I in surprise, while throwing away the

fag-end of my finished cigar. "It was by the merest chance that I didn't."

"Deuced lucky for you, however," answered broad-brim, "that another got your place; and all the worse for him!"

"You astonish me much," I said enquiringly, "pray how do you explain that?"

"Gentleman as occupied that seat yesterday," replied the coachman, lowering his voice and speaking gravely, "was killed—that's all!"

"Killed!" I cried, while feeling queer, at this intimation, though at the same time duly estimating the value of my good-luck, in not having been, the morning before, the occupant of the seat. "How, in the name of wonder, did that happen?"

"Happened this vay," said the coachman, who, I saw, wanted to spin out his story as much as possible, *ad longam;* while, along with this fault, he had a provoking style of interrupting himself by chirping to the horses, and *"cussing"* the reins, and growling at the thong of his whip, which every now and then would get fixed to some part of the harness, or the cross-bars of the leaders. "Happened 'xactly this way:—You see, Sir, this coach is the fastest coach in England—the fastest in the world, indeed, considering its journey on end, of upwards of two hundred miles (hish, hish; chirp, chirp); consequently, you sees, we hevery day meets with a haccident. One day it is a splinter-bar giving way—another day it is a trace getting loose—and another day it is the reins breaking—a wery bad haccident, indeed (cuss that thong, it has again got twisted to a buckle)—sometimes we have a smash—sometimes we have an entire spill—a werry aggravating circumstance (chirp, chirp); but hevery day, as I have said, we have something or other wot constitutes a haccident. Yesterday we had gentleman killed!"

"And how did that occur," said I, now all alive to the circumstance, from a sort of dread that "gentleman might be killed to-day again." "Was it from a fall, or a smash, or a spill?"

"Spill, Sir," replied the driver, "and I'll tell you as how it took place. It was not with me, but with the coachman as drives the next set of stages. You see there is a particular part of the road, where the hosses doesn't canter, as they should only do, but where they races. Its impossible to hold them in, Sir, and away they goes at something like twenty miles an hour, till they come to a hill and then they canter again—all right: yesterday, however, one of the leaders being a blind un, and the other a bolter, (chirp, chirp) they took it into their heads to make a sudden swerve across the road when they was a-going at the fastest, and this brought the off fore-wheel upon a jutting out bit of the kerb stone, which caused a sudden jerk, when off flew the gentleman on the box seat, who foolishly was not holding on, and he, striking with his head the sixty mile stone, from the General Post Office, was immediately a dead un; for, on being taken up, he never made a movement, and, consequently, the crowner's 'quest sits on him to-day."

"That is very sad, indeed," I said, beginning to think that after all the box seat was not so desirable as even a less pretentious one at the back would be. "And must we pass along the same bit of road to-day, and at the same pace?"

"For certain you will," answered the coachman, "for we never goes two ways. But bless your soul, there is lots of wery dangerous places of a like kind, and we're just a-coming to one!"

"Do you observe that 'ere white cottage, on a bit, on the near side," continued Jehu, by way of strengthening my nerves, so far as a warning went, "well, at that cottage we goes down a declivity, and there you will see how these hosses will then lash out!"

"I hope," said I, as coolly and unconcernedly as I could express myself, "that there are no bolters and blind ones to-day in the team?"

"Not exactly," replied the coachman, assuringly, "but there's a short-sighted un that shies at everything, and a bit-biter that runs off whenever he gets a chance, with the snaffle in his teeth, and that's about as bad!"

As the coachman made this pleasant announcement we arrived at the cottage, when I immediately observed that what he had intimated was true. The road did, indeed, descend fearfully, and the horses, in consequence, had the game to themselves. Although the coachman pulled the reins with all his might, they literally flew, while the coach rolled from side to side like a ship in a sea-way.

"It's impossible to bring them up with the reins," said the coachman, with the air of a martyr, "but we'll see if we can do so with the collars!" and thereupon he applied the lash to the leaders and wheelers in a way fearful to behold, relaxing, as he did, the reins at the same time.

"Don't be alarmed, however," he cried, as he observed me clinging to the iron rail of the box rather convulsively, "don't be alarmed, for the same sort of haccident never happens twice running, and you are as sure not to be killed on a milestone to-day, as if your life was insured. There," he went on to say, "didn't I tell you that I would bring them up with the collars; for don't you observe how peaceable and well-behaved they now are?"

The coachman was right, for we now indeed were going at an orderly pace, though still at the gallop, and very fast, which brought us fully within time, to the next stage, where, as usual, plenty of grooms were waiting to receive us, so complete and reckless of cost were the arrangements made for this celebrated coach, which, in that era, was to the road what the express train is to the railway now-a-days.

None of us, indeed—not even the coachman—were allowed to leave the coach, for as four men took out the exhausted horses, four other men placed in harness the fresh ones, so that we were enabled to start again after stopping, in exactly one minute ten seconds, by my watch.

In this start, however, I thought we were at last destined to have a *spill;* for, on the coachman having had the reins handed up to him, and he had cried "all right—let go!" while the four grooms started off from their respective sides, the leaders made a plunge (one of them almost standing upright on his hind legs) and then commenced to kick, which ended in the near one getting his leg across one of the traces, and then, indeed, there was a scene of rather an alarming nature.

It was the work of a moment, however, for the grooms to run forward; to catch each a horse by the head—to disconnect the trace, and fix it properly again—to lead on the horses a couple of paces—and, in a word, to make a proper start—while the philosophic coachman—who never took his eye off his cattle—exclaimed exultantly, "Thank God! we have got over our haccident for the day!"

The rest of the drive was pleasant enough, for although we continued to carry on at the same break-neck pace as before, I felt faith in what the coachman had predicted, that no further *haccident* would take place, so that galloping became comparatively, a normal state of affairs, and racing rather a pleasant occasional excitement than otherwise, and consequently, when we arrived at Manchester, very shortly after the time laid down, I felt almost disappointed that the journey was at an end.

At Manchester I staid but a few days, doing there, however, a fair stroke of business, and making promising arrangements for the future. This was, indeed, more than I had intended to do in this city, but everything seemed now to be flourishing with me, and, accordingly, when I took my seat in the mail coach for the place of my nativity, I felt a wonderful degree of happy equanimity.

On this occasion I chose the inside, the weather having again become threatening, and consequently did not enjoy the journey so much as I had done the one in the Red Rover, the mail being comparatively a jog-trot affair compared with that quick coach. Neither were my companions so communicative nor entertaining as the driver of the Rover had been. Two were evidently old stagers and commercial men, or what are called "bagmen," of an economic and managing turn; for, on the coach stopping at the end of the stages, and the respective coachmen presenting themselves at the window for their fees—that being the barbarous system of those days, so far as concerned the Royal Mail: a coachman for every stage, and consequently a fee for each—one of these gentlemen alternately paid for both, in the shape of a shilling, thus making the charge to each only sixpence, while I, not having a supply of the smaller coin, had to tip my shilling, my companion opposite having refused to enter into an arrangement similar to that of the bagmen, fearing perhaps, that if he did so, he might appear, in the eyes of the several Jehus, as being a bagman likewise.

This formed rather a serious consideration, on a journey that had at least twenty stages, and, consequently, I did not adopt a very flattering opinion of my exclusive friend, who ever and anon would draw a long silken purse, through the chinks of which the "yellow Geordies clinked," and pay therefrom the coachman a "bob," with the air of a millionaire.

He might have been one of that class, for aught I knew; but certainly he did not look like it—at all events, he had not been the architect of his own fortune—to quote the cant of the day—for he was a very young man, seemingly not over twenty, dressed extremely foppishly, and redolent of lavender water, which occasionally came in ambrosial gales from a rich Indian silk handkerchief which he sported.

He was, in my eyes, likewise, very ugly, although he wore a splended fur travelling cap. His eyes were small and winky; his nose flattish; and his mouth wide and simperish, with thin lips, occasionally displaying a case of large square teeth in front, guarded by tusks at each side, of a decidedly animal expression.

He, altogether, looked less like a man than a monkey; and this latter similitude was the more intensified, in my mind, by his having a sharp, *brusque* manner of turning his head from side to side, peculiar to the baboon race. Of course, I formed towards him a thorough contempt, which grew and grew, as we each needlessly paid our beggar-my-neighbour sort of fees to the ruthless drivers.

At last I got something like an advantage over my opponent, in consequence of the suggestion of one of the com-

mercial gentlemen, who recommended me to toss with the
coachmen whether I should pay them a shilling or nothing;
and coachmen being always fond of anything in the shape of
gambling, I found that the bait succeeded, particularly as my
good luck as usual stood by me on the occasion. I had likewise the satisfaction to observe that the process completely
disgusted my *gorilla* friend, who, no doubt, looked upon me,
in consequence, as being little better than a vulgar bagman.
And thus we proceeded on our dreary and unsocial journey,
passing over the cold Shap Fells, and so on to Carlisle, where
we breakfasted at an early hour, and where I got a supply
of sixpences, and my friend a supply of shillings wherewith
to contend again, the commercial men now leaving us, which
gave us the inside of the coach entirely to ourselves.

At last we reached the outskirts of Glasgow, passing the
locality where I had so long sojourned when a boy, and
which caused me to strain my eyes in order to detect the old
house in which, with my mother and poor Sissy, not to
mention poor old Jack, I had resided. Alas! it had given
way to a building of more modern architecture, and nothing
remained of that once happy, but latterly unhappy home.

And now we are trotting along the Gallowgate, as the
Eastern portion of the main street of this great City is
named, in compliment to the constitutional institution it led
to, and which, in former days, had its local habitation at
the Cross, or very heart of the City, in pleasant juxta-position
with its little brother "the pillory," upon which, almost
every Wednesday—that being the market day—poor unfor-
tunates, till within a recent date, which many men, who do
not consider themselves *old*, yet remember, were to be seen
undergoing the ordeal of exposure, while "papped at," by
the populace, with rotten eggs, spoiled apples, dead cats, and
all other descriptions of offal and filth, but which institution
has been done away with, in consequence of being considered
too barbarous, although its big brother, "the gallows," still
exists.

As the coach rattled along the streets, I observed that
many old landmarks in the shape of quaint houses, with
Dutch gables, containing carved work representing scrip-
tural scenes, and which had been the mansions of the
higher, and more aristocratic citizens, in bygone times, had

been removed, and new ones built in their places, and that
Glasgow had suffered, in its topographical appearance, a
complete transformation. So much, indeed, was this the case,
that when the coach stopped at the Bucks' Head Hotel, after
dropping its mails at the narrow cross street that led to the
then Post Office, I felt as though I were visiting for the first
time an altogether strange locality,—the only thing that
really assured me it was the veritable City of St. Mungo,
being an occasional emblazonment here and there of the City
Arms over a shop door, or window, with its peculiar and
pious motto,* which seemed actually to have been realised, so
greatly did it appear to have increased in magnitude, and
wealth :—

* NOTE F.—Glasgow City Arms. *See Appendix.*

CHAPTER XXXIV.

INTRODUCTORY DOGGERELS.

"Let Glasgow Flourish"—like its tree,
    That bears fish, bell, and bird;
Above all, let it flourish—"by
    The preaching of the Word."

Long may its fish swim in the Clyde,
    Its bird soar to "on High,"
Its bell ring sinners to the Kirk,
    The *Deevil* to defy!

The Goosedubbs Poet.

AND now I stood once more in my native City of Glasgow, after so many years of absence, and under circumstances so different from those in which I had left it. Then I was poor and dependent, but now, comparatively speaking, I was rich and independent; for, according to a calculation I had passed the time in the coach by making, I considered myself, one way with another, as being a man worth betwixt five and six thousand pounds, which was no mean sum to commence business with, particularly as I was well acquainted with that business, and versed in all the ramifications pertaining thereto, as well as other schemes which permitted of proper and safe applications of capital being made, when opportunities offered.

These I felt myself equal to cope with, perhaps better than most merchants in the place, in consequence of my experience abroad; for, at that period, it was not every one that ventured to face the dangers, not only of voyaging to foreign climes, but of the many maladies, in the shape of fevers, choleras, and agues incidental thereto, when he did reach his destination.

Of course a thousand little incidents at every step, presented themselves to illustrate the change that has been alluded to.   The very fact of my being now the occupant of an apartment in a hotel into which, when a ragged boy, I used to gaze as though it were a fairy land, while wondering

where all the good things that the waiters carried to the guests could come from, was one.   The circumstance of being bowed to, and spoken civilly, if not servilely to, by the landlord and waiters, as I strutted along the lobby, instead of being chased away from the window with a broomstick, as an impudent peeper and eaves-dropper, was another; and the feeling, indeed, that I was now a gentleman, and not a blackguard —that is, so far as apparel and position distinguish the gentleman, or the blackguard—and privileged to go and come, when and where I liked, was a third.

But I was overpowered with their amount, when, in the fall of the evening, I stole out to visit the old haunts of my childhood in the precincts of the Goose-dubbs and the Briggate, where I used to pick the pockets of passers-by of handkerchiefs, and likewise pick the gutters of garbage.   There, these scenes remained as of old, with no change for the better.   There seemed to be the same amount of drunkenness, of riotousness, and of squalor.   The very inhabitants seemed to be the same—neither older nor younger—with the same rude and coarse manners to each other; the same habits of cursing and swearing; the same mode of howling, and whistling, and quarrelling; and the same style of attiring themselves in rags.   The locality presented no pleasing reminiscences for me.   I had only

visited it impelled by curiosity to know if it still existed—if
it really had always existed—and if my knowledge and remembrance of it had not been the impressions of a dream,
instead of actual experience and reality.

Having satisfied myself as to these facts, and that the horrors
of the place owed nothing either to phantasm or imagination, I fled from it, and wandering, whither I cared not,
found myself at the harbour, and there indeed I discovered
that so far as regarded it, a very remarkable change had
taken place. Large vessels, in fleets, lay crowding alongside
of magnificent piers, where formerly there had only been
small river craft, and mean Highland wherries, and even few
of these, tied to grassy banks, which now were all converted
into the piers which have been alluded to; while these were
strewed, at the same time, with packages of rich merchandise
in the process of being embarked to, or imported from all
quarters of the globe.

Nothing could have presented to my mind a surer indication of the truth, that the rise and progress of this City of
the West were of the most substantial description, than what
I now viewed. I had read of them in newspapers which had
been sent out to me while abroad, I had heard them spoken

of and commented upon by people of all nations, that had either visited the locality or heard them described, but now I witnessed their development with my own eyes, and was enabled to realise their importance and solidity.

"This is the place," I said to myself, as I retreated to my hotel, in the dusk of the evening, "for a man that seeks to make a fortune, to connect himself with, for what is all that I have seen but the general wealth of a fortunate community who have it forced upon them, and thrice happy, therefore, will be the clever fellow who, in becoming one of that community, gets not only his own share, but, by his commercial management, the shares of others. Yes," I continued, "a fortune is nothing but the acquirement of the portions of others, in addition to one's own, and, therefore, I will go a-head with determination, to acquire these portions!"

The next day being Sunday, I resolved to take advantage of the circumstance, and to commence my new career in Glasgow as a regular church attendant, knowing the importance of having a character for such a habit in Scotland generally, and in this City in particular.

I may confess, however, that this was from no veneration that I entertained for the Church, or for church service; for my remembrance of the latter when, as a boy, I used to go in a forced sort of style with my father, to hear the clergyman of our parish expound, had not made an agreeable impression on my mind, but the very reverse. Then, the service was intolerably dull and disagreeable to me, and the only thing I relished about it, was the "Amen" which dismissed us.

Since then I had been but seldom within a church, having, while associated with Tom Throstle, generally spent the Sundays in excursions to the country while the weather was good, and in slumbering and smoking within doors when it was bad; and afterwards, when in South America, never having thought of such a thing as a church.

As the City bells began to jowl their sonorous summonses to church-goers, in all the varied and discordant keys that are so familiar to the inhabitants of large towns on such occasions, I issued from my hotel, dressed in my best suit of blacks—and which suit I had, by way of anticipation, obtained while in London from the most fashionable tailors, for the very purpose of attending Glasgow churches in, on Sundays, and probable dinner parties, and routes, on other days of the week—not to speak of possible funerals—when I came to be asked to them,—and, laying my course due east, was soon mingling with the decent and well-dressed populace, who, like myself, were respectively bound for some place of worship.

I was, however, struck with the circumstance, that instead of going with the stream, I was—in the route I had taken—going directly in the face of it; every one, with a few exceptions in addition to that of myself, being bound for the west. Nor did this phenomenon indicate any tendency to change until I had attained the High Street, and directed my course along it, when I found that I was proceeding more in consonance with the march of the wayfarers than before I had been doing, although what had been a river in the Trongate had here dwindled to a mere brook.

I, however, reflected that perhaps if any one, like the Apostle, had become a fisher of men for the nonce, and cast his angling tackle into these respective streams, he would have found that the smaller of the two could have produced the best fish, morally speaking, even as is the case with streams of comparative size, physically speaking—as all followers of Isaak Walton know full well.

Yes, in the broad stream I had left, it is to be feared that fashion more than religion was the inducement which led so many westwardly, and this fact I pretty satisfactorily realised on arriving at the church to which I was bound, for there I found the number of the congregation not only to be extremely small, but in appearance of very second, or rather third-class, quality. There was, indeed, but a sprinkling of people present, and, in consequence, the church had a very dull and deserted like appearance, which contrasted greatly with what I remembered of it; for, in former years, it used to be not only well filled, but on some occasions crowded.

While I was wondering if this change could have been effected by some subsequently appointed minister, of a dull and dry character, having "preached the church vacant"—to trench upon an old clerical joke—for the incumbent of its palmy days had long ago passed away,—the pastor of the parish entered the pulpit, and soon put this idea to rout; for he not only gave out the psalm with as great vivacity, and, at the same time, with as great impressiveness as if the church had been crowded, prayed with much earnestness and originality, read a chapter with masterly intonation, but preached a sermon that would have done credit to St. Paul himself—at all events as far as my opinion went.

He commenced his discourse with a general review of the greatness, the goodness, and the love of God, as evinced in all His promises, and in all His actions. God, he said, was not what many presumed Him to be, to judge from the way in which they addressed and seemingly tried to propitiate Him by means of flattery and fulsome adulation—mistakenly intended for adoration. He was not tyrannical, He was not vindictive, He was not capricious; and although in one of the commandments He was declared to be "a jealous God, visiting the sins of the fathers upon the children unto the third and fourth generation of those that hate Him," he thought this might be taken as being more a literal than a virtual translation of the ancient Hebrew language; but whether or not, it was qualified by what immediately followed in that same commandment, in respect to His "shewing mercy unto thousands of those who love Him, and keep His commandments." Besides, the preacher went on to say, we must keep strictly in remembrance the great fact which was our stronghold of happiness and hope, that He sent from Heaven, and to this world for the salvation of all, the great Head of our Church, His only begotten Son, our Lord and Saviour Jesus Christ, whom, while on earth, we reviled and persecuted, and at last crucified, whereby there was constituted the atonement, for a remission of the punishment that would have followed our sins, had He not "endured the cross, despising the shame, and been set down on the right hand of God" as an intercessor for us.

The reverend gentleman then branched from that, to the beauty and advantages of the Christian religion, which he treated in a practical way, and illustrated in a manner that must have been intelligible to all present, judging, as I did, from the impression it made on myself.

The ministers of this religion, he said, in their efforts to illustrate and disseminate its truths, as became their duty, had great difficulties to contend with. They had the passive resistance of the free-thinker, the wavering and timidity of the doubter, the cold candour of the casuist, and the bold temerity of the scoffer, like rocks a-head and around them to endanger their course.

They had likewise, within their own flocks, wherewith to harass their efforts and breed dispeace, the jealous, the gratuitously-meddling, and the sourly-intolerant, — people who, he was sorry to proclaim, were apt to say as it were, "Stand by thyself, come not near to me, for I am holier than thou!"

But although these very ardent individuals were prone to order their fellows to keep at their distance, they themselves, when it suited their whims, did not practice the same restraint; for they liked nothing better than to interfere with the unhappy persons he had first alluded to, and instead of expressing sorrow for their want of soundness, and mildly endeavouring to convert them by gentle suasion, they reviled and persecuted them, saying all manner of evil things against them. They even in their haste were apt to fall foul of, and load with abuse, a class—a most numerous and excellent class — whom he would call the real backbone of the church, namely, the cheerful Christians—those who blow not trumpets in the streets when they give alms, nor pray at the corners of streets, that they may be seen of men, but who practise both charity and piety in secret, —in the way set down by the great Author of our Faith. These intolerants, the preacher remarked, had much to answer for; they had the dispeace he had alluded to, to answer for; and they had likewise a most lamentable consequence, with which they themselves were concerned, to answer for; for those parties whom they got to loggerheads with, in retaliation, would enquire into the habits and practice of their opponents, and finding these inconsistent with their extreme rules, as certainly must be the case when undue strictness is attempted to be followed, would turn against them and brand *them* as hypocrites.

This state of things, the reverend gentleman said, he lamented much, and if he could be the means of rectifying it, it would give him real pleasure; for, passing over the facts he had expressed, as to the principles of the cheerful

Christian, he was prepared to say, he did not believe there were such things as hypocrites; and what was more, he did not think there was, at bottom, such a thing as an actual infidel, far less an atheist, in existence. There were many, no doubt, who acted as such, who made themselves ridiculous and offensive as such, and who marred their own interests and happiness, as such; still, when opportunity occurred for testing them, they invariably ignored their characters as such. He had found out, connected with many of those libeled individuals, deeds of unostentatious charity, of secret benevolence, and of magnanimous self-denial, that would have done honour to undoubted believers; and he never knew of an instance where they did not give their children—excepting in example—every opportunity of becoming true Christians; nay, they did not object to their children being serious, if not pious. With respect to themselves, however, when the day of trouble came, when health deserted the vigorous form; when the rose forsook the cheek, leaving the pale lily in its place; when the dimples departed, and the wrinkles came instead; when the imprudent boldness and conceit of youth, and even of more sedate manhood vanished, and the prudence and sobriety of age took the direction, then broke forth the long-suppressed, but latent sunshine of Christianity, to warm, to strengthen, and sustain the sinking soul!

"Ah, yes!" exclaimed the divine, breaking into a momentary enthusiasm, "this is always the case, sooner or later, and a happy thing it is so; for what an awful thing it would be if that sun should set, leaving the sinner unconvinced of its reality, and amidst darkness, solitude, and hopelessness, that he should perish for ever!"

The preacher having now attracted and deeply riveted the attention of his small congregation, as was indicated by the clenched hands, the suppressed breathing, and the eagerly directed vision towards him, of many around, took the opportunity, of "improving the occasion" by addressing a few plain words, as he would call them, to his hearers, and which he thought would now be applicable and appreciable. He then went on to point out that this was a commercial City, having a strictly trading community, who rejoiced in their character as such. To make money here was therefore considered a virtue, and to possess a fortune was to take a high and respectable position in society. Where was the individual, he would ask, amongst them, who did not feel this truth, daily, hourly, nay, momentarily suggesting itself to his mind, and in consequence, spurring him up to cope with his neighbours in the race for wealth, and thereby advancement? When a man in this City made money, what did he then not become? In spite of a neglected education he was at once received as a Solan and an oracle. With money jingling in his pockets, his rude and vulgar manners become pleasant characteristics. With a good account at his banker's he immediately found himself to be influential, and his will a law. He started at once from the shop to the saloon; his palm was grasped by the highest in the community; he was invited to the most sumptuous tables; his society was found pleasing; he, in a word, was a grand discovery, not only to others, but to himself, and as such, he became very happy and comfortable—at all events in appearance—no doubt!

But this, although a familiar occurrence, the preacher went on to say, in Glasgow, was by no means an every-day one. It was occasional, not regular; and, though many were the successes, many, many, on the other hand, were the reverses and failures; and, in consequence, the disappointments and mortifications attendant thereon. He had known of cases where men had spent years on years in the vain endeavour to acquire wealth; and, after labouring and calculating, and canvassing, and struggling, had ended in bankruptcy and beggary—their youth spent and thrown away, their health destroyed, and their energies paralysed: worse than that, they had neglected the one thing needful, and had, therefore, no resources to fall back upon, wherein they could find true consolation and soothing to their sufferings.

"But now," said the clergyman, "having pointed out to you the dangers and difficulties that attend the struggle for wealth, as it is practised in this City, let me call your attention, to a sure method of attaining it, and in no instance meeting with a failure, or even a check. As I have said," he continued, "you try to get wealth as a means for placing you in a respectable position in society, and making you influential, pleasing, agreeable, and useful. Now, the

practice and hearty adoption of true Christianity will do all
that better than money. Let a man be a Christian, in the
real acceptance of the term, as laid down by the great
Master who instituted it by sacrificing himself, and he
becomes at once on a par with, nay, above all these monetary potentates that I have mentioned. The Christian is
always a gentleman ; his manners are bland ; his demeanour
is dignified; his step is firm and elastic. His word is never
doubted; his opinion is never questioned; his influence is
never denied. He is, indeed, the true personification of
wealth—and wealth, too, of a kind that never takes wings
and flies away!"

Having illustrated his views further in a like way, and
concluded his discourse with an eloquent peroration, the
reverend gentlemen, after the usual prayer and psalmody,
closed the forenoon service; and I was soon thereafter in
the open air, threading my way to the street, along with the
meagre congregation that had heard this profitable discourse,
and most of whom, I judged from their appearance, if they
were men of wealth, must have been so in the Christian
sense, so ingeniously dilated upon by the clergyman, more
than in the deprecated pecuniary one.

I now bent my steps towards the West End of the City;
which was indeed quite a new territory to me, occupying as
it did what had been only cereal producing fields, and grass
parks, at the period of my departure for the transatlantic
world. These fields and parks were now changed into streets,
and crescents, and squares, containing large and commodious
houses, furnished in the most sumptuous and elegant style—
to judge from the peep I got through their plate-glass
windows—and appearing more like the palaces of nobility,
than the mere every-day mansions of commercial citizens.

I was struck on passing some of these houses to observe,
gazing from the windows, the faces of men whom I remembered to have been mere clerks in counting-houses when I
was a boy in Silvertop & Company's, and who now must have
become men of fortune, or, at all events, of good incomes,
if I might judge from the residences they now occupied.
Some of these individuals, too, had attained the dignity of
married men, and possessed families, for I remarked more
than one issuing from their front doors, attended by their

wives and well dressed trains of youngsters, averaging in age from five to fifteen.

They were all bound, seemingly along with many others that were issuing from their dwellings—and who formed, in consequence, rather a crowded procession—for a chapel of beautiful architectural elevation, apparently only recently built, and whose bell was "ringing-in" the congregation that was to attend the afternoon's services.

The bell, however, of St. Blythswood's Sanctuary, as the church was denominated, might have almost been spared the trouble of ringing-in, for no one seemed to require such urging, to fill the pews, as I might have judged from the crowded manner with which the doors were besieged by those who had sittings, and by the patiently hanging-on demeanour of a supplimental crowd, called "the strangers," who could only expect to be favoured with seats, or the privilege of standing, after the regular hearers had become accommodated.

Amidst the latter I took my stand, feeling curious to hear a preacher who could attract so large and respectable an audience, and which formed so striking a contrast, in respect to numbers, to that which, along with myself, had attended the excellent Mr. Sifter's forenoon service.

My first fear, indeed, was that I would not get admittance into the sanctuary at all, for couple on couple, and family on

family, and single men, and single women as well, came on,
flocking like bees returning to the hive after a hot summer
day's flower-sucking.

At length, just as the bell ceased tolling, the last of the
seat-holders entered the church, when the beadles appeared
to beckon the expectants to what accommodation they
could procure for them, and whom they managed remarkably
well to provide for, assisted, as I have much pleasure in
acknowledging, by the congregation, who in several instances
incommodated themselves to give room, by crushing, to those
who otherwise would have required to stand. Indeed,
I saw several gentlemen give up their own seats for the
benefit of ladies, and betake themselves to quarters where
they neither could be so comfortably seated, nor hear the
clergyman in an equal degree, to what would have been the
case, had they remained where they were.

And now all having become settled, and quiet, and
decorous, while a subdued and rather sombre shade pervaded
the elegant interior, in consequence of the windows being
filled with rich stained glass, that excluded the vulgar daylight considerably, and made it to some extent dark, the
clergyman, preceded by the principal beadle, carrying the
ponderous Bible, entered from the vestry, and immediately
mounted to the pulpit, where, with much solemnity and
good emphasis he gave out the psalm, which was beautifully
sung by a band of professional singers, whose united voices
almost equalled in volume, the strains of an organ.

I felt some difficulty in distinguishing the minister, as he
again rose, after the performance of the psalm, to enter upon
his prayer, in consequence of the gloom that pervaded the
church, and which I have already noticed. He seemed to
me, however, to be what is called a fashionable preacher, and .
was elegantly and neatly dressed, so far as the colourless hue
of "the cloth" permitted, for his gown was of the heaviest
and glossiest silk, his vestment of the finest pile, and his
wristbands, neckcloth, shirt breast, and clerical bands, of the
whitest and purest cambric and linen; while his hair, which
was raven black, was parted in the middle of his forehead,
and fell in hyperion curls over his shoulders, rather effemin-
ately, it might have been considered, but for his rather harsh
features, which again constrained his countenance into a

more manly expression, than otherwise would have been the case, had he been what is called "well favoured."

His prayer was at first calm and subdued, but as he went on, it became more excited and anxious. He addressed the Deity not in original sentences, but in scraps borrowed from many portions of the Scriptures, and which went to treat of the greatness and power of the Almighty, of His jealousy and revengeful feelings, of His determination to smite and punish, and of His terrible denunciations against all those who offended Him, and obeyed not His commandments. These, no doubt, he humbly deprecated, and craved might  be averted; but in no instance did he allude to the fact that a Mediator stood betwixt them and the fearful punishment that was threatened, and which circumstance, indeed, forms the great gift of Christianity to a perishing world.

As the divine proceeded, he became more energetic; and I noticed that he then seemed to care neither about the coherence nor connection of the doctrines he touched upon, provided what he said clinked well, and told thrillingly. I began, indeed, to look upon him as something of a ranter, or a bellower, but that I was forbidden to judge so harshly, in consequence of the serious and respectful attention with which his prayer was received by his flock.

There was, at the same time, something about the reverend gentleman that I thought was not altogether new to me. I had surely heard that nasal twang before. These sounds that filled my ears, were somewhat familiar. "Shades of departed days!" I at last exclaimed to myself, at a most sonorous and brimstonish *epocha* in the prayer, "can it be possible, that the individual who bobs and wags his black

curly "pow," in that aristocratic pulpit, is my old friend,
Nahum Gusset?"

It was so! And as if to impress the fact still more upon
me, the minister, who had now finished his prayer, opened
the Bible, and called upon us to read with him, the first
chapter of the Book of Nahum, which was not only in
consonance with his Christian name, but with the severe
sentiments he had been expressing in his address to the
Deity.

I had hoped, for the credit of my old friend, that, after he
had finished the reading of that chapter, he would have
drawn attention to the hope and consolation held out in the
last verse, and particularly in the first portion thereof—
"Behold upon the mountains the feet of Him that bringeth
good tidings, that publisheth peace!"—and construed that
into a promise of the coming of the Messiah, as the only
averter of such awful denunciations; but no—Nahum had
no such inclination. On the contrary, to make things even
worse, he shortly afterwards commenced his sermon by
taking for his text the second verse of that very chapter,
which is as follows:—"God is jealous, and the Lord revengeth; the Lord revengeth, and is furious; the Lord
will take vengeance on His adversaries, and He reserveth
wrath for His enemies;" and on that, he commenced a sermon, which, if his hearers believed in, they could scarcely
have felt comfortable. He, indeed, "spairged about the
brimstone cootie, to scald poor wretches," as Burns says, in
a most unscrupulous degree—denouncing all who heard
him as being gone in sin and misery—unworthy to look
up—fit only to cover their faces with their hands, and
blush; and, altogether, as being utterly lost, and past
redemption.

He no doubt alluded to what was the great panacea for
all this, but in such Biblical and mystical sentences, that I
scarcely believe any one of the congregation could (and perhaps he did not himself) understand what was his meaning.
Nevertheless, they took their promised doom wonderfully
well. As the reports of trials, where capital convictions have
taken place, sometimes say, "the coolest persons present
seemed to be the condemned culprits in the dock;" for, on
turning round to survey my neighbours stealthily, I found

most of them wearing extremely serene countenances, while not a few were smelling perfumes, and here and there an elderly one nodding in sleep.

Nahum, in the course of time brought his discourse to an end, but before dismissing the congregation, after "prayer and praise," as the Presbyterian saying is, he read to them a report regarding what he called "The St. Blytheswood Mission," and which seemingly was a pet institution of his own for carrying conversion to the heathen, and for which  purpose he called on all present to bestow liberally on leaving the church, in addition to what they might have given on entering, particularly if they had been unaware, or had forgotten that such an important collection was to take place; for, as he said on winding up his appeal, "charity covereth a multitude of sins," meaning probably that in this instance it would go far to condone those, for which they had but recently been put under the ban of his discourse.

And they did bestow liberally, for as we marched out I beheld the collection plates piled up with gold and silver pieces, interspersed with bank notes, to the exclusion of such vulgar coins as "poor bodies' pennies," or "bairns' bawbees."

Of course, I could not fail to be struck by what I had discovered, in regard to my old friend, nor could I help wondering at the good luck that had brought him from his mother's garret in the lane off the Trongate, to so great an elevation in the West End. I likewise marvelled that such nonsense as he had emitted, in the course both of his prayer and his sermon, should be acceptable to what was seemingly a rational and educated congregation, while the genuine and practical discourse of Mr. Sifter had, comparatively speaking, only four bare walls to hearken to it.

Above all, I could not but admire the wonderful power he seemingly possessed of causing the money of the congregation to pass from the pocket to the plate, in a way which now-a-days would have entitled him to the denomination of a "genuine spiritualist!"

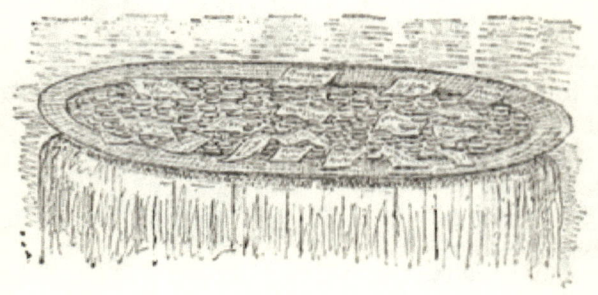

CHAPTER XXXV.

INTRODUCTORY DOGGERELS.

Sweet is the tinkling Sabbath bell,
As to the Kirk we throng;
But sweeter—even to Mess John—
Is the booming dinner gong!

The Goosedubbs Poet.

I DEVOTED next forenoon to the procuring of a comfortable lodging, a hotel not being exactly the place for a business man to sojourn in, who intended to become a resident citizen of the town, and to form a general acquaintanceship, although the system may suit "commercial gentlemen" very well.

I was rather successful in the accommodation I obtained, my landlady being the widow of a gentleman whom I remembered as an eminent and rather aristocratic West India merchant, reputed at one time to be rich, but whose business had succumbed to the new order of things, like that of many other "decayed houses," which could not cope with their *quondam* clerks, who opposed them, and cut them out, after gaining, at their expense, a knowledge of their business transactions.

I could not help contrasting the lodging I got in Mrs. Kingston's with that of honest Mrs. Gusset, the mother of the reverend Nahum, with whom Tom Throstle and I had lodged in former days. There was something so comfortable and neat in Mrs. Kingston's apartments, so genteel, and yet so subdued, so old-fashioned, and yet so fresh, while every service was conducted, without the slightest noise or bustle, or seemingly without putting her establishment to any inconvenience.

I knew, however, that this was in consequence of good management, and industry, on the part of Mrs. Kingston; for it was impossible, with the single servant, whom, I was aware she was only enabled, from her now restricted circumstances, to keep, and whom she always sent up to wait upon me, so tidily dressed, and so promptly attentive to my bell, that it could be otherwise. Indeed, I was forced to believe, that poor Mrs. Kingston laboured a good deal with her own hands, and did menial work too, although she was rather clever in concealing it; for, when she did make her appearance, no one could have told but that she had come

from the drawing-room instead of the kitchen, and from the manipulation of Berlin worsted work, instead of the scrubbing and black-leading of a goblet.

This was pride, no doubt, but still it was pardonable pride! Poor body, she could not forget that she had once been the wife of a rich West India merchant, and therefore she retained traditions sufficient to make her work hard in her old age, though in supposed secrecy—rejecting the aid of several sources from which she was entitled to have drawn assistance, in consequence of her husband's position as a burgess, and member of the Merchants' House, as well as that of several societies.

She had likewise retained all the family pictures—they having been valued in the bankrupt effects of her husband's estate, at a mere trifle—and, therefore, the dining-room, which I came to inhabit, was hung with representations of elderly gentlemen in court-dresses, and be-powdered bag-wigs, who grimly scowled at me, as I sat at their old mahogany tables, partaking of my chop, with the aid of the remnant of their crest-adorned silver forks and spoons.

Alas! that such things should occur—that a mere decade of years should make so many changes—a *quondam* pocket-picker of the Goosedubbs taking the place of the sugar aristocrats of the Squares! But such is life—particularly modern commercial life!

After securing the lodging of worthy Mrs. Kingston—the particulars regarding whom, that I have given, having been subsequently ascertained—I proceeded to wait upon a few business correspondents, who expected my coming, they having been "advised" to that effect, and others whose acquaintanceship I had yet to make.

I had given up the idea, even if I had the opportunity, of calling upon any of my former employers, Mr. Silvertop, my early patron, having, long ago, departed this life, and Mr. Bracepiece having given up business altogether, and become a residenter in another quarter; while both Mr. Gunter and Mr. Slide had retired from the active management of the house of Gunter, Slide, & Company, and gone to live on estates which they had purchased in the country, leaving the business to be conducted by their sons, who had sprung into commercial existence since I had left for abroad, and I, therefore, did not much care to trouble myself with them, particularly as I had now become, in some respect, their rival, if not opponent, in business.

On making the calls I had prescribed for myself, I had soon the opportunity of contrasting the domestic kindness of the Glasgow people to strangers, with that of the Londoners; for, the very first I visited, on learning that I was a new comer, and, without waiting for an order to excite his humanities, asked me kindly to partake of "pot-luck" with him that day; and all the rest, whom I subsequently saw, followed suit in the same way, asking me to name the days most convenient for me, on learning that I was engaged on those they had themselves proposed. I found myself, in consequence, in a position to give little trouble, so far as regarded the prime meal of the day, to my landlady, for some time to come.

"You'll find us in a very quiet way to-day," said my new friend, Mr. Garnethill, whom I had called on to begin with, and who, consequently, was the first to engage my affections for the hungry hour of five o'clock, as I *sauntered* arm-in-arm along with him, according to arrangement, from the Exchange, where I had met him, to his house in the

West End, he having undertaken to be my guide for the nonce. "You will find us in a very quiet way—for we expect nobody to meet you excepting Dr. Morse, our family

medical attendant—old calo-mile and chalk-mixture, as I call him, these being the great ingredients, or 'simples' to use his own phrase that he deals in—his bane and anti-dote, in a word—and a young friend of mine named Jackson, a writer, whom I employ professionally, and who is coming on rapidly in his business, and making a fortune, although, betwixt you and me, I suspect the birkie is managing that otherwise than by the law, and the slow process of extracting three-and-fourpences, and six-and-eight-pences, from the pockets of his clients; for I have reason to know, from a circumstance that recently came, by the merest chance, to my knowledge, that he is doing a good deal in the private discounting line."

"Do you mean to say," I inquired, "that he's a money lender?"

"Something in that way," replied my friend, "but call him what you like: it does not signify in Glasgow a button how one makes money, *if* he makes money, and particularly if one has some other business as a means of conferring a *nomme de plume* upon him. This young fellow calls himself a lawyer, and besides, he inherits a small landed estate in the suburbs of the City, which came to him by his mother's side, and, therefore, he is considered a genteel sprig, notwith-standing his trenching upon the preserves of Moses, and doing a little in the usurious way."

This candid description of the guest I was about to meet did not predispose me in his favour—not that I would have scorned to have done something in that line myself, had opportunity and a chance of making money presented them-selves in favourable guise—but still I was not partial to the profession of a money-lender, whom I was inclined to look upon as being naturally a screw, and a low fellow.

However, not being aware what might be Mr. Garnethill's position in regard to this one, or what might be his reason in consequence, for cultivating his acquaintanceship, I made no invidious remarks upon what he had been pleased to communicate regarding him to me; but on the contrary, changed the subject by inquiring as to his other friend Dr. Morse, whom I was likewise to meet.

"Dr. Morse," replied Mr. Garnethill, who, I began to observe, was a bit of a gossip, "is a very good fellow to make an acquaintance of, but may providence avert his ever getting my body to deal with, as a doctor, for I must say I dread him a great deal more than any disease that would attack me. As I have told you, he is our family physician, that is to say, he attends my wife and children, but for all that he never gets an opportunity of practising on me, partly from my scarcely ever having anything wrong with me, and partly from my never having abandoned the adviser of my bachelor days, worthy Dr. Glober of the Gallowgate, who, in contradistinction to Morse, only deals in herbs and vegetable decoctions, instead of metals and minerals, and, therefore, if he cannot cure me, at all events he does not kill me outright, but gives me a chance of my life."

"Do you mean to say," I inquired, "that Dr. Morse never gives that."

"If he does," replied my friend, "it is more from luck than good guidance; from nature and a good constitution carrying through his patients, than anything he prescribes to them, and then the whole town resounds with the wonderful cure he has effected!"

"If that is the case," I said, "why do you allow him to attend your wife and children?"

"Because, to tell you the truth," answered Mr. Garnethill, with a grim smile, and in a half confidential way, "I have no choice; the grey mare is the better horse at home, as you will come likewise to know, my young friend, when you get married, and become a good husband. But, thank God," he continued, "so far as my children are concerned, they are out of Morse's power for a while at least, my two girls being at a boarding school in Edinburgh, and as to my wife, she is, although ailing occasionally, pretty tough. But he'll kill her some day, my dear friend; he'll kill her, I fear, and I shall be left a miserable and disconsolate widower!"

As the worthy man said this, with a lack-a-daisical whine, I turned to look at him, expecting to see at least a tear moistening his eye, if not trickling down his cheek, but in this I was mistaken, for instead of a lachrymary flow, his physiognomy bore what I would call a very resigned-like expression.

"Ah! yes, my dear friend," he went on, however, to say, "you little know what we married men have to submit to in this City, for we are completely, one way or another, in the hands of the Clergy, the Faculty, and the Law, and all because it is fashionable. There's Dr. Gust of St. Blytheswood Sanctuary, why I have to fee him as heavily as I do Dr. Morse: what with my subscription to this mission and that mission, by contributions to this collection and that collection, and my advance (which of course never comes back) to this school and that school, not to mention an occasional testimonial to the reverend Doctor, in the shape of an embroidered purse, or worked pair of slippers, got up by the ladies of the congregation, and filled with sovereigns by the gentlemen—for in a case of this kind, slippers hold coins just as well and naturally as purses—while, at the same time, we have to hearken to a homily, appropriate to the occasion of presentation, from his reverence, which is as great an infliction as the extraction from our fobs of the filthy lucre, as perhaps the worthy gentleman will designate it, in his very next sermon, not alluding to the presentation, however, *particularly*, but generally."

"Talking of that," continued my friend, "I expect we will soon have another call in that way, for the Doctor a few days ago had a son, and that's too good an occasion for the ladies to lose. They first made up a purse for him (by our aid) along with a Bible, psalm-book, and gown, when he got the living; then another along with a silver tea service, when he was married; then a third, along with a cradle, when "his first-born," as he designated the brat, came; and since then, their name has been legion, along with articles varying from a gilded time-piece to a silver ink-stand!"

"Your pastor, Dr. Gusset," said I, not caring, for my

own reasons, to talk of him, as an old acquaintance, excepting in a general way, "must be a great favourite with the
congregation, when he gets so many kindnesses bestowed
upon him?"

"With the women only," replied Mr Garnethill, "and a
few uxorious gowks who are obliged to do as they are
ordered by their wives. But Gust, not Gusset," he went on
to say, "is his name, although I have heard it said that, like
other would-be aristocrats, who are ashamed of the fathers
that begat them, he has changed it, so as to have a more
fashionable sound. Our Smiths now are Smythes, our
Pokes are Pollocks, and our Meiklewames are Meiklams;
why then should Gusset not be Gust, particularly as it is
in keeping with his sermons, which, after all, are gusty
indeed."

"I had the pleasure of hearing him preach," said I, "at
St. Blythswood's yesterday afternoon, and I must confess
that what he said was in keeping with the joke you now
express. But, may I ask, does he always send you to the in-
fernal regions as he did yesterday, and does that add to his
popularity?"

"Ah! my dear fellow," replied Mr Garnethill, "our
friend Gust had his purpose to serve by that sort of sermon
yesterday—and he served it, as you might have noticed, by

the large plateful of notes and gold which he gained under
the auspices of his two fashionable and ruling elders, who,

dressed in white chokers on such occasions, are there for the
purpose of staring the congregation out of contributions!
The fact is, these collections are just the penitential sacrifices
of old Catholic days, bestowed in dread, though demanded
in modern style.　Had he not flashed the brimstone in our
faces, he would not have received half the sum he got.　But
stop till next Sunday, and after he has counted the amount,
to his satisfaction, and then we, the men, will be 'charitable
Christians,' 'whose bread thrown upon the waters will return
to us after many days;' and our wives will be 'saints in life,'
who have set their households in order, and have nothing
to dread!"

"Well, after all" I said, with the view of drawing my
gossiping friend a little further out, as to Nahum, in whom
I confess I was becoming interested, "your minister, in so
acting, shows great tact, and quite a business turn, but is he
always successful, and never seen through?"

"Well, I don't know but that he is," answered Mr. Garnethill, musingly, "for I fear he sometimes overdoes the
thing.　For instance, it has been noticed lately that his
graces at dinners—for he is a great diner out—are on a
regular tariff scale, according to the style of the 'spread,'
and that has caused prejudicial remark.　If he sees, to state
an example, that there is only one soup, and that the best
plate—the silver dish covers, let us suppose—are not out, he
merely prays that we may be thankful for the 'mercies now
spread before us.'　If, in addition, however, to the soup,
there should be a display of silver, thus indicating something
superior beneath it, he craves the Deity that it 'may be
blessed exceedingly, and that we may esteem it beyond price,
and with becoming gratitude to the Giver of all Good.'
But if there should be an inordinate display of plate—two
soups in silver tureens; the French corner dishes out, and
so on—with perhaps three or four 'sawlies'* to wait the
table, then there are no bounds to the reverend gentleman's

---

* The *sawlies* of Glasgow are as famous a body as what the *cawdies* of ancient
Edinburgh used to be.　They are men—generally *quondam* footmen, waiters, or beadles
—who gain their livelihoods by attending funerals in the forenoon, as mutes or *sallies*,
and dinners in the afternoon, as butlers and waiters.　There is a story told that a
certain plain-spoken individual once hurt the feelings of a Glasgow Bailie who was
entertaining his friends with an extra *shine*, by asking him if he might be allowed to
ring the bell for the *sawlie;* and hence the continuance of the jocular appellation.
It was something like exclaiming *memento mori* over the wassail cup!

pious enthusiasm, for under such circumstances he is observed to throw up his arms, exclaiming, 'bountiful Jehovah!' and to give a 'grace like a tether,' as Burns says!"

As Mr. Garnethill finished this characteristic anecdote regarding the worthy Nahum, we arrived at his door, being that of a very comfortable and commodious mansion, situated in one of the West End crescents, and adjacent to houses of a like description, when he immediately introduced me to Mrs. Garnethill, whom I found sitting in the drawing room, and with whom he left me alone, while he, no doubt, proceeded to his dressing-room, for the purpose of putting himself in dinner array.

Mrs. Garnethill I found to be a very kind, hospitable person, seemingly about the same age as that of her husband, which was a little beyond the prime, and notwithstanding that she wore a controlled expression of countenance, in consequence, no doubt, of the devout observances she indulged in, in common with other ladies of the fashionable locality in which she resided, as hinted at by Mr. Garnethill, she was evidently of a cheerful and communicative and inquiring disposition.

Her first inquiry at me, after Mr. Garnethill had explained that I was about to establish myself as a residenter in Glasgow, and she had got over the usual remarks upon the weather, etc., was, "Pray, whose church do you sit in?"

This I had much gratification in answering, while con-

gratulating myself upon the steps I had taken to enable
me to do so. I, therefore, replied that I had attended Mr.
Sifter in the forenoon, and Dr. Gust in the afternoon of
yesterday, my reason for so rambling being, that I had only
arrived the day before, and being comparatively a stranger
to the City, had therefore found my way to the churches of
these clergymen more by chance than from any laid down
plan.

"Oh! yes," replied Mrs. Garnethill, "it was very natural
for you to do so, but your better chance has been that which
led you to Dr. Gust in the afternoon, than to Mr. Sifter in
the forenoon!"

"Indeed?" said I, feeling rather surprised at this communication, "Why, I heard a very good sermon from Mr.
Sifter, and which edified me considerably. I must confess,
that of the two, I preferred him exceedingly!"

"Ah! my dear sir," interjected Mrs. Garnethill, "if
a lot of mere moral quibbles, strung together in fine
words, and delivered in glowing language, and with a
musical delivery, be a good sermon, then I grant that what
you say is correct. But ah! where is the consolation, where
the benefit of such vanities, and such latitudinarian principles—as Dr. Gust would call them? Will they cheer a
death-bed, or maintain a sinking spirit? Will they give us
hope while darkness lowers? Will they grant us peace,
when there is no peace?"

"Well," I answered, while feeling that it was necessary I
should be very cautious, if not a little hypocritical, with the
worthy lady, whose fanaticism was evidently of a chronic
and determined nature, "I must confess, that Mr. Sifter's
sentiments were more addressed to those who were healthy
than those who were ailing—to those who enjoyed intellectual vigour, than those whose brains were weakened
by disease—to those who yet have the world before them,
than to those who are done with it, and, therefore, have no
interest excepting in the world to come. But surely," I
continued, "notwithstanding this circumstance, Mr. Sifter
does not neglect the important considerations you have suggested, when there is necessity for them, and when his duty
points out to him that it is essential to act the consoler as
well as the teacher?"

"Consoler here! teacher there!" exclaimed Mrs. Garnethill, "he's neither the one nor the other; but, on the contrary, a mere moralist, and expounder of sentiments, that serve as an excuse to the materialist and the schismatic; but will such bring us to the true interests of religion? Will they bring us to the bosom and embrace of the Church? Will they above all, bring us to Zion?"

"Ah! my young friend," Mrs. Garnethill resumed, after a short pause, during which she had evidently been musing as to how she should keep up the conversation, for I was determined to be silent, in case of committing myself, "you did right to hear Dr. Gust in the afternoon, and notwithstanding your partiality for Mr. Sifter, I am sure you were pleased with him, for what he preached was considered a great effort. Indeed, it was remarked to me, by several ladies as we walked home, as being wonderful!"

"Oh! I by no means wish to depreciate Dr. Gust," said I, by way of setting myself right with Mrs. Garnethill, "on the contrary, I hearkened with the greatest interest to him, and went home much impressed with what I had heard. Indeed, I feel quite interested in Dr. Gust, and intend to cultivate his acquaintanceship, both as a clergyman and as a friend."

"I am delighted to hear that," said Mrs. Garnethill, who did not know, of course, my true reasons for wishing to learn more about the reverend gentleman, "and I particularly rejoice that you will not have to wait long for an opportunity of improving upon that very proper resolution; for it so happens that Dr. Gust is to dine here to-day, I having had the happy chance of asking him to do so, when he called here in the forenoon."

"Dr. Gust to dine here to-day," exclaimed Mr. Garnethill, as he entered the drawing-room at this moment, seemingly with rather a mortified look, as he heard the announcement, but which expression he banished immediately, as he continued, "well, I am glad to learn that, for in the first place, we'll have a better dinner in consequence, and in the second, my wife will have somebody that will keep her in talk to her satisfaction!"

The latter part of this speech was addressed to me "aside," as the playbooks have it, and was, therefore, not heard by the critical ears of his worthy spouse, whose attention, indeed, was otherwise occupied, as the sounds of feet in the act of ascending from below were heard, and the door

opened with a bang to admit the important and all-attractive person of the Reverend Nahum Gusset, or Gust, to give him his improved name, as he stalked into the room, with folded hands before him, and a solemn and important air, as much as to say, "I am the guest for whom you wait, but now let the feast proceed!"

My old friend, who evidently did not know me, on being introduced by Mr. Garnethill, and which is not to be wondered at, considering the great change that had taken place in my appearance, both from the development of bulk, and the endurance of a hot climate—after gravely bowing to myself and the rest of the party, in keeping with the dignity of his position as a popular clergyman, took a seat on the sofa alongside of Mrs. Garnethill, with whom he was soon engaged in a warm conversation, no doubt pertaining to spiritual subjects, and this gave me an opportunity of surveying another guest that had come, he being announced as Mr. Jackson.

For something in the shape of Mr. Jackson, not very prepossessing, I had been prepared by Mr. Garnethill in his explanation during the walk out, regarding that gentleman's profession and business practices; but I confess I did not expect to find in him the monkey-faced man who had been my fellow-traveller in the coach, from Manchester to Glasgow, only two days previously, and who had offended me by his exclusive reserve and puppyish manners—but such was the case.

Mr. Jackson himself seemed taken a-back and conscience-struck on being introduced to me by Mr. Garnethill, for he returned my stiff bow with an awkwardness that proclaimed he was not at ease. We therefore retreated, from each other as far as the dimensions of the room would permit, he to examine a cabinet, in which were placed stuffed birds and foreign shells, and I to study an album that lay on the drawing-room table, with a very rich and costly gilded binding, in the pages of which were delineated a number of vile drawings, intermingled with unnecessary scraps of doggerels that had been culled by some girlish hands, and denominated poetry.

These served my time for the nonce, inasmuch as they gave me an opportunity of glancing at Mr. Jackson occasionally, whom I observed to be attired in full dinner dress, which in my jealous eye made him look more than ever like a monkey, and one fit to dance on the top of an organ, while being ground by some of those *lazaroni* that render uncomfortable, squares in general, and quiet streets in particular.

At last Dr. Morse was announced, which still more relieved the ante-dinner tedium I had been suffering, particularly as I knew that he was the last guest expected.

The Doctor walked into the room, in a very unpretentious

manner indeed, and one that would not have led me to judge he was of the murderous character described by Mr. Garnethill. On the contrary, he looked as sedate and mild as a minister, and not as if he had either the dread of his dead patients on his conscience, or their blood on his hands.

I, however, remembered Byron's description of Lambro:—

> " He was, indeed, the mildest manner'd man
>   That ever scuttled ship, or cut a throat,
> With such true breeding of a gentleman,
>   You never could divine his real thought;
> No courtier could, nor scarcely woman can
>   Gird more deceit within a petticoat!"

and, therefore, resolved not to allow appearances to prejudice my judgment.

He passed on, after the usual salutations to the general guests, to where Mrs. Garnethill sat, and taking his seat at her side, other than that occupied by the Rev. Dr. Gust, he asked earnestly after her health, and at the same time deliberately felt her pulse, while he held his gold ticker in his unoccupied hand.

"There's a picture for you," whispered Mr. Garnethill to me, while pretending at the same time to be referring to something in the album, "my poor wife, betwixt Divinity and Physic, like Garrick betwixt Tragedy and Comedy, and each trying who'll get the mastership!"

At this moment the gong sounded, and the drawing-room

door sprung open, while the welcome announcement was made that "dinner was on the table." Dr. Gust accordingly, as the principal, or at all events as the most honoured guest present, led Mrs. Garnethill down stairs to the dining-room, while the rest followed—worthy Mr. Garnethill bringing up the rear.

CHAPTER XXXVI.

INTRODUCTORY DOGGERELS.

Send round the wine—no heel-taps show—
Fill—fill the glass again—
There's none to blame the toper who
Swills claret or champagne.

E'en ministers themselves may swig
Such drink till they get frisky;
But woe to the poor workman, who
Dares to get drunk on whisky!

The Goosedubbs Poet.

THE Rev. Nahum Gust, D.D., so far as I could judge, on this occasion, certainly bore out the character which his friend Mr. Garnethill had given of him to me, as we walked from town, for he pronounced a benediction over the pewter dish covers—the dinner not being sufficiently important, probably, for the silver ones—of rather a subdued and moderate nature, such as boiled haddocks and roast beef might have commanded in any ordinary company, ungraced by a clergyman, where like edibles were presented on the table. He nevertheless did great justice to these plain provisions, in which operation he reminded me very much of his old table habits when a student, with this difference, that he handled his knife and fork on this occasion better, and swallowed his wine more elegantly than he used to do his beer and whisky, when entertained by poor Tom Throstle and myself, in the olden time. He had, in addition, more control over his manners, and, indeed, conducted himself very like a gentleman, who not only respected himself, but felt that he was respected by those around.

He had, likewise, a very knowing way of ever and anon peeping through his glass, as he held it betwixt himself and the light, and of agitating the liquor with a circular motion, as *connoisseurs* do, when he would apply his konk to it, and having thereby, as it were, satisfied himself as to the genuineness of the wine's "bouquet," and proper colour, he would whip it off.

"This is the same old brown sherry," he said, addressing Mr. Garnethill, "that we have had from you before? And do you know," he continued, as that gentleman nodded his head to him, in token of assent, "it very much resembles some wine that I have tasted in our friend's, at No. 59 of the Square, only that I think yours is better, and more matured. May I ask if you have remarked that wine?"

"To tell you the truth," replied Mr. Garnethill, "I have not, and for this simple reason, that our friend in the Square never gives me an opportunity of tasting his brown sherry. He reserves it for his minister, and perhaps his doctor, and bestows upon his ordinary friends something plainer instead!"

"You are complimentary," answered Nahum, without showing himself in the least degree abashed by this plain bit of facetiousness on the part of Mr. Garnethill, "but if our friend does so, his kindness is thrown away, at least on me, for to tell you the truth, sherry is a wine that I do not much care about."

"That being the case," replied Mr. Garnethill, "we'll change the drink upon you, and I hope with something that will more meet your approbation!"

Here Mr. Garnethill gave the smart waiting woman that had been attending the table a peculiar hint, when she immediately procured from some cunning nook of the sideboard, a long-necked bottle, which she placed before her master, while all eyes were bent upon it, and in particular, those of the worthy Nahum and Dr. Morse.

This bottle, which the host announced as something superior in the way of champagne, was not like that of modern days, glossy and shining, as if it had just come out of a glass-house, with a white silvery head of tinfoil, but on the contrary, was dirty and cobwebbed, while its neck was enveloped in a huge crust of grim wax, almost impervious in appearance.

The opening of it, therefore, required some manipulation, which Mr. Garnethill forthwith addressed himself to, with the aid of a formidable carving knife and a pair of nippers, with the former of which he scraped the wax, making a mess of the table, and with the latter he snipt the wire, when the cork immediately bounded to the roof, with a crack that seemingly rejoiced the heart of the reverend Doctor, for on the bottle being transmitted to him, before being operated upon by anyone else, he immediately commenced to fill from it Mrs. Garnethill's long glass, slowly and deliberately, so that it should not be supplied alone with froth, but on the contrary, with good solid wine. He then, in like manner, poured the sparkling liquor into his own glass, and passing the bottle to Dr. Morse, he kindly smiled and nodded to Mrs. Garnethill, and then solemnly, and with an evident relish, swallowed the champagne, turning up the whites of his eyes, while he did so, as though he had been pronouncing "Amen" to one of his longest graces.

Dr. Morse, likewise, did full justice to the champagne, after which the long-necked bottle found its way to where Mr. Garnethill and I sat, and after resting a few moments there was duly returned to the head of the table, Dr. Morse, on this occasion taking upon him to fill Mrs. Garnethill's glass for the second time, although the worthy lady—very properly, as I thought, and perhaps as Mr. Garnethill, likewise, thought—protested against it.

"My dear madam," remonstrated Dr. Morse, by way of overcoming Mrs. Garnethill's scruples, "I am not pressing upon you any thing that will do harm. On the contrary, I am actually prescribing a medicine—and a medicine that I only wish all my patients could afford to take—without looking for a fee. Permit me, therefore, to fill your glass—

aye, even to the brim—and to recommend that you imbibe it
before the effervescence flies off, when all I have to say is,
that if it does you any harm, blame me!"

"My conscience!" whispered Mr Garnethill to me, as Dr.
Morse said this, "there's my dear wife whipping off, what
she knows perfectly well will lay her up to-morrow with a
bilious headache, during which she will make me miserable
with her complaints, and all because Physic says she should
do so, and Divinity approves it. Why, if required at their
hands, she would take arsenic just as fast!"

And as if still more to add to worthy Mr. Garnethill's
trepidation, the very next step that Dr. Morse pursued, was
still further to prescribe to the lady, twenty drops, as he
called them, but in reality a tolerable dram of brandy, which
he poured into the bottom of her champagne glass with his
own hands, while declaring that the same would "keep all
right!"

The doctor then took an equal portion of the esteemed
liquor himself, and passed it to the Rev. Nahum, who filled
up his glass to the brim, and tossed it off, while declaring that
he only did so because it was recommended by the Faculty.

"And do you now recommend brandy," here screeched Mr.
Jackson, with something like a satirical leer upon his
baboonish face, "as the universal panacea for all complaints,
doctor. The last time I had the pleasure of meeting you, it
was something simpler?"

"Scarcely that," replied Dr. Morse. "In general, I recommend to all my patients whisky and cold water, as being by far the safest, the plainest, and the most harmless drink they can take; but on special occasions, such as after champagne, or oleaginous condiments, or puddings, or sweets, I do not object to brandy, particularly if it be good—such as our worthy friend at the foot of the table always makes a point of keeping in his cellar."

"Why—what would you say to the cold water without

the whisky?" again intermitted Mr. Jackson, while a broad grin, that exposed his tusks, illuminated his countenance, at what he evidently conceived to be a very posing hit against the doctor, "as by far the simplest, the plainest, and most harmless drink of all: although, perhaps, it might be rather inimical to the practice of yourself and brotherhood?"

"I'll give you my opinion as to that," retorted Dr. Morse, "when you please to call me in, or I may even do that gratuitously, when you of the legal profession generously give advice that will save people the necessity of going to law?"

And here a general "guffaw" broke forth at what may be called the small passage of arms that had thus taken place betwixt the two professionals, which relieved Dr. Morse from the embarrassment that the ingenuity of his opponent was calculated to have placed him in, and at the same time gave Mr. Jackson a little *eclat*, not only as a wit, but as being, like Falstaff, the cause of wit in others.

And now the dinner proceeded rapidly, the more substantial dishes having been followed by sweets, which brought drams into requisition again, particularly on the part of Doctors Gust and Morse—but merely as digestives, as they pronounced them—the whole affair being crowned by toasted cheese, which had been specially ordered by Mrs. Garnethill, as a mark of respect towards her beloved pastor, "for she knew he liked it," and who washed down the same with a tumbler-full of double London stout, after which he declared he had dined completely to his mind.

On the port, sherry, and madeira being placed on the table, accompanied with a few dishes of dried fruits, Mr. Garnethill made a motion as if he were about to pass the decanters round; but his better-half, noticing this, immediately cried "hush!" and bowing to Dr. Gust, requested that he should return thanks.

This the reverend gentleman did at once, after which, notwithstanding his declaration only a few minutes before, as to the fulness with which he had dined, he immediately commenced to demolish a fair share of the dried fruits that were on the table, and, in particular, a dish of walnuts, the kernels of which he tipped with salt; and these evidently having re-invigorated his palate, he was enabled to pay his addresses to the port, which he ogled affectionately, and then saluted with a smack that might have become an English Bishop, let alone a Scottish Presbyter.

"Ah! this is the true Falernian," he exclaimed, "this is that divine juice, which cheereth the heart of man, and such as I can conceive inspired old Noah after the ark had grounded, and the waters subsided!"

And having thus delivered himself of a sentiment which I scarcely conceive a layman would have dared to utter, but which good Mrs. Garnethill listened to as devoutly as though it had been one of the inspired sayings, Dr. Gust went on to sip the "ruby bright," and to crack walnuts till it was time for that lady to rise, when he kindly accompanied her to the dining-room door, and bowed her out.

The conversation, after the lady left, became general, but still animated, particularly as Mr. Garnethill—no doubt, agreeably to surprise his reverend friend—introduced a bottle of port wine, of a still superior vintage than that of which we had been partaking; and, in order that full justice should be done to it, he allowed Nahum to decant it himself, in which operation he proved himself to be quite an adept, for it came forth as pure as amber, and without a bell upon it, leaving the crust on the side of the black bottle perfectly unbroken.

Nor did a single bottle suffice to satisfy the two doctors, notwithstanding the fact that they got the most of it to themselves, seeing that the rest of the party preferred brown sherry, and that, too, in something like moderation.

The reverend Nahum now got on a subject which, as I learned from our host, he was invariably garrulous regarding, particularly when the port was good, and he had people with sufficient patience to listen to him, and not contradict him—or, at all events, not to an extent beyond that which gave a filip to his loquacious combativeness—and that was the drunkenness of the lower classes.

"It is perfectly annoying, nay, it is disgusting," he said, filling his glass with the superior port that has been spoken of, and passing the bottle across the table to Dr. Morse, "to observe to what an extent, now-a-days, drunkenness is being carried amongst the working people. Why, one can scarcely get along on a Saturday evening, or even on the morning of the Lord's day, without being staggered against, by some of those wretches who have been spending their wages in vile whisky, and not only impoverishing themselves, so that they cannot afford to clothe their persons sufficiently, to appear decent at church on a Sabbath—that is to say, if they were willing to go there, but which, I fear, they are not—but endangering their souls, by their excesses, at the same time!"

"But how can you put it down?" said Dr. Morse, in a tone of hopeless candour. "See the efforts that have been made by the temperance and teetotal societies, backed by those of the Faculty, some of the brightest ornaments of which have granted a certificate that intoxicating drinks, or fermented liquors of any kind, are not necessary, either in a medical, or alimentary point of view; and, yet, according to Parliamentary returns, the consumption of spirits is greater than ever."

"Temperance—teetotal societies—Faculty certificates!"

interjected the reverend doctor with a sneer, "these can do nothing; nay, on the contrary, I sincerely believe they do harm. It is only the denunciations of the pulpit, the vigilance of the eldership, and the remonstrances of the missionary, aided by prayer, persuasion, and the threat of penalties, and supported by the police, that can do anything!"

"Yes!" he continued, after whipping off his glass and again filling it, "the minister must exalt his voice, and the magistrate must apply the rod, and if he has not power sufficiently to do so, a law must be passed strengthening his arm in that respect, so that vile concoctions such as beer, bitters, and whisky, may be swept from the land, or at all events consumed in such moderate quantities, and at such proper intervals, as will spare us the pain of seeing people staggering in the streets, wallowing in the gutters, or being carted in wheel-barrows to the police office, where a triffling fine, or a short incarceration, forms no punishment at all!"

And so the Rev. Doctor went on, listened respectfully to by all, while monopolising the whole talk, till he had exhausted the subject and the port wine, when he bethought himself that it was time he should take a "white wash" of sherry, and go to the drawing-room, and which resolution he proceeded to execute, followed afterwards by us all.

We had now tea, toast, and tittle-tattle, in the drawing-room, during the course of which, I had the luck to get into closer confabulation with my old friend, who still continued to prose away on his favourite subject, without receiving any contradiction from me. Happening, however, inadvertantly to address him as Dr. "Gusset," instead of Gust, I immediately discovered that I had aroused a new sensation within him, for he forthwith became silent, and retreating to a sofa which stood in a darkish corner of the room, he there seated himself, while darting suspicious, if not angry glances at me, which showed that I had struck some string

within the compass of his memory that did not vibrate
harmoniously.

I, however, took no notice of this little incident, but, on

the contrary, looked as innocent
as though nothing but what was
regular had happened. At the
same time, I felt I had set his
brain a speculating, and that in
course of time it would lead to
a mutual recognition betwixt us
of one kind or another.

Nor was I wrong in this surmise, for Dr. Morse, having had
a message sent to him to attend
some patient that had been
suddenly taken ill, on his leaving, the company commenced
to break up, and having paid my adieus to Mr. and Mrs.
Garnethill, and left the house, I was soon overtaken by the
reverend Nahum, as I walked along, who thrust his arm
into mine, and, naming me, asked if it was possible that he
had been sitting all the afternoon and evening with an old
and honoured, and dear friend, without knowing him?

"You have," I replied, "and what is more, you have, at
the same time, not been unknown to me, for I heard you
preach yesterday, and then discovered, that since I left my
native country and returned to it again, which was only on
Saturday afternoon, you had become a great, a popular, and
an honoured labourer in that vineyard, for which you were
so earnestly and so industriously preparing yourself when I
had the pleasure of being a lodger in your worthy mother's
house, regarding whom I beg now respectfully to inquire!"

"Ah! my very dear friend," answered Nahum, who
really seemed to be touched by the *quasi* complimentary
speech I had made, "you have taken me so aback by the
kind and eulogistic mode in which you have spoken, and
said, and asked so much, in the well chosen and ably
condensed words with which you have expressed yourself,
that I feel quite overwhelmed, and unable to explain and
answer as I fain would, what you have required from me
without appearing prolix and vain. I have, indeed, as you
have said, been exalted in the ministry beyond what I ever

expected, or perhaps deserved, but still such is the case, and the poor student, that laboured and studied while he was neglected and even reviled, has become honoured and bepraised, so that well may I exclaim 'the stone that the builders have rejected, hath become the chief corner stone!'"

"With regard to my worthy mother," he went on to say, "alas! that excellent and beloved woman has long been in her grave; although no doubt she is now a saint in heaven, for to me she was more than a mother, and to her I was indebted not only for a bright and proper example as to how I should act and comport myself, but for the means of attaining that education which has led me to so favoured and exalted a position in the ministry."

Here Nahum pulled out his white handkerchief and commenced to whine, while alternately eulogising his late worthy mother and blowing his nose; but which paroxysm I thought was more indebted for its vehemence, to the port wine he had lately imbibed, than to any actual sorrow that he felt.

I was led to judge thus uncharitably regarding him by what followed, for lowering his voice, and banishing his whining suddenly, he said, "By-the-by, my dear friend, I have one thing to remark to you. You called me 'Gusset' before the rest of the party to-night, instead of Gust. Now I wish to explain to you that although the former designation is one that I will never cease to honour,—it being that of my worthy father whom I only remember in connection with the days of my boyhood, for he used to *larrup* me well for neglecting my lessons and playing the truant at school—but it was all for my good; excellent man, rest his soul!—and likewise that of my still more esteemed mother, who never *larrupped* me at all, yet I wish now to be distinguished by the name of Gust, instead of Gusset, the difference betwixt them being merely created by the dropping of two redundant letters, thereby rendering the surname more terse and distinguishable, and the pronounciation of it more euphonious and musical. Besides, my dear friend," and here I suspect he spoke his real sentiments, " Gust is a much genteeler name than Gusset, the latter savouring so much of the seamstress, which to some extent my excellent mother was, for she was very eydent, as we say in Scotland, with her needle. Not only so, but in these politic times it is quite usual to modify, or lengthen, or shorten, or even alter names where such is considered opportune. It was a practice, too, amongst the priests of the old Catholic Church, and why should it not be so amongst those of the Reformed Church?—therefore, my friend, I request that after this you will designate me Gust and not Gusset. Yes, even the ' Reverend Na-um Gust,'— Nahum being pronounced soft, in the English style, and not hard, like Naw-hum, as in the vulgar Scottish, and which my very soul detests and abominates!"

And having thus given me a broad hint that, with all his professions and pretensions, he was actually ashamed of the mother that had been so kind and considerate to him, she having, to my certain knowledge, almost starved herself, while labouring at the same time, in the most menial manner, in order to give Nahum a college education, he suddenly changed the subject of conversation by asking where I had taken up my quarters.

To this I answered that I had engaged the apartments of a Mrs. Kingston, and that I was now on my way to them, I not having in fact yet occupied them, else I would have been happy to have asked him to step in and see them.

" Mrs. Kingston?" said Nahum, on my making this communication. " My dear Sir, I know her well, a most excellent worthy woman, and one of my congregation, never absent forenoon or afternoon—a very pillar of my church, I may say, and whose mite is always forthcoming when required. I am glad, both for her sake and yours, that you have got her rooms, and, as a proof of my joy for the circumstance, I will accompany you there, as it is on the way to my own house, and introduce you to her good graces, by speaking favourably of you to her, as an old and esteemed friend!"

" But hark you!" he continued, while giving my arm rather a severe pinch—what, indeed, I would call a port-wine pinch —" not a word to her about Gusset, nor about my dear and

honoured mother, nor about the days of my studentship, for
all these must pertain to oblivion, if you value my future
friendship!"

To humour my reverend friend, I hastily promised obedience, for we now stood at Mrs. Kingston's door, the bell of
which had been rather violently pulled by the obliging Nahum,
which brought the widow herself to answer it, and then
what a shaking of hands on the part of him and her, took
place, interspersed with not a few goodly compliments, which
Nahum evidently excelled in, and which seemed never to
fail him, particularly when addressing the fair sex. "My
very dear and worthy Mrs. Kingston," he said, while his face
wore a most lugubrious smile, and he at the same time made
her arm go up and down like
a pump handle, "I have just
learned, from my valued
friend here, whom I met, by
the merest chance in the
world, at the table of our
respected acquaintance, Mrs.
Garnethill, that he had taken
up his abode with you, and
therefore I have volunteered,
on my way homewards, to
call in upon you, and com-
mend him to you, as one
who is well worthy of your
best consideration. And as

all our deeds and all our actions should be commenced pro-
perly as Christians, I will just take the opportunity of in-
augurating this happy occasion, by stepping inwards, and
favouring you with a mouthful of prayer!"

Here Nahum, without further preliminaries, brushed past
Mrs. Kingston, and, stalking into her dining-room—which
was destined for my sitting-room, and which she had, in
expectation of my coming, taken care to have in the best
order, and well lit up with a full blaze of gas—coolly took a
chair, and bending before it, an act which, out of seriousness
on the part of Mrs. Kingston, and decency on that of myself,
was duly imitated by both of us, he commenced to pray aloud
in a way not only very complimentary to the lady and me, but

to himself. Indeed, the reverend gentleman's prayer might
have passed for a very good after-dinner speech; and, to
ascertain that it had proper effect, particularly on the widow,
he every now and then turned round, and took a look at
her—her back, in the attitude she had becomingly assumed,
being to him—which motion had so ludicrous an effect, that
I with difficulty restrained my laughter, as I "twigged" him
with the tail of my eye.

Of course, it will not be expected that I should give a
recapitulation of the prayer. It is sufficient to say, that it
seemed to serve the turn of my friend, and was evidently
much appreciated by Mrs. Kingston, who, at its termination,
arose from her knees, not only with an extremely grave
expression of countenance, but with tears in her eyes.

This might be accounted for, by the circumstance, that, in
the course of his prayer, he had alluded to her former
elevated position, in contrast with her now reduced and
widowed state, but which latter, as he whiningly expressed
it, was so much more the better and happier of the two, in
consequence of her having become, more a believer and a
church-goer than ever.

"Ah!" said Mrs. Kingston, as she addressed Nahum,
seemingly in return for the compliments he had paid her,

and who received the same becomingly, as he sat on the
chair, before which he had recently kneeled, with his eyes
cast reverently on the bright
mahogany, and his hands
clasped meekly before him.
"Ah! you have ever a word
of consolation and hope for
the unfortunate and oppressed,
and I take it very kind that
you should have stepped in
thus unceremoniously and
plainly with your young friend
to visit me, and, as it were,
introduce me to him; for, although I had seen him before,
it was only this forenoon, for
a few minutes, and I might

say, therefore, he was comparatively a stranger to me; but
which he shall be no longer."

"But," continued the widow, "now that you have so
opportunely and pleasantly, thus favoured my humble dwelling with courtesy and worship, will you allow me to offer
you a cup of tea, or a glass of wine, or any refreshment that
I may have in the house, seeing that my new lodger has not
had time to lay in supplies, so as to be enabled to entertain
you in that way?"

I fully expected that Nahum, on receiving such an invitation, under the circumstances, would have looked upon it as
a mere act of conventional civility, and have declined it, while
taking himself off, but in this I was mistaken; for, evidently
knowing something of Mrs. Kingston's domestic resources,
and what would still farther add to her joy on the occasion,
he answered, "Tea we have already had, *usque ad nauseam*,
and wine, I might say, if inclined to be facetious, but which
I never am, *ad burstum*, (here he tipped me a most uncleri-
cal wink), and therefore we, or at least I, must decline
these; but, if it is not going too far, and putting you to too
much trouble, my worthy friend, I would not be disinclined,
particularly if you pressed me, to taste, by way of refreshment after the Word, a little of your old Jamaica Rum, such
as on rare and interesting occasions like this, you have been

in the habit of treating me with, and the recollection of the
superior flavour of which makes me smack my very lips!"

"That you shall not want!" cried Mrs. Kingston, evidently
pleased with Nahum's euology upon her rum, while she
jingled a bunch of keys that hung at her girdle, and selected
one of them, which was evidently that of the cellar door,
"That you shall not want, though it should be the last
bottle that I had in the house!"

And away she went hurriedly from the room, while Nahum
leered humorously and evidently delightedly at me, as he said,
"Now you will have a treat, for I can assure you there is
nothing like it, in the way of old, well-selected, and genuine
spirits, in the whole west of Scotland, it being some of the
ancient stock that belonged to her husband; and it was even
old when he laid it in, some ten or fifteen years ago."

Mrs. Kingston now re-appeared,
bearing two cobwebbed bottles, one
of which she placed on the sideboard,
and the other on the table, the latter
of which Nahum immediately un-
corked, he being good at that sort
of work, as well as praying.

"It is the genuine stuff," he exclaimed, after he had withdrawn the
cork, and placed the mouth of the
bottle to his nose, for the purpose
of inhaling the aroma, "the real
elixir vitæ, and as refreshing to my
olfactories as the breezes of the Red
Sea used to be to the early pilgrims!"

He then poured into a tumbler a goodly allowance of the
liquor—equal, I should say, to about a couple of ordinary
glasses—and dashing after it a quantity of cold water into the
tumbler from a considerable height, without spilling a drop,
till the concoction actually frothed, he proceeded to quaff it
off, with great gusto.

Another and another imbibation followed this preliminary
one, betwixt the intervals of which he said many pleasant
and courteous things to Mrs. Kingston and myself, which it
is not necessary I should repeat, and after robbing the
bottle of about half of its contents, he started to his feet,

declaring that if he did not go home, Mrs. Gust would become alarmed.

But Mrs. Kingston was not done with her kindness to him, for, wrapping the other bottle in an old newspaper, she followed him to the door, and urged his acceptance of the same.

This, Nahum, after a few protests, gracefully agreed to, and putting the bottle into his pocket, he took my arm, I having resolved to see the worthy gentleman home in case of accidents. He then bid adieu to Mrs. Kingston, who was perfectly enchanted with the honour he had done her, in thus visiting her house.

As we walked along, Nahum commenced to speak confidingly and unreservedly to me, and which, although a little thickish, in consequence of his coming into the air, was to something like the following effect :—

"My deashaw, p'raps you'll think me too familiar with my flock, butitch my shystem, and a very goodstem itish. Yesh, the quinsiconce sis they all love their pashtor, and I love them. They're very fond of me, and show their reshpect ash you've seen. Probly some consider me 'xacting—yesh, a've defamers, but I doncare that for them. (Here he snapped his fingers). I'll show what I can do. I'll bring them to book. I don't shee why there should'nt be Hildebrands in the Presbyterian Chuch as well as in the Romanshuch, aye and Tetzells and Beckets, too—and why shouldn't I who've got not only a Brish, but a Europation? The factish, my deashaw, am paid very ill. Only four hundred ayea, poor beggarly stipend 'tish, and they 'spect me to do everything for that, to baptish them, marry them, and bury them, dirty low pigs that they are. But for a few 'clections, 'scriptions, and preshentations, don't know how I'd geton. But I'll make them pay—Yesh!—I'll apply what I call my three B's —brimshtone, Belzebub, and the bottomlesh pit—to them, if they don't come down! My deashaw, you're my friend, my old friend, and thishish in confidensh—so don't say word 'boutit—only you'll see!"

And so honest Nahum maudlingly went on, as it were thinking aloud, till we reached his own house, the bell of which he jerked as if it had been that of his steeple, when a servant girl opened the door. He then affectionately and kindly squeezed my hand, while hoping to see me soon, or at all events, not later than next Sunday, at St. Blythswood's, where I would always be sure to get a seat in his "ownspew," as he expressed it.

He then staggered along his lobby, and the door of which being duly shut, I returned to Mrs. Kingston's.

CHAPTER XXXVII.

INTRODUCTORY DOGGERELS.

Lucky's the one whose stomach tough,
  Needs not the doctor's skill;
For ten to one, before he's done,
  He will the patient kill!

The Goosedubbs Poet.

I GOT on very thrivingly in my native city, both commercially and socially. Indeed, I may say I was killed with kindness, as the phrase is, for every one seemed to strive with another to show me the extreme of hospitality.

I soon, in consequence, began to consider myself a man of importance, and it is more than possible, therefore, that I may have assumed a greater air and a more vain bearing, as I read the commercial news in the Exchange, than I should have done, considering what were my antecedents.

I, however, had not forgotten these, neither was my conscience altogether at rest, amidst my feastings and revellings in the comparatively high life to which I had attained. Many and many a time, would former scenes, in which I had performed a certain part, and which it is not necessary I should again particularise, rise to my mind, and cloud my brow, even as the apparition of Banquo did that of Macbeth. I was ever, indeed, in a state of anxiety. I felt like a thief whom the baton of the constable might arrest at any moment; or, to be more classical, I was a Damocles over whom the sword hung by a single hair.

I cannot say, I am sorry to confess, that this anxiety arose so much from compunction, or remorse, within my breast, as to the manner in which I had acted towards my mother, poor Sissy, and my father, who had now, individually and collectively, been for such a length of time, a "dead letter" to me, as from a dread—notwithstanding the years that had elapsed, and the almost certainty I felt myself warranted in entertaining, that they had either emigrated or ceased to exist: for I had made every inquiry, in my own *discreet* way, as to their whereabouts in this country—that they might appear some day to beard me in the very presence of my newly-acquired acquaintances of the higher order, and to brand me as a low-sprung individual like themselves, and

who, in justice to themselves, should return with them to the humble haunts from which I and they had sprung.

It was the possibility of something suddenly in this way happening, that haunted my imagination, and made me miserable. Even as I sat at the polished boards of my entertainers, and while the joke and the laugh went round, in which I took part—for it was wonderful how I had assumed ease and coolness in this my new department of life—I would feel a small slim form bending over my shoulder and whispering into my ear, something like the following warning:—"Take care that we do not appear in these very halls to claim thee as our own! Thou art an impostor, a cheat, and a pretender! Thy smiles are false, thy sentiments are hypocritical, thy opinions are insincere, and thou art only to the present company what thou hast been to us! That friend to whom thou bowest so complacently, and offerest so many small benevolences, is only precious in thine eyes because he is rich! That bright-eyed damsel whom thou flatterest with thy attentions is only propitiated because she is well connected! All around, in a word, are only esteemed according to thy idea of their pecuniary standing, and thy appreciation of their market value! Let a change come over these qualifications, and they will fall in thy estimation accordingly—to be neglected, avoided, and lastly, despised, as we have been!"

I might have reasoned with the phantom, that thus vexed my soul, by retorting:—"And so, on the other hand, would *they* use me, were I falling in *their* estimation. It is altogether a matter of social reciprocity. I am only admitted here because I am commercially valued myself, higher than perhaps I ought to be, and I am no more false to them than they are to me!"

Had the phantom's powers, however, been restricted to reasoning, possibly I might have been able to cope with it. Unluckily, however, it was stronger in another point than that which I felt myself able to confront it on, and that point lay in its power, should it appear in the flesh, of claiming me as a part of itself; in other words, as a low-bred *parvenu*, who had risen from the gutter, and only required to be proclaimed as such, to be driven ignominiously back to the same level!

I went on, however, in my career of good fortune, adding to my stock of superior friends and acquaintances, and to the extension of my business, which every day promised, more and more, to make me ultimately what is known by the desiderated *soubriquet* of a "millionaire." To such an extent was this the case, that I found myself fast surpassing even those friends whom at first I supposed to be unsurpassable. I found myself, in short, getting amongst those who had solid silver dish-covers, instead of " Brumagem " plated ones; who kept plush adorned flunkies, instead of print-gowned waiting-women; and who drove in their own carriages instead of street hackneys.

Even my friend, Garnethill, could not penetrate into the circles where it was my good fortune to have the *entrée*, although there, I occasionally met Dr. Morse, and the Rev. Nahum Gust, who, as the fashionable physician, and popular clergyman of the West End, were privileged to kill bodies, and save souls, even in the most elevated quarters.

And, talking of these gentlemen, perhaps it may be as well, before going further, that I should narrate what was the consequence of their prescriptions, and advices, and attentions, to worthy Mrs. Garnethill, at the dinner, given by the husband of that lady, in his own house, as has been succinctly described by me in last chapter.

On that occasion, as has been observed, Mr. Garnethill did not altogether approve of the manner with which Dr. Morse and Dr. Gust plied his wife with champagne and brandy; indeed, as it were, he protested against it, by making severe remarks on the subject to his guests, at the same end of the table as he himself occupied, and, in particular, on what he prophesied to me, would be the consequence to the lady, in the shape of a bilious attack, and utter prostration; but which, although she might have had a pretty good guess from former experience, of what would be the case, she set at nought, from a superstitious and pious feeling, like that of many excellent people similarly situated, that what was prescribed, and approved of by medical men and ministers, could not be wrong.

The sequel turned out, however, different to what she expected, and, as will be seen, a great deal more serious than what even her husband dreaded; for, on calling on him next day, at his counting-house, to inquire for the lady, and to pay my respects to him, in return for his kindness, he informed me, that ere we were well out of his house, she had been carried to her bed alarmingly ill, and that Dr. Morse had been summoned to her in the course of the night, to rectify, if possible, what Mr. Garnethill pretty boldly hinted, was the result of that gentleman's own folly!

Next day, on calling again, I found the lady no better; and so on—the next—and the next day after that; the symptoms, by that time, as Mr. Garnethill, with tremulous voice, told me, having become perfectly alarming.

To do the honest man justice, he appeared to be most

uneasy about the state of his better-half, and perhaps he had good reason for being so; for, as he explained to me, the disease had now assumed the appearance of confirmed constipation, for which Dr. Morse was treating her with his favourite practice, in the shape of four grains of calomel every four hours.

"I would fain," said the distracted husband, "call in my own old-fashioned medical man, Dr. Glober of the Gallowgate, only my wife has a prejudice against him, because he is neither a genteel, nor a religious man; that is, because he has neither the whining speech nor the canting manner of Morse, who is always ready, if his specifics fail him, to give a prayer, and that my wife considers makes all right; besides," continued Mr. Garnethill, "Dr. Glober's practice is diametrically opposed to that of Dr. Morse, for he has a thorough antipathy to mercury, and so, I fear, if I were even getting over Mrs. Garnethill's prejudices, and introducing him, that the two physicians would quarrel."

I fully sympathised with my excellent friend in the dilemma in which he seemed to be placed, but could offer him no advice, in consequence of my ignorance not only of such matters, but of the Medical Faculty of Glasgow, the only one that I had seen in the shape of a doctor within its walls, having been during my youthful days, and he was a little humpbacked apothecary, who occupied a small, low-roofed and dark shop, near the Goosedubbs, and sold doses of salts, senna, and camomile, as well as liniments of train oil, turpentine, and sulphur, at a penny each. This unpretentious practitioner was considered quite an adept in his way, and the people had great confidence in him, for although I had heard of many cures that he performed, I never heard of his killing any one.

It would have perhaps been well for Mrs. Garnethill, had she had Dr. Griper of the Goosedubbs, as this little medico was named, to administer his penny doses, instead of Dr. Morse's sovereign ones; for, what did result from the latter, might probably, in consequence, have been averted, even though the little humpbacked doctor and his shop should have gained no fame thereby.

The catastrophe alluded to, I was unhappily myself a witness of, within a fortnight from the time I had experienced Mr. Garnethill's kind hospitality, and three days after I had seen him at his counting-house, he subsequently having confined himself to his dwelling-house, in order to be near his wife in her alarming state, when he told me that Dr. Morse, in desperation at the stubbornness of her complaint, was actually then administering twelve grains of calomel every four hours!

Even from the little I knew of medicine, and although I had been in hot climates where this ingredient used to be prescribed to greater extent than is usually the case in cooler ones, I thought such practice was exceeding the fullest latitude admissible to a medical man, however celebrated, and therefore I felt considerable anxiety regarding the patient, which urged me to call at Mr. Garnethill's private house, for the purpose of learning what these fearful doses were likely to result in, and with which view, I wandered forth in the dusk of the evening, on the occasion alluded to.

My intention, when setting out from my lodging, had been merely to call at Mr. Garnethill's door, and on hearing a report of the state of matters, to have passed on without

seeing any one, or, indeed, leaving my card. But on pulling
the bell (which I found was muffled, and in consequence I
did not hear its sounding), rather I fear too violently, the
door was immediately opened widely, while the servant girl,
in a very excited state, and seemingly rather confused,
exclaimed, "Come away, Sir, quickly, quickly!" and tripping

up the stair, which led to the upper or drawing-room flat, she
further ejaculated, "this way—this way, Sir, and as fast as
you can, else all will be over!"

I was so much taken by surprise, and bewildered by this
proceeding on the part of the girl, that I did not think of
questioning the propriety of her thus leading me up stairs so
unceremoniously, or asking her for an explanation thereof.
Indeed, I did not know where she was conducting me to; I,
therefore, as it were, followed her, more instinctively than
willingly, for had I reflected for a moment—that is to say,
if I had got time to do so—I would most certainly have
shrunk from intruding into the locality in which I subsequently landed.

This was a large bed-room into which I was ushered,
before I knew where I actually stood, so sudden and impul-
sive had been the action that had led thereto,—while, to add
to the confusion, the girl screamed out, "here he is at last!
here he is at last!—perhaps it is not too late!"

What she meant, at last flashed on my mind, perhaps aided
by what I saw before me. The girl had mistaken me, in the
excitement of the moment, for an additional medical man

who had been summoned, and was momentarily expected,
and had, therefore, without consideration, brought me into
the scene which I shall now attempt to describe.   On a bed,
the curtains of which were all drawn aside—for I afterwards
learned that the patient, only a few minutes before, had
cried out, "More air!—more air!—oh, give me air to
breathe!" and which had led to the circumstance—lay the
emaciated and prostrated form of poor Mrs. Garnethill, her
head being supported by a nurse, while the expression of her
countenance betokened what was very shortly about to take
place, for her eyes were turned up in their sockets, her
mouth was open, her features were pinched, and though she
still breathed, there was a rattle in her throat.   She was
not alone.   At the end of the bed stood my much-to-be-pitied
friend, Mr. Garnethill, grasping the footboard, as if to support himself, and absorbed in the most profound grief; while
on either side of the couch of death, knelt respectively Dr.
Gust and Dr. Morse, with arms extended and fingers
sprawling, while both howled out prayers which jarred
against each other.

I stood rivetted to the spot, without the power of either
advancing or retreating, and perhaps I felt there was no
necessity for my doing either, for seemingly no one noticed
me, and this gave me time to collect my scattered senses,
and to look around.

On a small table placed at one side, were two decanters

labelled as containing port wine, one of which was empty, and the other half exhausted, and a pitcher marked "chalk mixture," while on the mantelpiece stood a bottle of brandy, likewise half empty, and a large phial, with the warning announcement on its flat side, that it held, or had held "Laudanum—Poison."

These were the ingredients with which, up to a few minutes before I arrived, Dr. Morse had endeavoured to arrest the dart of the King of Terrors, who was now just about sending it home, and finding the same a failure, he had abandoned them, and, as a last resource, had thrown himself on his knees, to join his friend Gust in praying—leaving the servant girl that had ushered me up, to do the last office usual on such occasions, namely, to wet the departing individual's lips with a moistened feather.

It was a painful scene to be sure, but not one that was destined long to endure, for in the course of a few minutes, the suffering lady gave a long and a deep gasp, as a convulsive movement passed through her attenuated frame, and she ceased to breathe, while Dr. Morse, springing to his feet and grasping her wrist, so as to feel her pulse, pronounced her dead!

At this moment the reverend Nahum approached Mr. Garnethill with holy though stereotyped words upon his tongue, but that distressed gentleman turned from him, seemingly with disgust, and throwing his head upon my shoulder, while he grasped my hand, burst into tears.

I allowed my friend to indulge himself in this position for a few minutes, feeling that nature to be relieved must get vent in some way or other. After which, on getting a hint from the same servant girl who had ushered me in, and who was now perfectly cool, that it would be necessary the room should be left to her and her other female coadjutors, I

slowly led Mr. Garnethill to the drawing-room, but to
which neither Morse nor Gust followed; on the contrary,
they passed down stairs (rather sneakingly I should say), and
so from the house, while a man with a black straightening
board, and a woman with certain white linen garments—
probably grave clothes: so promptly and so judiciously are
these things always managed by the softer sex—passed up
stairs and into the chamber of death to take their place.

In the drawing-room, the door of which I carefully
closed against intrusion, Mr. Garnethill threw himself upon
a sofa, and, burying his face in his hands, became absorbed in
grief for some minutes, during which period I did not care
to disturb him, but after the paroxysm had seemingly
passed away, he became more composed, and inclined to
speak.

"Ah! my friend," he then exclaimed, "they have managed
the matter, and killed my poor wife at last! Little did
I think," he continued, "when I expressed my misgivings as
to Dr. Morse's medical treatment so lately, that my worst
fears regarding them would be so soon realised: but such is
the case!"

Mr. Garnethill then went on to tell me regarding the
illness of his wife, and the particulars of her symptoms from
day to day, in which he seemed to take a melancholy pleasure, which, as I had often remarked, is generally the case
with bereaved relations. He detailed to me the doses of
calomel Dr. Morse had administered to her, and which he

calculated had reached the aggregate of two hundred grains; the disease during the period, becoming more stubborn thereby, instead of yielding. At last it did yield, and then with a vengeance, for its very antithesis succeeded, to stop which again, Dr. Morse actually made the poor patient—she that for a fortnight before, had tasted scarcely anything beyond the vile calomel, but slops—swallow a bottle and a half of port wine, half a bottle of brandy, a large phial of laudanum, and no end of chalk mixture. "What has been the consequence?" he nervously cried, "why, in endeavouring to right the ship, which careened to one side, he has overweighted her on the other, like a thoughtless captain, and down she has gone!"

I could not but allow that there was too much truth in the reasoning that had suggested the similé to my friend, but still I endeavoured to mitigate his criticism by pointing out that medical men were often driven to desperate resources in desperate cases; and I appealed to his candour, by asking if he would not have approved of the treatment of Dr. Morse, even in the face of his former prejudices, had the lady recovered. I then called his attention to the fact that even the learned and logical Dr. Johnston, who would never allow, during lusty health, that the physician could be of any service, and maintained that in every case, it was nature, and not the doctor that brought through the patient; yet when he was overtaken by the disease which ultimately carried him off, was glad to overcome his scruples and be surrounded by medical men, whose nostrums and bitter perscriptions he greedily partook of.

Mr. Garnethill admitted the justness of my remarks, and subsequently became more tranquil and collected, which, with the assistance of a couple of tumblers of whisky toddy that we each partook of, resulted in a pleasant predisposition on his part to sleep, in which state I accompanied him to his bed-room, where I had the pleasure of seeing him tumble into his couch, seemingly pretty comfortable, while declaring himself "perfectly resigned,"—upon the ascertainment of which pleasant consummation, I left the house.

We buried Mrs. Garnethill a few days after this, both Dr. Morse and Dr. Gust being present at the funeral, and from the latter we received two enormously long prayers, in which

he dwelt most pathetically upon the domestic and religious
virtues of the deceased, and in particular upon her great
Christian charity, and liberality in furthering the advancement of religion, which I understood to be a sort of
acknowledgment of the numerous contributions on the part
of the lady, from the purse of her husband, towards the many
testimonials of Bibles, gowns, inkstands, and slippers, that had
been presented to himself, the particulars regarding which,
collected from Mr. Garnethill's former remarks, I have
already narrated.

Dr. Morse looked extremely grave and solemn on this
occasion, adorned as he was with white choker, of remarkable purity, broad weepers, and deep crape, but this did not
prevent him from emulating his reverend friend in tossing
off a bright bumper of sherry, and snapping up some exceed-

ingly nice cake and comfits
that were handed round
betwixt the prayers, by the
"sawlies," which set the
funereal company a munch-
munching, and smack-
smacking, and had rather a
ludicrous effect, in the
otherwise silent and solemn
apartment.

In the coaches, which
followed the hearse to the
Necropolis, if I might judge
from what took place in
the one within which I
rode, accompanied by other three gentlemen, there was
much pleasant gossip regarding the general topics of the
day, and in particular regarding the great attention that had
been bestowed on the deceased, by Dr. Morse, whose celebrity
in consequence, I observed, had been greatly enhanced
thereby, if that could be possible. There was much praise
likewise bestowed upon the prayers of Dr. Gust, which
were pronounced "beautiful and touching in the extreme."

After the funeral, I was invited to dine quietly with Mr.
Garnethill, along with two or three intimate friends, including the reverend Nahum, who gave us two long graces and

a prayer, varied as these were with good viands and good
wine, and wound up with some whisky-toddy, (there being
no ceremony on this occasion,) after which we solemnly left
the house, and in the evening I went to a small private
musical soirée, where we had cards, quadrilles, songs, and a
supper, and where, by-the-by, we were waited upon by two of
the very sawlies who had officiated at the funeral, only they
now exhibited none of the weepers, nor hats with broad crapes
flaunting behind, like flags of distress, with which they had
been adorned, while heading the melancholy procession in the
former portion of the day.

CHAPTER XXXVIII

INTRODUCTORY DOGGERELS.

> Let not the evil-doer think
> Time will his deeds efface;
> For, when he least expects—they'll rise
> To stare him in the face!
>
> *The Goosedubbs Poet.*

BUSINESS in Glasgow was, at this period, in a very prosperous state. The working-classes were all well employed, and everybody, connected with the upper circles, was making money. There existed, therefore, much contentment, great self-satisfaction, and no small quantity of domestic intercourse and sociality, throughout the community.

This was indicated by the attention that was bestowed by the upper classes publicly to municipal matters, and privately to dinner parties. Indeed, there never was a period known when Town Council debates and proceedings were more warmly attended to, in the forenoon, or fat feeding and feasting, harmoniously pursued, in the afternoon. It must have been a rare time for butchers, bakers, pastrycooks, wine merchants, and last, though not least, for our friends, the "sawlies," who got good employment in consequence of these parties.

I came in for a pretty good share of the entertainments going, and was asked to not a few of the dinners given by Town Councillors, and other great men, where I had the pleasure of meeting, occasionally, the Bailies, and even the. Lord Provost himself; and although, at first, I felt the conversation to be dry enough, if not vulgar and uninteresting, where little else was talked of excepting municipal subjects

—and where "my speech on this point," and "your speech on that one," and this one's "motion," and that one's "amendment," were the peculiar topics of conversation with men, who could scarcely pronounce the English language correctly or grammatically, and who evidently had read little or nothing beyond the newspapers, I came to like it well enough, particularly after having duly scanned the Town Council debates, in order to be properly posted up on the local subjects of the day, and, in self-defence, as it were, to be able to join in conversation regarding these.

So well did I get on in this way, that, much to my surprise, as the annual period came round for embryo councillors to be fixed upon as candidates for the approaching election,

I found myself waited upon by a deputation, who looked upon me as one who would form a very eligible sort of candidate, for an important ward that was expected to be vacant, and which, it was the desire of the electors, or at least a majority of them, should be filled up by what was rather anomalously denominated a "Liberal Conservative."

It seemed I had earned this mongrel political character in a very easy, simple, and happy way, by voting, on the occasion of a parliamentary election—when two Whig or Radical, and two Tory or Conservative candidates had solicited the honour of the representation,—for a Whig on the

one hand, and a **Tory** on the other, and as both these gentlemen had been successful, my discrimination, in thus giving
my vote, had afforded great satisfaction to all concerned.

As to my real sentiments on political matters, these I had
kept to myself, and regarding them had never committed
myself: partly from really never having made up my mind
as to which side I should espouse, and partly from an
intuitive caution I possessed, and which induced me to
resolve, if possible, to be on good terms with all parties. So
far as my private ideas went, however, I rather, of anything,
leant to the liberal side, particularly as that side advocated
free trade, and which, from the experience I had acquired,
both abroad and at home, in business, I saw, if carried out,
would do the country, and particularly myself, much good.
When I observed so many rich men, however, in this City,
who had sprung from the gutters, like myself, professing
conservatism, and subscribing to this and that fund, for the
purpose of rolling back the tide of sentiment in favour of
free trade, that had set in, and munificently contributing to
monuments in honour of deceased statesmen, who had
resisted every liberal proposition that had been advanced, I
could not but consider that I chose the safe path when I
followed their example, particularly as I noticed that at all
parties, which I attended, they were invariably paid great
respect to, by men of all political professions, not even exclud-
ing that of extreme liberalism itself. These gentlemen were
always placed at the head of the table, on the right hand of
the lady of the house, and had the nicest and rarest tit-bits
presented to them; while, in conversation, if what they
mooted as their sentiments were not assented to, they were
not disputed, or, at the worst, received with a respectful
silence.

I, therefore, rejoiced in the reputation I had acquired as a
liberal conservative, seeing that it gave me a very comfortable sort of *status* in society, and particularly as it secured to
me the goodwill of both sides, which was proved by my being
placed at the head of the poll, to the prejudice of a far better
man, and accordingly returned as representative for the ward
that had so greatly honoured me.

I paid great attention to my duties as a municipal councillor—that is to say, I was rarely absent from the meetings,

either of the Council itself, or of the committees; and especially, I went to all the dinners I was asked to, and any other little fetes that were given, such as the presentation of the freedom of the City to any great man—on which occasions a dinner generally took place, or the celebration of the Sovereign's birthday, or the sail down the river for the purpose of inspecting the lighthouses—the said lighthouses never being inspected at all, unless the partaking of a full feast, under a tent, on a rural island, where one of these lighthouses quietly rears its lamp, be an inspection, and the guzzling of turtle-soup, curded salmon, young lamb, venison, saddles of mutton, rounds of beef, tarts, puddings, blancmanges, creams, and early fruits, form an inquiry into the economics thereof, prompted as the intellects of the Town Councillors and their friends invariably are, in that inquiry, by sparkling champagne, choice hock, port, sherry, madeira, and claret, not forgetting brandy, liqueurs, cold punch, and the never-failing whisky-toddy.

In the Council, I took care never to open my mouth in the way of a speech, and if I made a remark, it was only for the purpose of suggesting an explanation from others, or asking a question; and as I was so lucky as invariably to vote with the majority, or to refrain from voting when the question was complex, I got along very pleasantly indeed.

In this way, a couple of years happily passed over, during which time I had voted, eaten, drank, and toasted myself into a very good position, so that on the occasion of a new election of Magistrates and office-bearers, I was not surprised to find myself chosen as a fit hand for the honourable situation of Deputy Water Bailie, which, although not considered a very high appointment, was looked upon as a sort of stepping stone to something more dignified and more important on a future occasion.

In the meantime, I may mention, I had extended my own establishment, and got a house of my own, which enabled me to give parties, and to entertain my fellow Town Councillors, and business friends, more in consonance with the style of my compeers, than would have been the case had I remained a lodger with Mrs. Kingston.

I was induced to take this step partly from a desire to make more show and appearance, than I could have done as

the inmate of a mere lodging-house, no matter how well conducted, and partly from the circumstance that worthy Mrs.
Kingston had found it convenient to give up this mode of
subsidising her small income, in consequence of a piece of
good luck that befel her, in the agreeable shape of a considerable reversion from the estate of her late husband accru-
ing to her unexpectedly, and which placed her in comparative
independence.

The good lady, however, in breaking up her establishment,
was enabled to be of great service to me in forming mine,
and I, therefore, found myself extremely comfortably located
in a moderately-sized self-contained house, well furnished and

plenished, with her old servant as
my cook and housekeeper, assisted
by a lad in livery who waited the
table, cleaned the knives and forks,
and acted as my *valet de chambre.*

I felt myself to be now rather
an important man, while my
time, from the several avocations
I pursued commercially, munici-
pally, and magisterially, was well
occupied. I discovered, however,
that the two latter rather trenched
upon the portion of this important
element, that was due to the first
named, and I, therefore, hailed with
some degree of relief the close of my first turn of duty, as
Deputy Water Bailie, and the substitution of my principal on
the bench, which enabled me to get away, on a business tour,
to Manchester and the manufacturing districts of England,
and which I expected would, for its performance, occupy a
considerable portion of time.

I, no doubt, was a little chagrined in thus being urgently
required to set out for the south, as it so happened that the
Lords of Justiciary were just about to hold an important
assize in the City, and I had every reason to expect I would
receive an invitation to dine with them in virtue of my office
as a Burgh Magistrate, if I remained, the same being considered a great honour.

Set off, however, I did, leaving the enjoyment of this

distinction to others, who, no doubt, appreciated it much, nor did I return till fully six weeks afterwards, when I found that, although I had been disappointed in the pleasures pertaining to the exercise of hospitality on the part of the Judges, I was about to be called upon to perform certain onerous and responsible functions, connected with the business they had gone through, on the occasion of the assize alluded to.

This was rather painfully brought to my notice in the following way:—I had only, on the day in question, arrived early in the morning by the mail from the south, and at an hour which, instead of permitting me to take repose—to which I was predisposed by a sleepless night, spent in a crammed four-inside seated mail coach, with dusty roads outside, and a stifling atmosphere within—called me at once to business, after merely enjoying the refreshment of dressing and breakfast.

These business duties I had got over, and had returned to my house, where, after a light dinner, I was about to retire to my dormitory, when the bell was rung with a startling and ominous vehemence, and which being duly opened by "buttons," the City Chamberlain entered in rather an excited state. His object was to mention that the execution of a man and a woman, who had been tried and condemned for robbery and assault, under aggravating circumstances, at last assizes, was to take place at eight o'clock next morning, at which, it would be necessary that I should attend, as one of the Burgh Magistrates.

I felt rather surprised and taken aback by this summons, while wishing to be excused from the performance of such a duty, on the score that I was not one of the City Magistrates proper, but only that of an inferior Court, appointed for a special and limited purpose, and that as such I had never, at the Town Council, been recognised otherwise than as an ordinary member.

The Chamberlain was prepared for this objection, and told me he had consulted the Town Clerks on the subject, who were unanimous in the opinion that I was eligible to act, on such an occasion, as one of the Magistrates to whom the duty of seeing the sentence duly carried into execution, had been remitted, by the warrant of the High Court of

Justiciary, seeing that the Court at which I presided was a regular Burgh Court, and as such had been recognised from time immemorial. At the same time the Town Clerks admitted that it would be better, and beyond objection, if one at least of the regular City Magistrates attended, as had always been the case on such occasions.

It now came out, however, by the admission of the City Chamberlain, that the presence of one of the Bailies, let alone that of the Lord Provost, at this execution, was rather problematic. The latter dignitary had a week before, proceeded to London, accompanied by other two of the Magistrates, for the purpose of superintending a bill connected with the City, while being carried through Parliament; another was absent on matters pertaining to his own business; other two had deliberately gone from home in order to be out of the way on the painful occasion, and the last remaining one was confined to his own house by a severe "bilious attack," which he found would very possibly prevent him making his appearance at the hour of cause. Under these circumstances, the City Chamberlain had no resource left, but to fall back upon me; for, as he stated, the dilemma he was in, had already got wind, and he feared that unless a Magistrate or Magistrates were present, the agent of the prisoners would appear to protest against the execution, and he did not know what might be the consequences. He, therefore, appealed to me most urgently not to desert him on such an occasion, no matter what might be my scruples, not only as an act of necessity, but as one of duty and loyalty.

I saw the difficulty in which the Chamberlain was placed, and while thinking that he went too far in asserting that I was qualified to act, as had been represented by the Town Clerks, I reluctantly resolved to accede to his request, and to make my appearance, but only on his solemn promise that he would do all he could to obtain the more proper attendance of the desiderated Bailie already alluded to, and which the Chamberlain did not quite despair of managing, for he let out to me—of course in strict secrecy—that Bailie Bowser, the gentleman in question, had a wonderful facility of getting over such ailments as he was now suffering under —he being subject to them—if properly attended to, by his medical man and his butler; and these individuals he had subsidised for the purpose, with the best hopes of a favourable result. The fact was, that the worthy Bailie was rather prone occasionally to get drunk for days at a time—or, as the vulgar expression has it, "to go on the batter"—during which period, he was liable to disappear, and not come to light again, till he had fairly seasoned himself; and this the Chamberlain, rather humourously, hinted to me was one of these ailments, or as they were leniently denominated, " bilious at tacks."

The Chamberlain now left me, after a pleasant gossip on town politics, over a couple, or three tumblers of whisky-toddy, and I then retired to bed fairly knocked up, but unfortunately not to sleep, for I tossed and tumbled all night, and rose next morning at an early hour, unrefreshed, with a splitting headache, and a galloping pulse,—the results of the varied uncomfortable thoughts which had passed through my disturbed mind, during that wakeful night, and particularly those connected with the disagreeable duty I had undertaken to perform, and which had brought back to my recollection scenes that had long slumbered, and facts that, although they might be temporarily suppressed, could never be forgotten.

Nevertheless, the next morning, as the bell chimed half-past seven o'clock, I found myself at the side wicket of the Jail, through which I was instantly admitted by the official on duty with that stereotyped respect which is ever awarded to the magisterial gold chain and badge, and which I took care, rather ostentatiously, in consequence of my being only a Deputy Water Bailie, to display, when I was duly bowed and ushered by the Council Officer into the Court Hall.

As I passed along the corridor, I happened to cast my

eyes to the side, when I beheld the dismal "gallows-tree" erected at the front of the portico—the same old acquaintance on which poor Barney and my *quasi* stepfather had suffered so many years before, and seemingly in much the same state as then—with its heavy cross-beam from which two nooses again dangled in the air, and while waving to and fro, in the morning breeze, seemingly awed to silence a considerable crowd of people, of all sexes and ages, that had assembled as usual, with that inexplicable curiosity which is always attendant on such occasions.

On entering the Court, I was relieved to a considerable extent of the anxiety that weighed on my mind, by finding that Bailie Bowser, through the praiseworthy and excellent management of the Chamberlain, had arrived before me, and had already taken his seat on the bench, where I was requested by the Chamberlain, in a whisper, likewise to do so, although, on placing myself beside the Bailie, I thought I perceived on his maudlin and phlegmatic countenance, an expression of jealousy, if not scorn, towards me, which I took to be the consequence of his looking upon me as being an inferior judge, of an inferior court, instead of, like himself, a regular City Magistrate.

I, however, took my seat, after acknowledging his dry recognition, when, like the rest of those present in the Court-room, we became silent, during which uncomfortable period, I had time to look around.

The morning being darkish, the Court Hall had been dimly lighted up with gas, which enabled me to observe that there had been placed on a table, a carafe of water, and a bottle of wine, flanked by two cut crystal glasses. These were intended as refreshments for the felons, and were the remnants of a barbarous species of humanity, which aimed at granting spirituous comfort along with spiritual consolation, the one being now represented by the bottle in question, and the other by the Chaplain of the Jail, who, however, instead of doing his duty in the Court, more appropriately and probably more efficiently, did it privately with the culprits in the condemned cells. Around, were a number of individuals who had been led from curiosity to attend this sad scene, and who, being of the better order of citizens, had obtained the privilege of getting within the Jail. There were likewise some members of the press with their pencils and note-books, taking down every particular, so as to make the description of the execution, in the second editions of their newspapers, as racy as possible to those who were so humane and genteel as to scorn to be present at such a degrading scene, but who would read all about it at second hand, with great interest and avidity.

In addition, there was present a large concourse of persons who gave themselves out as the representatives and members of a society, having for its object the suppression of capital executions; but how their principles should have permitted them to be present on this occasion, as I believe they were likewise so, on all similar ones, I have been puzzled to discover, even to this day. It possibly may have been in consequence of their determination to witness, with their own eyes, the horrors of such scenes, so as to enable them to be represented graphically and truthfully to the public; for, no doubt, if the community could be made aware that exhibitions of the kind, so far from tending to morality, or acting as a warning to those spectators, who crowd the front of the gallows, as though they were beholding some fete, instead of a fellow creature being put to death, was the very antithesis of that desirable result, capital punishment—at least in public—would be at once, abolished.

All, however, were very orderly and very silent, and, in consequence, the assembly had rather an imposing and awe-inspiring air about it, particularly as most of those present were attired in mourning, and many wore weepers, and crape hatbands.

Time, however, while I had been remarking, had fled rapidly away, if not with us, who sat rather painfully in the silent Court-room that has been described, at all events, with those who were the most interested in its prolongation and proper application, on the melancholy occasion, for now the bell of a neighbouring church steeple sonorously pronounced that the fatal hour of eight o'clock had arrived, calling upon us thereby to prepare for more exciting and heart-rending action, connected with the doleful scene.

We now heard some distant sounds coming silently as from the very bowels of the earth, which attracted the attention of all towards a trap-door, situated behind the bar, and which yawned ominously with large, gaping, dark mouth, that did not allow us to see even the trap stair which led to it from the cells below.

The sounds were those of footsteps, at first faint, but gradually becoming louder, as the party to whom they pertained, made their way up the stair.

A thrill at this moment went through the whole assembly, silent as the grave although every one was, and this was rendered the more acute, when a deep groan was heard, as if it had been rent from the very bottom of a breaking heart. What must it then have been to that of the individual who uttered it, when it touched so sympathetically the hearts of those who heard it, for all were evidently deeply affected, and as for myself I felt as though I would have dropped to the earth?

Bailie Bowser, alone, seemed to retain his equanimity and self-possession, fortified, as he probably was, by a good stiff morning dram which he had partaken of, if my olfactory nerves were not mistaken, for he rose dignifiedly to receive the approaching party, as they appeared at the orifice of the trap-stair, and I, as well as the Chamberlain, rose along with him.

The first that emerged to the light was the Governor of the Jail, dressed in black, who came to deliver his prisoners into the hands of the Magistrates; then two officers; then a man bent down with grief, and groaning heavily, betwixt other two officers; then a woman, with her head enveloped in a shabby black scarf, likewise betwixt two officers; then the Chaplain of the Jail; the whole being brought up by the Executioner, and a number of red-coated men carrying halberts, as a sort of show of strength, in case of resistance or tumult on the part of any one.

The felons having been allotted seats, the Governor of the Jail approached Bailie Bowser, and addressing him, stated that he now produced the person of William Bald, and Cecilia Bald, his wife, found guilty of a capital crime at last assizes, and handed over to his charge, to be produced on this day, and at this hour, and to be delivered into the hands of the Magistrates of Glasgow for execution.

"And I," said Bailie Bowser, addressing the Captain of Police, "hold in my hand the warrant of the High Court of

Justiciary for said execution. Captain!—are you prepared to do your duty?"

At this moment, and ere the Captain of Police could give the usual formal reply, that all was prepared, the male prisoner lifted his head, and with a voice betwixt a groan and an ejacula-tion, exclaimed, "Oh! gentlemen! Oh! Sir! Oh, my Lord! hear one word from me before you proceed. I confess to being justly convicted, and condemned, for the crime I have committed, but, before I die, let me protest that my poor wife is

as guiltless of participation in it, although she has like-wise been condemned for it, as the child unborn. It was I that did all the evil; it was I that perpetrated the felony, assisted by others, who have escaped; and it was I that forced her into the pawning of the stolen property that implicated her in the transaction. Had she not done as I desired her, in the rabid state in which I was, I would possi-bly have murdered her; and thus compelled, she did what she ought not, and wished not, to have done. I am the only culprit—I—I alone ought to suffer!"

This speech made a great impression on the assembly, and, of course, on myself, but much as it was calculated to do so, there was another circumstance that commanded my interest still more; for, as he proceeded, I discovered that the penitent culprit was no other than my old acquaintance the "Bald Billygoat," now distinguished by the more rational title of William Bald, and which, I believe, was his real name. But although he was thus known to me, I confess I did not feel great pity for him—remembering his antecedents—and I, therefore, turned my gaze upon his wife, who till this moment had sat like a draped statue, representing the perfection of silent and resigned misery.

An officer at this period of the drama, or rather tragedy, however, was now pouring out wine into the glasses that already have been spoken of, and having filled them to the brim, with that conventional generosity which distinguishes the process on such occasions, he proceeded to present them to the culprits, and this rendered necessary the removal of the scarf from the face of the female.

It was the work of an instant, but in that instant what did I not behold to humble, to degrade, aye, even to condemn me, and to fell me to the very ground, but the wan and emaciated features of my poor, wronged, deserted, and despised sister Sissy!

What further passed became a blank to me,—my head swam, my brain reeled, darkness filled my eye-balls, and in a moment I dropped to the floor of the bench, as if I had been seized with a fit of apoplexy.

So far as concerned me,

"Chaos had come again!"

CHAPTER XXXIX.

INTRODUCTORY DOGGERELS.

Sweet convalescence—kind relief—
  Assuager of our ills—
Deliverer from pain and grief,
  And slops, and draughts, and pills.

How fondly do I hail thy smile,
  As I sit up in bed,
And order out the physic vile,
  And roast beef in, instead!

The Goosedubbs Poet.

MANY days passed before consciousness returned to me, and when that was the case, I found myself stretched in bed, and the room darkened, while the icy digits of Dr. Morse

were applied to my pulse, as he assured my worthy friend, Mr. Garnethill, who was likewise at my side, that I was decidedly better, and had fairly "got the turn."

On attempting to move, however, I at once found out how great was the extent of my exhaustion, for strength had fairly deserted me, and langour and weakness had taken its place.

I was, however, free from pain, and what was better, from an awful nervous agony, that had attended me throughout my illness, and which, although my reasoning and observing faculties had entirely been suspended, had been of the most acute description. I had no perfect remembrance, but only an impression of it; still that was sufficiently painful, and I shuddered when I let my revived, though still weakened mind dwell upon it for a moment.

The doctor, observing my return to mental sensibility, at once forbade me from attempting to speak, and, indeed, ordered Mr. Garnethill, who had been most attentive throughout the course of my ailment, to leave the bed-room, if not the house, lest he should be tempted to converse with me; and he likewise enjoined a strict rule upon my servants as to silence, while stating to all, that if a relapse took place, it could not fail to be fatal to me.

I had, therefore, to submit to continued restraint for several days further, at the end of which period, having regained considerable strength, I could no longer control my curiosity, to learn what had been going on during my illness, —which had been a brain fever—and particularly what had been the concluding scene of the drama in the Court Hall; and I, therefore, summoned my servant-lad to my presence, when I peremptorily desired him to instruct me with regard to these, so far as he was able.

The young man, who, for his age, was rather intelligent, and well educated, although a little timid in acceding to my request, in consequence of the restrictions that had been put upon him by Dr. Morse, found it impossible to resist my importunity, and therefore proposed that, instead of giving his own account of the matter, he should post me up, as to the particulars connected therewith, by reading the newspaper reports that had been issued with regard to the execution, the copies of which, that had come to my house—for I was a regular subscriber to all the journals of the day, whatever their politics might be, thereby making myself popular with the Press—he had very properly preserved, from a presentiment that they might afterwards be required, in this very way.

He, therefore, with my approval, commenced to read these, whilst I kept myself as calm and self-possessed, amidst the bed-clothes, as possible.

I found they narrated the full particulars pretty accurately, and graphically, up to the period at which I have broken off—with too good an excuse, I hope it will be admitted—in my own account, when the lad read on, as follows:—"At this trying moment, the feelings of all present were sensibly touched to the core, while sighs and sobs escaped from not a few. Indeed, so greatly overcome, by the affecting scene, was our worthy Deputy Water Bailie, who occupied a seat on the Bench, along with Bailie Bowser, that he was suddenly taken ill, and had to be carried out of Court, in a fainting fit, and immediately conveyed to his own

house, where, we believe, he continues to be seriously indisposed, under the care of medical attendance, to which we earnestly hope his ailment will yield."

The report then went on to say, that it was to be regretted the excellent and humane Bailie had not been able to bear up for a little; for what took place, subsequently, must have relieved his excitement greatly, a messenger having, shortly after he was struck down, arrived express from the Post-Office, despatched specially by the attentive Postmaster—to whom, in consequence, the thanks of the community are especially due—with a letter addressed to the Magistrates, from the Secretary of State for the Home Department, containing a respite for the female prisoner, who, in consequence, instead of being conveyed to the drop, along with the male prisoner, had been remitted back to prison, there to be retained, till the resolution, as to her further disposal, should be fixed upon.

The report concluded with a long account, written in the usual stereotyped style, that distinguishes such penny-a-line narratives, of the conduct of the male felon on the gallows; how he ascended to the drop with the greatest firmness; how he addressed the multitude, warning them to take a lesson by his fate, which had been brought about by his neglecting good advice, and particularly by breaking the Sabbath day; how, nevertheless, since his condemnation, a new light had been revealed to him, that had turned his heart to the proper way, and which now, he felt assured, was leading him to a blessed immortality; how his prayers had so far been already heard, that the partner of his condemnation, though not of his sin and guilt, had been spared at the eleventh hour, and rescued as a brand from the burning; how he was, therefore, enabled to hope, like another penitent, when placed under similar circumstances, that the promise would be extended to him, "This night shalt thou dwell with me in Paradise;" how the executioner had then adjusted the rope; how the signal had been given; how the bolt had been withdrawn; and how the Bald Billygoat had been launched into eternity!

A farther supplementary account, divided from the chief one by a dash, gave a limited biographical account of the prisoners, and stated the many notorious deeds that had been committed by the male one, who, for years, had been quite a pest, as a thief, a burglar, and a highway robber, in the west of Scotland. That for some time, lately, however, and previously to his ultimate detection and conviction, the narrative went on to say, he had taken himself up, and becoming a member of a temperance society, at the earnest solicitation of his wife, had conducted himself very properly, whilst following his occupation as a tradesman, and which had enabled him to maintain both himself and her—although she likewise worked very hard as a mill-spinner—in comparative comfort. Unluckily, however, in an evil moment, he had broken his pledge, and taken to drink again, which had led him to the commission of his old pranks, for the last of which, namely, highway robbery, attended by aggravated circumstances, he had been convicted, and had suffered accordingly. With regard to his wife, the narrative stated that, in the indictment, she had been accused of aiding and abetting her husband, in the commission of the crime; that she had been sworn to, by a witness as one of two women who had been present at the robbery, and who had held the person that was robbed, while he was rifled by the man of his money, watch, and other property, and afterwards savagely attacked by him. The victim of the robbery, it was true, could not himself say that she was the identical woman; and the witness who had sworn to her identity had rather wavered in his cross-examination, which were favourable circumstances in her case; but, unfortunately, it was proved beyond doubt, that, subsequently, she had pledged the watch in a pawnbroker's office, for a sum much below its value, and this, coupled with a rather severe charge of the Judge, had induced the Jury, after a long consultation, to return a verdict of guilty against both criminals; but, in her case, with an earnest and unanimous recommendation to mercy.

The recommendation alluded to had, of course, been duly forwarded by the Judge to the proper quarter, but, as it was understood, accompanied with no opinion, on his part, as to whether it was worthy of consideration or not, and it therefore had not received the attention of the Home Office which it otherwise might have been favoured with. This delay had led to petitions being got up in her favour by several humane parties, and particularly by the Society for the Suppression of Capital Punishments, whose memorial was accompanied by the report of an inquiry that had been made into the particulars of her career by a committee of its members, when it had been elicited, that there was much to excite pity and sympathy in favour of the culprit. It had been ascertained, for instance, that she had, all her life, been an industrious and hard-working girl, and that she had commenced her course of labour when little more than a child, in consequence of her father, who was a sailor, having gone to sea, and been detained for many years abroad, during which time nothing, beyond their own exertions, had been available for the maintenance of herself and mother, the latter, in fact, being ultimately supported by her. That on the return of her father from abroad, she had hoped to have been in better circumstances, but his health having given way, she had actually then, instead of being subsidised by him, been obliged to assist both him and her mother, to effect which more substantially, she had been induced, in an evil moment, to marry the male prisoner, William Bald, formerly the scape-grace that has been mentioned, but at the period in question, a much reformed and well-employed tradesman, who paid his addresses to her, and under the most sacred promises of continuing in his good course, and—what worked upon her feelings more than all—from his having shown the greatest consideration and liberality towards her parents, she had consented to become his wife, although there was a great disparity of years betwixt them, he being much her senior.

The report then went on to say that on inquiry being made into the character of the witnesses that had been brought against her at the trial, and through whose testimony she had, in fact, been convicted, it had been ascertained they were of the most worthless and degraded description. That, in short, these witnesses were thieves and pick-pockets, and very possibly themselves might have been the accomplices of the male penitent on the occasion of the robbery, instead of the poor convict being so; for it was notorious that they had often previously been seen in William Bald's company, drinking and rioting, while in no instance could it be proved that his wife was given to these vices. On the contrary, amongst her neighbours she was considered quiet and retiring in her manners, and of so sober a disposition as to be looked upon as being rather distant and unsocial than otherwise. That she had been known, so long as she possessed decent garb, and before that had been disposed of, to supply her severe necessities, to attend public worship in one of the churches in the neighbourhood, and to partake of the communion, as was certified by the clergyman and one of the elders of said church; and that on examining the little store of ragged clothing which had been found in her dwelling, and taken possession of by the police, there had been found a Bible, and some well-thumbed pamphlets, and books of a moral and religious description.

Amongst other facts connected with this inquiry, on the part of the Society for the Suppression of Capital Punishments, a most important one had been elicited, namely, that one of the witnesses had stolen and pawned a little golden Malay chain, which, it was ascertained, had belonged to the poor criminal herself, and which it was proved had been bestowed upon her by her father before going to sea, and this the Society had urgently called the Home Secretary's attention to, it was believed with the best effect.

The report concluded by stating that, no doubt the serious

and glaring fact of her having pawned the property that had been taken from the man who was robbed and assaulted, had been brought home to her, beyond dispute, but that she might have been induced so to act, under threats from her husband, of doing her personal injury if she refused, and which indeed he, in a declaration and confession, spontaneously made before one of the Magistrates, and which had been forwarded to the Home Office, had acknowledged to have been the case.

The petitioners, therefore, had prayed for the clement consideration of her case, by the Secretary of State, with a view to a mitigation of her sentence being granted by the Sovereign, particularly as it had been ascertained that her defence had been very loosely got up, in consequence of her having been unable, from extreme poverty, to fee counsel, and, therefore, had only been defended by those appointed by the Court for paupers, and who, although they, no doubt, had done their duty as far as they could under the circumstances, had yet been unable to bring forward such mitigating testimony as was necessary, and which is always forthcoming to those who can afford to pay.

The petition and narrative containing the foregoing particulars, it was stated, had been rather late of being forwarded to the Secretary of State, and, therefore, it had been much feared they would have failed in the effect desired. Indeed, all hope of a favourable result had been departed from, when it was ascertained that on the day previous to that appointed for the execution, no communication had come from head-quarters to the Magistrates at all, although it was known that the Lord Provost, who, as had been already stated, was in London, was interesting himself to the utmost, to obtain a mitigation of the sentence. This, however, at the very latest moment, he had been enabled to obtain, not, as was hinted, from any humanity, or feeling of leniency on the part of the Secretary of State, or perhaps from any inquiry into the real circumstances of the case—that functionary's leisure, it was understood, being much engrossed, in consequence of there being at the time what is called a "Ministerial Crisis" existing—but from the Provost having represented that a commutation of the sentence would, by giving general satisfaction to the lower class of voters, greatly strengthen the party that supported the Ministry at the general Parliamentary election which was expected to take place. "This, however," the editor of the paper said, in conclusion, "was only a rumour, and might be taken by the reader for what it was thought worth!"*

A paragraph, in a subsequent number of the paper, mentioned, that "the sentence on the prisoner Cecilia or Sissily or Sissy Bald, lately under condemnation to death, and who had been respited during the Sovereign's pleasure, had been commuted into banishment for life, and that it was expected she would, in a few days, be sent to London, along with a batch of other convicts, for transmission to the penal settlements."

This was all that I could learn in the meantime from the papers, regarding the exciting incidents which had taken place, and which were of so much moment to me, but in the course of a few days afterwards, and when I had become so well as to leave my bed and sit up, and, indeed, instead of slops, enabled to partake of something more palatable and substantial, I had the pleasure of reading a paragraph to the effect that "the public would learn with satisfaction that the health of the much respected Water Bailie had greatly improved, and that he had almost completely recovered from the shock which his benevo-

lent and humane feelings had received on the occasion, etc., etc., at which I rather chuckled in the sleeve of my *robe de chambre.*

While thus chuckling, however, I could not help feeling—in spite of the relief which the reading of the newspaper reports had afforded to my mind—a considerable depression of spirits, that greatly controlled the joy I otherwise might have indulged in. I had been rescued, as it were, from a gulf which, on looking back upon, I observed to

---

* An incident, with similar circumstances, actually took place, connected with the same locality, within the present century.

be still yawning for me; and though for the moment I was safe from its dangers, I still was not free from the contemplation of its horrors. I was, in short, in doubt as to what Sissy had in her power to say of me; for though, so far as I could observe, she had in her communications—if from her communications any part of the narratives that have been alluded to, were taken—never revealed anything regarding me, nor, indeed, had she even given her maiden surname, while her Christian one, in the indictment, had partaken more of a gratuitous, than a literal rendering: still she had much in her power, and there was no saying to what extent she might use that power.

On thinking over the scene in the Court House, I reasoned with myself on every little circumstance that had taken place in the brief and harrowing interval, from the removal of her scarf, to my losing consciousness. I recalled her heart-broken expression of countenance, which revealed her total mental prostration, and absence of hope—her vacant stare, amounting almost to idiotical submission, but which contrasted violently with the sharpness of vision which evidently returned to her, on her eyes meeting mine. From that particular incident I could not but feel convinced, that she had recognised me, as unexpectedly, but as decidedly as I had recognised her. Indeed, it had been that look that had had the severe effect upon me which has been described. It had pierced me to the quick. It had paralysed me mentally, as well as physically; and it had brought me to the dust as though it had been the stroke of a thunderbolt, instead of the mere flash of a human being's eyeballs.

Still, there was no expression of malignity in that terribly penetrating glance. On the contrary, it indicated more of pity than any other sentiment; and yet that apparent pity was severer than if it had been malignity. It was like Byron's curse, the very antithesis of what such an unholy thing, generally, is understood to be,—"that curse was forgiveness!"

As soon as I was perfectly well again, and able, with the assent of Dr. Morse, and the good wishes, expressed in various prayers, of the Rev. Dr. Nahum Gust—who was the only one that, during my illness, had done anything for the good of my wine merchant, inasmuch as he had never failed, in making his daily calls, to partake of, at least, a couple of glasses  of my best brown sherry—to leave my house, and take an airing in a carriage, I resolved to put in practice a decision I had come to, which was neither more nor less, than to have an interview with my sister, and which I knew I would be enabled to accomplish, even privately, both as a Magistrate and as a Member of the Jail Committee, without let or hindrance, and without even leave from any one; for which purpose, at the earliest day possible, I desired my coachman to drive me to the North Prison, where I understood she had been again incarcerated, as a preliminary to being banished.

I intended, of course, to go about this in the most prudent and delicate manner possible. I had not decided upon the exact language I would use on the occasion, or the sentiments I might express—knowing how futile all such resolutions generally are, and how much better it is to trust to being regulated by the circumstances of the moment than any set plan—but I had made up my mind as to the basis on which I would treat, which I need scarcely say was that of pecuniary profuseness, to be extended to her, after she got to the colony, if such could, in any way, be made to bear.

Of course, I could not conceal from myself that there was danger in what I proposed to undertake, for if it turned out a failure, there was no saying what the consequences might be; still I trusted in my good luck as usual, and having made up my mind to the step, I felt rather decided as to carrying it out.

I, likewise—let me here confess—trusted not a little to the generosity of poor Sissy herself, for I could not banish from my recollection her many kind and benevolent acts, even to me—whatever, in her eyes, their requital may have been—her irrefragable good nature, and, above all, her naturally pious turn of mind, all of which had been testified to, as her characteristics, in the report of the Society for the Suppression

of Capital Punishments, and I, therefore, argued that I would
be pretty safe in putting confidence in her.

On arriving, however, at the prison, and after summoning
the Governor to my presence, I learned what I had never calculated upon—the papers having been silent on the subject—
namely, that about a week previously, she had been drafted
along with some other convicts to proceed to Leith, and there
be shipped for the Thames, where she likely would be put on
board a convict ship, then lying at Greenwich, and about to
sail for the antipodes. So that poor Sissy, instead of being
in Glasgow, as I had thought, was at that very moment probably, tossing on the German Ocean, in the midst of an
easterly gale, which at the time was reported as being general along the Eastern Coast.

CHAPTER XL.

INTRODUCTORY DOGGERELS.

Amidst the silence of the night,
    What harrowing thoughts come o'er us,
Should conscience, with it's lantern bright,
    Light up our deeds before us.

In vain we shut our eyes to these,
    In vain we try to banish
Those phantoms of realities,
    That grow instead of vanish!

The Goosedubbs Poet.

My nicely arranged, and cunningly concocted little plan having thus been summarily frustrated by the remorseless current of circumstances, connected with the sad career of poor Sissy, I felt myself for the moment rather non-plussed and placed in uncertainty, as I stood listening to the Governor's report relative to the causes which had led to her so hurriedly being sent off, and which principally, he explained, was in consequence of the prison having been more crowded than generally was the case—the want of accommodation having, in fact, caused him to place her in a cell with another woman during night time, while remaining under his charge, instead of in an apartment by herself, as would have been more consonant with the regulations of the establishment, had such been possible.

This he communicated to me entirely as an official matter, but he little knew how I was interested in the fact otherwise.

However, to carry out the spirit of my visit, as much as possible with a continued official appearance, I now intimated to him that I would make an inspection of the establishment —a duty which my position, as one of the Jail Committee, indeed, pointed out I should do—while feeling at the same time, a sort of prescient conviction, that I might learn something regarding Sissy, by viewing even the four bare walls of the cell she had occupied.

To this the Governor bowed a respectful acquiescence, and immediately, at my request, ordered a warder to accompany me in the inspection proposed. This the warder did, in the usual style of such officials, by unlocking and throwing open the several cell doors, as he passed along the "galleries," as they are called, leaving the poor inmates thereof

exposed to my gaze, and who were immediately locked up again, when I had satisfied myself, as to any particulars I required regarding them. In this way I got through a good number of what are called the silent cells, and at last came to those connected with hard labour, in which I found various inmates, working at the trades or occupations they had been accustomed to pursue, while free.

One of these was an elderly female weaver, plying away at a web, and, having a curiosity towards such description of manufacture, I proceeded to examine her work, with more deliberation and expenditure of time than I had bestowed on that of others, while the warder went forward, making locks clank, and doors bang, pertaining to cells further on.

This left me alone for a moment with the woman, who, lifting up her eyes from her work, seemed rather surprised, while at the same time she proceeded to address me, (although for prisoners to speak to any one, was against the rules of the establishment, and punishable by the infractors thereof being deprived of their meals), in a hurried whisper to the following effect:—"I have an important communication to make to you, which I cannot reveal here. Meet me on Monday week, at nine at night, beside the Monument in the Green. I get out of Jail on that day!"

To this startling announcement I made no reply, though doubtless I looked rather astonished, as indeed I was. This she observed, and possibly thinking I was doubting her sincerity, she was evidently perplexed, particularly as the returning steps of the warder were heard approaching the cell again.

A moment more, and she would not be enabled to say another word, but that word she did say.

It was simply "Sissy," and scarcely had it been pronounced, ere the door was closed upon her, and locked and barred as before, while I went on, to examine a few more cells, but with little heart for the job, for by this time I was knocked up with fatigue, in consequence of my still feeble health, not to say that I was considerably upset by the utterance I had heard, under such peculiar circumstances, of that simple, though eventful name.

I would fain have made a few inquiries at the warder, and indeed had, for the purpose, put my hand in my pocket, knowing how a little of the "filthy lucre," to quote my esteemed friend Dr. Gust's favourite expression, can relax jaws, and even, when the case is extremely urgent, open bolts, bars, and locks, of the heaviest and firmest description; but, when I reflected that the queries I would necessarily put, could not fail to reveal an inordinate anxiety and interest, in the criminal inquired about, that even the exceptional concern I had displayed regarding her fate,—and which, of course, was publicly known—in the Court Hall, on the eventful morning when I was struck down in unconsciousness, possibly would be insufficient to account for, I prudently refrained from doing so, and merely "tipped" the warder a small remuneration, instead of what otherwise might have been a "bribe," and for which that official evinced respectful gratitude.

I then declared myself duly satisfied with the inspection I had so far made, and having entered a short report regarding it, in the book, kept for the purpose, I left the prison, and returned to my vehicle, being duly attended thereto by the Governor, when I was immediately conveyed home, to be sharply rebuked by Dr. Morse, who called shortly afterwards, for venturing so far, while declaring that the effects thereof, had brought back febrile  symptoms, for which he prescribed a four grain calomel pill, but—remembering the fate of poor Mrs. Garnethill—I substituted for it a concoction of my own, in the shape of choice *eau-de-vie*, hot water and sugar, which made me all right again, much to the satisfaction of the Doctor, who, on calling next day, declared there was nothing like a judicious application of that blessed medicine calomel, particularly to the systems of those persons requiring it,—and I was one of these.

Had he said "deserving" instead of "requiring," perhaps he would not have been so far wrong; but as I had no notion of meeting my deserts at this particular time, I did not choose to take them from his hands, considering that I was sufficiently punished in submitting to his visits, which were running up to a pretty severe bill, as I afterwards found out to my cost.

During the interval, which lay betwixt this time and the Monday week following, the date for meeting, which had been so mysteriously named by the elderly female weaver, in

the Jail, and which embraced a period of fully ten days, I was
kept on the rack of suspense, while wondering what she
could have to communicate about poor Sissy.

At last, however, the appointed night arrived, and though
it was cloudy and coldish, I resolved to carry out the undertaking, come what might, particularly as I was, notwithstanding the attentions of Dr. Morse, greatly better now in health,
and, indeed, almost quite well again. I, therefore, called a
vehicle, and desiring it to be driven to within a short distance
of the "Green," where I got out, I soon found my footsteps
pressing its clammy sward, while the crescent of a six or eight
days' moon, struggling amidst heavy clouds, dimly revealed

to me the tall grim Monument that had been named as the
place of meeting, and to which I now hurriedly directed my
course.

As I passed along, I could not help recalling to my mind
many reminiscences connected with that Green. It had once
been my play-ground, where, in company with the tadpole
miscreants of Glasgow, now forming the necessary under-
stratum of society, in the shape of blackguards, burglars,
and highway robbers—with the exception, perhaps, of a few
lucky ones, who, like myself, might have, in the great
cauldron of inscrutable Fate, boiled up to the surface—I had
enjoyed many happy days. In it I had experienced the

humanity of worthy Mr. Silvertop, who had been the primary means of my "getting on in life." And in it I had witnessed the execution of two particular friends, the remembrance of whose antecedents, in connection with an early portion of my own, I would—had it been possible—have fain blotted from my remembrance for ever.

These, and a hundred other incidents rushed on my mind, as I bent my lonely steps towards the Monument, making me wish that the coming ordeal was over, and that I was safe at home again.

On reaching the spot, although the City bells had tolled nine o'clock a few minutes before, I found that silence and solitude reigned around. There was no one present that I could see, nor, indeed, did even a distant step indicate that any one could be within a considerable distance of me, so, to divert my mind from tedium, I struck a light, and commenced to smoke a cigar.

Presently, a form rose, as it were, suddenly from the turf, and approaching me at a slow pace, I was able to descry that it was a female, robed in a dark cloak or duffle, as that description of garment is called, but although I looked pretty hard at her, she appeared as though she would have passed me without recognition.

This manœuvre, however, I found to be only that of prudence, for after walking a few steps farther, she turned round, and addressing me, uttered the name "Sissy," by which I knew her to be the same woman I had seen in Jail.

"Well," I said in reply, "what have you to communicate regarding the person to whom that name belongs, and be quick and truthful in what you say, for remember I am a Magistrate!"

" I have nothing whatever to say," she answered, "the person who desired me to utter that word was, like myself, a prisoner, unknown to me personally, and I only took in hand, for the price which she paid me, to deliver this letter to the Deputy Water Bailie, whom I know you to be—for you once sentenced me to thirty days imprisonment—and having done so, I have only to be off from the Green again in case of mishaps; for there are rangers now in it, which was not the case in former times."

As she said this, she delivered the letter into my hands,

and was for turning away, but I requested her to stay a moment, while I put a few questions to her as to how she had come by the word "Sissy;" what was the payment she had alluded to as having been received for this service, that made her so careless about any further reward; and under what circumstances she had taken it in hand? To which she replied that she had been desired only to use that word as an effective method of attracting my attention; that she had been paid for her present undertaking, by receiving the better portion of her fellow-prisoner's meals, and some of her clothing; and that she had taken it in hand as a kind of reciprocal duty, due from one unfortunate to another, and, therefore, had now executed it, adding as a clincher to this sentiment, that "there was honour amongst thieves!"

She, in addition to my urgent inquiry, stated that she knew nothing further, excepting from *clash* and rumour, amongst the prisoners, regarding Sissy, which she had obtained at meal-times, and during exercise, the only periods they had an opportunity of being together—and which she cared little for, as she was determined to have nothing to do again with such characters, if it were possible for her otherwise to earn an honest penny, and thereby procure a respectable maintenance.

I could not but admire the philosophy of this poor wretch, and being satisfied with the way in which she had executed the commission she had undertaken, as well as gratified that she possessed no sinister knowledge that could be of disservice to me, I put into her hand five sovereigns—the only money which, from prudence, I had brought with me.

This unexpected and welcome sum seemed perfectly to electrify her. She almost danced for joy, and relaxing from the stiffish and almost independent demeanour she had before displayed, she showered upon me heartfelt blessings, while she said, "This will now enable me to become an honest woman; for it will furnish a little shop that will be the means of my doing a decent and upright business!"

She then bent her way across the sward, till her form had almost disappeared, when she turned round, and ejaculated, "God bless you!"

I was pleased with this, although, remembering my many

sins, I felt like Macbeth, and "could not say Amen, when she did say God bless thee!" At all events, I did not attempt it, but hastily returned to my cab, and so was driven home, glad that I could get there, with nothing worse having befallen me.

As may be anticipated, I was not long, after getting into the quietude of home, of perusing Sissy's letter, which instantly commanded my full interest and attention. It was written in a fair scratchy hand, and though there were a number of mis-spelt words in it, and many slips of grammar, which I do not care to give here literally, it was perfectly readable and comprehensible. It was simply addressed to "The Deputy Water Bailie," and was to the following effect:—

"Sir,—I am constrained by gratitude for the interest you evidently took in my case in the Justiciary Court Hall, under peculiar circumstances lately, to address to you the following lines. I have been little accustomed to receive sympathy from any one, and, therefore, can appreciate that on your part, which seemed so strong as to bring upon you sudden illness, from which, however, I have to thank the Giver of all goodness that you are now recovering, as I have since learned, with heartfelt gratitude to Him, who is the Healer of bodies as well as the Saviour of souls. Sir, it is because I wish to stand well in your estimation, that I now take this method of communicating with you; and I hope in doing so, that I will not be considered as sinning against, or hurting any one. I am a bruised reed, plunged in the depths of misery and misfortune, and I have only the consolation of a pure conscience, notwithstanding what has been brought against me, and the awful and humiliating position in which I have stood, as one of the most despised outcasts of society, to keep me from falling into a state of utter despair. Pardon me, if I state my reasons for thus far presuming to lift up my head, when perhaps I should rather lay it amongst the dust, and desire to be forgotten, and particularly for attempting to vindicate myself to you, who are so far placed above me. Sir, I was early in life, left to buffet with the world, in penury and ignorance. I had a father who could do little for me; a mother who could do nothing; and a brother who did not choose to do anything. I had, therefore, no choice but to toil at the meanest of occupations, and amongst the poorest, I might say, the lowest of fellow-labourers. Still I attempted to conduct myself properly, and to maintain a fair character, and in this I was so far successful. My father's return from sea, after a long absence, in poverty and ill health, brought upon me, in addition to the care of my mother, who by this time had become paralytic, an additional burden. I did my best, however, not only from a desire so to do, but in obedience to the holy Fifth Commandment, to maintain them, and myself in comfort and decency, but found it a hard struggle, although we went to a distant locality, where work was plentiful, and rent and food cheaper, than in this City. There, we found an old acquaintance, who had been before that, every thing that was bad. He, however, had reformed; was in excellent employment; had saved a little money, and was so clever a tradesman, that he possessed all the likelihood of continuing to do well. I was induced to marry him, although I loved him not, being persuaded by his promises, and particularly by the regard he showed my parents, whom he engaged to support, and never to see in want. He fulfilled to the letter that undertaking, and, in consequence, our little cottage became a heaven on earth, although my poor father was often saddened by something my brother had communicated to him, when he saw him abroad, regarding my mother and me. My father, however, never would state what that was, and carried the secret to his grave, where, along with my mother, he lies in the churchyard of ———, but from whence, I hope, yet both will have a glorious resurrection. Oh! that I had followed them to such a blessed repose, as it would have spared me what took place subsequently. My husband losing the companionship of my father, to whom he really was attached, and unfortunately we had no family, became careless, and in spite of all my efforts to make his home happy, he left it, to seek for work in this City, employment at ——— having become scarce, in consequence of a depression in trade that had taken place. Here, unfortunately, he fell in with his old and bad companions again. He broke his pledge; became a fearful drunkard—even worse than before—plunged into vice and crime, and being convicted of these, the result was what you already know. In endeavouring to drag him from the whirlpool of danger, into which he had plunged, I myself got involved in the fearful vortex, and had almost perished like himself. All, however, I can say, and will say, is that I am innocent, and for the proof thereof, will only refer to what he declared in the Court Hall in your presence, and which, doubtless, did not escape your attention.

"Sir,—I have done with all that I have to state regarding myself. What I only wish further to say is, that I do not blame my brother for what he has chosen to do, in regard to either myself or parents. He was far above us in learning and ability, and possibly had too good reason for his actions. I loved him fondly, and still love him, for he once was kind to me, and gratitude will never allow me to think otherwise than dutifully, and affectionately of him. Even in my condemned cell I prayed for him; and, under whatever circumstances I may be placed, I shall continue to pray for him, though the naming of him will be confined to these prayers and to the secrecy of my own breast; for never will it be known to any human being that so worthless and degraded a creature as I am, has a brother that has reason to be ashamed of her! Indeed, Sir, even before my degradation, I had acted determinately up to a resolution which I had adopted, of never revealing his name, or my connection with him, to any one; feeling that though my character was then unblemished, he was so far placed above me in society, that he should not be afflicted by constrained consideration for the like of me, unless it should please God to ordain otherwise.

"Sir, for yourself, as a Magistrate that has felt for me, I will pray that you may long enjoy the happiness and dignity of your position, while hoping that you will not despise the expression of the good-wishes of one, even so abject and unworthy as I am."

This document, which had attached to it the single letter "S.," I read, and re-read, and, as may not be wondered at, it filled my mind with varied and conflicting emotions, towards which the silence and privacy I was placed in, ministered not a little; for, before I had mastered its contents, it was

far into the depths and solitude of the night, or rather morning. It gave me both pleasure and pain; for from it I learned that I had now nothing to fear regarding the secrecy of my low origin being divulged, while, at the same time, I had ascertained that all my former terrors and apprehensions, as to that disagreeable contingency happening, might have been spared. An alteration of feeling, likewise, began to pervade my soul, as the light now dawned upon me, which revealed these important facts, consisting of gratitude towards poor Sissy, and mortification that I could do nothing to prove that gratitude. Here had been a poor devoted creature, suffering all the pangs of poverty and want, and yet she could refrain from any attempt to relieve these pressing difficulties, upon high principle and Christian resolution. Not only so, but that she might relieve him, whom she dreaded to injure, and who had acted so very differently to her, she had as it were starved, and rendered herself naked, while, at the same time, making the communication which conveyed that relief, in the most delicate and kindest manner possible.

Well might these thoughts have agitated and perplexed me! Well might they have driven sleep from my eyes and slumber from my eyelids; for, ere I had exhausted them, they had changed in my mind the respective positions of poor Sissy and myself in relation to each other most decidedly, and so far as regarded myself, most humblingly. Our attributes had been transposed in fact. Instead of being the munificent and patronising benefactor, I had proposed to be, I had become the craven and abject recipient of bounty and forgiveness; while she, on the contrary, was the dignified dispenser of relief, and indeed of mercy!

Oh! how silently, and yet pityingly, she rebuked me; and when I had retired at last to my couch, to reflect still further, on what had been revealed to me this day, how her form, with the resignation of a martyr appealing to heaven, amidst the smoke and flames of persecution, stood, in my mind's eye, at the foot of that couch, and haunted my guilty conscience!

In person, she was far, far away, tossing amidst the billows of the ocean, while I lay on a bed of down; but with that apparition ever present—and which I in vain shut my eyes to—it was still a bed of thorns and misery!

CHAPTER XLI.

INTRODUCTORY DOGGERELS.

Lead down the dance!—
O'er life's expanse,
We do but dance, from day to day:
Till cruel Death
Stops short our breath,
When to the grave,—we dance away!

The Goosedubbs Poet.

I SOON after this—what with taking great care of myself, and what with refraining altogether from taking the prescriptions of Dr. Morse, who, nevertheless, duly called once a day, in his carriage, at my house, to write them out in dog-latin, but which, instead of being sent to the apothecary, to be made up, were invariably consigned to the fire, and the worthy Doctor never a bit the wiser—became perfectly re-established in health, and likewise to a great extent in spirits; for, in pursuit of the latter, I had resumed intercourse with society, and the season being rather gay—indeed gayer, it was remarked by every one, than it had been for many years previously—I had many opportunities of diverting myself in the way of dancing and dinner parties, of which I took as much advantage as possible, all my friends being emulous to show me attentions in that way, in consequence of my recent dangerous illness, which I found had added not a little to my importance, and popularity: though, I must confess that very often, amidst the bustling scenes connected with these entertainments, a severe qualm of

conscience would come over me, and render me for the
moment dejected, if not miserable.

In eastern countries, we are told by a popular author, it
was once the custom of entertainers to place in their gilded
saloons, amidst their guests, draped skeletons, which, on

being discovered, while startling them, no doubt, had, at the
same time, a moral effect upon their feelings, as the circumstance reminded them of certain serious topics, that eastern
ethics required should not be forgotten.

The apparition to me of Sissy at times, while placed under
like circumstances, was even as those skeletons were to the
Orientals. Sometimes it would appear in the smile of a
damsel; sometimes in the rustle of a silken garment, although
the poor creature had never touched such a fabric, far less
worn one; sometimes it would be developed in a painting on
the wall; and sometimes it would be suggested by a strain
of music.

The visitation, if such it might be called, was evanescent,
but still it had the effect of controlling any undue hilarity
I might have been prone to indulge in; and in consequence,
on all such occasions, I was rather subdued and serious in
my deportment, than otherwise.

Nor was this characteristic in my manners of disservice to
me. I rather think it was of great use, for I felt conscious
that I was often treated with great respect, while others, my

superiors in social qualifications, were unappreciated. My silence and reserve, indeed, I found to be generally much more attractive than the volubility and wit of others, particularly amongst the male portion of the company, though even the females did not altogether turn the cold shoulder to me, when I essayed to pay staid attentions to them.

I would have been rather *non-plussed* had such been the case with the latter; for, sooth to say, at this particular epoch of my life, I had begun to have very serious communings with myself as to the value of this more estimable portion of the sexes. To be plain, I had turned my thoughts towards matrimony, for I felt that I was now getting up in years, and that my habits were assuming something of a definite shape, which I feared might result in confirmed bachelorhood, if not checked. And this tendency was not lessened by the circumstance, that I had a very comfortable house, a very useful and clever servant lad, that knew my way; and, in particular, a very trustworthy and attentive housekeeper, who attended to my linens, darned my stockings, aired my night clothes, not forgetting my night cowl, and never neglected, from the beginning of November to the end of April, to place a hot water bottle at the foot of my couch, before I retired for the night.

And then she cooked so well, and sent up the dishes so tidy and so hot, that my dinners were talked of by my friends for months afterwards, and contrasted favourably, by some of my married acquaintances, with those of their wives, even to their very faces, thereby endangering that *entente cordial*, which it was my desire to strengthen instead of weaken, betwixt myself and the "better-halves" of my married friends, knowing as I did the value of their good opinion, as matronisers and advisers of their unmarried sisterhood.

I found, indeed, that the rashness of their husbands in praising my "bachelor dinners," had led to a little jealousy on the part of the worthy dames, which soon indicated itself in hints and inuendos, if not satirical allusions, to my "bachelor exclusiveness and selfishness," in robbing them of the society of their husbands, while they were left at home to mope with the children, or meditate upon the ingratitude and cruelty of men in general, and of myself in particular.

I felt the full force of these arguments, and the danger that lurked underneath them, and therefore to propitiate the worthy matrons, and, so far as I could, make all right again, I arranged, after deferentially consulting them, that I should give a special dinner party, to which they should be all asked, along with their husbands; and which came off with great success, the entertainment ending with a dance in the drawing-room, to which a reserve of their sons and daughters, and their daughters' sweethearts, were duly invited, when no stint of waltzing, quadrilling, and gallopading took place, I having had the hardihood to furnish that apartment with a piano, which kept them hopping and flirting till midnight, when my housekeeper, who deemed her character at stake, surprised them with a *petit soupé* that might have been creditable to a *restaurateur*, let alone a private *provideur*, though only got up on the spur of the moment.

This, however, was the means of perfectly overcoming the matrons, for, while assorting their shawls and hoods in the lobby, previously to raising the siege, they declared they had never been so delighted by anything of the kind before, and that the only thing I required, to obtain their thorough good will, was a wife, a remark that Barbara, my respected housekeeper, or as they dubbed  her for the nonce, Mrs. Barbara, who was now attending to their comforts in the way of robing—as though all her housekeeping exertions had been mere "bairns' play,"—did not seemingly relish at all.

Whether the said Mrs. Barbara approved or disapproved of the suggestion, however, it made a deep impression on me, and, I confess, caused me to blush not a little as I shook the various "tabbies" and their daughters by the hand, while wishing them safe back to their respective places of abode, on the way to which, I did not doubt they would severely criticise my domestic arrangements, including the quality of my tables, chairs, crockery, china, crystal, plate, mirrors, and Brussels carpets, as I had found generally to be the case, particularly with those dowagers who had an opportunity of seeing bachelors' quarters, and had daughters in the nuptial market.

That my establishment, however, had met with approval, was proved by the fact that, for weeks afterwards, I was bombarded with cards of invitation to dinners, quadrille parties, routs, and soirees, without number, to overtake which I was under the necessity of sometimes attending three " occasions" of an evening, that sort of thing being considered quite fashionable amongst the young men of that day, and perhaps is practised even by those of this one.

A party, however, was to come off about this time, which I resolved not to damage by any such snobbishness; but, on the contrary, to devote the whole evening to, I therefore flatly declined several inferior quadrille shines, set for the same evening, the invitation to this superior one having been issued for upwards of three weeks before it was due, thereby causing much sensation and eager expectation in "fashionable circles."

It was indeed *the* party of the season, and both gossip and rumour understood it was to be got up in magnificent style, towards which purpose, the first confectioners, the foremost decorators, and the most superior " sawlies" had been pressed into the service—it being the " house-heating" of Councillor Tweel, of the wealthy firm of Tweel, Braid, & Company, Haberdashers and Silk Mercers, who had just taken possession of a splendid mansion in the West End, and had fitted it out with new furniture, new plenishing, and new every thing; so that it was not to be wondered at, if it had become the subject of admiration, if not of envy, amongst all the matrons residing in the locality of St. Blythswood, as well as other fashionable quarters.

Mr. Tweel I was not particularly acquainted with. I had met him at the Town Council, which he had only lately joined, having been ushered into public life when rather up in years, by being returned for his own ward, by a considerable majority, over an old representative, in consequence of his greater wealth. Riches in fact, formed his peculiar qualification for the responsible position he had acquired; and it was well that he had something to recommend him, as I never heard a more stupid or clumsier speaker than the honest Councillor, amongst even the boobies that formed our corporate body—he being ambitious to be an orator, and yet having neither education, information, nor even verbiage, to assist him in attaining his object. Still he would speak, to

the great amusement, if not scorn, of his brother Councillors; and, notwithstanding his absurd attitudes, his indifferent grammar, his misnomers, his stammering, his hesitation, and his apparent want of aim, he went on persevering in his questions, his motions, and his amendments, with a pertinacity worthy of the best of causes.

Of course, his being rich gained for his person respect, and for his speechifying-efforts toleration, in the Council, which otherwise would not have been the case had he been poor. Still, for all that, the laugh and the jeer could not be suppressed, when he was more than ordinarily absurd, and consequently, he occasionally stood in the humbling difficulty of not being able to obtain even a seconder for his motion, or his amendment, as the case might be.

I suppose it was from my having felt pity for his plight under some such circumstance, or regard for his monetary standing, and thereby backed him, in one of his unmeaning questions, which the Provost declined to answer, on the plea that he did not understand it—although he must have understood it as well as I did—that I gained the Councillor's favour, so far as to be invited to his approaching rout. At all events, I had reason to consider it a great compliment, particularly as no other member of the Council had been invited.

Councillor Tweel, nevertheless, had not forgotten that body, of which he was so important a member, for he had, about the same time, issued invitations (in which I was likewise included) for an official dinner, as it was called, which was to be given by him at St. Blythswood Terrace, two days after the ball—the said dinner, however, being understood to be merely one of those stereotyped municipal entertainments, where Provosts and Bailies, and ordinary members meet, dressed in white chokers and black vestments, to discuss a sumptuous "feed," and pledge each other in the best of wines, and perhaps pass a few compliments in the way of special toasts, to the healths of officials, but without the least feeling of friendship or real regard being felt at heart towards any one, and then go home to tell their wives all about the dishes, and the plate, and the dessert, and how many "sawlies" had waited the table—but who are now denominated "waiting-men;" and whether there were entrées, or French side dishes; and if the soup had been cold, and the fish underdone, and the ices had melted; and what like the silver-plated epergne was, and whether the flowers in it were real greenhouse cut ones, and not artificial muslin or wax ones; and, in particular, how Mrs. Muff, or Mrs. Duff, was dressed, and who took the lady of the house down to dinner, and how she conducted herself amongst so many gentlemen—all which particulars are of the utmost importance to the questioner, as it possibly may happen, that at the very time, her husband, Councillor Buff, may be contemplating the giving of a dinner too, and she would like to know as to those of others, so as to be able to equal, if not excel them, in *her* entertainment.

The evening on which Councillor Tweel's "re-union," as the ball was fashionably styled, was to take place, at last arrived, and, having dressed myself in a new suit, got for the occasion, I popped into a cab betwixt nine and ten o'clock, and was driven to St. Blythswood Terrace, which I found in a blaze of light and crowded with vehicles, while a host of people stood about the door, which was kept clear by a couple

of policemen, some being there from curiosity, to "see the grand ladies and gentlemen," and some, no doubt, to pick pockets, a pastime which I myself once was an adept at, but which fact, now that I had become a Magistrate, I strained to bury in oblivion, as I passed hurriedly from the cab to the corridor, where I was duly divested of my hat and happings by the beadle of St. Blythswood Tabernacle, and then passed up the elegant staircase, brilliant with gas, and adorned with flowers and evergreens, towards the drawing-room, while a sawlie below, and a sawlie above, shouted out my name, by way of announcement, as though I had been a peer of the realm.

On reaching the drawing-room door, which had been taken off its hinges for the occasion, thereby permitting a commanding vista of the gay scene within, rendered imposing by waving silks and nodding plumes, belonging to a

numerous company, most of whom were moving to the
strains of a small but excellent band, I found Mr. Tweel
standing to welcome his guests, with his large hands
enveloped in pure white kids, that looked not unlike boxing
gloves, in consequence of the substantial flesh and bone
within them, while he bowed and smiled most hospitably to
all comers.

To me he was particularly kind, if a warm and rough
shake of his said capacious "mawley" could be considered a
proof of such sentiment, in addition to an earnest inquiry as
to my health, after my recent illness, and to which I
responded with becoming acknowledgments, by which time
the music and the dancing had ceased for a little, when he
proposed to lead me to Mrs. Tweel, no doubt as an especial
compliment to me, as a Bailie, and particularly, as he said,
that she desired I should be introduced to her as an old
acquaintance, when I should arrive.

I was a little surprised at this information, but soon found
it explained in a way I had not reckoned upon; for, on proceeding to Mrs. Tweel, who was seated at the head of the
room on an elegant ottoman, like a Sultana, and attired in
a remarkably rich and fashionable dress, relieved with a
profusion of glancing pearls and glittering diamonds, I was
utterly confounded to find that the person who bore the
name was no other—though much changed in consequence
of the matronly stoutness she had acquired—than my old
friend, the elegant and adored Miss Tucker, who, previous to

my emigration, had almost broken my heart by becoming
Mrs. M'Chuckie!

I could not help being a good deal discomposed by this
discovery, and perhaps I blushed, and looked a little awkward
in consequence, while going through the ceremony of bowing
and shaking hands, like a mere automaton.

The lady observed my confusion, and perhaps being prepared for it, hastened to relieve the pains I felt, by kindly
pressing me to take a seat by her side, while a quadrille was
being arranged by a portion of the company, which diverted
attention from us, till the music had struck up, and the party
had commenced dancing: when she turned towards me with
the kindest and most patronising manner possible, and said,
"Ah! Bailie, this is indeed a pleasant re-union, one that I
looked forward to, though perhaps you did not; for I have
heard of your success in life, and of your worthy promotion
to so high a position amongst your fellow-citizens!"

To this I bowed a bland acknowledgment, which possibly
exhibited, at the same time, on my countenance a look of
curiosity, for she went on, as if in reply, to say, "Ah! dear,
dear, what a change has happened since the old happy days,
when I formerly used to meet you—of course you heard of
my first husband's death?"

To this pointed query I was under the necessity of reply-
ing that I had not, while excusing myself for displaying so

much ignorance by pleading, that in the distant locality I
had gone to, I had not had the opportunity of regularly
seeing the Glasgow newspapers, and had probably, in consequence, missed those ones, in which the sad announcement
would be made, in the usual obituary columns.

"Ah! yes," she answered, "it must have been so, for it was
duly recorded at the time, and there likewise was a paragraph stating his many virtues and business qualifications,
and which he greatly deserved; for he was a kind husband to
me, and a friend to every one, so that I may say when he
died, he did not leave an enemy behind him in the City."

I bowed an acquiescence to this eulogy, although with a
mental reservation, and, at the same time, to a certain extent,
with truth; for, I kept in view that, at the period to which
she referred, I had left the City, and the country too, though
I had not forgotten or forgiven the maulings Tom Throstle
and I had respectively received at the M'Chuckie's hands,
and which, so far as I was concerned, made me learn the
news with wonderful composure, notwithstanding that Mrs.
Tweel communicated it, slightly sobbing, and with a richly
sewed handkerchief applied to her eyes, in which I did not
observe the slightest approach to a tear. She, however,
pathetically continued:—"Alas! alas, Bailie! it was a sad
trial, for he was barely spared to me above a year, and he
left me with only one pledge of his affection—that is she, in
the middle of the room, dressed in the pink satin petticoat,
with lace skirt over it, and pousetting with the gentleman
in the blue coat—you will know her by the likeness to her
dear father, and I will introduce you to her, after the
quadrille is over!"

I looked, and observed a raw-boned and gawkyish-looking
girl, dressed as described. Her age was apparently about
nineteen, although she could not, by my calculation of the
time that had elapsed since her parents' marriage, have exceeded seventeen; while, in the gentleman, I recognised my
disagreeable friend, Jackson, who was capering and skipping
about in great glee, seemingly much delighted with his
partner and himself, and looking more like a dancing monkey
than ever.

I resolved, therefore, although not much struck with Miss
M'Chuckie's beauty, to dance with her as much as possible,

if for nothing but to annoy Mr. Jackson, for I noticed that
he evidently admired her, by the way he followed her with
his bleary eyes, when she was crossing over, and afterwards
ogled her, when poussetting, on her return.

Miss M'Chuckie, however, I found to be greatly in demand; for, on the dance being finished, and her mamma had
summoned her to her side, for the purpose of introducing
me to her, I could only procure an engagement with her for
a country dance far on, and which she duly registered in her
"*carte*," thus leaving me, in the meantime, to exercise my
shanks otherwise, or to continue to chat with her mother,
who, as presiding goddess of the entertainment, occupied her
ottoman as a fixture.

I, however, broke away from the restraint such an ordeal
would have imposed upon me, and found my way to the
negus room, where I fell in with another old friend, namely,
Mr. Quince, whom I met at the first party of ancient days,
that introduced me to gay life, and, at the same time, to the
adorable Miss Tucker. Mr. Quince, like myself, had been
successful in business, having risen from a clerk, to be a
partner with his employers, Messrs. Spicer & Company, and
had evidently waxed independent, if I might judge from his
appearance, which was that of a respectable elderly gentleman, to whom the grand scene around was nothing in
particular. I found him however, as before, very communicative, and ready to furnish me with information
regarding everybody, and consequently, I learned from him
all particulars as to the career of Mrs. M'Chuckie, now Mrs.
Tweel, with whom he had continued in pleasant intimacy,
from that day to this, and hence was one of her guests on
the present signal occasion.

According to Mr. Quince, Mrs. M'Chuckie on becoming a
widow, found that all along—that is previously to her marriage
with the M'Chuckie—she had been secretly admired by her
employer, Mr. Tweel, of Tweel, Braid, & Company, in whose
show-room she had exhibited, upon her handsome person,
the shawls, cloaks, and draperies, that had brought this
eminent firm into such great repute, for that especial
description of goods. She likewise discovered that Mr.
Tweel had almost gone out of his reason, like others, when
she married M'Chuckie, and had never forgiven himself for

K 2

not being the first to ask her—a misfortune which he did not
lose the opportunity of retrieving, as soon as he again got
the chance—for, ere her grief was well exhausted she became
the happy wife of Mr. Tweel, who, though much her senior
in years, and indeed, understood to be a confirmed old
bachelor, made up for these disadvantages, by taking her to
a handsome home, which had resulted in a still handsomer
one—of which this occasion formed the "heating"—and a
carriage to the bargain.

By the time I had swallowed my negus, and likewise this
interesting little bit of gossip, of which the foregoing is only
an abridgment, for Mr. Quince, like others of the same kidney,
was rather diffuse, I found, to use a commercial expression,
that I was almost "due" to Miss M'Chuckie.   I accordingly
returned to the drawing-room, where she was relinquished

to me by Mr. Jackson, evidently with no good will, and I
had soon the pleasure of leading her to the head of the room,
where she was allowed to lead off the first country dance of
the evening, in virtue of the normal etiquette that was
observed on the occasion, and during the dancing of which
she was watched by Mr. Jackson, who did not choose to
engage another partner, evidently with feelings not of the
pleasantest description.

At the end of this dance, the band struck up promenade
music, indicative of refreshments being requisite for the
ladies, and possibly, porter for themselves, and accordingly

I invited Miss M'Chuckie, as others did their partners, to proceed to the negus room.

As we passed along, I by chance directed my eyes towards a lady, who sat alone in propinquity to some ancient dames, in what was rather a neglected corner of a sofa, for to it I had observed no gentlemen proceed for partners, during the time I had been present.

There was nothing particular in the appearance of this young lady, only that on lifting her eyes, which till then had been cast down, as if she were listening to the music, unheedful of the gaiety around, I was startled to observe they were like those of Sissy, and I thought that the expression of her countenance was also like hers. The circumstance, however, was purely accidental; for, in a moment the resemblance had vanished, and I found that I had merely been visited by one of those dreamy reminiscences that occasionally haunted me in such scenes, to warn me as it were, that like Philip, I ought not to forget my infirmities!

I, nevertheless, felt a keen desire to know something further of this neglected one; and as soon as I had disposed of Miss M'Chuckie, after getting her again to enter my name in the first vacant part of her *carte*, for a forthcoming dance, I had recourse to my useful friend, Mr. Quince, who told me all about the young lady, and then introduced me to her.

"She's only the governess," he said, "of Miss M'Chuckie,

and her half-sisters, the Misses Tweel, which accounts for her being allowed to keep her seat so long amongst the ancients; for our Glasgow chaps soon find out 'who's who,' and a governess, no matter how amiable and pretty she may be, has, under such circumstances, little chance of being taken up, if there's an ugly girl, whose father is reputed rich, to be got, and whether she can dance or not. Bless your soul, Sir," he continued, "every maiden here has a ticket pinned to her gown, stating her market value, though your uninitiated vision may not recognise it!"

Mr. Quince went on to say that, notwithstanding, the governess was a very nice sort of person, intelligent and well-informed, and one whom, on getting into conversation with, I would find a most agreeable companion, as he had done,—he not being a dancer—she would very possibly be allowed to retain her seat the whole evening, unless he could induce some "useful young man," as a great favour, and out of charity, as it were, to lead her up to a reel, or country dance, or any other trifling affair of the kind.

On being introduced to Miss Gentle, that being her name, I found Mr. Quince had not overstated her qualifications. She was, indeed, worthy of her name—gentle, unassuming, and well-informed—with a musical voice, and subdued manner—again reminding me of poor Sissy, but pleasantly— that quite charmed me. She was dressed simply in a plain white muslin gown, and, unlike the ladies around, had not a single jewel on her person, or ring upon her finger, while her well-proportioned hands and neck were like alabaster of the purest kind. She danced well too, and waltzed prettily, so that, when I led her to her seat, I felt that I had not been unfortunate in making her acquaintance, however I might have lost the opportunity of cultivating that of several reputed heiresses who polked formidably, waltzed wantonly, and galloped *gailliardly*, as the hyper-critical Mr. Quince expressed it, on commenting on the circumstances of the evening, afterwards.

I would have fain led Miss Gentle into supper, which was now announced, only that I was precluded from obtaining that pleasure by the arrangements of Mrs. Tweel, whereby she impressed me into her own particular service. It was a great honour, no doubt, that I should have been selected to conduct her to the banquet, and take my seat on her right hand, at the head of a table that actually groaned with good things, consisting of all the varieties and luxuries of the season. What a show it was to be sure of French cookery, pastry, and confectionery, and what a contrast these formed to the substantial roast beef, and boiled mutton, that formed the edibles of the supper, on the occasion of our ever-to-be-remembered first meeting, not forgetting the "penny-pies" and the "twopenny-tarts" that the attentive and loving M'Chuckie had pressed upon her, as he leered at her with his one eye, while filling my soul with envy, hatred and jealousy!

We had no toddy or punch, as on that boisterous occasion, but we had champagne and crackers, which, although not so exhilarating, to a certain extent animated us, and put us in spirits, so that when the company returned to the ball-room, where I had the honour of dancing with Mrs. Tweel herself—the only occasion for such a display she allowed herself to indulge in, this evening: and that out of especial compliment to me—we found ourselves less stiff, and under less restraint than before.

Mrs. Tweel, it is true, unlike Miss Tucker, did not cut and caper, and bound, and pirouette; but on the contrary, moved backwards, and forwards, and sideways, in the

controlled and fashionable mode of the day, like a balloon—
in consequence of her matronly *embonpoint*—out on an
airing, but still she enjoyed herself, as did the rest of the
company, with the exception of Mr. Jackson, who was
evidently annoyed at my being so distinguished by the hostess, and particularly at my dancing and waltzing more than
he approved of, with Miss M'Chuckie.

And thus Mrs. Tweel's grand "re-union" pleasantly pro-
gressed, till it was far on in the morning, and the guests
were becoming rather knocked up, and *blasé*, when, to
remedy this misfortune, we were summoned to another repast, in the shape of most delicious and rare soups, served
out in beautiful French china *saucières*, appropriate for the
purpose, and which were found most refreshing. This delightful variation of the luxuries of the fête, Mr. Quince
informed me, was suggested by what had taken place at a
splendid entertainment of the kind, given by the Duchess of
Dumbarton, and, he presumed, would be generally adopted
at other fashionable routs during the season, "unless," as
that jocular gentleman added, " the Duchess should choose to
introduce rump-steaks and porter, and then, of course, these
will become fashionable, instead !"

Mr. and Mrs. Tweel's "house-heating" was indeed a great
success, and on its being wound up, somewhere about three
o'clock in the morning, there was scarcely one of the guests,
I am sure, that would not have been glad to have had it
encored.

CHAPTER XLII.

INTRODUCTORY DOGGERELS.

> Behold the important Councillors,
> Who, in the forenoon, puzzle
> Their civic brains, with town's affairs;
> And in the evening—guzzle!
>
> *The Goosedubbs Poet.*

Mr. and Mrs. Tweel's grand ball created much talk, and no small quantity of envy, for many days afterwards, particularly amongst those who had not been present at it; indeed, some of the latter were malignant enough to designate it vulgar, which, by-the-by, I found was a term that people in this part of the world were very prone to apply, not only to the entertainments, but to the characters of each other, while of course, never taking the impeachment home to themselves; on the contrary, it is understood here, as universally throughout the globe, that when one makes a charge of vulgarity against another, the charger is to be considered a very superior and genteel personage.

I don't know, besides, any place where, in addition to the accusation I have named, the antecedents of the unfortunate calumniated ones are so acrimoniously resuscitated, for the purpose of propagating the calumniations, as in the City of St. Mungo. Invariably, I have found, that after the Pattertons had given an evening party, the Flappertons, on inquiring into, and commenting upon it, would stumble on some such circumstance—to remind themselves, and instruct their auditors—as, that old Patterton had been a porter, and Mrs. Patterton a mantua-maker; while, after the Flap-

pertons' dinner, the Pattertons would tell, that Mr. Flapper-
ton had once carried a pack, and that his wife's mother had

been a "sweetie wife," with
a stand at the Cross, where
she sold apples and gundy to
the bairns.

In the same spirit, the
M'Staves would insinuate
that the Cleavers came from
the Cowcaddens, where their
father was a butcher; and to
balance this, the Cleavers
would communicate, in an
equally Christian spirit, that
the M'Staves were originally
working-coopers, though now calling themselves extensive
timber merchants.

It was not, therefore, to be wondered at, if I heard many
inuendos expressed at the expense of the Tweels; and that,
I was told in a whisper, and as a great secret, various little
particulars that I knew better about, than my informants did
themselves. I was, however, "all ears and no tongue," and
consequently had, at least, the satisfaction to know, that Mr.
and Mrs. T. suffered nothing at my hands, whatever I might
have had in my power to state about them.

With something like a feeling, under these circumstances,
that I was a friend of the family, I found my way, two days
after the date of the rout that has been recorded, again to St.
Blythswood Terrace, at the very aristocratic dinner hour (for
that era) of half-past six, when I was welcomed by Mr. and
Mrs. Tweel, with all the civilities due to an old and valued
acquaintance; and, notwithstanding what envy or scandal
had insinuated, namely, that this feast would be just a
reproduction of the luxuries, in another shape, of the former
display—reminding one of what Hamlet says about "funeral
baked meats coldly furnishing forth marriage feed," &c.—I
found such not to be the case. There was not a consumable
element that I could recognise as having been present on the
former occasion. The soups, as a matter of course, were
new. The fish had evidently swam the day before. The
joints might have been in the larder, but never on the table

before. And as for the side-dishes, the sweets, the pastries, the blancmanges, the jellies, the ices, and the dessert, they were all of a different cast entirely. The only things that were not novel were the smiles of the host and hostess, the enormous plated silver dish-covers, the plush livery of the butler, the rather ample laced coat of the coachman—he being made available for the occasion—and the staid physiognomies of the sawlies.

The table, indeed, presented an imposing sight, after we had marched down the magnificent staircase, and along the encaustic-tiled lobby,—betwixt two rows of waiting men or sawlies, some of whom looked as well as, and indeed might have passed for, councillors themselves: as possibly some day they may become, if they should take up "cook-shops," now genteelly designated "*restaurants*," and make money—into the dining-room, the Lord Provost conducting Mrs. Tweel, the Reverend Nahum Gust Miss M'Chuckie, the Senior

Bailie Miss Tweel, and myself Miss Gentle, while the rest of the Council, with their stiff white necks, followed, and, along with a few other private friends, amongst whom Mr. Quince was conspicuous, dispersed themselves towards this, or that side of the table, to find seats, as they best could—all which being duly arranged, we then got a grace from Nahum, wherein he quite outstripped himself; for, as he stood, before the bright dish-cover—which could not prevent the escape, notwithstanding its amplitude, of the delightful savour of some delicious preparation that lay beneath it—with his arms extended at full length, his eyes

turned up in their sockets, and his voice sonorous with gastronomic gratitude, he appeared the very perfection of what a Chaplain, at a civic feast, is understood to be. It was certainly worthy of the occasion, and must have cost the reverend gentleman some preparation, for it was not only eloquent, but lengthy, two qualifications which, however appreciable at other times, seemingly were not so at this particular one; for scarcely had his welcome "Amen" been pronounced, than every one was drawing in his chair, and bringing his person into comfortable position, while dividers were dispensing soup, and sawlies were passing and re-passing, and lips were sip, sipping, the reverend Nahum's holy ones being about the first at that duty, notwithstanding the provoking length of time he had kept ours from it.

I must do Mrs. Tweel the justice to say that this dinner was the best I had ever been at before, so far as luxuries and expensive dishes could make it. We had real turtle soup, which everybody took, and white soup, which all declined. We had a noble salmon, caught that morning in the Forth, and brought express from Stirling, it being the opening day of the fishing season, and therefore valued, as the gentleman on my right, who was a bit of a guzzler, told me, at something like 5s. per pound; and beautifully dressed white fish, that an unfortunate sawlie in vain endeavoured to find a customer for. We had lamb, although it was just out of January; and early pease, although the ground was covered with snow; we had venison, we had game—we had, in a sentence, everything nice, that arrangements could have anticipated, or cash have commanded.

And then what superior wines. How the hock sparkled, and the champagne creamed, and how the guests tossed bumpers of these off, particularly the Provost and Nahum, who pledged each other more than once, across the bows of Mrs. Tweel, who sat serenely, as though she had been the figure-head of a Cunard liner.

Under such luxurious circumstances as these, one might have had some difficulty in supposing, that any person present could have had the smallest room for fault-finding or grumbling; but such I actually discovered not to be the case, for, on turning to my guzzling companion, who had been paying great attention to the work before him, and who had touched my arm with the view of uttering a remark, I was amazed when he made, in proof of this fact, the following confidential communication—"Noo, Bailie, if I had just a bit o' cheese and a drink o' porter, I wad say I *waz* dined!"

Of course, to keep up intercourse after that with such a Goth, was out of the question; so I resumed conversation with Miss Gentle, who by-the-by, in justice to, I must tell, had conducted herself very differently to most of the company, including even her pupils, the Misses M'Chuckie and Tweel, for she partook of the good things but sparingly, and without any particular selection, with the exception that she seemed to prefer what was plain, to what was rich.

In her I found a most agreeable companion—instructive without being pedantic, communicative without being conceited, and humorous without being vulgar. Indeed, she

had all the attributes of a gentlewoman, so that it was easy
to perceive that though she held the humble position of
a governess, she had been carefully educated and superiorly
brought up.

I really, therefore, felt regret when, after the dessert had
been discussed, I heard that ominous rustling of silks which
indicated that the ladies were rising to leave, and observed
stately Mrs. Tweel stalking towards the door, with crossed
arms and folded fan, followed by her daughters in like

fashion, the fair procession being brought up by plainly
attired Miss Gentle, who had no fan at all; while one of
the gentlemen opened the door respectfully, and all the rest
stood up, with their table napkins in their hands, as though
they were flags of distress, expressive of the sorrow felt at
the *exody* that was taking place.

This void, however, was soon remedied by Mr. Tweel
taking his better-half's vacated chair at the head of the room,
and Mr. Quince becoming *vice*, after which arrangement the
wine was more vigorously pushed round, and the company
became less staid in their communications with each other.

The Provost, shortly after this, called for a "special
bumper," and with very good taste, in a few preliminary
remarks,—for giving which he apologised, while excusing

himself on the plea that this was "the inaugural dinner" of Mr. Tweel to the Council, in the splendid mansion, within whose walls they now partook of his munificent hospitality, &c., &c.,—proposed the health of Mrs. Tweel, and "her fireside."

This, of course, led to other toasts being proposed, in short speeches, wherein so many compliments were reciprocated betwixt one Councillor and another, that an uninitiated one would scarcely have believed such a thing as a "bickering" or a "heckling" could ever have taken place at a Town Council meeting. We were all, in short, "esteemed representatives," "honourable members," "worthy Magistrates," and so on.

Nor did the reverend Nahum remain silent on the occasion, though he was more than ordinarily brief, the reason for which was explained to me by Mr. Quince, who asserted that in parties like this, the wine was always particularly good, and the time short, and Nahum, knowing this, was not the fool to throw either away. He, however, true to his purpose, ran a tilt against the sins and evils of the day, amongst the working-classes, from those venial ones, which consisted in attending philosophical lectures, tending to atheism; dancing soirées, driving to demoralisation; and singing assemblies, leading to lewdness; to the more outrageous ones of Sabbath desecration, demands for political power, and indulgence in intoxicating liquors: crying evils, which he hoped his friend the Lord Provost, aided by a Christian Council, would use his earnest efforts to put down, and for which he would receive the approval of his own conscience, the commendations of the community, and the prayers of the clergy!

Nahum, having thus dutifully acquitted himself, now, by way of practical illustration of a portion of his philanthropic precepts, commenced to do full justice to Mr. Tweel's port and claret, by swallowing full bumpers thereof, every time the decanters came round, a duty which I have no doubt he would have continued to exert himself in, but that time fled fastly, and that the Provost was now looking anxiously at him, after passing, without partaking of their contents, the bottles twice or thrice, as much as to say, "Of course we can't budge before the clergy!" which hint being observed by Nahum, he gave effect to it by calling for a "white-wash," and proposing that we should join the ladies.

After the reverend Nahum's white-wash, which consisted of a jolly glass of brown sherry he led the way, arm in arm with the Provost, to the drawing-room, on the passage to which my friend Quince told me to be prepared for a musical treat, as a beautiful new harp, the gift of Mr. Tweel to his step-daughter, was to be introduced that night, it having just come the day before, from London, and unluckily too late for the ball that had taken place; but which misfortune was to be remedied, so far as it could be done, by the Council having their ears regaled by its harmonious twangs, on this occasion. It was a very fine instrument, Mr. Quince said, and had cost the honest haberdasher no less than two hundred pounds, for he had seen the account, duly receipted, with two and a half per cent. discount for cash taken off, with an accompanying letter from Mr. Tweel's correspondents in London, which stated it was the finest that could be got for money, being a duplicate of one that had been furnished to the Duchess of Dumbarton at three hundred guineas. This difference in price, Mr. Quince supposed, was in consequence of the Duke not being so flush of money as the draper, and therefore taking it upon credit—"a thing which, of course, a Glasgow Councillor would never do!"

Accordingly, as soon as the sawlies had served us with

coffee, tea, and cakes, the said harp was duly brought forward from its corner to the middle of the room, by Plush and Jehu, when Miss M'Chuckie took her seat at its side, where she might have passed as an admirable representation of Hibernia, if she had only had a little of the brogue, and less of the Scotch west-country accent.

Having arranged her drapery and her person to the best advantage, she proceeded to run her fingers over the strings of the

harp, bringing out very good tones indeed, quite in keeping
with its price and magnificent appearance—for it displayed
an enormous quantity of carving, and gilding, and inlaying;
and, after an appropriate symphony, she commenced in a style
rather *forté* to warble a song, the music to which Mr. Quince
informed me in a whisper, was composed by the gentleman
who had given her instructions at a guinea a lesson, but
which I really thought was a little familiar to my ear.

As to the appropriateness of the words, they—considering
that she had seen the harp for the first time, only the evening
before, and that it was span-new—may be judged of from
the first verse, which was as follows:—

> " My gentle harp, my early friend,
>   While o'er thy chords I weeping bend,
>   Say why thy melancholy lays
>   Remind me so of early days!"

How the harp, under the circumstances, could have been
her early friend, it was difficult to conceive, and as to
her weeping, there was not a tear in her eye.

Miss M'Chuckie, however, went on with a long argument
and remonstrance with her harp, as to its cruelty in making
her so miserable, and ended by importuning it as follows:—

> "Then harp, oh! change thy notes of woe,
>   Nor cause the burning tears to flow,
>   For why with melancholy lays,
>   Remind me so of early days?"

As the last cadence died away—as romance writers say—
Miss M'Chuckie rose from the harp, and Plush and Jehu
replaced it in its corner, while the Lord Provost and all the
Council made a soundless motion with their kid covered
hands, as if clapping them in applause, and one or two
exclaimed " very sweet" and " very beautiful," amidst which
Miss M'Chuckie placed herself at the grand piano, an
instrument that Quince likewise announced to me, as having
cost at least as much as the harp did, and as if to put us in
good spirits after the lachrymose song, thumped out of "Collard
and Collard" a fantasia that fairly drowned all our voices,
and reduced us to silence.

A rather awkward silence followed the fantasia, that
almost threatened a break-up of the company: for by this

time carriages were rattling before the front of the house, though none as yet had been announced. To avert this catastrophe, however, Mr. Quince rose, and after a few remarks to, and remonstrances with, Miss Gentle, who was evidently not inclined to make any musical display, prevailed on that young lady to allow him to lead her to the piano, upon which she played very sweetly and tastefully indeed. To sing, of course, she was invited, but being averse to this, she compromised the matter by giving a Jacobite chant, as

Quince announced it, and which was to the following effect —although I regret I can only render it here imperfectly, having written down when I got home, so far as I could, its substance, and submitted it to my friend, the Poet of the Goosedubbs, who put it into rhyme:—I never having attempted such a thing myself, since composing the song which brought upon me the revengeful retribution that followed, at the hands of the malignant M'Chuckie:—

"The setting sun resigns his sway to Night;
    But ere he vanishes beyond the hill,
He casts a parting glance intensely bright,
    Tinting with gold the vista: nor until—
    O'er wood, and waste, and water-fall, and rill—
His latest beam hath all but died away,
    Doth the scene lose its richness, for it still
Retains, though mellowed more, a lingering ray,
That lights again my heart, and lonely Invergray.

"Alas! the sun hath set on Invergray,
  And now it is deserted: though, of old,
It held within its walls the great and gay:
  The high—the humble, if but brave and bold,
  Who fought alone for loyalty, nor sold
Their services for lucre, in the day
  When Majesty was menaced—as 'tis told
In history, in legend, and in lay—
Such were the terms on which all met at Invergray.

" Rent are those massive towers, and turrets light,
  Where beauty sate in hope, or fear, to weave
The holly, or the cypress, for the knight
  Who fought to triumph, or who fell, to grieve
  His country, and his ladye-love, and leave
A fame, perpetuated to this day,
  In minstrel's verse. Ah! who could then believe
Such times of chivalry would pass away,
And spare naught but the stones, and name of Invergray?

" Frail bearer of that name, well mayest thou mourn,
  As sadly wandering by those hoary halls,
Thou viewest the stately pile where thou wert born,
  Fast crumbling into chaos, and its walls
  Tottering with age, as one on other falls
In mouldering destruction and decay:
  Alas!—such is the doom that, too, enthrals,
And drives thee hence, to exile far away—
The last, and ruined heir, of ancient Invergray!"

This chant delighted me, although it seemingly did not
enchant the Provost, for he yawned most ungraciously in the
midst of it: as much so indeed as the members of the
Council generally did, during any of the dry and long
speeches for which he was eminent. The lengthened jaws
of the Provost likewise set those of others a-going. Mr.
Tweel yawned; Mrs. Tweel yawned; and even the gentle
Miss M'Chuckie yawned, although she attempted to conceal
the fact with her richly lace-embroidered handkerchief.

A continuous announcement of carriages now took place,
followed by a universal shaking of hands, and bidding of
farewells; and Mr. and Mrs. Tweel's grand dinner party to
the Town Council, became a thing of the past!

CHAPTER XLIII.

INTRODUCTORY DOGGERELS.

> The feast is o'er, the guests are gone,
> While home all joyous wander,
> Leaving the fagged-out host to snooze,
> As they his efforts slander!
>
> *The Goosedubbs Poet.*

I HAD the honour, as was generally the case when I met Nahum at dinner, and the distance was not so great as to render a vehicle necessary, of seeing the reverend gentleman home; and, as we now had become very great friends—for I had lately subscribed handsomely to several testimonials which had been got up for him, by his congregation and admirers—he was, even more than usual, communicative and patronising to me, on this occasion.

"My dear B'lay," he said, as he bent the weight of his capacious body on my arm, "'low me to congrat'lt you on your success—nomstake 'bout it—that's fact—you've won the heart and 'fections of Miss M'Chuckie. Vile name M'Chuckie, and sooner she changes it the better, ha! ha! Evident she'sn love with you—never keeps her eyes off—follow 'tup you dog!—follow 'tup! and she'll marry you—that'st say, I'll marry you; no, I won't,—but I will—ha! ha! That'st say, I'll tie the knot. Ten thousandsh—nomstake Tweel 'll bleed to that—glad to get rid of her—forshakes own daughter—(hick)—wish I'd chance—wouldn't hesitate instant—but never will have chance—Mrs. Gust will take care of that, nomstake: Dr. Morse will take care'f that—never gives her cal'mel—ha! ha! But you stick in—ten thousandsh pounds, ha! ha!"

"You're joking, my dear Sir," I replied, when I found the

reverend gentleman in this promising mood, "I rather think the young lady's affections are engaged already, if not her hand, to Mr. Jackson."

"Jackson!" exclaimed Nahum scornfully. "No, no—she'll never throw herself, and her tenth housand pounds away, on that baboon — that chimpanzee — that oran'tau!" ("that gorilla," I daresay he would have added, had that most ferocious of all the ape species been known at the time.) "No, she must have a man, and not a monkey; and that man's yourshelf if you like!"

"Well,—but, to tell you the truth," I answered, "I do not like: if there is any lady in the family that I admire, I would say it is Miss Gentle. What do you think of her?"

"Miss Gentle!" exclaimed the reverend gentleman indignantly, "why, she's only a governess, and a beggar—hasn't a penny; and she's an Episcopalian to the bargain—I hate 'piscopalians—Romansh in disguise—no, no, never think of that—won't do—leave the like of her to Jackson!"

By this time we had reached Nahum's mansion, where he

wrung my hand, and left me, exclaiming, however, as he supported himself on the railings of the short stair, that led to his door—"don't loose chance—tenth housand pounds —wish I had it—ha! ha!" and so on.

I was just turning away, as Mr. Quince, who had been following leisurely, came up, and I was on the point of inviting him to proceed with me to my house, for the purpose of having a chat and a "qualifier," after Mr. Tweel's superb entertainment, in the shape of a glass of whisky-toddy, when he proposed that I should accompany him to what he denominated "The Herring-bane Club," where, as he said, that decoction was to be had in the greatest perfection.

In answer to my queries, he instructed me, that the Herring-bane Club claimed to be one of the institutions of the day, or rather *night*, and was attended by the richest and most aristocratic—if such a thing as aristocracy existed—in the City. That its rules and regulations, though of the most perfect description, were unwritten, and that, in consequence, it was one of the most harmonious and best managed clubs in the empire. "Our system of ballot," he said, "for the entrance of members, is peculiar. We never use black balls at all; and, therefore, every candidate is successful in obtaining the honour of entrance. When blackballing does take place, it is managed, not by ebony pease, as is the case with those clubs, where dandies stand or sit, all day long, at large plate-

glass windows, and seemingly do nothing but ogle, and cause to blush, modest ladies, who are obliged to pass that way; but by a system perfectly *unique* of its kind, namely, by the disapproving members entirely deserting the Club House—which I may mention is not a building, to which the Club is thirled—and leaving the rejected member the whole of it to himself, where he becomes so solitary and deserted, that he ceases, in fact, to be a member. The effect of this is wonderful: for, in consequence, all the members comport themselves to each other so pleasantly, and so much to the general taste and satisfaction, that a blackballing may be said never to be put in force at all.

"But I will leave you to judge for yourself," continued the cynical old fellow, "for here we are at the splendid portico of our elegant Club House, and if you will please to follow me, I will have you entered and passed at once."

He here made a dive down three or four steps, and I following, we entered a door with a ricketty porch, that admitted us to a gas-lighted passage, leading to an inner bar, where sat a buxom hostess, who was handing out tumblers, hot water, and other "paraphernalia, pertaining to fuddling propensities," as Mr. Quince expressed it, which were carried away by a greasy-looking waiter, for the benefit of the members of the Club, whose joyous and noisy accents we heard at the same time.

We then entered a low-roofed room of moderate size, with a sanded floor, where, at the head of a plain and even unpainted fir table, sat a gentleman with his hat on, puffing from a cutty pipe, and whom we scarcely could see, in consequence of the wreaths of smoke that surrounded himself and his companions, who — likewise smoking — occupied the sides of the table.

The company was in the midst of some debate or other, and so engrossed were the members with their subject that they paid no attention as Mr. Quince and I took chairs, and assorted ourselves at the table as we best could, while being served, by the waiter, with tumblers "hot from the oven," and, consequently, in prime condition for the preparation of the drink, for which the Club was famous.

I had now time leisurely to glance around, when I discovered that the gentleman at the head of the table was one of the first merchants of the City, and reputed to be worth half a million sterling, although, perhaps, that amount was, as usual, magnified. He was supported, right and left, by other wealthy individuals whom I knew, either by repute or otherwise; while around were gentlemen of more moderate calibre, in the way of riches, some of whom were comparative strangers to me, but all were in great glee, and very happily inclined.

I may mention, however, that many of the gentlemen present were not rich—a few, indeed, I knew myself to be the very reverse of that—still they were respectable, and at all events well liked; amongst the latter, particularly, there being men celebrated for their wit, their *bonhomie*, and their literary attainments, and whom I regretted to observe paying sycophantic deference to their rich companions, merely on account of these riches, but for a portion of which, in return for their *bon-mots*, and *double-entendres*, and racy jokes, they would wait a long while, indeed.

All drank whisky-toddy, towards the brewing of which there was no lack of suitable elements on the board, and as they mixed their tumblers, they tossed into a small basket, which was placed in the middle of the table, the price of the same; which admirable system, while leaving no dispute as to "the lawin'," freed all from any restraint, as to going and coming, when they liked. It, no doubt, was one of the rules and regulations of the Club that Mr. Quince had eulogised, but, whether or not, I approved of it very much.

To give an idea of the conversation that was carried on and the topics that were treated of, would be rather difficult; for they varied very much, and rapidly, in consequence of the free and easy manner with which they were conducted—none seemingly caring whether a debate was carried to a conclusion, or a story to an end. The company, too, seemed to be under no restraint of manners or discipline, for they came and went as they liked, this one leaving when it suited his convenience, and that one entering, and drawing in his chair, and propounding his ideas as it suited his whims; and this conduct apparently gave no offence, nor ruffled the equanimity of any one.

As to the quality of the language used, it must be confessed it was rather rough, and interspersed with coarse and unnecessary oaths, that would have matched those of the troops in Flanders, in the olden times, so graphically commented upon by "My Uncle Tobby."

One gentleman, in particular, swore most gratuitously, and I would say, offensively, although he did not disturb a countenance, and far less obtain a check; and on my remarking to Mr. Quince as to the absurdity and impropriety of this, he explained that the display was only an imitation of a sporting nobleman, who had many good and kind qualifications to counterbalance his bad propensities in this way; indeed he was notorious for his condescendence and wit, and, in consequence, was extremely popular amongst the sporting bloods of this community, many of whom, he was glad to say, adopted his better habits; but this rude fellow, who was a great admirer of his lordship, being but a *gowk*, unfortunately imitated only his worst ones, and which "I must confess," said Mr. Quince, "notwithstanding his stupidity, he is very successful in doing, although he causes himself to be laughed at and despised, by those who are even little better than himself. Riches, however," continued Mr. Q., "cover a multitude of sins; and he being rich, is accordingly tolerated!"

Mr. Quince and I sat on, if not exactly enjoying the scene, at all events trying to do so, for it was an ever varying one, in consequence of the numbers that went and came, each of the latter presenting some new feature or peculiarity that at the least made him an object of curiosity. Amongst others, who should appear but my friend Jackson, in company with the guzzling gentleman who had sat next to me at dinner at  Mr. Tweel's; but the former, who, till he had reached the middle of the room, had worn rather a hilarious counten-

ance, the moment he saw me assumed a grave aspect, which
evidently indicated that he would rather have wished I had
not been there.   His self-assurance, indeed, was quite upset,
and though he rattled away with others, in badinage and
bragadocia, it was perceptible he was ill at ease, and did
not relish the fun he had come to enjoy.

This was made still more apparent by the shortness of his
visit, for he had scarcely swallowed a glass of the standard
nectar of the Club, and which must have scalded his lips
and throat, in consequence of the rapidity with which he
tossed it off—ere he sounded a retreat, while casting at me,

as he passed to the door, a glance which it was impossible to
say whether it consisted most of malignity or of jealousy.

His companion, too, who had taken his seat next me, and
on the score of our former juxtaposition, at Mr. Tweel's
table, had claimed me as an acquaintance, and consequently
had commenced a gossip on the incidents of the dinner, and
particularly regarding the dishes and the cooking, seemed
taken with surprise at Mr. Jackson's sudden exit; for, as he
confidentially told me, he had found that gentleman waiting
for him on his return home, to hear all about Councillor
Tweel's grand "feed," and, after discussing a couple of
tumblers on the head of it, they had retreated to the Club to
pick "a herring bane," as he felt rather "yawpish" *after
wanting so long*!

His disappointment, however, was compensated by what took place, for by this time the hour had arrived, which, by the rules of the Club, permitted members to partake of the delectable refreshment, for which the institution was famous, and from which it indeed took its name.

Accordingly, the chairman having given the greasy waiter a significant nod, that official was not long of placing upon the bare boards of the table—any thing like a table-cloth seemingly being considered an unnecessary adjunct—a large platterful of salted herrings, which, to do the landlord justice, were of the finest description, being large and plump, while at the same time, they shone like silver. He likewise placed around, plain white earthenware plates, knives, and three-pronged iron forks, ("ony body that wanted silver anes," as the chairman announced, "being at liberty to take his fingers!") the whole being completed with an ashetful of laughing mealy potatoes in their coats, and smoking like a volcano.

To this mess, on an order being given by the President that the company should "fa' to, and peg awa'," hearty devotion was immediately paid, my guzzling friend, notwithstanding the enormous dinner he had partaken of, being the most marked worshipper. Indeed, I may say that all present showed themselves to be in excellent case, and the possessors of first-class appetites: the circumstance of many wearing white chokers, and evening dress—thereby indicating that they had "dined out"—being no bar to their performances, in this rather coarse gastronomic display.

For myself, I confess that I enjoyed my herring amazingly, and polished my *bans* as well as the best of them, notwithstanding that I was not accustomed to partake of suppers, and, indeed, far from being hungry, when I first entered the Club-room—a phenomenon that Mr. Quince accounted for, on the principle that "eating is infectious, and only wants a beginning."

"But, if you wish to see the thing in real perfection," said that gentleman, "only stop for an hour or two, till the '*drunken hunger*' comes upon them, and then you will have your astonishment exercised, for this feast of herrings and potatoes may be called only a whetter, to what will follow. Then," he continued, "poached eggs, devilled bones, anchovy biscuits, Welsh rabbits, roasted oysters, and any other provocative, that the whims of irritated stomachs can suggest, will be the order of the day, or rather morning: for, the 'wee short hour ayont the twal' will have long passed, ere such indulging will be brought to a termination!"

I, however, did not stay sufficiently long to see this exhibition to perfection, although I did so to such an extent as enabled me to judge of the subjects and sentiments that came on the tapis for discussion, and which did not display much amiability on the part of the members of the Herring-bane Club; for, the party by this time having become less changeable, and more concentrated than it had been, there ensued an earnestness of gossiping, amounting to scandal,

that quite amazed me. Every young lady, for instance, that was creating a sensation in fashionable circles at the period, was brought forward for criticism, and this not of the most charitable description. Her fortune and expectations, were condescended upon; her manners and accomplishments ridiculed, and, if defended, it was done in such a way that the defence was worse than the libel. Her style of singing was imitated; her mode of dancing was caricatured, one active gentleman being particularly good at displaying gyrations that were understood to represent this, on the sanded floor, and altogether, as Mr. Quince expressed it, she was taken to pieces and put up again, in a way perfectly disgusting, though much to the amusement and diversion of the company.

But young ladies alone did not monopolise the attention of the dissectors on the occasion, for, young gentlemen as well were brought forward to be operated upon, in a no less severe manner. This, perhaps, was not so cruel, considering their sex, and it might have done good, had they been present, in subduing vanity and puppyism; while, at the same time, it would not have partaken so much of the appearance of injustice, if not cowardice, as it otherwise did, on the principle of the poet, that it is beneficial "we should see ourselves as others see us!"

And if young gentlemen were not passed over, neither were old or elderly ones, though what was said of them was more in a commercial than social spirit. Many of those who were reputed rich, I now learned for the first time, were not so, and, consequently, that those who flirted with their daughters—the young ladies that had been primarily discussed—under the impression that they were ingratiating themselves into the affections of heiresses, or expectants of riches, were under a complete delusion. Some of these gentlemen, we were told, while keeping up great style and giving grand parties, for the purpose of getting their daughters off, were on the borders of the *Gazette*, and probably would be appearing in the "sma' print" very soon. Some could not get their bills discounted; some had no bills to discount; and some, if they had bills, were doing so at a most usurious rate of discount!

It is impossible almost, to give even a faint idea of the fearless and scarifying way, with which the gentlemen present discussed the positions of their contemporaries, and dealt with their characters, their means, their prospects, and their faults; for as to virtues, none were allowed to any of them, and, indeed, if I had judged from what I had heard, I would have been disposed to consider that there was not such a thing as a commercially respectable, or morally decent man, woman, or child, in the City.

I, consequently, rejoiced that the rules of the Herring-bane Club granted to me the privilege of leaving without ceremony, or the necessity of bidding adieu, when I liked, and which privilege I now felt myself inclined to take advantage of, although my friend Quince refused to stir, very possibly from a desire to be present, when I myself should be brought forward for anatomising, or, what was more likely, when his particular friends, Mr. and Mrs. Tweel, and Miss M'Chuckie, and the grand dinner party, that had just taken place, were submitted for due criticism and slander, as assuredly would be the case.

I, therefore, with relief found myself plodding on my solitary way homewards, my mind being pervaded with many and varying reflections upon what I had witnessed and heard. "Here," I said to myself, "is something to make one both humble and proud—men who have attained wealth and position, and yet they can find no pleasure but in descending to low enjoyments, and in abandoning themselves to indulgence in coarse drinks, coarse food, and coarse conversation; who, while degrading themselves, degrade the characters of others, so as to bring all on a level of meanness and humility. Talk of the manners and corruptions of the Goosedubbs after this!—why, I have seen the latter, all re-enacted here, with this simple difference, that the performers instead of being ragged and poor, are well attired and rich—transpose the garbs and means of the one to the other, and you could not detect a difference!"

Although I felt convinced, however, that the major part of what I had heard, had been gross exaggeration, I could not divest myself of the prejudice it had engendered within me. It caused me to look with contempt upon many, whom before I had admired and respected, so much had the poison entered my mind.

Under these circumstances, it may not be wondered at if, on reflecting on many of the young ladies I had been in the habit of viewing as the incarnation of perfection, and their parents as the realisation of all that was desirable to be connected with, I beheld them now as something dangerous and repulsive: so much are we disposed in such matters, to be guided, or perhaps misguided by the opinions and sentiments of others. To me it appeared, therefore, that the most desirable maidens one could concentrate his regards and affections upon, would be those who were totally unknown, and who had neither fathers, mothers, sisters, nor brothers—orphans in short, whom one could marry, without at the same time marrying an "illustrious" family.

One individual alone presented herself to my fancy as embodying that desirable reality. It was she, whom of all others, that I could think of, the members of the Herring-bane Club*—perhaps from her insignificant position as a poor unpretentious governess—were not likely to condescend upon with their slander and ridicule. She, therefore, shone out in my estimation as something to be appreciated and idolised, not the less that I had really conceived a tender regard for her previously.

I, therefore, after this eventful day, of high and low entertainment, retired to my couch to think, and ultimately to dream, of Miss Gentle.

* NOTE G.—Herring-bane Club. *See Appendix.*

CHAPTER XLIV.

INTRODUCTORY DOGGERELS.

All potent love! to thee—enslaved,
And bound in silken chains—
We yield our precious liberty,
And e'en our very brains!

The Goosedubbs Poet.

I AROSE next morning with my mind perfectly made up, in respect to Miss Gentle, whom I now looked upon as the only one whom, with justice to myself, and even with justice to herself, I could form a matrimonial alliance with, that promised happiness, contentment, and satisfaction.

Of course, I never took into consideration for a moment the idea that Miss Gentle could object to my suit; but, on the contrary, I assumed that I had only to propose, and I would be accepted.

Perhaps—by those who know the world better than I did—this assumption will be looked upon as having been rather gratuitous, if not foolhardy; but when it is remembered that I had risen in life with but one idea steadily kept in view, and that I had associated entirely with people who were seemingly guided by the same sentiment, namely, that money was all-in-all and every thing, I may be held excused for having come to such a vulgar and arrogant conclusion. Miss Gentle, besides, I looked upon—as she was looked upon by others—as a poor and dependent governess, who was earning her maintenance, if not in a mean, at all events in a humble way, and, however well-bred, well-educated, and accomplished she might be, as holding a position that she would be but too happy to exchange for one, where she would be at once placed in comparative affluence and inde-

pendence, and to some extent, on an equality with those
who, under the pretence of being excessively kind and
generous to her, every moment snubbed and mortified her.

I, however, felt considerable perplexity, as to how I should
go about my suit. Ladies, I knew, however willing to gain
husbands, required to be courted, and to court a lady who
lived in a family as a dependent, and where she could neither
command her own time, nor her own privacy, formed a difficulty that, I saw would require the exercise of all the wit,
and all the dexterity I could command.

Neither was this difficulty lessened, when I reflected on
what my friend, the reverend Nahum, had communicated to
me, in the fulness of his patronising heart, and which, with
the usual vanity of a bachelor in want of a wife, I had
adopted, to wit, that Miss M'Chuckie herself was disposed to
set her cap at me, with the approbation of her mother and
stepfather, and, therefore, it was doubly necessary that they
should be kept in ignorance of my admiration of Miss Gentle;
although, at the same time, I had a suspicion of its being
possible that, after all, in doing so, Miss M'C. was only

aiming at the augmentation of that contending bevy of
admirers, and lovers, which every lady likes to think herself
possessed of, notwithstanding the possibility that one, in
particular, commands her heart and affections.

Whether this surmise might be true or not, it added to
the complexity of my position, particularly as I saw that
any rash proceeding, or false step on my part, might seriously

compromise Miss Gentle, if not both of us, in the eyes and esteem of the Tweel family.

Nevertheless, I determined to proceed with my suit, and therefore behold me now, transformed from a commercial and money-making man into a lover, and—ah! rare circumstance in these days of gain-grabbing and greed, even in the most sacred pursuits—a lover, too, who proposed to devote himself to one, and that sincerely, who had neither fortune nor rich connections. Indeed, I may mention, what perhaps I should have stated in its proper place, that she had neither father, mother, brother, nor sister, which circumstance I learned from an explanation with which she was pleased to modestly reject a compliment I aimed at paying to her chant of "Invergray," and which she did in an apologising way, by saying that she had chosen it, as being the most melancholy of her stock, in consequence of having heard that day from a poor old uncle—her only living relative in the world—who, to use her own words, "was now prostrated with infirm health and pecuniary difficulties, which, when contrasted with the brilliant scenes she was in the habit of witnessing, as an inmate of Mr. Tweel's house, almost broke her heart."

Fate, however, so far, seemed to be propitious to my views. At the very first municipal meeting that took place, namely, about a couple of days after Mr. Tweel's dinner, and at which meeting—notwithstanding all the delectable viands that had been gulped, and the heart-warming wines that had been quaffed by his brother representatives, he was interrupted by the Provost, sneered at by the Magistrates, and coughed down by the Councillors, so that he made but a sorry appearance—as usual, it was my good fortune to come to his assistance, and which lucky service, on my part, was successful in rescuing him from a mortifying defeat. I, therefore, was not surprised at receiving, what indeed I had been working for, a kind invitation to visit his house in the evening. This, however, was no more than a repetition of what Mrs. Tweel herself had desired, for over and over again, as I bade her adieu at the conclusion of the eventful night, or rather morning of the ball that has been recorded, she expressed a hope that I would "pop in, in a friendly and old-fashioned manner, as became an old friend," not to mention that Miss M'Chuckie had promised to sing to me a dozen of her newest songs, when under less restraint, and I, in consequence, with pleasure, looked upon the same as being a general invitation.

At this quiet meeting, as indeed, similarly was the case, at a dozen subsequent ones, I came on even better than I could have expected: Miss M'Chuckie squalled her lays, twanged her harp strings, and banged her piano keys; and if hearts could have been carried by such furious attacks, I dare say she might have brought me to a declaration of love in a very short time, as perhaps she did with other visitors, who came to these family parties, as well as myself—Mr. Jackson being one of these, and if I may be allowed to reveal such precious secrets, evidently one of her most attentive and devoted admirers. No one was so useful and nimble as he, in bringing forward her harp—indeed, he did it better than even Plush or Jehu could have done it—no one was so dexterous in turning over the leaves of her music book, and just at the proper note; and no one was so suggestive of the songs she should sing, and particularly of those that suited the harp, or the piano best, and at the same time, her voice: according as she accompanied herself with either of these instruments—for she wandered from the one to the other, as it suited her whim—the perfect representation of a spoiled child of song.

She sang, I must allow, rather well, but still to my mind, it was more in what is called a "professional style," than a private one: what became indeed more a saloon, or hall, than a parlour, or drawing-room, although the latter, in Mr. Tweel's house, might have commanded the appellation of "hall" or "saloon," so extensive were its dimensions, and elegant its proportions, and which Miss M'Chuckie's voice could have filled, had it been even double in size. Her voice, too, was rich, although it had nothing of the sweetness of Miss Gentle's, whose singing, in my opinion, was the very perfection of harmony and taste.

Miss M'Chuckie's performances, however, seemed to electrify Mr. Jackson, although I could perceive, notwithstanding all the ease and confidence he assumed, while going about his little attentions to her, that he was far from being comfortable when I was present, and particularly when she was pleased to select any song as a "favourite of mine," and which she

M 2

often did, while she was not *blate*, as the Scottish saying has it, in declaring it so, and, in consequence, a "favourite of her own."

On such occasions, Mr. Jackson could not conceal his mortification, and he would then direct to me a glance that spoke a thousand revengeful feelings, but which I received with the calm composure of a lion looking at a monkey.

. Poor man, he little knew how indifferent I was to all the blandishments and allurements of Miss M'Chuckie, and how much my heart was concentrated upon that unobtrusive

 figure that sat so modestly and retiringly, at her "scam," in the quietest corner of the magnificent drawing-room she could select; while the rest were distributed—here, there, and everywhere — laughing, chatting, flirting, and trifling: unless when it pleased them to have a "quadrille on the carpet," and then Miss Gentle got leave to monopolise the piano, and to turn over her own music leaves to the bargain, excepting when I did so; but which prudence forbade me practising too often.

But if I had reason to congratulate myself on the blindness Mr. Jackson displayed as to my supposed attachment to Miss Gentle, and which, had he known, I flatter myself would greatly have relieved his mind, how much more had I not reason for consolation in noticing that all others were likewise innocent of any suspicion of the kind? No one, indeed, seemed to dwell, for a moment, on the possibility of a governess having an admirer, or if they did, they could only suppose, that such might possibly be the parish schoolmaster, or the music master, or the tutor of the family, who got a guinea a month, and his tea with the children, after the lessons were over.

And what surprised me not a little, though it did not elate me, was the peculiar circumstance, that even Miss Gentle did not seem to have any idea that she could attract, and far less that I could be the attracted one. It was true that she received the little attentions I paid her, evidently with gratification, and even gratitude, but still it was as if she considered these were bestowed more from a feeling of polite benevolence towards a respectable inferior, than from a desire to be gallant and courteous to one who was rated as a sweetheart, and, as such, one with whom she was on a perfect equality. In proof of this provoking fact, I would sometimes, in very quiet evenings, find myself, before I well knew what I was about, alarmingly alone with Miss M'Chuckie; but whether that was from chance or design, I could only surmise. First, Mr. Tweel would slip out of the room, probably with the intention of indulging in his pipe—for the honest councillor "blew a cloud,"—then Mrs. Tweel would follow, very likely to look after domestic duties; and then Miss Gentle would disappear, attracting with her the two Misses Tweel, who yet went early to bed, when I would be most awkwardly left *tete-a-tete* with Miss M'Chuckie, to relieve which predicament I kept her squalling most unremittingly, till Mr. Jackson, like a godsend, though looking a thousand daggers, would make his appearance, — little knowing, however, how welcomely he was received by me—when things, once more, became "all serene."

And seeing I have got on the subject of Jackson again, I may now mention that, about this time, I received some information regarding him, from my old gossipping friend, Mr. Quince, which rendered it necessary that I should be on my guard in my intercourse with him at St. Blythswood Terrace. Indeed, that information went to confirm a suspicion I had entertained for some time previously; namely, that he was no other than the son and representative of the worthy lady, who, in my boyish days, had employed my mother as a washerwoman, and to whom, as a small return for her patronage, my father had presented the learned ape Jaques to their said representative, who was now her successor in the property.

The circumstance was trifling, to be sure, for at the period in question Jackson had been a mere bantling, and possibly in consequence knew little, and now remembered less, connected with the matter; but inasmuch as a possibility existed, should old reminiscences be revived—and nothing leads to such revivals so much as quarrels: when "who's who," of course, then becomes the natural question—that he might come to discover the secret of my low origin, and thereby obtain a powerful advantage over me, I judged that, if I kept in view the prudent proverb, which says, "let sleeping dogs lie," and acted in keeping therewith, I would be doing a wise thing.

I accordingly conducted myself to him as civilly as possibly could be the case, on my occasional visits at Mr. Tweel's, notwithstanding his pertness and jealous conduct towards me, in consequence of his evidently deeming me his successful rival in the affections of Miss M'Chuckie.

And so time wore away: and winter brightened into spring, and spring blossomed into summer, and the period came, for those Glasgow people who considered themselves fashionable and aristocratic, to paper up their windows and flee to the coast, amongst which migratory West-End grandees, the Tweels were always the very first, for they had one of the largest and finest of *chateaux* situated at Rover's Bay, built in imitation of a baronial stronghold, that frowned over a territory of no less than one acre, two roods, and thirty poles, of arable ground, interspersed with beautiful groves and rockeries, subject to the payment of a yearly feu-duty to his Grace the Duke of Dumbartonshire, amounting to—but nobody has any business with that, unless Castle-Winsey, which is the name of the chateau, should come again into the market, when all such "further particulars" will be found in the advertisement.

This mansion, I had been told, had equal accommodation to that in Mr. Tweel's town house, if not more, and was as richly and expensively furnished. Indeed, when the family went to it, they required to take nothing with them but their body-clothing, and Miss M'Chuckie's harp, there being even harmoniums, and grand pianos at Castle-Winsey, of the finest description.

I had almost feared that the flight of the Tweels to Castle-Winsey would impose a truce upon my intimacy with them, and that thereby I would be debarred the pleasure of seeing them again for a long time, while what was worse than all, I would be deprived of Miss Gentle's society. But these fears were happily allayed, on the occasion of my seeing

them off in the steamboat, by a kind invitation which I
received from Mrs. Tweel, that I would visit them at the
coast, on the very first Saturday I could make it convenient
to do so, and remain with them till the Monday following,
"or as much longer as I chose to honour them with my
company!"

Of course, this was a mark of hospitality and favour that
was not to be thrown away, and I therefore accepted the
invitation with pleasure, while promising to arrange with
Mr. Tweel—who required, on account of his business and his
public avocations, to be often in Glasgow, and for the purpose to keep a portion of his house at St. Blythswood Terrace open—as to the period of said visit.

In seeing the Tweels off, however, I had another object
in view, besides that of merely complimenting them with
adieus, and that was to slip into the hand of Miss Gentle
a small packet, which I had prepared beforehand, containing
a present, and on the outside wrapper of which I had written
her name, while the inward one bore this much more senti-
mental and loving address:—"To the one whom I adore!"

I meant this packet, as may be supposed, to be an unmis-
takable indication of my regard for her, and as it contained
a beautiful pearl necklace, with ear-rings to match, I determined to consider her acceptance or rejection thereof, a proof
of the light in which she would judge my suit—the ornaments
in question, being of too great a value to be looked upon as a
mere passing compliment.

A happy opportunity occurred, as I stood with the party
on the steamer's deck, as she lay at the quay, previously to
starting, for the presentation of this packet to Miss Gentle,
by the arrival—and the consequent bustle occasioned thereby
—of Miss M'Chuckie's harp, in the music-seller's pianoforte
van, which had been called into requisition for the purpose
of transmission, and which, from the carelessness of the
driver, had only reached the quay after the steamer's bell
had been rung, and the vessel was just about to be set under
way. Taking advantage, therefore, of the family dismay at
the lateness of the instrument's arrival, and of the risk it
was now about to run, while in the embraces of rough
porters and tarry-fingered sailors, I requested Miss Gentle
to take possession of the packet, while slipping it into her

hand, and before she could give me an answer, I sprung ashore, and in a few moments thereafter, with a face glowing with blushes, I was waving my hand to Mrs. Tweel and Miss M'Chuckie, and kissing it to Miss Gentle, as the steamer pattered away, the only thing that disappointed me being the circumstance that the latter lady seemed to be neither put up nor down, by the gallant act I had just performed.

For some days afterwards, indeed for a week, I was kept in considerable anxiety lest I should have the package returned to me; but when, after meeting Mr. Tweel once or twice on his return from Castle-Winsey, and finding that he did not pull it out of his pocket to return it to me—for heads of families at the coast are always looked upon, remorselessly, as being common carriers—I began to take confidence, and to re-assure myself as being on the fair road to become the happy *affiancé* of Miss Gentle; so that I felt rather impatient for the happy Saturday on which I was to visit Castle-Winsey, and which, as fortune would have it, was not long in being fixed upon, by the worthy Town-Councillor.

CHAPTER XLV.

INTRODUCTORY DOGGERELS.

> Welcome! bright Spring, that comes to chase,
>   With zephyrs fresh and *lowne*,
> The wintry frosts and fogs away
>   From good Sanct Mungo's town!
>
> Allured by thee, our routs are stopt,
>   Our wassail and our clatter,
> And—papering up our windows—we
>   Adjourn to "doon the *watter*!"
>
> There—bless'd by sunshine and by shade,
>   In many a cozy nook—
> We pass the time, excepting when
>   We fish, or flirt, or "*dook*."
>
> Till—having gained fresh health and strength,
>   And possibly grown fatter,—
> We leave the coast, to seek again,
>   The joys of "up the *watter*!"
>
> *The Goosedubbs Poet.*

I DO not know how lovers in general may feel, who are situated as I now considered myself to be, namely, under offer, as it were, to the fair one in whom were concentrated for the present, all my hopes and fears as a matrimonial aspirant, but this I know, that on the eventful Saturday which was fixed upon, for my accompanying Mr. Tweel to the coast, I felt my nerves in a twitter, as the steamer which conveyed us—like one of those "argosies with portly sail," Shakspeare speaks of, but propelled with steam instead of wind, though containing, as her prototype did,—

> "Grand signiors, and rich burghers on the flood,
>   Who overpeer the petty traffickers"—

approached the pier at Rover's Bay, when that gentleman—  while surveying the spot through a beautiful new mother-of-pearl opera-glass which I had lent to him, and which he had seemingly no thoughts of relinquishing: the same having been purchased by me in the hope of being admired by, and consequently presented to Miss Gentle, as an additional mark of my esteem— called my particular attention to a number of gaily dressed people standing upon the brink of said pier, waving white handkerchiefs, whom he declared to be a portion of his own family, who had evidently come to welcome us.

I would fain have requested from Mr. Tweel re-possession of the glass, so as to have gratified myself with a glimpse, though it should only have been momentary, of one whom I esteemed so greatly, as to look upon her, as being worthy of becoming my companion for life: but I did not deem it prudent to do so. Accordingly, the honest man, who seemingly never thought for an instant that any one—even its owner—could have wished to see through it, retained it, while at the same time, as he grinned with delight, he provokingly kept exclaiming:—"There they are, the dear creatures, and how charming and lovely they look! Ah! Bailie, you little know what happy dogs we married men are!"—or words to that effect.

Of course I fully expected that the object of my adoration would be one of these, and I was preparing to command, as far as I could my own, and soothe the blushes that I presumed would very naturally suffuse her cheeks on the occasion of this, our first meeting since my sentiments towards her had been revealed—as I really considered them to be—when, alas! I was doomed to disappointment, for Miss Gentle was not there at all, and instead, I beheld the tall Miss M'Chuckie and her fat mother, both being dressed in the most flaunting fashion of the day, and sweeping the pier, as they curtsied, and kissed their welcoming hands to us. This was a sad disappointment to me, and what I reluctantly was forced to consider a bad omen, although I tried to account for the

circumstance, by representing to myself that, possibly Miss Gentle's duties as governess had kept her at home, attending to the tuition of the younger branches of the family, whose education, of course, was as strictly attended to at the coast as in the town. I likewise, to some extent—suggested partly by hope, and partly by vanity—tried to console myself by supposing, that Miss Gentle might have been kept back by a preconcerted arrangement on the part of Mrs. Tweel and her daughter, in consequence of jealousy towards that young lady, on my account!

We stepped on shore amidst the roar of steam, and the confusion attendant upon the landing of the passengers, to receive a hearty welcome, while Mr. Tweel gave his arm to his wife, leaving me to bring up the rear with Miss M'Chuckie, who, as we walked along towards Castle-Winsey, which was at no great distance, drew my attention to a broad banner, that floated over its towering battlements, while stating that it had been hoisted in honour of me!

I found the plenishing and splendour of Castle-Winsey all that had been represented; indeed these, I should say, were on a scale more suitable for a nobleman than a Glasgow haberdasher, while the dinner was every thing that could be desired, the ladies having dressed for it, just as ornately as if it had been a ceremonious occasion, although no person beyond myself, and the members of the family was present. Miss Gentle, of course, was there, as plainly and tastefully attired as ever; but what mortified and surprised me, after I had got over the awkwardness of meeting her, was to observe she did not

wear the pearl necklace I had presented to her, but on the contrary that it encircled the already summer-embrowned throat of lank Miss M'Chuckie!

This was rather a stunner to me, and entirely took away my relish for the good things that composed the feast, my mind being taken up with the discovery I had made, while I puzzled myself to account for it.

At first, I thought it was what, in genteel parlance, is called "a sell," but on looking at Miss Gentle, her countenance bore such a calm and ingenuous expression, that I repelled such an idea, and I, therefore, concluded that it must have occurred in consequence of some mistake, arising from her not comprehending properly what I said, when I presented the package to her in the steam-fizzing and hurry-skurrying, attendant upon the vessel's threatened departure from the quay; and which, as I have already explained, left me little more than time to get ashore.

Nevertheless, I had to bear my perplexity as best I could, and not only that afternoon and evening, but during the silent hours of the night, the interim having been spent in boating and fishing,—during which process Miss M'Chuckie stuck to me, like a limpet to a rock,—and afterwards in tea-drinking and music, till it was time for the ladies to retire, leaving worthy Mr. Tweel and me to drink grog and smoke cigars, while I trembled every moment lest he should question me, as to my "intentions" towards his step-daughter.

Luckily, the worthy haberdasher did not broach the subject, but contented himself with one, far dearer to his heart, namely, his last speech at the Council, the prosy details of which he inflicted again upon me, till I actually yawned in his face, and that acting at last upon him as a hint, he seized a silver-plated bed-room candlestick, and staggeringly marshalling me to my chamber, left me to my repose.

Repose, however, was not for me, if forty disturbed winks be not an exception to that; for I tossed and tumbled all night, and walked up and down my bed-room as daylight broke, and gazed out of the plate glass windows at the silent waters of the frith, and envied the sea mews; and finally arose about half-past seven o'clock, and found my way to the garden, so that I might indulge in a reverie amongst the rockeries and shrubberies, which, considering the extent of ground attached to the castle, were exceedingly well got up, some parts of the limited demesne,

being almost as umbrageous and retired, as though it had been in the heart of the Highlands.

I longed, of course, to be delivered from the uncertainty I was placed in, and was cudgeling my brains to devise some plan to have a private interview with Miss Gentle, when, as if to prove the truth of the wise and philosophical saying of Sancho Panza, that "while we are pondering, the hare starts up," who should appear before me, as I approached a sequestered nook, but Miss Gentle herself!

I was rather surprised with this unexpected meeting, and so was she, but after explanations had taken place, and it was discovered that it was in consequence of both of us being early risers, the awkwardness attendant thereon wore off, and we then entered into a pleasant chit-chat, every subject from the castle to the cliff; from the swallows to the solan geese; from the little burn that meandered through the grounds, to the sea that received it within its embraces, being condescended upon, before we came to that which I daresay was principally uppermost in both our minds.

And when we did come to that, it was in the most by-the-byish sort of way possible, the subject of the burn having led to that of the sea-shore, thence to shells: from that to oysters, and from oysters to pearls: which marine elements, of course, could not fail to usher in the pearl necklace.

"Ah yes," Miss Gentle had replied to a very learned and prosy treatise I had uttered on conchology and sea gems, "pearls are very pretty things indeed; and, therefore, even rated in the Scriptures as 'of great price,' no doubt in consequence of the difficulties and dangers encountered by the poor fishers who dive for them; but talking of such costly commodities" she continued, "I hope you are pleased with the way in which I have executed the commission you entrusted me with?"

I did not know how to answer this question, partly from its abruptness, and partly from that embarrassment which is ever attendant upon lovers. She, however, did not wait for my reply, but went on, probably by way of relieving my perplexity, to say that she had not done what had been alluded to, on her own responsibility alone, but had laid the matter before Mrs. Tweel, and which she considered she was bound to do, in the delicate and dependent position in which she stood, as a governess—who, properly speaking, should not meddle in such matters—previously to handing the necklace to Miss M'Chuckie, and Mrs. T. having approved not only of the step, but of my suit, and subsequently Miss M'Chuckie having likewise seemingly approved them, by a graceful and grateful acceptance of the presents, she was now delighted to be able to congratulate me on the happiness that was before me, and which she trusted would be attended with a blessing to all concerned!

All this was stated in the calmest and most innocent manner possible by Miss Gentle, indeed, so much so was this the case, that I saw at once a comedy of errors had taken place, and entirely too, through my own over-caution, if not stupidity, though perhaps it had been, at the same time, furthered by Miss Gentle's extreme modesty and absence of vanity, in never, as evidently was the case, having supposed for a moment that she was the esteemed one, and not Miss M'Chuckie. What to say, therefore, in reply, I did not know, but stood gaping, and I daresay looking the very reverse of the happy suitor Miss Gentle expected I should have been, which being noticed by her, she rather anxiously inquired if I approved of what she had done, while adding a hope that no mistake had been made.

"Indeed, there has been," I answered, "but the mistake lies altogether on my part, from the ambiguous way I now perceive I have gone about this matter. I really intended the necklace for another instead of Miss M'Chuckie, and I may add, one that is infinitely dearer to me than twenty Miss M'Chuckies can ever be—that valued one being, in reality, no other than yourself!"

"You astonish!—indeed, you alarm me, Bailie!" replied Miss Gentle, "by what you now state, for had I entertained the slightest idea of what your real intentions were when you entrusted the packet to me, I would have acted very differently to what I have done; and in a way that, while averting the dilemma, in which this unfortunate occurrence, I fear, has placed us all, would have spared you the loss of this valuable trinket!"

"Never for a moment speak, or think of the value of such a trifle," I convulsively rejoined, "though it were ten times what it was, for that is a matter that can easily be remedied. Let Miss M'Chuckie, then, keep the necklace, as a mere present to a Miss: and, with your permission, I will substitute something really worthy of my esteem and regard for you!"

"You entirely mistake me," replied Miss Gentle, while assuming a dignified manner that I did not expect in one who stood in her dependent position, and far less was prepared for, "I meant merely to say that had I in

the slightest degree suspected your real motive in making
this presentation, I would have studied how I could least
offensively, and with proper delicacy—while acknowledging
the honour you proposed doing me—have undeceived you as
to what you possibly conceived my sentiments regarding you
as a suitor were, by returning it in a respectful, but at the
same time a decided manner!"

This was a staggerer that almost upset me, but still I
managed to stammer out, while feeling as if the rocks would
sink beneath me, "am I then to understand, Miss Gentle,
that I am deceived—that is to say, that I have deceived
myself—in this matter, and that I am in the unhappy position of being rejected and spurned by you?"

"My dear Bailie," answered Miss Gentle, with an air that
was apparently meant to be kind, but which was not the less
galling on that account, "there is no necessity for your
going so far—that is, for your endeavouring to draw from
me an answer that might have in it characteristics of so
severe a nature, as you would invest it with, and which, if I
were to confirm, either positively, or tacitly, would not, I
think, on my part, be becoming a gentlewoman, far less one
that has been so honoured by you. What I would have you
rather to assume is, that the proposed offer of the gift has
been but a delicate, nay, it may be called an elegant, method
of ascertaining the existence of what might, or might not,
have led to more serious relations; and, it not having been
accepted, therein no harm has been done, beyond what may
be treated as a mere joke or pleasantry, that fractures no
friendships, and breaks no hearts!"

"I would never forgive myself," I answered, "if what I
have so clumsily done, interfered with any friendships, and
particularly if it severed friendship betwixt one whom I so
greatly regard, and myself. As for breaking hearts, such
things, in this now artificial world, are exploded. Still, pain
may be felt that, in ancient and poetical days, might have
amounted to that!"

"Alas!" replied Miss Gentle, "I am the last that should
inflict pain, however unwittingly, on any one, seeing that it
is ever too much present in my own bosom, to warn me from
an act of the kind. It is not, however, on my own account,
but that of others, that I am forced to bear it; and particu-

larly of an only relative, whose misfortunes have produced such a complication in his, and my family matters, that, at at the end of my engagement with Mr. Tweel, which happens soon, I will require to exile myself, while becoming a nurse, I may say almost a menial servant, to that beloved relative, but to relieve whom, even in the slightest degree, will be a labour of love, and I hope of consolation."

"I tell you this in confidence," she added, "to show how humble an individual Marion Gentle is; and, therefore, how little to be regarded, as a means of causing either pain or pleasure to any one!"

As Miss Gentle said this, she hurriedly, and somewhat alarmedly—for foot-steps were heard approaching, though whose they could be, the dense foliage concealed — extended her pretty little white hand to me, which with reverence I kissed, and, after "dropping a curtsy," that might have become a countess,—for notwithstanding the humility she had expressed, there was an aristo-cratic, if not haughty demeanour, about her, that even the controlled bearing of a governess could not conceal—she turned, and tripped off, while I stood rivetted to the spot, looking as stupid as one of honest Councillor Tweel's sculptured woodland divinities, that were stuck in appropriate nooks around, though not so merry, and certainly not so picturesque.

I was disturbed in a brown study or reverie I had fallen into—wherein I alternately had been ruminating on the disappointment I had met with in Miss Gentle's resolution, and on the predicament I stood in, with regard to Miss M'Chuckie, as the innocent accepter of what I had designed for another—by a sharp and familiar pat on the back; and on turning round, I found it had been administered by Mr. Tweel, who, on beholding my grave and serious countenance, exclaimed, "Why! what can be the matter with you, Bailie?—you look by all the world like a love-sick swain, that has been telling his tale of woe to the rocks and the waterfalls, or what is more appropriate to our commercial notions, like a merchant comtemplating the unfortunate results of some of his speculations with "Bills-Payable," in perspective, and nothing to meet them with, excepting the *Gazette*, or a compounding with creditors, at the best. Indeed you put me in mind of poor old Bob Bumbazine, of Brown, Bumbazine, and Company, who failed in the year 'sixteen, and cut his throat, after taking in our house to the tune of three thousand odds, on which they only paid three shillings a pound! But cheer up," he continued, as he observed I did not join in his merriment which savoured so much of the shop, "you, of all men have no reason to despair, either in love or business, and therefore it must be something else that is making you look so serious this morning!"

Much as I detested my friend's allusion to business in so coarse and unfeeling a manner as his taste, or wit had dictated, I did not shrink from the subject, so much as I did from that of love, with which he commenced; for I considered it the mere preliminary to an attack upon me, regarding my intentions towards Miss M'Chuckie—perhaps in consequence of his being crammed by Mrs. Tweel, after a morning's curtain debate, as to what he should say. I therefore adopted the former as the preferable one to talk upon, while at the same time, from knowing my man, I saw in the conversation I might draw him into, what, if properly managed, might set him on a new scent altogether, and keep him from coming to too close quarters with me, on the other.

I accordingly maintained my grave countenance, and in reply, gave him to understand that however he might be inclined to indulge in facetious remarks as to business misfortunes, I was not. On the contrary, I said that all men engaged in commerce should not "whistle till they were out of the wood," for there was no saying what "a day or an hour might bring forth," especially in such times—and this was actually the case—when the bullion in the Bank of

England was daily decreasing, the discounts at the highest
rates allowed by the usury laws, and the foreign exchanges
enormously against this country. I then entered into a
discourse upon the fearful effects of over-trading—evils that
at present were bearing hard on the commercial community:
the same being the gist of a circular on the subject that I
had lately received from Messrs. Pull & Hawl—and ended
by hinting that if he had a few thousand pounds at his
command, I would not care to give him the best interest
going, for the use of them, till better times arrived.

I hit the nail on the head exactly as I wished to do, by the
knowing method I had pursued in this matter. Mr. Tweel
immediately became restive and fidgetty, while declaring
that he never entered into such subjects on Sunday mornings,
and therefore begged to "adjourn the debate" upon them
till another favourable moment presented itself for their discussion, particularly as it was now nine o'clock, and the
breakfast gong was sounding!

We accordingly bent our way to the castle, where, what
with tea and coffee, muffins and crumpits, ham and eggs, and
so on, the balance of the morning was passed till it was time
to go to church, when we all set off, to walk towards it, along

the dusty road, the only remarkable thing that I noticed being
the circumstance that Mrs. Tweel, instead of so manœuvering

that her daughter should be my companion, stuck to me
most kindly herself, and which special mark of friendship
I attributed to a conference she and her husband probably
had indulged in at my expense, previously to our setting
out.

Whatever may have been the cause, I did not get any
farther opportunity of flirting with Miss M'Chuckie, nor, as
may be supposed, did I seek such gratification. Indeed,
we spent but a humdrum and mopish sort of a day and
evening, the ladies seemingly being disposed to remain quiet,
and possibly serious, in their own retired quarters; so that,
although the lunch was excellent, and the dinner as sumptuous as ever, I was very glad when bed time came, and
gladder still when next morning early—the fair ones having
sent their adieus by deputy—I found myself progressing
rapidly up the Clyde, along with Mr. Tweel, from whom I
parted at the landing-place, and did not see again for some
time, except at meetings of the Council.

CHAPTER XLVI.

INTRODUCTORY DOGGERELS.

He's clever who keeps out of scrapes,
  And knows what he's about;
But he's cleverer, who, when in a scrape,
  Knows how to wriggle out!

The Goosedubbs Poet.

ALTHOUGH what I had stated to Mr. Tweel, on the eventful Sunday morning at Castle-Winsey, that has been narrated in last chapter, regarding the badness of the times,—and which statement ended with a hint that immediately alarmed his susceptibilites, both domestic and commercial, just as I wished it to do,— may be considered by those, who have had the patience to peruse these pages, to the extent they have gone, to have been a mere joke or trick, on my part, to effect a purpose: still there was a great deal of truth in my observations, as a panic which took place a few days thereafter, not only in the business circles of Glasgow, but in those of London, and, indeed, throughout the general trading communities of the country, fully proved.

One of those crises that occasionally occur, in short, was just about happening, after a period of great prosperity, which was destined to shake the whole commercial world, and even to stagger politically, by its effects, the institutions of nations, while, at the same time, displacing monarchs, and throwing dynasties like chaff to the winds.

The symptoms of these troubles were making their appearance—as I had divulged to honest Councillor Tweel: but who, though sharp enough in his own immediate business, had not head sufficient to comprehend their general nature— iɪ the horizon of the money market, like clouds in that of nature, and portending—ominously to those who were skilled in such predictions, though, perhaps, only discomfortably to those who were not—storms and convulsions, that could not pass over without leaving havoc, and in many cases, ruin behind.

By those who were up to the reading of the commercial barometer that gave warning of such predicaments being at hand, of course much good could be done, by the exercise of timely caution and wise preparation; but even as at sea, there are captains of ships who will drive on, without attending to symptoms that should induce them to shorten sail, instead of setting more: so on land, there are merchants that even in the face of appalling bank returns, and rising rates of discount, will continue to trade without restriction in their transactions, till they are brought up with a shock, and thrown on their very beam ends.

It is true that many, even if they were willing, could not act otherwise. Sails cannot be always lowered, or indeed reefed, even by those who are inclined to do so, and for this simple reason, that gales too often disarrange the very machinery that assists such manipulations; while many are induced to act upon a theory—and one that sometimes proves good in practice—that to escape from being engulphed altogether, it is necessary to "crowd on," as the nautical phrase has it, with a still greater pressure of canvas, and, like the stage mariner, represented in Dibdin's song:—

> " To sail with the gale
> From the Bay of Biscay, O!"

So far as regarded myself, in the ominous circumstances

that had arrived, I was peculiarly situated. I had not over-traded. I had made a remarkably good balance at the end of the preceding year, and I was in excellent credit with all the manufacturers and others, from whom I had been in the habit of purchasing goods, for the purpose of sending abroad.

Unfortunately, however, I had been actually too cautious in my mode of doing business, which had been that of purchasing entirely with cash, so as to get bargains at the cheapest rate, and, at the same time any discount going, while those drafts that I received from abroad I never discounted, but retained till they came to maturity, when I got payment of them myself, if due in Glasgow, and transmitted to my friends Pull and Hawl, if payable in London, the latter placing the proceeds to my credit.

I thus was but a poor customer to the local banks, the managers of which, indeed, knew little about me, with the exception of the one in whose establishment I kept an account, merely as a receptacle, or safe as it were, for the money I required for present use, and as I studied economy in such matters as much as possible, seeing that the interest allowed on these accounts was moderate, I kept my balance smaller than perhaps prudence should have dictated, although, of course, always on the proper side of the ledger.

In consequence of these circumstances, when the bad times burst around us, and first-class firms were stopping payment, and bills were being protested to an inordinate extent, I felt I would be in rather an awkward predicament if I required assistance, or in other words, advances on bills, from the bank.

Nor was it long before such a predicament as I feared, came about; for having purchased a lot of goods at a very reduced price, suitable for a market, from which I had received for such, uncommonly tempting quotations, I found it would be necessary that I should discount some bills-receivable I had on hand—a practice as I have already stated, that had been quite unusual on my part—and having handed these to the bank, with which I had so long had an account, to my perfect surprise, I found the manager quite indifferent and chary about them; indeed, so much so was this the case, that with difficulty I got him to cash even those which were payable in London, although the accepters thereof were

of the very first standing. As to the others, the verdict was simply "not convenient!" so I had to return with them to my office, very much chap-fallen, and, indeed, disgusted—particularly as the manager had been rather sharp, if not rude, in "putting me through my facings."

When the day of payment for the goods therefore arrived, instead of being able to give cash, I could only offer part in that commodity, and part in the local bills that had been rejected by the bank, endorsed over to the payee, leaving, for reasons that I need not explain, a balance of about fifteen hundred pounds, for which I tendered my own promissory-note, but which, although at a very short date, my creditor did not seem to relish at all.

He, however, received it as well as the others, upon my assuring him, that by the time they were due I would be in receipt of bills, now on their progress from the other side of the Atlantic—all first class, and drawn on London—to an amount that would pay the few I had on the circle here, ten times over.

I thus got him pacified, but as it turned out, only for a couple of days; for at the end of that short period he returned to inform me that, do all he could, it was impossible for him to get the fifteen hundred pounds promissory-note "melted," unless I got a good London name attached to it, when he felt sure all would be right.

I was rather annoyed, as may be supposed, at this untoward incident, and after fuming a little at the banks, and growling at the manufacturer, I asked him if the name of Pull and Hawl, attached to the Bill as a guarantee, would satisfy his scruples, to which he promptly replied that such would be the case.

I accordingly asked him to leave the bill, so that I might be enabled to transmit it to that firm, for the purpose proposed; but on sitting down after he had left, to write to Pull and Hawl on the subject, I could not for my life concoct a letter that to my satisfaction explained why I wished them to do me the favour in view. My powers of composition, indeed, seemed entirely to fail me, and, consequently, in the endeavour, I spoiled an enormous quantity of good post paper. Somehow, the preliminaries of one letter looked too much like pleading poverty, consequently it went rumpled into the waste-paper basket. Then, that of another seemed too independent, and it accordingly met a similar fate. Again the peroration of a third, was inconsistent with its beginning; while the fourth was altogether a jumble of nonsensical explications, bad grammar, and incongruities.

I, thereupon, threw down my pen in despair, rushed to the reading-room, and wasted the rest of the day in gossip, and in reading the dismal accounts of the state of trade in the provinces, as well as the list of bankrupts in the *London Gazette*.

These were certainly rather extensive, and indicative of the distress throughout the country, to remedy which, the commercial articles in the newspapers submitted many propositions, while urging upon the public the exercise of patience, calmness, and forbearance, but which I thought rather calculated to augment the haste, agitation, and severity that were deprecated. There were many letters, too, in the general columns of the press, from those who felt "the shoe pinching their corns,"—as a facetious editor expressed it, in commenting upon them—wherein the Bank Charter Act was assailed as the cause of the evil, and free trading in banking, and an unlimited issue of notes called for, as an undoubted panacea for the evils complained of.

The next day, on going to my office for the purpose of renewing my task, I found I was as unfitted for it as ever, and I began then to think that I had undertaken an engagement which I should never for a moment have contemplated. This was soon made apparent by a circular, which I received by that days London mail, from Pull & Hawl themselves, announcing a further rise in the rate of discount at the Bank of England, an alarming account of the state of the

exchanges, a desponding description of business in general,
and of their own in particular, and a melancholy anticipation
that things would even be worse before they were better.
And this circular was accompanied by a private letter, in
which retrenchment in business was recommended, and
dependence on the assistance of London agents particularly
deprecated!

I was much puzzled by all these circumstances, and so

perplexed and confused,
that I felt as if I were
becoming insane, aggra-
vated as my feelings were
by the unfortunate issue
of my suit towards Miss
Gentle, which I could
never get out of my
mind.   Indeed, I may
say that, to some extent,
I was actually mad, as
what I am about to re-
veal will possibly make
apparent; for as the time
approached, when my cre-
ditor had engaged to call
again for his bill, I had actually the temerity to endorse it,
in my own handwriting, with the name of Pull & Hawl,
trusting, however, to the circumstance that, as it was payable
at my own place of business, I would have nothing to do
but to retire it, when it became due, in the usual way,
without any body being the wiser, or myself the worse,
for the transaction.

. Whether or not I was right in this anticipation, the sequel
will show!

I had scarcely committed the rash act, and presented the
bill to the manufacturer, who came sharp at the time
appointed, than I began to repent the proceeding, not perhaps from dreading any ulterior effects, that might be contingent thereon, as from seeing, on reflection, the improvi-
dence of the step, which was far from being that of a business
man, and particularly of one who was ambitious to rise in
the world as a great merchant.

Not only so, but on further contemplation, I saw I had committed a crime, in the eye of the law, which might bring me to disgrace, and a fearful fate, if ever found out. The more I contemplated what I had done, the more I became miserable: during which state of mind, I beheld myself as occupying a baser position than even poor Sissy had endured, and probably was now enduring; indeed, I felt it would be only a just retribution, and something of an atonement to her, if I came to take, as a condemned criminal—and that, too, under the official administration, and contemptuous pity, of my brother bailies—a like place to what she had occupied, under the appalling circumstances in which I had last beheld her!

What was done, however, could not now be undone, and so I consoled myself as I best could, trusting to the chapter of accidents, and particularly to my good luck, which as yet had never failed me, excepting in love, to get me out of the difficulty, and this I began to feel certain would be the case, when something like a month had passed away, and there was only another to come, ere the bill would be retired: against which result, I was now perfectly prepared, in consequence of having received remittances, to an amount far beyond what I had anticipated, or even required.*

I was engaged in my office, one afternoon, reading over some business letters I had written, previously to sending the same to the Post-Office, and then going home—where I had engaged, to dine with me, in a very quiet way, my friend Councillor Tweel, whom I had not met privately for a long time before — and probably turning over the little disagreeable matter of the bill, in my mind, while resolving that I would never commit such an unjustifi-

* NOTE II.—Mercantile forged bills. *See Appendix.*

able error again—when the clerk who was remaining to
close the office, on my vacating the inner room, which I used
as my *sanctum sanctorum*, came to announce that a gentleman wished to speak to me on particular business, and—of
all gentlemen in the world—no other than my monkey-faced
friend, Mr. Jasper Jackson, writer, lawyer, money-lender,
usurer, and so on, as I had been accustomed to hear him
designated, and perhaps to designate him myself, when in
scandalising mood.

Immediately, a disagreeable qualm came over my conscience,
that almost deprived me of my presence of mind. I, however, had resolution enough to conceal my feelings, and, at
the same time, sufficient judgment to see, that whatever
might take place betwixt Mr. Jackson and me, should not
be witnessed by a third party. I accordingly desired the
clerk to show him in, while intimating that as I might be
detained a little longer
than usual, I would lock
up the office myself, and
thus not require the
young man to wait on
me.

Jackson now entered
grinning from ear to
ear, with an evidently
forced politeness, that
made him look liker one
of the ape tribe than
ever. At any other time
I question if I would
have been civil to him,
but feeling, like the seer
of the poet, that "coming events cast their shadows before,"
I constrained myself to assume something of a tolerant air
towards him, and consequently desired him to be seated, while
speculating in my mind as to what he could have to say.

I felt assured it could only be something sinister, for the
character he possessed, pointed to that. Nevertheless, I
entered into chit-chat with him, as if I felt nothing but what
was fraternal and philanthropic towards him, while touching
upon the ordinary commercial topics of the day—such as the

falling price of consols, the rising rates of discounts, the decreasing amount of bullion in the bank coffers, and so on. I then remarked that the weather was particularly mild and salubrious, and that, therefore, the Tweels would more than likely be enjoying the coast extremely. After which—a rather awkward pause having taken place—I asked him the reason of my being so agreeably honoured by a call from him on this occasion?

He did not keep me long in suspense, for with that easy impudence, which some people make themselves believe is graceful self-possession, he chatteringly said, "I hope I will be pardoned, Bailie, for troubling you at this late period of the day with business matters; but I have been so much engaged, that I really had not time, till now, to call upon you—(hem, hem)—the fact is, these are very nervous times, as you have just been remarking—(hem)—very nervous times, indeed—and, therefore, for one business man to call on another to speak confidentially with, perhaps may be excused—(hem)—what I have come about, at present, however, is merely to ask you if you know a firm of the name of Pull & Hawl, in London?"

"Pull & Hawl?" I replied, while I felt the blood leave my cheeks, "certainly I do; they are my agents in London, and very respectable people!"

"Well! I am glad you say so," he answered with a would-be dignified bow, "and therefore all's right, so far. Will you tell me, however," he continued, while drawing from his pocket, and unfolding the bill for fifteen hundred pounds, which I lately had granted, "if this name which, you will observe, is appended to this promissory-note of yours,—and which, I may mention, has come into my hands in the usual course of business—is their signature?"

I felt a cold sweat come over my frame as he said this, while feeling as though my fate lay in his vile hands. Still I answered coolly, "I will relieve you of all doubts as to that, Mr. Jackson; for if you feel anxious about it, I will give you a check for the amount, on your handing it to me!"

"Anxious about it?" he replied, while rising to his feet and approaching me, with a provoking impertinence, that assuredly would have tempted me to knock him down, had I been differently circumstanced, "it is not I, that should

feel anxious about it, perhaps, if all were known. What I
ask you is this—is this signature"—here he threw himself
into a theatrical attitude, while striking the bill with his
dexter paw, *a la* Kean,—"is this signature, I say, in the
genuine handwriting of the firm of Pull & Hawl, and
appended as a guarantee to your bill, or is it not?"

But in striking the bill again, at the end of this bold query,
during which his agitation had become supreme, he rather
overdid his part, for the bill flew out of his hand, and as
good luck would have it, towards me; and before he could
recover it, although he nimbly enough made a snatch for the
purpose, I had caught it, and in a moment crumpled it up
like a ball, which I held in the palm of my hand, in such a
way as that nothing but extreme force could have torn it
from me: and that I did not think he possessed in a superior
degree to me. Still, he seemed determined not to be outdone
if possible, and, in the attempt showed such an activity, and
also a disposition, more like that of the inferior animals than
of the human ones—for he jumped round about me, and even
over me—that I became confused and alarmed, and therefore
ejected the bill from me, as it were, to save my skin, towards
the fire-place, forgetting in my distress that, as it was
summer time, there was no fire on.

It did not, however, even go into the fire-place, but struck
the wall, and deflecting therefrom, finally found a resting-
place on the dusty top of a cabinet containing documents,
where I hoped it would be out of Jackson's reach, till I could
get time to pacify him, and bring him to a reasonable parley.

In this expectation, however, I was mistaken, for in a
moment, with one spring from the floor to the mantelpiece,
and from that to the cabinet, he bounded after it with an
activity almost superhuman, and before I could have even
winked an eye, was on the top of the latter, where he seized
the now dusty pellet, and immediately secured it beyond the
reach of my power. He then, apparently having satisfied
himself that all was right, assumed a defiant attitude by
sitting down on his hams, and spreading out his arms, with
his hands resting on the cornice of the cabinet, while
grinning and gibbering triumphantly at me!

I was mortified exceedingly at the chance I had thus
lost, of gaining re-possession of the unfortunate bill; but

still being determined to make another effort, I coolly opened my desk, and taking therefrom a pistol, which I was in the habit of keeping there, and cocking it, although it was unloaded, I desired him to deliver up the document, or else I would "blow his brains out!"

This little bit of highwayman dodgery, however, did not daunt the intrepid Jackson. His ire was up, and so was his pluck. "Fire!" he cried, "if you dare, and add the crime of murder to that of forgery. Fire! I tell you, if you have the bravery to do so : you will at all events thereby attract some one to my assistance with the noise, and then we will bring this matter to an issue one way or other!

I confess I was somewhat relieved by this bold speech of Jackson, and particularly by the concluding portion of it, which comprehended the expression "one way or other," for it contained, as I thought, the germ of a compromise, and that, if other chances failed, might eventually be the means of getting me out of the difficulty.

I consequently uncocked the pistol, and returned it to the desk, while I said "No, I won't fire, if for nothing but for the sake of old recollections, and the remembrance of your mother who was kind to me in my youth, and whom I therefore respected."

"My mother!" he replied, "Oh, ho!—You knew my mother, did you?—then allow me to inform you that what you tell me, now convinces me of what I have all along suspected, namely, that you are, after all, but the son of our washerwoman, and a low-bred fellow, if not worse!"

This unexpected homethrust stung me to the quick, and almost overset my reason, while filling my breast with rage and mortification, so that I believe, had the pistol been loaded I would have acceded to Jackson's invitation, and brought him down with a vengeance; for in addition to the severity of his remarks, he had revealed to me, that he was in possession of the secret of my origin, and for aught I knew to the contrary, might be aware of other particulars connected therewith, which, if promulgated, would effectually ruin my standing in the City. These facts actually made me forget, what even might be considered a worse predicament to be in, than what I have stated, namely, my complexity in the bill transaction, so that I gave way to my rage by ventilating on him all the malevolence of language and slander I was master of. I accused him of being a usurer, a cheat, and an impostor; a scamp, a coward, and a ruffian; a puppy, a perjurer, and a pettifogger; and finally wound up the catalogue of his faults by declaring that he was a public laughing-stock, despised by all gentlemen, and detested by all ladies—by the latter of whom, indeed, he was not looked upon as a man, but as a monkey!

Having exhausted my supply of such "Billingsgate," I paused, fully expecting that Jackson would have descended and grappled with me, when I hoped to overcome him, and regain possession of the bill; but in this surmise I was mistaken, for instead of showing fight, he indicated a very different disposition. My acrid sally had, in short, had a most wonderful effect. It had overcome him. His weak point was his personal appearance, and through that, I had subdued him, if I might be allowed to judge by what took place, for the pert, impudent, and almost diabolic phiz, that a moment before had been grinning in victory over me, became overclouded and abashed; his chin dropped upon his breast; his body doubled up; he folded his hands over his skull; and he appeared the very personification of despair and humiliation; while, at the same time he alternately gasped and groaned, as though his heart would break, as I wonderingly and hopefully waited, to see what these paroxysms would produce.

In a few minutes, he roused himself from a quietude that had succeeded this ebullition, and descending from his perch, more deliberately than he had gone up, approached to where I sat, while I, thinking he might be inclined to take revengeful amends upon me, placed myself in an attitude of defence.

I might have spared myself this trouble, however, for instead of making any hostile attack, he dropped upon one of his knees before me in the attitude of a suppliant, and catching hold of my hand, exclaimed:—" For the sake of all that is dear to you—for the sake of your own mother, that has been spoken of, and for the sake of mine, whom you say you respected, oh ! never say what you have now insinuated, again ! Take all that I hold dear on earth. Take this unfortunate bill, and tear it in a thousand pieces, without my having recourse for its payment. Take her, to whom my whole soul and heart have been devoted, but whose affections you have robbed me of, and make her your

bride. Take my estate and riches, if you like; but never horrify and agitate me as you have done, by the utterance of such injustice, and such scandal!"

I now saw that I had my antagonist completely in my power; that the tables were turned; and that I, instead of he, was master of the situation; for, as if to prove his sincerity, he had produced the bill, and spreading out its wrinkles as he best could with his trembling hands, had placed it on the desk before me, remaining, however, in the prostrate attitude he had assumed.

" Well, Jackson !" I said at last, after I had recovered
from the agreeable surprise, which the unrehearsed scene
in this little private drama had created within me, "since
you are now inclined to act thus reasonably and properly, I
will be the last man in the world to reject this proffered
compromise on your part, so clap your name on the back of
the bill, and I will give you a cheque upon the bank for
the amount, which you will get the cash for to-morrow, and
then we will talk further on the other particulars of your
proposition.

He arose from the floor, and taking a pen, endorsed the
bill, while I drew out the cheque referred to, and presenting
it to him, he put it in his pocket—although in such
an absent way that I do believe he was almost unconscious
of the act.

" And now," I said, with my mind at last comparatively
at ease, " since we have happily got over preliminaries:
touching this little joke of mine which seems to have
affected you so much, you must allow that you were the first
aggressor, by casting in my teeth that my mother was a
washerwoman !—but I know what you are going to say,"—
I continued, as I observed from the expression of his countenance that he was about to commence an apologetic
explanation—" as the proverb has it, ' the least said's the
soonest mended,' so let us make a paction at once:—that
never again will we open our lips on these silly subjects
which have given offence, respectively, to both of us, and if
you like, let us be friends instead of enemies henceforth, for
I have that to say, and to propose to you, which perhaps
you will find a thousand times more important to your
interest and happiness, than such absurdities !"

" Agreed !" he cried, while he grasped my hand and
wrung it energetically ; " Jasper Jackson is the last man
that will refuse such a fair offer, and should either of us ever
break the covenant we now enter into, let it be war to
the knife !"

I returned his friendly grasp as he said this, and requested
him to be seated, having made up my mind, in the meantime,
how I would treat the other subject he had touched upon,
while knowing full well his sentiments towards Miss
M'Chuckie, whom he seemed to suppose I had snatched from

his embraces. I was, however, determined to make capital (as the saying is) of it, at the same time, so as effectually to keep the whip-hand over him, in case of any ulterior risk occurring to interfere with the arrangement we had made. Assuming, therefore, a very simple and almost surprised look, I coolly said, "you have been pleased Mr. Jackson to broach a very tender subject, and one that I would not have dared to enter upon, but for your choosing to draw me into it—so pray, may I ask, if you mean to charge me with anything unfair or sinister in regard to my intimacy with the Tweel family; for if I remember rightly, you used the expression that I had *robbed* you of your bride?"

"My dear Sir!—My dear friend!—if you will allow me to use that familiar term!" gasped the subdued Jackson, "I meant nothing wrong by that term—I had learned that Miss M'Chuckie had accepted from you a valuable trinket, and considering the circumstance to be a proof that you were her accepted lover, I conceived her to be lost to me, and that I thereby had been robbed—though in a figurative sense—of the chance of obtaining her hand, which I flatter myself I once enjoyed."

"But it does not follow," I replied, "because a gentleman offers a present to a young lady, that he is going to marry her. No doubt I have had thoughts of matrimony, like other young men, but still I am free to confess, that so far as I am concerned, Miss M'Chuckie's heart is still her own. At all events, she is not engaged to me!"

Mr. Jackson's face brightened up at this declaration, for evidently it gave him joy, if not hope, so I thought I would improve upon it, by saying—"What would you think, instead of my robbing you of a bride, if I rewarded you with one, and so far from being your rival in the affections of Miss M'Chuckie, if I became your 'black leg,' and so made you the happiest man in the world?"

"Think?" exclaimed Mr. Jackson, while making a motion as if he would again have sunk on his knees, "I would not think it too much to become your slave, and to serve you in any capacity; not only through life, but to all eternity, if such a thing were possible!"

"Well, a bargain be it," I replied, "and so give me your hand on this new contract. I will do my best for you, and

as a commencement of the good work, will be glad if you will
walk home with me to dinner at my own house, where you
will meet Mr. Tweel, who is to be with me in a very quiet
way, and as he is a party worth propitiating, connected with
the matter, you can benefit by the opportunity that will be
thus afforded you, in making yourself as agreeable to him as
possible."

"My generous friend!" cried Jackson, as I uttered this
proposition, and which he evidently considered a guarantee
of the sincerity of my friendship towards him, "this is
really too much, and beyond what I could ever have expected, or dreamed of. I, therefore, accept your invitation
with all my heart and soul; for although I have another
engagement, I will make it subservient to this much more
important and pleasant one, if you will favour me with
half a sheet of note paper to write an apology upon."

This I handed to him, and after he had written the note
—which with difficulty he did, in consequence of his joyful
agitation—I despatched it by a special messenger, and then
locking the office, I walked home with him—who would have
believed it!—arm-in-arm, while surprising not a little, a number

of mutual friends, who had
been aware of our rivalry,
by the singular circumstance,
some of whom actually turned and looked after us, as
though they could not trust
their eyes!

We had, however, a very
pleasant walk to my house,
our conversation being on
numerous subjects mutually
agreeable to us, but nothing
was said as to our singular
rencontre in the office, with
the exception of an explanation which Jackson begged
leave to make, "just," as he said, "to remove everything
that might stand in the way of our increasing cordiality,"
and which was to the effect that on visiting me, he had
never intended to insinuate anything sinister against me,

but carried away by the heat of his temper, he had used an "unparliamentary" expression, which he had intended to apply to the party to whom I had granted the bill, and not to me, and which he was sorry for.

This of course, I received graciously, while thinking to myself that truth often lies in a mistake, as well as in a joke, notwithstanding the aptness of the proverb in respect to the latter.

On reaching my house, we there found Councillor Tweel, who had arrived before us, waiting impatiently for his dinner; for the worthy gentleman was blessed with a healthy appetite at all meal-times, and particularly at the afternoon one, when protracted a little, as on this occasion it had been, in consequence, as I explained to him, of business that Jackson and I had been transacting. Excellent man, he little dreamed to what extent his own domestic matters were connected with that business!

He, however, received our apologies blandly and kindly, appeased as his hunger immediately thereafter came to be, by a little repast quite to his mind, and which was sent up by my housekeeper, Mrs. Barbara, in her best style. This, accompanied as it was, by a bottle of Madame Cliquot's champagne, and followed by some of my prime port, and my rarest claret, put him, and indeed all of us, in the best of humours, it being proper to be remembered, that both Jackson and myself laughed at all the councillor's jokes, whether they were funny or not, and hearkened to the rehearsal, or rather repetition, of several of his windiest and dreariest Council speeches without yawning. I even had the temerity to hint, that on the first occasion for the election of Magistrates, which, in course of time, would take place in the Council, it would only be a natural thing that he should be chosen a bailie, and which appointment—what with his popularity in the City, in consequence of his well-known hospitality, and the opportunities he had for entertaining the Council in his magnificent mansion at St. Blythswood Terrace—would more than possibly lead to his acquiring the highest dignity going, namely, that of Lord Provost; which suggestion being well backed by Jackson, the honest councillor fairly took the bait, and as he imbibed his liquor, began to assume such a maudlingly important and official-like air, that I

verily believe he would not have objected, had we addressed
him as " My Lord!"

We indeed spent a very happy afternoon, for all of us
were in the greatest glee.   Mr. Tweel, in consequence of the
renewal of our intimacy, and the deference shown to him by
Jackson and me, as the future great man : Jackson, by the
prospect of getting a bride, quite to his satisfaction, and on
whom he doated with the ardour of genuine love: and I,
from having got quit of a disagreeable matter that had been
keeping me miserable, uncertain, and anxious, for weeks,
but which now, thanks to that good luck which ever stood
my firm friend—however it
might seem for a time, to
desert me—had vanished.

It was, therefore, with
great satisfaction, while the
ten o'clock bells jowled in
the several steeples around,
that I bade good evening to
Messrs. Tweel and Jackson,
as they staggered away from
my door, arm-in-arm—their
clay well moistened, and their
hearts glowing — and I returned to my parlour to
ponder over the events of the
day, the only drawback to
my happiness now, being the
pinching thought that I was
not, like the latter, enabled
to look forward with hope to that which was uppermost
in my mind, at all times, and in all situations, and which
became the more intense, the more it appeared to be removed
from my grasp.

CHAPTER XLVII.

> When burglars break into a bank,
>   To a settlement they're sent;
> But, when "*financiers*" break a bank,
>   They get a settlement!
>
> *The Goosedubbs Poet.*

I WAS, the very next day, waited upon by *my friend* Jackson, he being anxious to report to me as to how he had come on with Mr. Tweel, after that gentleman and he had left my house, and to consult me regarding what he should further do, as a suitor for the hand of the (in his eyes) adorable Miss M'Chuckie.

According to that report, he had elbowed the honest councillor home, and, notwithstanding all the port, champagne, and claret they had imbibed in my house, they had discussed three tumblers and an "eke" of whisky-toddy in Mr. Tweel's, so that after becoming "as thick as dog-heads," and as benevolent towards each other, as if they had been brothers, he had been obliged actually to assist the worthy gentleman to his bed-room, where he left him snoring, before he could get well out of the apartment.

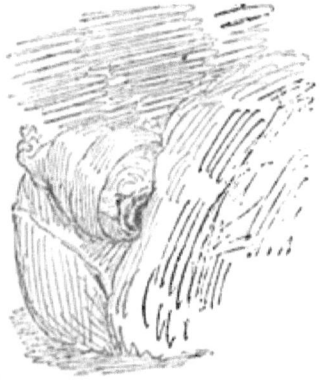

Still the councillor had never alluded to the one subject that Jackson was most interested in, namely, his step-daughter; far less had he asked him to visit his family at Castle-

Winsey, notwithstanding several hints he had given him, and in consequence, Jackson, who like other true lovers, thought the object of his adoration must be as dear and as admirable to every one who beheld her, as she was to himself, was beginning to think that perhaps some new suitor had in the meantime come in the way to cut him out, and to be even a more formidable rival to him than he thought, at one time, I had been.

I rallied Jackson on this view of the case which he had taken, by representing to him that "Rome was not built in a day,"—that "faint heart never won fair lady,"—that "hearts, like castles, were only to be taken by storm," and by dozens of such like consolations, as are generally ventilated by patrons, holding the position in which I stood to him, to dependents groaning in that, to which he stood to me.

"With regard to the circumstance which you seem to put so much stress upon," I continued, "namely, that Tweel has not invited you down to the coast—what of that? There is a good inn at Rover's Bay, and it is open to every one. Why not take your traps and go down to it, when you have a mind; and, being there and in the neighbourhood of Castle-Winsey, as a matter of civility you will call, when, of course, you will be entreated to remain to dinner, which will give you an opportunity of seeing and wooing Miss M'Chuckie, as well as if you had got a special invitation!"

I was not altogether disinterested in giving this advice to Jackson, for if he went, I felt that he more than possibly would report all about his visit to me, and thereby I would ascertain something regarding Miss Gentle, whom, of course, I now had no opportunity of seeing, or indeed learning about; for Tweel I saw was of opinion that I was not the rich man he had considered me at one time to be; and, therefore, not worth asking down to Castle-Winsey again, as a desirable suitor for his step-daughter.

Jackson approved of this idea, and resolved to put it in execution, so I went on with other suggestions, which were simply to the effect that he should follow up his suit by making presents to Miss M'Chuckie, the state of his finances being such, that the cost thereof could be no great object to him.

"You have hinted," I said, "that I have presented Miss

M'Chuckie with a necklace; well it cost only eighty guineas; what do you say to bid above me, with a diamond bracelet worth a hundred?"

"A hundred!" exclaimed Jackson, "I would not grudge a thousand—no, nor ten thousand—if by so doing I could gain her hand!"

"Bravo!" I answered, "the poet says 'none but the brave deserve the fair'—had it been his luck to have been acquainted with you, he would have altered the expression 'brave' to that of 'rich'—but softly," I continued, "there is no necessity for running away with the harrows. Something moderate will be best to begin with, in extent not exceeding the amount I have mentioned. As to your thousands, why if they are cumbering you in any way, and the security I am enabled to offer pleases you, I dare say I could employ them, if granted at fair interest!"

I made this bold suggestion half with a view to test the sincerity of Jackson's profession of the day before, and half in earnest, while expecting that the result would be similar to what followed the like proposal—though in joke—to Mr. Tweel, but to my surprise, Jackson stood the test.

"I promised to place at your disposal, yesterday," he said, "nay I proffered to you anything and everything I had in the world. From that I will not shrink. So name what you want in the way of accommodation, and if it be not beyond my means, I will satisfy you!"

I confess I was overcome, and even affected, by this generous offer, it being so greatly beyond what I had ever dreamed of, and perhaps, too, beyond what my conscience told me I deserved. I, therefore, thanked him heartily, while telling him that all I would ask would be an occasional "lift" in the way of discounting a bill, should these pinching times render it necessary that I should make the application.

"My dear friend," said Jackson, "the times may be pinching, but to you whose slave I have become—to speak in the spirit of our yesterday's covenant—I will reveal, as part of my duty, how they may never be so. Listen, then, to me, and have that film which has hitherto blinded your financial eyes removed for ever!"

He then commenced to give me a long treatise on banking, the mysteries of which he seemed perfectly acquainted with, and although I could not quite follow him, he made it apparent to me, that to be a good financier, it was necessary one should know and understand a little about those establishments called banks, wherein there are men, as he said, " nick-named bankers," desirous to give money on certain terms, while without, there are men desirous to *get* money from those bankers on any terms !

"Now, just let us," he continued, "contemplate these establishments—these magazines—these mines, as I may call them—for a minute, and perhaps we will arrive at some idea regarding them, which not only may entertain, but perhaps become useful to us. And remember we are not singular in doing so, for 'legion' is the denomination of those who gaze at the architectural piles, day after day, while feeling awed by their frowning porticos, their towering pillars, their ornate carving and sculpture, and their defying strength: perhaps wondering, at same time, if it can be possible that there should be people so fool-hardy or idiotic as to contemplate an attack—by way of getting possession of the lucre within —upon any of these impregnable strongholds of wealth!"

"And yet," further continued Jackson, as he warmed on

his subject, while I sat admiring his eloquence, "even these Algerine Forts — these Gibraltar Rocks—these Dumbarton Castles, will yield at last! Some morning we will waken up to read—as we discuss our ham and eggs—that a daring and successful burglary has been committed on this or that bank; and which, while astonishing everybody by its unexpectedness, its secrecy, its boldness, and its ingenuity, will reveal the fact that even the hardest masonry, the firmest bolts, the heaviest locks, and the strongest safes, must succumb to good generalship, though the general should, as an atonement to the humiliated bankers, swing for it !"

"But even as these banks," still further continued Jackson, "may be assailed by, and made to yield to, the tactics of the burglar, they may still more successfully be assailed and subdued by another, and even more formidable description of tactics ; for it is my design to reveal to you a method of getting to their very cores—to the inmost recesses of their safes—to the hearts of their strong boxes—where you may revel in, and deal with the riches they contain, at your leisure, and as you like, while running—unlike the unhappy burglar that has been alluded to—no risk whatever, but on the contrary, receiving the smiles and the thanks of obliged bankers, for so doing!

"These tactics," added Jackson, "are the tactics of the financier, and in order to explain them fully to you, it will be necessary that I first reveal a few particulars in regard to banks and bankers, for which it is necessary that I should command your attention and ears, for a few minutes."

He then went on to explain that banking, as practised, was nothing but a huge system of pawn-broking, with this difference, that instead of the pledges being good solid property, they were in most cases, mere names, the value of which was only according to the stability and soundness of the parties they represented.

Treating them, however, under the more dignified appellation of "banks," he said, if one would just look for a moment into circumstances connected with the banks pertaining to Scotland alone, he would find that in the aggregate, they possessed a paid-up capital of no less than ten to eleven millions, while in almost every case their proprietors, at the same time, were responsible for the banks' transactions to the whole amount of their substance and fortunes. This bank had a capital of two millions. This other one, had one-and-a-half millions; and this third and this fourth one, had each at least a million—all paid up in hard cash, and deposited: *when they commenced business*—in the coffers of the respective establishments. They had likewise the power to issue notes, representing from four to five millions, which, although a false capital, was yet a great subsidy to the means the banks had for doing business transactions, and consequently, gave

them a supplemental addition to their capitals, that made the
aggregate enormous.   Not only so, but there was another
element connected with banking, that went to swell the
amount of the working means of banks—far beyond what
even the paid-up capitals and this issue of notes afforded—and
that was the deposits, which in some instances exceeded the
real capital fivefold. The aggregate deposits of the Scottish
banks, in fact, Jackson calculated to be upwards of fifty
millions; which, added to the real capitals, and the average
circulations, made a grand total of working means amounting
to betwixt sixty and seventy millions!

" Now," said Jackson, " let us just consider for a moment
how this enormous amount of capital is to be worked, or
rather let us consider how it really *is worked!*   If properly
done, it should be on a system as complete and safe as that
on which ordinary pawnbrokers do their business; but as to
that I will leave you to judge by what I will bring before
your notice. This I will illustrate, not by a general vidimus of the action of banks, but like Sterne with "slavery,"
by taking a single instance, and dissecting it to the core.
Let us select, for instance," he continued, " the very
bank which, in this morning's paper, is paraded before the
public as the paragon of success and stability, in consequence
of having declared at its annual meeting, which was held
yesterday, a dividend of ten per cent., after carrying over
eighty thousand pounds to account of ' Rest,' which is stated
to be now upwards of three hundred and fifty thousand pounds.
Now, here you will find in the statement of Assets and
Liabilities, that the present capital of the bank is one million
five hundred thousand pounds; that the note issue amounts
to four hundred thousand pounds odds; and that the deposits
amount to five millions and a-half: making the handsome
aggregate of upwards of seven millions four hundred thousand pounds! How is this fearful sum to be worked ! Why,
by a single man, and you know very well that he is a block-
head—a vain, conceited, arrogant, silly ass !—and yet he has
nearly eight millions in his hands to do with, as his caprice
or his folly dictates; for, as for the directors—pooh !—you
know what they are ! Well, this fellow has to keep this
eight millions spinning, and, after tossing it to and fro, and
sending it here and there—east, west, north, and south—to

America, to Russia, to Australia even—he has to collect it all together, once a-year, in figures—as has been done here—and out of the shakings thereof, to pay the usual dividend of nine or ten per cent. to the delighted shareholders, who look upon him as the greatest Solon in the country! No wonder that he dines out every day; no wonder that he is always placed at the right hand of the hostess; no wonder that he gets the first of the tit-bits; no wonder that every one defers to him, when he opens his oracular mouth, and laughs when he pleases to joke, for he is their autocrat and patron, at one and the same time!"

"But how is this despot," continued Jackson, "with this enormous power of eight millions, enabled to command time thus to dine out every day, and occasionally, likewise, to entertain at home?—how is he always to be seen in his bank parlour, as if that commodity were as plentiful with him as money?—how is he ever smiling and ever pleasing,

excepting it may be when he refuses to discount some 'poor devil's' bill, and drives him from his presence dumfounded and abashed, as though he had been attempting sacrilege?—simply because he has his own system of acting—that is, of conducting business. Of course, the world, and particularly the grateful shareholders, who annually get their ten per cent. of dividend, believe that system to be something superlative; they think that he knows every thing about the people whom he favours with discounts, or trusts with advances; they consider that, in turning over this and that bill, and scrutinising, as it were, the hand-writing thereon, and the watermark of the paper on which it is written, he detects therein its genuine worth, as a fortune-teller discovers, in the palm of a hand, or the colour of an eye, the fate of his dupe. Let us examine, however, how this may be. I do not deny that, in such inquisitions, he may sometimes be really in earnest, and consequently right in coming to a conclusion thereon; for, properly speaking, that ought to be the ordeal all securities, great or small, should be submitted to. But how, as a regular proceeding, could one man do such a thing in all cases? It is simply impossible. Were he to attempt it—that is properly—so far from being able to dine out, he would scarcely have time to munch a biscuit,—and as for sleeping—why, that would be entirely out of the question! My dear friend, consider for a moment, that he has eight millions to keep on the move, from year to year— that is upwards of twenty thousand a day, Sundays included—how, in the name of common sense, can a human being look properly into so many transactions as are necessary to circulate that amount, and be master of them all—as he pretends to be, and as his constituents think he is?"

"I grant you," Jackson went on to say, "that I am bringing before you the extreme view of the case. Were I to propound what I have said, to your confiding directors and shareholders of banks, they would tell me that it was all bosh, and they would very satisfactorily—particularly to themselves—explain how all could be done by the wonderful system that is pursued by, and is patent to joint stock banks —for doesn't the Board meet once a-week, and isn't the manager daily in the bank, from ten till four?"

"Let them continue, however," added Jackson, while he tipped me a knowing wink, "to go on in their happy delusion—let the directors enjoy their elevated and exclusive positions—let the managers wield their autocratic sceptres— let the shareholders indulge in their auriferous dreams: it is for you and me to profit by the advantages which the singular circumstances that I have revealed—and which simply amount to infamous management—spread before us, and invite us to enter upon: thereby to enrich ourselves beyond compute, ere they awaken to the reality of their true position, and discover, to their amazement and horror— as assuredly they will some day—that all along they have been but enjoying a fool's paradise!"

"But how is this to be done?" I inquired, as Jackson brought his comments to an end, "for although you have

made it apparent to me, that there is much truth in what
you have said, I cannot see how it is possible to get hold of
any portion of this mass of wealth which you have described,
and which, I will confess to you, I could make good and
honest use of, were such in my power?"

"By the simplest process in the world," answered Jackson,
"by putting your name to bills, and exchanging them for
the good solid money, that the managers have at their disposal, and which, in fact, they are ever seeking to dispose of,
as they sit in their parlours, picking their nails, and waiting
for the chance."

"Bills?" said I, while I thought I would checkmate Jackson by what I had to say on that point. "They don't want
bills at all, at least so my experience teaches me; for only
the other day, a few bills, for trifling amounts, that I presented—and the first, too, that ever I troubled the bank
with—were peremptorily rejected, and that, in the most
offensive and humiliating way, although they were as good
and sound as their own notes. Besides, you know what
took place with the unfortunate missive that has been the
means—happy, I hope—of bringing you and me together?"

"I am keeping all that in view," said Jackson, "and
will illustrate what I wish you to understand, from the very
circumstances you have now mentioned. To come to the
point at once then, however it may surprise you, the reason
of your having been denied the accommodation you wanted,
was simply because you had been too modest with the banks.
You had not asked enough!"

"Not asked enough!" I cried, while I indeed felt surprised
at Jackson's confident allegation, "do you mean to tell me
that I would have been better received, had I asked more?"

"I did not use the expression '*more*,'" replied Jackson,
without wincing, "I said '*enough.*' I am talking seriously
to you on this subject, and you must not pervert my words!"

"But it would have been quite enough!" I retorted, "nay,
it would have been more than enough, when I take into
consideration the funds I was daily expecting, in the shape
of remittances from abroad, and which, if I could have
received but a few days earlier, would have enabled me to
dispense with discounts for a time, altogether!"

"My dear fellow!" coolly replied Jackson, "be not offended

if I again attempt to put you right, for you are now—in your simplicity—perverting my meaning, even as you did my expression. It might have been enough for you, but it was not enough for the banker. What did *he* care for this bill for a hundred pounds, and that bill for two hundred—aye or even for fifteen hundred, or two thousand?—no more than a wholesale grocer does for such an order as a quarter pound of tea, or a single pound of sugar. It is quantity that is desiderated—something in amount, which, with as moderate trouble to the banker as the small transaction would require, will furnish that official, so far, with the means of making up a dividend—it may be only an apparent one: what about that?—wherewith to propitiate the expectant shareholders!"

"I begin to comprehend your meaning!" I cried, "a light commences to break in upon my obtuse mind, and I think I now understand you. I should have offered my banker eight, or ten thousand pounds in amount of paper, and then it would surely have been worth his while?"

"Well!" answered Jackson, "eight or ten thousand pounds would have done very well to begin with, provided you had chosen the proper period for the transaction—for nothing is truer than what the Scriptures say, 'there is a time for all things,'—but having begun, you must not stop; and what will you say, when I tell you, that to ingratiate yourself fully into the affections of the banker, you would require to go on, till you got upon the circle, bills, extending to fully a couple of hundred thousand pounds, or perhaps three, in amount!"

"Three hundred thousand pounds!" I shouted, while I actually thought Jackson was joking, though his serenity belied that, "what could I do with three hundred thousand pounds, even if I could get it? Why, it would take a Paterson or a Law to employ such an amount at Darien, or the South Sea Islands!"

"That's your look out!" replied Jackson, "not the banker's—for you could scarcely expect that he should furnish you both with the money, and the idea as to how you should use it. But after all, what is there to alarm you in the working of two, or even three hundred thousand pounds? Have I not explained to you that we have men

called bankers, or bank managers, who are yearly working sums, varying, say from two millions to ten millions,
and producing therefrom, apparent dividends, to their shareholders of five to ten per cent. Why should you not be
as clever as they are, particularly as you have to deal with
only about a thirtieth part of the sum that cumbers them?"

"But it is by far too much," I rejoined, "and beyond
what I would desire, even if I could use it to advantage.
I dare say I could work ten or twenty thousand, and what is
more, without any danger to the bank!"

"Aye!—true,"—replied Jackson, "I know that perfectly.
But you must look at all sides of the question. You could
work as you say twenty thousand, without danger to the bank,
no doubt, but not without danger to yourself; and therefore
to assure that latter desirable end, you must have from your
banker, either hundreds of thousands, or nothing. There are
no safe half measures in such transactions!"

"I confess you are again beyond my reach," I said, "and
therefore I must require that you explain further."

"I will simply do that," answered the patient and
instructive Mr Jackson, "by a suppositious case. Let us
suppose, for instance, that you become a money-borrower,
that is a "financier," and have always on the circle connected
with our favourite bank, bills, or an overdrawn account,
to an extent not exceeding, say twenty thousand pounds.
Well, something particular takes place in the money market
—the bullion is leaving the country—the exchanges are
getting against us—or it may even happen that some impudent and officious director looks into your account—for
there are occasionally such—and in consequence the manager
gets a "rounding," and is ordered to curtail transactions with
you—for be it remarked, the very manager that can be so
overbearing and cruel to what should be considered the best
friends of the bank, namely, the decent tradesman, who
comes with his small bill, will quail and sneak to his
directors. Under such circumstances, he will probably do
as he is ordered, particularly as he can do so easily, in consequence of the sum at issue being only twenty thousand
pounds; for, if the putting on of the screw even brought
you down, the balance of loss, after deducting the dividends
your estate would pay, would form no great hardship to the

bank, though it might possibly ruin you. If, however, the
sum at issue were two hundred or three hundred thousand
pounds—the larger the better—what could the manager do?
—simply nothing. He might send for you, and talk big,
and fluster a little, but it would end in your learning that
he was in your power, instead of you being in his, and,
therefore, on you would go as before, flush and comfortable,
though all around in the shape of well-doing tradesmen—
many of them probably shareholders in his very bank—were
pressed as in a vice, and from hand to mouth for want of
money : and yet he, the banker would not, or could not
give it to them, even to the smallest extent. No, no ;
believe me, moderate credits are dangerous things—safety
alone lies in their being of such amount, that any interference with them would be attended with greater danger
to the bank, than to you !"

"But then," I, as it were, unwittingly replied, "what a
fearful thing it would be if, notwithstanding, a reckoning
did take place. Why, what would the shareholders—what
would the public think?"

"Ah!" exclaimed Jackson, "if you are going to take it
in that way—if your bowels of compassion are to be moved
at the very commencement, and as it were anticipatively,
there is no use in commencing at all. As well might a
general of an army, when he places his troops in the field,
and before he issues his commands for the commencement of
hostilities, have qualms as to the damage about to be done
by his muskets and his guns, as a financier have misgivings
as to the effect of his monetary operations. No!—such fears
are baby fears, and must be discarded when you lift your
pen, as those of the soldier are when he draws the sword!
As to what the public may say or think, should you fail,
always keep this commercial maxim in view, that the larger
the sum you fail for, the more respectable will it be considered, and the more sympathy will you command. There is
nothing so contemptible as to go down for a small sum, for,
under such circumstances, you are sure to be despised by
your creditors, and, in particular, by those who are not your
creditors—not to mention that you are likelier to get a
favourable settlement if you fail for a gigantic sum, than if
you fail for a paltry one!"

"But," said Jackson, by way of conclusion to his monetary oration, "I have simply told you these little facts, and thrown out these little hints, as a mere matter of friendship to you. It is for you to take them into consideration, and if you think proper, to profit by them. I would not have done so, but for your having favoured me with your confidence as to your commercial position at present, and honoured me by asking my assistance. That, as I have said, so far as it lies in my humble power, is at your disposal. I have, however, endeavoured to show you, that a perfect El Dorado lies before you, if you like to enter upon it, and mines far beyond those of Peru or Mexico in richness, are at your disposal. Mistake not, however, the meaning of anything I have stated. As I have said, there is a time for all things, and therefore, the coming of that time is a matter that must be studied. Not only so; but in addition, there is a method to be pursued—it is the 'open Sesamé' of the cavern, and not known to every common robber! That, however, I will reveal to you if you like; and even as the roads which lead to the dazzling mines I have named require a guide, so will I in addition, be your guide, and lead you on to those diggings which lie so temptingly betwixt this and the Saltmarket!"

Mr. Jackson here took his hat, and reminding me that I had promised to assist him in selecting a diamond bracelet, which he proposed to present to Miss M'Chuckie as a love offering, invited me to accompany him for the purpose, to the shop of old Jem Peebles, a dealer in precious stones and bijoutry, and who, although as ugly and ungainly in his appearance as Jackson himself, had nevertheless a rare assortment of these valuables, so pleasing and precious in the eyes of the fair sex.

I accordingly accompanied him to the shop of Mr. Peebles, where we were not long in fixing upon a lapidarian gem that met the approval of both his fancy and mine, even as we expected it would delight that of Miss M'Chuckie.

This determined upon, I retreated from the counter, to Mr. Peebles' fire-place, and as I stood with my back to the mantelpiece, I had a rare chuckle, within my sleeve, as I beheld the two ugly fellows bargaining about the price, and almost rapping their twisted skulls together, in their keenness to reduce, or augment the same, as the case might be.

At last they settled: the money was paid, the receipt was granted, and afterwards I walked home with Jackson, who was delighted with his bargain, he having invited me to dine

with him, along with Mr. Tweel, at his lodgings, and where we passed again, a very happy and a very vinous night—the only difference being, that instead of Jackson seeing the worthy councillor home afterwards, I had that pleasure.

CHAPTER XLVIII.

INTRODUCTORY DOGGERELS.

Ye Bank shareholders who delight
  In yearly ten *per cent.*,
What would you say, if you but knew
  The way your millions went?

No doubt, you think them safely placed,—
  According to your Rules,—
Nor squandered amongst rogues and knaves,
  By donkeys, and by fools!

The Goosedubbs Poet.

I PONDERED very deeply on the monetary instructions where-with Jackson had favoured me. Indeed, they were never out of my mind, and I became very thoughtful in conse-quence. Indeed, I learned after-wards, that my solitary and abstracted-like appearance had attracted the notice of my friends and acquaintances.

I had no reason to doubt the sincerity of Jackson's views. They were proved by the figures with which he had backed his assertions, and by what I knew myself to be the case; for it was notorious that the banks were in the habit of giving inordinate accommodation to certain houses, whose positions were quite mys-terious to the general public, and the subject—particularly in straitened times—of no small surmise, if not gossip.

Still I hesitated even to contemplate the subject with

fortitude, far less with determination, no matter what the
temptation might be. I was, no doubt, most ambitious to
acquire money—as ambitious, indeed, as any that were
around me, and these were not a few—while every day I
was in the habit of seeing and learning regarding men that,
by dint of bold operations, were kicking fortunes before them
like footballs, and with the applause, too, of rivals, who
retired before them, as though borne down by the very
boldness of these operations.

Hitherto, the business I had carried on had been safe,
and, at the same time, successful. It had placed me in what
many would have considered a happy position, and what I
would have considered so myself, but that I beheld others
whom I could not look upon as being my match in ability,
deferred to and reverenced, on account of the greater wealth
they possessed. I longed, therefore, to gain an equal footing
with them on the envied platform of auric aristocracy, and,
in contemplating such an aim, became, in consequence, as
discontented and dissatisfied as though I had not possessed
a penny.

It is true that this unenviable state of feeling had become
much modified at the time I had made up my mind to marry
Miss Gentle, and during the delightful though illusive period
when I considered her within my reach. Then, I was disposed to have conquered all my ambitious views, beyond
what were perfectly legitimate and safe: to have considered
her affection as a sufficient substitute for the respect that I
saw paid to inordinate riches: and her love as a requital for
all the dangerous chances I might forego. For such a prize,
in short, I was prepared to have become a steady, prudent,
and safe go-a-head merchant, cheerful with what I possessed,
though, no doubt, not disinclined to have had that cheerful-
ness and that possession augmented, if it so pleased Providence that such should be the case.

When, however, I awoke from the day-dream I had been
allowing myself to indulge in; when I discovered that I
was the rejected of Miss Gentle—the rejected, too, of one
whose humble position as a governess I had calculated
upon, as likely to make her an easy conquest — these
philosophical ideas at once were upset, and I returned
to my old lucriferous train of thought, the former one

being but weakly retained by the lingering hope that some happy circumstance might occur to induce her to relent in her determination, ere I suffered the iron fairly to enter into my soul.

Alas! even the slight tenure of this hope was likewise at last torn from me; for Jackson having come one morning to report regarding a visit to Castle-Winsey that he had made, in consequence of an invitation, he had fairly *dinnered* —to use a Glasgow Town-Council verb—out of Mr. Tweel, revealed a circumstance that I had not calculated upon, although I might have done so, had I kept in view all that Miss Gentle had said to me on the eventful Sunday morning when I last had an interview with her, and which capped my despair, and brimmed my cup of grief. It was simply to the effect that she had left the family of the Tweels, and had gone whither they knew not—and whither, as it seemed, they cared not—for, as Jackson said, Mrs. Tweel was very much huffed, and placed on her high horse about it, she having entertained a hope that Miss Gentle would have entered into a re-engagement; instead of which, on the very day on which her contract ended, she had left, "with her bundles and her bandboxes," telling them they would never see her more, and not leaving even her address, which possibly she was ashamed to do, as no doubt she was going to her "beggarly, though proud relations; who never wrote her excepting through the medium of franks, procured from peers or members of Parliament, in order to save postage!"

This bit of information I only got from Jackson at the fag-end of his narrative regarding his own matters, and then I had, as it were, to *dig* it out of him piecemeal, he never having had the slightest idea of the cause of my interest in Miss Gentle, and, in consequence, was not particular as to the taste with which he communicated it. It was, notwithstanding, sufficiently conclusive to me, and filled my mind so much with sadness, that I longed for his absence that I might indulge in my sorrow and mortification, silently and alone.

Jackson, however, had no notion of gratifying me even thus far; on the contrary, as if to add to the poignancy of my feelings, he chose to revel in amplifications of his own hopes and

aspirations towards Miss M'Chuckie, who, as very naturally
might be expected, was all-in-all to him, even to the exclusion
of the supposition that any other woman could be dear to any
other man.

But Miss M'Chuckie, I picked up from his narration,

had been very cautious
in her intercourse with
him. She had played her
part well; and although
she had accepted his hun-
dred-guinea-bracelet — presented to her by Jackson
on his knees—she had not
compromised her affections
or her independence, in the
slightest degree. She was
still a free woman, and
what was more, she was
free to retain the bracelet,
whatever course Mr. Jackson's suit might take—happily
for himself or otherwise—and for this simple reason that
so prudent had he been, and so determined she should
become the possessor of it, that he had asked her to accept
it only on the terms she had accepted my necklace, and as
she was pleased to say that these had been viewed as those
of her "father's friend," of course the bracelet had gone, on
a like understanding.

Mr. Jackson thus made it apparent to me that the young
lady had been influenced in her conduct by a laudable
desire to have two strings to her bow. And then he took a
hearty laugh at the idea that she should pin her faith on me
for a moment—knowing my sentiments as he did—while I
in return laughed, though not heartily, on ruminating how
she might hoodwink both of us!

Still, I was not sorry that Jackson's suit promised to be
but a slow affair. Indeed, I would have been annoyed had
it been otherwise, for the simple reason that so long as it
hung on the balance, I could reckon on his being bound to
me, in consequence of his having assumed so sanguinely that
not only my advice, but my influence was great, connected
with the matter.

He was nevertheless exceedingly cheerful. His hopes exceeded his fears, and in this happy humour I found him, in consequence, to be exactly up to the mark for what I desired him to execute, after the lapse of a few days, during which period I had at last resolutely made up my mind as to how I should proceed, in the new field of ambition he had opened up to my view, and which I now felt a yearning desire towards, as a sort of solace for the mortification and chagrin that rent my aching heart—now rendered thoroughly desperate and hopeless by Miss Gentle's last act—and which I had persuaded myself would separate me from her for ever!

This was nothing more nor less than to go "slap-bang" into high speculation—"to make a spoon or spoil a horn" —"to draw the sword and throw away the scabbard"— to take my place, in a word, with the highest monetary magnates in the City, or to fall to the level of the lowest!

When I communicated this fact to Jackson he was quite delighted, and taking me by the hand, he congratulated me on my high resolve. "Don't despair!" he cried, "don't flinch for a moment; but go in and win!"

"In two months from this date," he continued, "money which now commands the highest rates in Lombard Street will be a perfect drug, and going a-begging. Then, will be the time for you to strike in with a galaxy of bills that will perfectly dazzle the eyes of our northern usurers. In the meantime, you must purchase your commodities; but what these should be, must be left entirely to yourself. I am not a man of manufactures or of raw materials—I study not price currents—I calculate not the relative value of production and demand—I enter not into statistics of imports, and exports—and above all, know nothing about supply or consumption, and far less regarding stocks on hand. I alone read the horoscope of the money market, and watch the passages, or eclipses of monetary stars, in so far as they influence earthly houses—even as the movements of planetary stars influence heavenly houses, if I may be allowed to use the jargon of astrologers—therefore, all I have to say, my friend, is— ponder you well on what *you* understand, and I, on the other hand, will do so on what *I* understand; and the result will assuredly be fortune to you, and satisfaction to both!"

I learned from this speech what, indeed, Jackson had before explained to me would be the case; namely, that he would not join me in any speculation, for this simple reason, that such was not his system. Nor was it reasonable to expect that he should do so. He proposed only to be my adviser—my guide — nay, more, my Chancellor of the Exchequer. What beyond that could I desire? Most go-a-head men in Glasgow had their advisers in the same way, their "writers," as they are called, to draw out their contracts; to keep them right in their bargains, to draft their important letters; thereby making up for their own deficiency in education. These writers, indeed, might be called their Lord Chancellors—the keepers of their consciences—but how much happier was not I: to possess one who combined within himself, not only the functions of that high office, but those of the more important, though humbler minister, I have named!

Jackson was now, therefore, my Lord Chancellor, my Chancellor of the Exchequer, my first secretary, my law adviser. Nay more, he was my *factotum*, and although with my usual caution, I had guarded against any real danger that might be contingent on the position I had placed myself in, and thereby assured myself, as it were, against his having a handle over me, I at the same time had no reason to doubt either his honesty or faithfulness.

My first operation was in the cotton market. At this period, that commodity—in consequence of the check speculation had received by the bank restrictions, some months before—was quite a drug in the market. To quote a broker's circular, "it was selling fifty *per cent.* below what it could be grown for." I therefore thought that I ran no great risk if I "went in" for a thousand bales, and accordingly did so. The next day, however, it went down a sixteenth of a penny a pound—a very alarming fall, under the circumstances—so to remedy that, I went in for another thousand bales, and which transaction perhaps helped to steady the market, for it was reported as bearing that character, for a couple of days, "at former quotations," and this gave me great hope, and induced me to go in for a farther thousand.

These hopes, I am happy to say, were realised. The market rose the same afternoon, a sixteenth. Next day it rose another sixteenth; and the next again an eighth: making altogether a rise of a halfpenny per pound, which, on my three thousand bales—had I realised—would have made a profit of about fifteen hundred pounds!

I did not however realise, as the sum was scarcely up to the mark that would have satisfied me; and it was as well that such was the case; for, next morning, on calling at my broker's, I was surprised and delighted to be informed that cotton in the Liverpool market had suddenly sprung up another halfpenny, in consequence of a packet-ship having arrived, which reported frosts to have occurred in the Southern States of America, and which were expected to have damaged the growing crops.

I flew to my friend Jackson, to talk over this, when he told me, that as to such circumstances having effect on the produce, and consequently on the price, I must judge for myself. All he could say was, that his advices from London, went to indicate that money again would not be easy there for some time to come, as the shipments of bullion to the continent were considerable.

I, therefore, judged that the wisest thing I could do, would be now to realise—in which decision my broker agreed with me—and I thus, within a week from the time I had commenced as a cotton speculator, coolly put into my pocket three thousand pounds, without having been required even to pay any thing to account, although I had been perfectly prepared to do so, without any financial difficulty: the balance I had at my credit in the bank, and the quantity of bills, all payable in London, that lay in my coffers, being more than sufficient to have liquidated what was required; but which the lucky promptness of the speculation rendered perfectly unnecessary.

This commencement was satisfactory, but still it was mere child's play compared with what I had made up my mind to do. It was but the preliminary rattle on the keys, or symphony, before I came down, like some of those musical Signors, with their formidable fingers, on the piano, in those fierce fantasias, that occasionally delighted our fashionable and musical gentry, of the West End.

Next day, I opened—in person: to show that I was a thoroughly business man—an account with the bank, which Jackson and I had fixed upon, as being the most eligible for doing business with, in the way he proposed, on a grand scale, when the proper time should arrive, by lodging ten thousand pounds. This had an immediate effect; for, on presenting myself with my bundles, the manager himself came out of his room to shake hands with me, and to intro-

duce me to the teller who was to receive the deposit; and after I had signed the signature book, and received my pass-book, he again shook me by the hand, while thanking me for the confidence I reposed in his bank, hoping at the same time that this "inauguration" would lead to a still more intimate acquaintanceship.

Honest man! he little dreamed how sincerely I echoed the sentiment in my own quiet way!

I may mention, however, that Jackson had previously seen him privately, to represent to him the advantage of getting such an important account as mine, and to offer his assistance in the procurement of it, as a very great favour. He likewise invited the banker to dinner, at his own house, for the purpose of introducing me to him personally—an act of kindly courtesy which the man of money showed he duly appreciated, by asking us both in return, to dine at his own

house, shortly afterwards, when, I need scarcely say, the
"spread" was magnificent.

Thus things went pleasantly on, while I watched the
markets, not only for cotton, but for any other description
of produce or material, that it might be desirable to invest
in. Prices current, I may say, were never out of my hands,
and comments upon grain, sugar, pig-iron, copper, and so on,
were more interesting and pleasant reading to me, than the
best Parliamentary speeches, or even the novels of the day.

Jackson, in the meantime, went to London for a very
necessary reason; namely, to arrange with eligible parties
for drawing upon, their principal recommendations for the
purpose being the sounds of their names, and for the use
of which he agreed to pay according to quality. Thus
the firm of Savery, Patty, & Company, although represented
by the owner of a cook shop in the Minories, was to receive
three-quarters of a per cent. on the amount drawn upon
them; while Tarleton, Lace, & Company, haberdashers,
were to receive one per cent.; and Pincher & Quid,
tobacconists, were to receive one-and-a-quarter per cent.

In all, he bargained with from fifty to sixty persons
for this useful purpose, all being of the most varied professions—from that of man-milliner, down to dogs'-meat merchant—and many of them females: the arrangement being
that they were to accept the bills that were to be drawn on
them, some in red ink, some in blue, and some in common
ink; and across, or under the drawers' name, as should be
directed!

Of course, he had considerable trouble in this commission;
for not only had he to study the handwriting of the parties,
to satisfy himself that it was business-like, but their literary
attainments, in case of grammatical errors: as well as their
habits, for fear of their soiling the paper, and thus possibly
spoil valuable stamps; for, as he suggested, "it would never
do to present to bankers, bills that were smeared with
tobacco juice, or spotted with grease, or that had a perfume
of cavendish, c'naster, or short cut returns!"

On his return, therefore, from London, things were in a
very promising way towards a real commencement, for in
addition he had consulted the money oracles, who thought
that the late panic had exhausted itself; while bullion was

slowly but surely returning to the cellars of the Bank, and
the rate of discount—in consequence of that circumstance, as
well as the restriction in trade operations generally, that had
taken place—was likely to fall.

To add to my temptation to speculate, cotton had, in the
meantime again fallen to its old price, the reports as to frosts
having injured the growing crops, having turned out to be
untrue—indeed, a speculators' hoax—though a new and care-
ful estimate of these crops, privately received, went to prove,
that their aggregate would be less than that of the year
before, by at least a hundred thousand bales.

I knew therefrom that whenever money became more plentiful, cotton was sure to go up in price, so I went in for five
thousand bales. A week after, on the mere head of the
expression "continued firmness," I went in for other five
thousand; and on the week after that, in consequence of a
rise of a sixteenth, and the lowering of discounts by half a
per cent., I further went in for an additional five thousand.
Thus I was a holder of fifteen thousand bales of cotton at
almost the lowest quoted market prices.

Shortly after this, Jackson judged that the time had come
for doing a little in the "bill way," and he judged rightly;
for the banks were complaining of the small business they
were doing, excepting in the way of receiving deposits, the
influx of which had become so great, that they had
issued a joint advertisement stating they would not allow
so much interest on these, as they had been doing, by one
per cent.

I therefore made up a batch of bills—the majority of
these being drawn on, and accepted by the parties in London,
I have already alluded to, as having been engaged for the
purpose by Jackson—in other words, "wind bills:" the residue, however, being genuine bills connected with my own
legitimate business—and with these I bent my way to my
new friend, the banker, personally to superintend the interesting process of their being melted into solid money.

The batch altogether amounted—I was going to state "in
value," but my conscience will only permit me to say "in
figures"—to upwards of thirteen thousand pounds, and they
were all duly stamped, numbered, marked as entered, and
domiciled—to use a favourite commercial expression connected

with such missives: so that they formed as pretty a little
business looking budget, as could have been desired.

Still I felt a little nervous, as I approached the bank, and
more so as I passed under its frowning portico, although
the result showed that such was an unnecessary alarm; for,
on presenting myself before the great man, he treated me
with the utmost courtesy,
and received my batch of
bills as if it had been a
presentation copy of some
delightful work, from the
perusal of which he anticipated much pleasure, in-
stead of a bundle of trash,
so gracefully did he handle
it, and so blandly did he
smile.

There was no attempt on
his part at official or affected
scrutiny; no turning over,
from front to back, of the
several bills; no humphing
and hawing; no critical
pausing. On he went, on the contrary, with the initialing
of them, as fast as his pen would allow; and, if he did make
a remark, it was most encouraging and assuring. "Scrub and
Co.," he would perhaps interject, "a capital house—know it
well. Bolus & Squill—most respectable. Sapples, Slop, and
Co.—excellent—all good bills: thanks to you for bringing
them here!"

He thus finished them off, much to his seeming satisfaction, and certainly to mine; after which, he invited me to
accompany him to the telling room, in the way to which, he
brushed aside, as though they were paupers, a lot of poor
fellows who were waiting, with their hats in their hands,
in the misgiving hope of getting their *small*, but possibly
good bills discounted, and passing on, introduced me to an
accountant, while he handed to him the bunch, saying aloud,
"London Bills—you understand!" which I took to be an
intimation that they were to be discounted at the lowest rates.
And so, with a warm shake of the hand, he left me, while I

only waited on, to get the deductions calculated, and the balance placed to my credit: after which I returned to Jackson to narrate what had passed, and to be congratulated on the success of this, my first transaction in the discounting line, while having a talk and a hearty laugh over the satisfactory way with which we had so thoroughly *done* the banker ! *

* Note 1.—Inordinate Bank accommodation. *See Appendix.*

CHAPTER XLIX.

INTRODUCTORY DOGGERELS.

"Where's your estate?"—says Dick to Nick,—
"'Tis in the shire for sport;"
"Where's your estate?"—says Nick to Dick,—
"'Tis in the Bankrupt Court!"

The Goosedubbs Poet.

IT is not my intention to afflict the patient reader who may have borne with equanimity the dry commercial particulars that have been recorded in the foregoing couple of chapters, or the impatient one, who may have wisely skipped them over, with further details of all the speculative transactions with which I essayed to arrive at the niche of ambition that I had proposed for myself.

Better far than that, would it be for me at once to give a fair transcript of my day-book in which these were all duly entered according to their dates: or of my ledger, where they were more compactly, if not so lucidly—excepting to those initiated in accountant-ship,—duly posted.

My desire, however, I protest, is to be perfectly candid and communicative: as much so, indeed, as any honest gentleman could be, who has matters of the kind to reveal, either for the satisfaction of his feelings, under the superintendence of his conscience, as

is the case with me, or for the satisfaction of his creditors,
under that of the sheriff, as might have, on the other hand,
been the case with me, had things not turned out differently,
and in such a way as to render the latter ordeal, happily for
all parties concerned, perfectly unnecessary. I will, therefore, while hoping to be forgiven for the diffuseness I have
already indulged in, attempt to atone for the crime, by giving
a mere vidimus of my subsequent transactions, although I
continue to dread that even such may be found dull enough.

Business, shortly after the period I have treated of, became
very brisk, in consequence of a revival of trade, induced by
cheap money, and bank facilities. One would have thought
that every person had thrown off his languor, and put on the
shelf his proneness to growl, which had been the characteristics of mercantile people for such a length of time previously. Factories set their steam hammers a-going again.
Mills started their engines, and whirled once more their
throstles and spinning-jennies; and all looked like a hive of
bees, busy and intent on making honey, in the sunshine that
prevailed.

The commercial news from London—in what are called
the money articles of the papers—were, likewise, most in-
spiriting; while the Board of Trade Returns showed great
increase in shipments over the same period of the former
year, and indeed, were all that could be desired.

For myself, I was over head and ears in business. I
bought and sold, and traded in everything wherein I thought
I could turn a penny;—cotton, pig-iron, sugar, grain, coffee,
tallow, tobacco, were only a few of the elements I speculated
in. I bought them in cargo and in bulk, in transit and in
store, in scrip and in warrant, and re-sold them and re-bought
them without ever seeing them, perhaps, excepting on paper.

As for bills, I was soon up to Jackson's mark in these; at
all events, to such an extent, according to his philosophy, as
made me independent of the bank, happen what might; for,
on summing up my bill-book, I found I had on the circle,
upwards of a hundred and fifty thousand pounds in amount,
and still the confidence of my banker in me appeared to be
unshaken. Once, and only once, did he venture to hint to
me that he would like if I would curtail the quantities I was
sending in, and thereby reduce the amount, if it were even

only temporarily, "just in case any disagreeable remarks should be made on the matter by his directors;" but I soon brought him to his marrow-bones for daring to perpetrate such an insult, by offering, on conditions humbling to the bank, to rebate my discount account to any amount he chose!

My good luck, it so chanced, stood by me at that critical moment, for on the very morning in question, I had received letters from two banking-houses in London, stating—merely for the sake of correctness—the balances they had at my credit, and—"as they were writing"—offering to discount any quantity of bills "similar to what I had formerly sent," that I might find it convenient now to send.

I may explain, however, that these balances were lying with the said London bankers, to meet bills which they had respectively authorised my correspondents in New Orleans and Charleston to draw against cotton shipments from thence, and were thus equal to bullion: and that the bills I had negotiated with them were genuine ones (and not "kites,") which I had got from abroad, in connection with my old legitimate business: all being accepted and payable by houses in London, as stable as themselves.

These London balances amounted, in the aggregate, to upwards of sixteen thousand pounds; but my purpose for keeping so large a sum in such a position, I, of course, kept to myself. It perfectly astonished the honest Glasgow banker; and, coupled with the offer that had been made to me to discount further—which I took care to show him—completely knocked the nail I aimed at hitting, on the head. He made a thousand apologies—offered to discount as much paper as I chose to send him—begged I would forget what he had blunderingly said—and asked me to dine with him on an early occasion, but which I declined, on the plea that I was already engaged.

But, nevertheless, the banker, after all, was doing a very good stroke of business with me, and it would have been well, if all his transactions with others had turned out as pleasantly as the ones in question did with me. The bank never lost a penny by me. Indeed, no bank did. My speculations, it is true, were vast and various. By some of these I lost heavily. By others I made nothing : but, on the whole, I did well; for, on balancing my books at the end of the year, and after allowing a fair margin, for any risks on unsettled accounts that possibly might accrue, I found I could congratulate myself on being a man worth—I like to be correct and particular—no less a sum, in the aggregate, than £115,795. 7s. 2½d!

I am free to confess that I made the bulk of this magnificent residue, not by means of my own, but by those of other people—by a borrowed capital in short. I will not even deny that if I had possessed such a sufficiency of capital of my own, as would have enabled me to go into the speculations I did venture upon, and which led to this wealth, I would not have done so. As a proof of this prudent, but selfish fact, the moment I had struck my balance, and commenced to realise in my mind, as a fact, the substantial circumstance that I was worth upwards of a hundred thousand pounds—although, when in the fever of my speculative career, I contemplated such an amount as nothing—I began to shrink from the idea of imperiling it. To be plain, I could sport with the means of the capitalist—with the savings of the industrious—with the pittance of the widow—with the portion of the orphan—but I could not afford to do so, with what I now considered as my own moderate, respectable, but solid little fortune !

The more I turned over these considerations in my mind, the more determined I became to realise, and particularly as I saw others, who had been going on in a like career of dangerous adventure to that I myself had been indulging in—but without being fortified by the philosophical instructions of a Jackson—figuring in the *Gazette*, and becoming the talk of the town.

I therefore went to Jackson, shortly after this, to communicate how well I had done, and, at the same time, to express my resolution *now*, to become cautious and prudent.

In so doing, I was not without dread that he would disapprove of the step I proposed. That he would look upon me as "henning," and that, in consequence, he would deprecate the idea, and persuade me to go on as I had been formerly doing. For I may whisper in the ear of the reader, whom I am now making my *confidante*, that I had still a lurking suspicion that his friendship, after all, might have been simulated, and that his real aim in showing me so much favour, might have been—like that of the Evil One in patronising his victims—to lead me into a labyrinth of difficulties, and there leave me floundering and undone!

I only state this to show what commercial gratitude sometimes amounts to, and how sinisterly one mercantile man may view the actions of another, even though these should have been the making of him. I could point out many men who have been nursed into riches, by friendships like what I have alluded to, who now cut their *quondam* patrons on the streets — yea! I could point to a poor "done-up" banker that still exists—perhaps starves in self-imposed exile, and who continues to be banned and execrated, as much by those who owe their success in life to the monetary facilities he extended to them, in his halcyon days, as by those who were the actual sufferers from his mismanagement, and have a right thereby to growl at him!

If but a small subscription, for his behoof, were got up by the former, who really owe him, at least, a memorial, the *pauvre diable* might be comfortable for the residue of his unhappy life. But will such a thing be forthcoming?

To that question I fear the answer will be nay!—for although there may be some, who have a sneakingly grateful sort of remembrance of his "saving qualities," it might hurt their credit to acknowledge these. However:—

> "When Nero perished by the justest doom,
>   That ever the avenger did inflict,
>   Some hand, unseen, placed flowers upon his tomb"—

and so, when our poor friend is dead, he may obtain a few *immortelles* from those I have alluded to. In the meantime, the garland that has been wrought for him, savours more of hemlock and hemp, than of oaken leaves and laurel!

But, on reaching Jackson, I found I had been doing him gross injustice, even as had been the case with me, on former occasions; for, so far from being adverse to my acting as I proposed, he highly approved of the same, and indeed urged me to take certain steps towards the consummation of my views, beyond even what I considered necessary myself.

"Had you been in the same position as a capitalist," he said, "when we first laid our heads together, in friendly confidence, to what you are now—or rather will be, when you have fairly realised—instead of pointing out to you how you could finance, I would rather have suggested how you might have invested. The latter measure, however, I then left to your own judgment, because I saw that, as a mercantile man, you had a knowledge of what could be done with certain commodities, at a certain period, although with risk, that would enable you more quickly to reach the desired goal, than by any thing I could point out, and your success confirms the truth of my judgment thereon. Now, however, that you have something to lose—that is, something of such an extensive bulk, that one could never forgive himself for committing such an error as losing it would amount to—it is my duty as a friend, to applaud and confirm you in the prudent and safe steps you propose to take."

Mr. Jackson then went on to point out a number of investments that he could safely recommend for the safety of the comfortable fortune I now possessed, ranging from government and municipal bonds, down to railway debentures and local securities; but, on my remarking that he had not mentioned joint-stock bank shares, which I thought he most naturally would have suggested, in consequence of the attention he had paid to the working of such institutions, he burst into a loud laugh.

"No, no! my friend," he cried, "these are the last things I would advise any one, I have an interest in, to endanger his means, by purchasing. Banks are all very well to deal with, when you have a purpose to serve; but when you have attained that purpose, avoid them, as you would a pestilence, or a trap! They pay good dividends to be sure, but for good dividends read bad security!"

"But, what would you think," he went on musingly to say, "of trying the best of all investments, where security is an object, as it now must be with you—namely, land? It is true that the return from this description of investment is small, but it is sure, and though we are threatened with a repeal of the corn laws, which some people think will considerably hurt the value of land, though I don't, have we not the railways to make up for that twenty-fold, by causing what is distant to become near, or in other words, by transporting, as it were, our corn fields into the hearts of our cities, and our cities into the midst of our corn fields?"

I confess, I rather liked this last suggestion of Jackson, particularly as it entirely harmonised with a little piece of latent vanity that, for a long time, had reposed in my bosom, and which had caused me to indulge in many a dreamy resolution to gratify, when the ambitious views I had of making a fortune, came to be realised. To have a landed estate—to be a laird—to be esquire of so and so—I indeed looked upon as forming the *summum bonum* of human grandeur, and worthy of all the toil I could undergo, and all the risk I could run, in mastering so desirable an attainment.

"Well, then," said Jackson, when I had communicated the substance of these ideas to him—"that being the case, let us give the matter immediate attention. Already, I am primed with something that promises to meet your requirements, and regarding which, months ago I thought of speaking to you."

"Look here," he continued, as he drew from one of his drawers a small map, "this is a sketch, showing a short line of railway, which it is proposed shall be made to connect the main line, lying betwixt this city and Drumfiddle, with the upper district of Stratharden. Now, if this line goes on, as I have every reason to believe it will, it will open up a large mineral district, and render several estates, that lie on its banks, worth double the value they now possess, in conse-

quence of the facilities it will afford for bringing to market,
not only the agricultural elements they now produce on their

surfaces, but the coal,
lime, and iron-stone
they may have in
their bosoms, and
which, as yet, have
never been worked,
in consequence of the
very want of convey-
ances, which will now
be supplied by the
proposed railway."

The district indicat-
ed by Jackson lay in
a contiguous county,
about forty miles dis-
tant from Glasgow.
It possessed several
estates that were at the time in the market, and which
were duly advertised, so as to attract the attention of capital-
ists. The estate, however, that Jackson regarded with the
most favourable eye, was a joint one, or rather a batch of
estates, called Stratharden and Lammerlee, and, according
to the advertisement, possessing considerable pictorial beauty,
along with great crop-producing qualities, while the purchase-
money was moderate, considering the improvement it was
capable of attaining, with the outlay of a little additional
capital, in the way of drainage.

"This estate," said Jackson, "which I find belongs to an
all but ruined nobleman, I have already been inquiring about
for a client, who, however, finds it is beyond his mark,
the price being ninety thousand pounds. What do you say
to turn your attention towards it, if the amount does not
fear you?"

Mr Jackson then went on to tell, that he had seen it himself, though cursorily, but so far as that went, he was much
pleased with it. If the railway went on, he said, it would
run through a portion of it, and thereby, though adding to
its value, subject the promoters of the line to a heavy com-
pensation that, when paid, would greatly reduce the pur-

chase-money, while, at the same time, a station would require to be formed at the town of Stratharden, that would be enormously convenient to the proprietor. However, as to all these little particulars, and a great many more, he thought the best way to ascertain them, would be for us to pay a personal visit to the spot, and judge for ourselves; and if I would undertake this at an early day, he would have much pleasure in accompanying me, as thereby it would be combining business with pleasure.

I readily agreed to this proposition of Jackson, and a day being fixed, we separated, he being in great glee, in consequence of having, that morning, in addition to the delight he anticipated from the proposed excursion, had a most gratifying interview with Miss M'Chuckie—as he informed me in the strictest confidence—when that young lady had accepted from him a similar and additional bracelet to the one he had already bestowed, and this time without any prudish stipulations. "Not only so," added Jackson, while he rubbed his hands with glee, and skipped about, while dancing and making antics, "but she actually—would you believe it?—allowed me to snatch a kiss!"

CHAPTER L.

INTRODUCTORY DOGGERELS.

> Where are the knights and mail-clad hordes,
>   Of Scotia's ancient chivalry?
> Where are the high and mighty lords,
>   That formed her old nobility?
>
> All gone—or going—to the dogs:
>   Naught left but their gentility;
> While usurers and wealthy rogues,
>   Form now a new nobility!
>
> *The Goosedubbs Poet.*

It was upon a beautiful spring morning that Jackson and I, fortified with our respective carpet bags, railway wrappers, and silk umbrellas, took our seats in a first-class com-

partment of the 11.45. A.M. train for Drumfiddle: from thence to be conveyed to the town, or rather village of

Stratharden, which lay at a distance of some ten miles from said station—by a neat *"po-shay"* that had been ordered to be waiting for us, on our arrival there.

Jackson was in an uncommon flow of spirits, in consequence of the success of his love suit, demonstrated as that in his estimation had been, by the reward he had obtained from his sweetheart—as divulged in the concluding portion of last chapter—although I thought it was but a moderate return for a couple of bracelets, which had cost him as many hundreds of pounds. I could not but marvel indeed, that a man who was so well up to the value of investments, should have been so easily contented with the meagre interest he was receiving in this case.

That, however, was perhaps not a fair way of reasoning. Had I judged of Jackson's satisfaction by what I myself might have been disposed to accept in the same way—had I been successful—I would possibly have approached nearer to the true mark.

Leaving that to the fates, however, we rattled away in the post-chaise, admiring the beauty of the country we were passing through, till we arrived at Stratharden betwixt the hours of three and four o'clock, when we found a gentleman waiting for us, whom Mr. Jackson had apprised by post of our coming, and had desired to be doing so—namely, one Mr. Job Stapfurrow, a very important person in the district: he being by trade and occupation, in the town of Stratharden, something betwixt an auctioneer and a land measurer, and perhaps a bit of lawyer to the bargain, or, more properly speaking, partaking to all these three professions together, and even a great many more.

Mr. Stapfurrow was a man betwixt the age of fifty and sixty, but he looked older from the way he dressed, for he wore a worsted wig and a woolly beaver hat, while his body habiliments indicated that they were of the home manufacture of the place, —at least as far as I could judge by a survey of them—from the coarse friese coat that covered his upper man, to the hodden-grey stockings and tacketty shoes that protected his lower extremities; while to shelter all from the weather, he carried under his arm, a bulky old-fashioned cotton umbrella.

He was, however, what is called in that district a "sicker body," very cautious in what he said, and inclined to be reserved in conversation, but when he did speak, it was to the purpose.

Jackson had, it appeared, engaged Mr. Stapfurrow to guide us in our inquiries, in regard to the estate of Stratharden and Lammerlee, he being, as he said, up to its agricultural value, from having, for the last thirty years, been engaged in measuring its surface, for the purpose of estimating growing crops, which he afterwards exposed at auction, when he invariably was appointed the undisputed umpire on the occasion, in case of any misunderstandings taking place betwixt the bidders.

Our experience of Mr. Stapfurrow's abilities did not belie Jackson's judgment. He remained with us to dine: a very neat little repast in that way having been got up at an hour's notice for us, at the "Stratharden Arms," the only hotel in the village, and where we engaged a pleasant parlour for the afternoon, and comfortable bed-rooms for the night.

Mr. Stapfurrow, it is true, was rather dry at first. He seemed to have a disinclination to draw in his chair to the table, which was painful to us. He laid down his knife and fork, too, after putting food in his mouth, across his plate, and placing his hands on his knees proceeded to munch as though he had been hired for the job; and he eyed his glass of sherry askance and with suspicion, while partaking of it in driblets, and as though it had been poison.

To help this state of matters if possible, Jackson ordered a bottle of champagne, and the effect was most gratifying. On Boniface making his appearance with the long-necked bottle—for of course on such an occasion no one but a land-lord could presume to remove the wax and untwist the wire —the old man seemed to be completely filled with awe, and on the cork springing to the roof, and the sparkling liquid being poured out, his eyes flashed with delight. "Ah!" he exclaimed, after he had gulped the first glassful over his

throat, "and this is champin'?—aweel it's grand stuff! I
never tasted it before, even when I hae dined wi' Lord
Stratharden; for ye maun ken he's no haughty, although
properly proud, and will often insist on my taking something
with him, when I'm about the place. Od! but ye Glasgow
gentry are great folk, when ye can afford to indulge in what
even our nobility grudge to themselves! I don't think
there's such a thing as a bottle of champin' in a' Lammerlee
Keep, or even ever was in Invergray Castle, afore it was
brunt and deserted!"

"Aye," said Jackson, as he ordered the old gentleman's
glass to be replenished, in order to keep his tongue a-going,
"I suppose money is not so plentiful with the barons of
Stratharden and Lammerlee, as it used to be in the olden
days, when they made their fountains run with claret and
canary?"

"Alas! no," replied Mr. Stapfurrow, "things are wonderfully changed since then; and not only with our lord, but
with others throughout the country. Our nobility, in fact,
are nobility only in name. They hae nae power, and even
on their estates, ane wad think that a wheen Embro' writers
reign in their stead!"

Jackson, who in the meantime had been making the
bottle circulate, and had, in particular, paid great attention
to the wants of Mr. Stapfurrow, who, however he might be

chary of sherry, had seemingly no misgivings as to champagne; for he did not remonstrate against another bottle being ordered, nor object to his glass being replenished therefrom, again and again. Jackson, I beg to say, here began a long categorical chain of questioning at the said Mr. Stapfurrow, who having now thrown off his taciturnity, seemed to take a pleasure in answering, while I certainly did so in hearkening.

His queries were numerous and varied, and though, of course, all about the estate that has been named, and its proprietor, not very regular: for he jumped from one subject to another, as his whim dictated; from the state of the drainage that existed on the mound, to the minerals that were cropping out in the glen; from the farmers' rents, to the minister's stipend; and from the public burdens on the lands, to the private income of the landlord.

From the answers to these pertinent queries, I was led to infer that the gentleman, or rather nobleman, who held that distinctive position, was not in the most comfortable pecuniary circumstances, and that, indeed, he was fast approaching the unhappy climacteric, when, if he did not leave the estates, the estates would leave him, notwithstanding the fact that he rejoiced in the aristocratic appellations of Richard, Henry, Charles, Plantagenet, Tudor, Stuart, Baron of Stratharden and Invergray, and held in his veins the blood of the royal houses, indicated by these names, in virtue of being collaterally descended, through a long and unbroken line of ancestry, from the union of Margaret Tudor, daughter of Henry VII of England, with James of Scotland, in 1503.

I likewise learned from the brisk conversation that was carried on betwixt Mr. Jackson and Mr. Stapfurrow, that Lord Stratharden had principally been brought to this melancholy pass, through bad health, which had forced him to relinquish an office he held connected with the House of Lords, he being one of the representative peers of Scotland, which, though moderately remunerative, had been of the utmost moment to him, considering that his estates were heavily burdened, and, therefore, after paying interest, left little or nothing in the shape of a residue to him. Indeed, over and above, he was considerably in debt, and to liquidate the same, and save a small sum, wherewith to procure an annuity, he was willing to part with the estates for the sum that had been named, with the exception of the superiority over Stratharden and Invergray, which he was desirous to retain if possible, in consequence of holding from these his titles.

"Ye see," said Mr Stapfurrow, as he brought his information to a conclusion, "he's a proud man—a wonnerfu' proud man, indeed—although a real gentleman, and therefore hau'ds on to this sma' exception like grim death, although the value of it is nothing, or but a trifle at best. But for it, he could have sold the estates twenty times over ; for the rich folk that hae looked at them, hae been most numerous. However," he continued by way of encouraging me not to be intimidated thereby, as the other rich people that he had alluded to, had been, "he's willing to part with Lammerlee, without this exception, seeing that no title is attached to it, though such was once the case, but it did not descend to heirs female, as those of Stratharden and Invergray do ; and, therefore, a purchaser through it, will obtain a' the county honours he can desire, if on sic like nonsense he sets his heart !"

"But I'll tell you what," he concluded, " the best thing you can do, is to see Lord Stratharden himsel', and hae a crack wi' him on the subject. He's bien and weel now, and can walk about wi' a stick, instead o' a stilt, as was only the case a month ago. Ye needna' be afraid o' seeing his lordship—he's wonnerfu' come-at-able, and will be glad to have an interview with you, whether it leads to business or not !"

Both Jackson and I thought this an excellent proposal, and, therefore, adopted it at once, particularly as Mr Stapfurrow undertook to see Lord Stratharden that evening, he being entitled to put himself in communication with his lordship in this way at any time—in consequence of being referred to in the advertisements as one who would show the estates, and furnish what particulars were wanted—and apprise him that he would be waited upon by us next forenoon.

Mr Stapfurrow accordingly, after fortifying himself with a glass of whisky, which he seemed to take more kindly to than either port or sherry, left for the purpose, while Jackson

and I, having nothing particular to do, killed the evening
with a walk, in the course of which we took a good survey
of the estates, without intruding upon any privacy pertaining
thereto, too closely. We were much gratified, however, with
what of them we saw, and found they bore out, so far as we
could judge, all that had been said in their favour by Mr
Stapfurrow, so that when I retired to my couch, after agreeing
with Jackson that we would not stickle about the terms
demanded, I all but felt myself to be the Laird of these fair
lands, *vice* my Lord Stratharden!

Next forenoon, after breakfast, we were again waited upon
by Mr. Stapfurrow, who came to announce that Lord
Stratharden would be ready to receive us forthwith; so away
we went, duly ushered by that important personage, who, as
we walked along, pointed out all the important features, and
bounderies, and marches of the estates, his talk being, at the
same time, of the "craps," the pasturages, the fallows, the
trenchings, the rotation of crops, and so on, which the
several farmers who cultivated these beautiful fields were
bound by their leases to follow out, and which having been
arranged under his superintendence, were of course the very
best that could have been fixed upon.

We, in a short time, having left the main road and
diverged to the left, found ourselves in an avenue, which in
ancient times had been guarded, at its entrance, by a noble

gateway, and a couple of porters' lodges, in the shape of towers, but all of which were now in a ruinous state, the former—which was still capped by lions *couchant*: the same representing the crest of the family—having been denuded of its massive doors—while a simple rough paling was substituted—and the latter being roofless and tenantless. The gateway, indeed, formed a fitting illustration of what we had learned regarding the former glory and present ruined position of the poor lord, who feebly clung to the broad acres it still pretended to guard.

The avenue, however, was beautiful and winding; and at many points presented remarkably fine vistas, one of which revealed in the distance a pretty old tower, with an addition attached to it in the shape of a more modern wing, which stood on the edge of a wooded dell, through which the little river Arden flowed meanderingly and beautifully, according as it met on its way to the ocean, peninsular or rocky resistances and interruptions, all of which, however, added much to its varied charms.

This tower, as Mr. Stapfurrow informed us, was called Lammerlee Keep, and in it, and its adjunct, Lord Stratharden resided, it being the only habitable mansion on the estate, although there were several others of a much grander and extensive description, but all of which were now in ruins.

As we neared the Keep, I proposed to Jackson that he alone should accompany Mr. Stapfurrow to Lord Stratharden's presence, as a preliminary to my being introduced to

him, if such should be ultimately necessary; for, to tell the
truth, I felt some delicacy in approaching the poor man on
such a business as we were about, namely, that of divesting
him of his property, while Jackson had no such hesitation,
treating as he did the affair as a mere business matter.

This proposal Jackson approved of, so leaving him and
Stapfurrow to go right on to the portal, I struck aside, and
falling upon an old track, I carried on till I came to the
back of the tower that overlooked the dell, and from which
sprang up some noble trees, on whose tops there was a
rookery, the black inhabitants of which, now all busy with
the construction of their nests, croaked in pleasant though
monotonous harmony, that added much to the solemnity and
loneliness, if not melancholy dulness, of the scene.

The old tower, and supplemental wing on this side had
several small windows, and in particular—pertaining to the
latter portion of the building—an oriel window, commanding
a magnificent view of the glen and surrounding country, one
of the sashes of which I observed was open, probably in consequence of the weather being more genial and warm than
usual, considering the early season of the year.

As I stood admiring the scene, I was startled by hearing
sounds proceeding from the open sash, which revealed that
some one occupied the apartment, and that one a female; for

they were evidently the tinklings of a spinnet, or, at the best, those of a very old and wire-drawn piano, whose best days were long past, although its notes were still in tune, strictly speaking. Its tones, however, contrasted sadly with what I had been accustomed to hear, and compared alone, with those of the instrument on which Jackson's adored one, Miss M'Chuckie, was accustomed to thump, was, in my mind, almost ridiculous.

This disadvantage, however, was compensated otherwise; for these feeble tinklings were accompanied by a melodious, though not strong voice, that sweetly warbled a song, the concluding stanzas of which—being all that it was my good fortune to hear—were to the following effect:—

> "The Spring brings forth its buds and flowers,
>   The birds crowd ilka tree ;
> The earth drinks up the balmy showers,
>   That fall on Lammerlee.

> "But never more within its dell,
>   The Spring's return I'll see,
> For I must bid a last farewell
>   To bonnie Lammerlee !"

I was rivetted to the spot by what I heard, while a number of ideas rushed through my mind, engendered by these simple lays, and that modest voice, which evidently pertained to one that did not dream any person heard her, for, on the conclusion of the song, silence ensued, varied only by some farther tinklings of the old instrument, that indicated a vain attempt to make it more musical. I, therefore, moved on, fearing that, if discovered, I would be looked upon as an eavesdropper, and it was well that I did so; for, on turning the corner of the tower, which brought me to its eastern side, I observed Jackson and Stapfurrow, accompanied by an old and feeble gentleman, leaning upon the arm of the land measurer, while with the other he used a staff to support his tottering gait, and whom, as he approached, Jackson, as it were by deferential signs, introduced to me.

This gentleman, of course, proved to be, as his noble and affable appearance indicated, Lord Stratharden; but what was my agreeable surprise, when, at the same time, I discovered in him, an old acquaintance: he being no other than

the gentleman who had, on my visit to the House of Lords,
some years previously—as has been duly narrated—kindly
piloted me from the House, after the breaking up of the
debate, and whom I had subsequently seen at the St. Paul's
Coffee-House, on his occasionally dining there, when I made
a sort of passive and silent coffee-room acquaintanceship with
him, which ended in my snobbishly offering him pecuniary
assistance—the remembrance of the polite but dignified de-
clination of which, had often given me great pain.

He now, however, put an end to the false impression that,
it seemed, I had adopted, by at once, after recognising me
and kindly shaking me by the hand, referring to the circumstance, which he was pleased to say he considered one of
the kindest things he had ever met with in the course of his
life, and which he had often thought of, whilst fearing that
he had not evinced sufficient gratitude for the disinterested
offer.   " Ah! my young friend," he exclaimed, " generosity on
the part of others, at the time, had been such a stranger to
me, that I was quite taken aback by the ingenuous disposition you then displayed, to one so thoroughly unknown to
you, as I must have been, and who had no claim upon you,
unless it was, that you discovered in my tongue a touch of
my native doric, which, in spite of the length of time I have

lived in England, will occasionally betray my nationality, and therefore felt your sympathies enlisted towards a brother Scot. Heaven knows!" he continued, "it was not pride that induced me to decline that fair offer; but I hope that proper principle, which should always incline one rather to starve than accept what possibly he could never repay, and which was actually the case then, as I was very poor—indeed, as I still am—a circumstance which it would be idle in me to attempt to conceal, seeing that the purport of my now meeting with you again, amounts to an admission of what all the world is at last perfectly acquainted with!"

I felt really affected, and indeed so did Jackson, and certainly Mr. Stapfurrow—who rubbed his eyes and sniftered a little—by this frank and at the same time dignified admission of the aged nobleman, but which being perceived by him, he attempted to remedy, by gaily—or at all events as gaily as he could—going on to say, "But it is perhaps as well after all, that it should be so. The world would stand still if changes did not take place, and as it happens that at this eventful period the necessity of these changes, with my fortunes, present themselves in a way that cannot be resisted, what should I do but submit, with proper humility and obedience, to a Gracious Providence that rules over every thing, and designs all for the best. A new qualification of greatness is springing up around us—a fresh aristocracy is rising in the land—a youthful nobility is being inaugurated in the realm—it is incompatible then, that old worn-out greatness, and bygone aristocracy, and senile nobility should remain! No! it cannot be—our day has gone by—we have 'like the poor player, strutted and fretted our hour upon a stage, and now we must go down for ever!'"

"But permit me," he yet went on to say, after a moment's pause, "my dear young friend—for I will take the liberty of addressing you as that, in virtue of the friendship which you once evinced towards me—to take your arm, while I conduct you to my house—and, thank God! I have still a house over my head—for it is not meet that we should stand thus outside, although the day is warm and balmy, and you so near my hall-door."

Lord Stratharden accordingly transferred himself from Mr. Stapfurrow to me, not, however, without a bland explanation to that gentleman, that my being his old friend, and as it were his guest, should be held as his excuse for doing so.

We then moved round to the front of the tower, and entering a low door, whose sides displayed formidable shot holes, that had formed a mode of defence in ancient days, we found ourselves in a narrow lobby that conducted to a spiral or cork-screw staircase, which again led to an apartment on the first storey of the modern part of the building, and which appeared to be the dining-room, if I might judge from the style of its several articles of furniture, which were all old, ricketty, and worn-out, but at the same time neatly arranged, scrupulously clean, and well burnished, so far as "elbow-grease" could make them so.

Compared, however, with the splendid furnishings of my friend Mr. Tweel's dining-room, in St. Blythswood Terrace, or even with those of my own, "oh! what a falling off was there"—what a feeble-looking and thin-legged table—what crazy though high-backed chairs—what a sprawling though bright grate—what spindle shanked fire-irons: shining as though they had been rubbed, till they looked wire-drawn—what a worm-eaten sideboard—what a threadbare and faded Turkey carpet!

Still there was comfort in the old apartment, and though the roof was low, and the walls covered with dark oak-panelling, relieved but dimly by some old family portraits of severe-looking armour-clad warriors, and bewigged and ermined lawyers and statesmen, thus proving that the House of Stratharden had contributed, in its day, to the army, the bar, and the senate, it had a wonderfully genteel appearance, for it had nothing savouring of the hotel, or the steamboat cabin about it, which Mr. Tweel's grand *sal à manger* certainly had.

There had likewise been considerable neatness displayed in the arrangement of some faded draperies, which were disposed around the room, and over the tables and couches, shabby though they were, with little pieces of knitted and sewed work here and there, as well as *bouquets* of spring flowers at several points, all of which showed that a tasteful female hand superintended the household.

Lord Stratharden having invited us to take seats, at once entered into business, by informing us that he was aware of what we had come about, having had the same intimated to him the evening before, by his friend and agent, Mr. Stapfurrow, and as he knew we were thoroughly business men, he expressed a hope that we would use no delicacy in putting what questions we deemed necessary to him, regarding the property, and any matters relative thereto.

Thus invited, Jackson at once commenced with some rather pertinent queries, which, although they made me blush, his lordship answered in the fairest and most straightforward manner.

At last, the delicate part of the negotiation came to be spoken of, namely, the price; and Lord Stratharden having named the same sum that had been stated in the preliminary correspondence which had taken place, as that which he still stuck to, I began to hope that what at last had become far from being agreeable to me, would come to an end, seeing that I had instructed Jackson, the night before, to at once close with it.

In this, however, I found I was mistaken, for Jackson, in the true spirit of a lawyer, who was determined to do the best he could for his client, scouted the demand rather rudely, while attempting to depreciate the estimates that had been submitted, as well as the many advantages connected with such a purchase, that had been pointed out.

I rather feared that this would have discomposed Lord Stratharden—Jackson's display of zeal having been so different to what had been displayed on the part of his lordship —candour and fair dealing being markedly the latter's characteristics.

Lord Stratharden, however, lost not his equanimity: on the contrary, he appeared to become more polite and reconciling than ever. "I cannot gainsay," he said, "the perfect propriety of your endeavouring to make the hardest bargain you can with me, but, on the other hand, I hope you will concede to me a reciprocal action. The fact is," he continued, "I am rather hemmed in, in my position as a seller, for the margin betwixt the amount for which the estates are liable in bonds, and the sum I ask, is all that I have to depend upon for my future support, and that being small, I am, as it were, compelled by a dire necessity to be firm. I might, perhaps, if hardly pressed, rather than break off this negotiation, and after looking into matters, and seeing how ends may meet, be induced—indeed I may say, compelled—to concede a hundred, or a hundred and fifty pounds—for in this out-of-the-way county, we country people still deal in 'luck's-pennies'—but even small sums being now matters of moment to me, I fear I dare not say more; much as I respect your client, and fain as I am to favour him."

I was greatly touched by this speech, and expected that Jackson would have been likewise so, for the sum the poor nobleman spoke of, as being of such moment to him, was in reality—and Jackson, likewise, knew this right well— nothing to me; but to my perfect horror, the manikin would go on, with his gratuitous zeal for my interest, while my very head swam, and my indignation arose.

At last I became wrought up to such a degree, that I could stand it no longer, and therefore determined to interfere—out of order, and perhaps out of courtesy too, though such conduct might be to Jackson, as my agent—for I had, with my usual commercial 'cuteness, by this time seen exactly the position of poor Lord Stratharden, and it may be, at the same time, a way of reconciling all difficulties connected with the matter on hand—aye, and difficulties beyond that, best known to myself, but of which more anon!

"Lord Stratharden!" I therefore said, while addressing

that nobleman, "if Mr. Jackson will permit me to speak, seeing that as yet, I have not interfered in this matter, and where, perhaps, he will allow, I have some little interest in, and right to do so, I will bring it at once to an easy issue, by making to, instead of receiving from you, a proposal, and it is simply this:—That *you* will act in this affair, both for me and for yourself, as becomes an honest and upright man: as I have perfectly satisfied myself you are. That you, in a word, shall receive from me the amount you have named, and which I am perfectly prepared to place in your hands when required—or even more, if it be necessary, —to be appropriated entirely as you shall see meet: for the redemption of the debt on the estates: for the procurement for yourself, what you desire in the way of an income: and, in short, for the re-establishment of yourself in independence and the enjoyment of your lands; and in return for this, all I ask is, that you will covenant to me proper assurance for the advance, either in the shape of revocable mortgage, in the usual way; reversionary investment in the estate to take effect at your death; or repayment of the monies otherwise, when such period arrives, according as our arrangement shall prescribe. I will leave the whole matter to yourself: all I have, in conclusion, to assert, being, that while placing myself unreservedly in your hands, I am perfectly candid and sincere in what I say and offer!"

As I said this—without looking at Jackson, who for aught I knew might have thought it nothing but an ebulition of insanity: for to tell the truth I felt as though I were in a sort of frenzy at the time—I arose, and seizing my hat, indicated that I would retire to give Lord Stratharden time to digest the proposal which had been made. The noble lord, however, arrested me in this movement, for he likewise rose, and seemingly affected by my unexpected offer, even to the loss of speech for the moment, threw himself into my arms, while the tears flowed fast from his eyes, and on to the very lapels of my coat. "My dear and generous young friend," he at last exclaimed in broken and sobbing sentences, "how shall I express my sense of the munificence you now display towards one who has so little claim upon your friendship, or indeed on that of any one? How shall I be sufficiently grateful for—how can I ever repay such disinterested kindness?"

But what he would further have added was arrested by the
approach of some one, whose progress was indicated by the
sound of hurried steps, moving along a passage that lay on the
other side of the wainscoat, and who was possibly hastened
and alarmed by what was passing, for Lord Stratharden's
"big manly voice" now broken and uncontrolled, and therefore "turning again towards childish treble"—in consequence
of his emotion—might have led any one to suppose that he
had suddenly become indisposed.

A moment more passed, and the door flew open, while a
lady rushed hastily into the appartment, and towards the old
gentleman, exclaiming at the same time, "my uncle!—my
dear uncle!   Alas! have these fearful spasms returned
again?"

That lady was Miss Gentle!

CHAPTER LI.

INTRODUCTORY DOGGERELS.

Sweet is our first and youthful love,—
Accepted when declared,—
But sweeter the long-cherished love,
Of which we have despaired.

The Goosedubbs Poet.

My friend Jackson was seemingly struck with surprise by the unexpected visitation of Miss Gentle. I myself certainly was not; and for the simple reason—which I am bound to divulge in this book of confession and penitence—that I had already, in commercial phraseology, "discounted" in my own mind, the contingency. To be plain, I had, with the acuteness of a lover—and who are more intensely so, than "your" disappointed ones?—become assured, perfectly to my own satisfaction, that the melodious, and to my partially inclined ear, the beautiful and charming voice, that accompanied the notes of the old cracked spinnet or piano, which I had heard under the open window, was no other than that of the one individual—of all in the world beside—to whom my heart and soul were knit, with a sincerity and intensity that nothing could exceed: no, not even the attachment of Mr. Jasper Jackson to Miss M'Chuckie, and that is saying much: with a love, in short, inexhaustible and undiminished—notwithstanding the many engrossing and commercial transactions I had lately been engaged in—and rendered all the more ardent, that it was seemingly hopeless, and the object of it beyond my ken, as well as my reach.

To say that I would have given half my fortune for the possession of such a gem, as I had at last brought myself to estimate Miss Gentle as being, by dint of contemplation, and reasoning against reason: as lovers in all ages, and at all ages, will indulge in: would be saying nothing. Indeed, I really believe I would have given *all*, if by that I could have attained the purpose, and been contented—for the prize thus gained—to have toiled as a clerk, or slaved as a porter!

Of course, I am speaking of what my desperation really could have driven me to, had I actually been placed in an extremity, that would have forced me to make an unredeemable election, one way or other: not of a still-born sentiment, that, like a moon-struck and love-lorn suitor, I would have preferred to put in practice. No, no! love in a cottage, or in a garret, or in some undefined place, known only to such an extremist as Lord Byron, when he exclaims—

> " Oh! that the desert were my dwelling place,
>   With one fair spirit for my minister,—
> That I might all forget the human race,
>   And hating no one, love but only her!"

is all very well, if you can do no better; but it is much more preferable, if such gratuitous and disagreeable difficulties, connected with lodgings of so ill-furnished a nature, can be got over, and no sacrifice be required to be made after all!

This confession, too, will perhaps be considered as a reasonable explanation of the unexpected and munificent offer I had made to Lord Stratharden; for, compared to giving up the half of my fortune, let alone the whole of it—as I have hinted I might have been induced to do—for the obtaining of such a prize as Miss Gentle, it was a very cheap and economical procedure, towards the aim I had in view.

To be sure, Jackson not being in my secret, considered that I had fairly lost my senses on the occasion, and tried to persuade me afterwards to qualify some portions of my offer, and to modify others; but I was inexorable. I had left the matter, I said, to the discretion and honour of Lord Stratharden, and would abide by the result of his decision, whatever that might be: the only management connected with the matter that I would allow to Jackson, being the arrangement and engrossing of the bargain, in legal phraseology and proper form, after it was fixed, and which he was well fitted to do, as a lawyer and property conveyancer of considerable experience.

It was after expressing deliberately these terms for the second time—the latter being in the presence of Miss Gentle, to whom the cause of Lord Stratharden being so nervously affected, and which at first she supposed had been in consequence of a sudden return of his illness, had been explained to her—that I left Lammerlee Keep, and returned with Jackson to the village inn, where we proposed to remain till next day, so as to give Lord Stratharden twenty-four hours to make up his mind as to what he would elect, in regard to the proposed arrangement about his estates, and which we feared would barely prove a sufficient period of time, for such an important purpose. But scarcely had we reached the Stratharden Arms, and before we had time to order dinner, it being yet early in the forenoon, I received a note from his lordship—brought by a boy

who rode a pony—to say that he had come to a conclusion on the matter, which he thought would please all parties, and this he wished to divulge to us, as soon as possible, for which purpose he begged we would return to the Keep, and remain afterwards to dine with him.

This promptitude on Lord Stratharden's part, I thought, boded good, and therefore I proposed that Jackson should immediately take the pony and return to him, leaving the boy to walk, while I would follow deliberately, and be with them, by the time they had drawn up the minutes of agreement on the subject, which, of course, there could be no dispute about; for as I said to Jackson on his leaving me, over and over again:—"Whatever his lordship proposes to be done, *must* be done, without remonstrance or reservation, of any kind!"

I, however, experienced some surprise, as I approached the Keep again, to observe Jackson coming to meet me, and to tell me that Lord Stratharden's proposal actually beat mine in generosity; that his terms, in a word, exhibited so much liberality, and even simplicity of character, that, lawyer though Jackson was, and keen as any business man should be, who had the interest of his client at heart—he had not had the conscience to minute the said terms, till he had seen me on the subject, as he was sure I would never agree to them, unless they were made more in consonance with his lordship's interest!

This, of course, was a thing, under such pleasing circumstances, that could be very easily remedied, and, therefore, with one stroke of my pen, or rather pencil, I altered figures that made the arrangement in Lord Stratharden's favour a very different thing to what he was disposed to have been satisfied with; while, at the same time, my own position remained in the matter, very fair and very satisfactory, all things properly and deliberately being considered, from certain points of view, which there is no use in entering upon here.

Things being thus delightfully settled, so far as business was concerned, we all met in the drawing-room previously to dinner: Mr. Stapfurrow cautious and subdued as ever, and looking occasionally askance, now at Lord Stratharden, with the respect and veneration due to a peer of the realm, and then at me, with the awe and consideration excited towards a rich man: Mr. Jackson, with the ease and impudent assurance of a managing lawyer, who could either patronise or tyrannise, as his self-interest dictated: myself, full of hopes and fears as to what all this might happily result in, or dismally farther disappoint me: Miss Gentle, affable and winning, but, at the same time, dignified and controlled, while rather a thoughtful, but cheerful smile sat on her countenance: and Lord Stratharden, evidently relieved by a matter that had long preyed on his mind, having been satisfactorily brought to a conclusion: and inclined, in consequence, to be hilarious, while subdued by what was due to his guests, and likewise to his rank.

Of course, the conversation was a little awkward at first, for, do as I could, the subjects that suggested themselves, all came to be associated with something trying to the feelings. The beautiful view from the little drawing-room window, Lord Stratharden agreed with me in pronouncing exquisite, as though it would not be proper, on his part, to be indifferent to the qualities of a territory, that one day was to be mine, if indeed it was not already so: the remarks I made on the old spinnet, drew from Miss Gentle a sigh, while she explained, that it had been her grandmother's, and in bygone days of the family's greatness, considered a wonderful instrument: while the admiration I expressed of the pictures only brought back old times, to contrast, as it were, remorselessly with the new ones.

I was greatly relieved, therefore, when an ancient looking butler, dressed in rusty habiliments, that would have been a great deal. the better of an airing at a good fire, to take the wrinkles and creases out of them, came to announce that dinner was ready, and Lord Stratharden asked me to lead his niece to the dining-room, where we all soon came to be most comfortably settled and attended to; for notwithstanding the antiquity of worthy Adam's appearance, as the butler was named, he waited the table remarkably well—as well, indeed, as any "sawley" in Glasgow could have done it—while he evinced a quietude and arrangement in his method of service, that were quite pleasing.

Adam was evidently no apprentice at the work before him, and though, possibly, in consequence of being obliged, by the necessities of the times, that had been making such inroads upon the fortunes of the house of Stratharden, to put his hand to more onerous labour than that pertaining merely to

the office of a nobleman's butler, so as to enable him to be
retained, he would not have, in my opinion, disgraced the
richest livery that could have been placed on his meagre
person, and blown-away shanks.

Then, what quaint-looking old table plenishings he had
to manipulate amongst: bright blue china plates, without
sufficient edges, wherewithall to hold mustard and salt: thin
silver forks that almost bent with the handling: tiny shanked
gravy spoons that looked as though they would double up:
and knives that had been rubbed on boards till they scarcely
had any metal left in their blades at all.

The crystal and crockery too, were of a very *antique* description, although pretty, and such as I had seen knocked down, at
sales as articles of *vertu*, for very high prices, to people who,
no doubt, intended them to pass as family-ware, that had
belonged to their own *quasi* aristocratic forefathers!

But there was one element, the oldness and quality of
which could not be gain-said, or doubted, and that was
the wine, for it was such as Jackson declared he would
have gone a hundred miles to partake of, he being no bad
judge of what was superior in that way, and therefore he
paid his addresses to it with great gusto; while, as to the
dinner, nothing could have proved more satisfactory: it being
neat, savory, and well-cooked, without being over-abundant,
as generally was the case with the formidable feasts we had
been accustomed to, in our own city.

Lord Stratharden did the honours of his table as might have been expected from a nobleman of his standing. His conversation was spirited and intellectual, and his manners bland and deferential; while those of Miss Gentle were exactly what could have been looked for, from a lady entitled to sit at the head of his board, and, in consequence, every one present felt perfectly at ease.

Miss Gentle, however, did not sit long, and when she did retire, I felt as though the scene had become eclipsed, although it did not appear to make much difference to Jackson, who, with such wine as he now had before him—and certainly our landlord did not stint it—seemed inclined to prolong his *tete-à-tete* with his lordship, for an indefinite period.

I, therefore, being differently inclined, rose after a short period, though with what purpose in view, I scarcely knew myself: for although Lord Stratharden intimated that tea would be forthcoming in the drawing-room, I rather shrunk from the ordeal of facing Miss Gentle alone, with that unaccountable diffidence and misgiving, which only lovers, and particularly despairing ones, can feel, and duly appreciate.

In consequence, instead of bending my way to the drawing-room, where I judged Miss Gentle to be, I directed my steps to the outside of the mansion, impelled as it were, by a desire to fly from society altogether, and indulge in solitude and melancholy; for to tell the truth, Miss Gentle's manner to me, although everything that politeness and hospitality could dictate, I had construed into being rather cool and discouraging.

Not only so, but some ideas had suggested themselves to my mind, which went far to indicate that an insurmountable bar lay in the way of her ever being mine. She was poor, no doubt, but no poorer than when she first dispelled my hopes of happiness in the garden of Castle-Winsey; she was dependent, but for all that she had now the roof of her uncle, assured to her by the arrangements he had made, to protect her, and her love to command his affection; above all, she was the heir-presumptive to his titles, and one day, if she lived, would be a lady of the land in her own right, and entitled to take precedence of many of the highest nobility in the list of the Scottish peerage.

I, therefore, wandered forth dejected and downcast, and soon found myself following a path, that led to, whether I cared not, so that it conducted me to where I could indulge in my grief, alone and unseen.

Pursuing this path, however, I soon came to a spot, that for a moment diverted me from my immediate thoughts. It was on the brink of a precipice that overlooked the dell, through which the little rivulet Arden rushed with its ever-warbling current, and commanded an extensive and gorgeous view; to further the spectator's enjoyment of which, a small rustic summer-house had been built, of bark and heather, on its extreme point.

I stopped short, as I approached this spot, and seating myself on the trunk of a felled tree, again plunged into the thoughts that had been besetting me, and which did not become more assuring, by being indulged in. So much so was this the case, that insensibly, as I arose to pursue my solitary walk, I heaved a deep sigh, which to my astonishment, I heard re-echoed from the inside of the summer-house, and this exciting my curiosity, I immediately stalked towards the portal thereof, where I beheld sitting, alone and blushing, no other than Miss Gentle, whom I now found I had been unconsciously intruding upon.

I felt awkward by this discovery, and, starting back, would have fain redeemed the impropriety I suspected I had committed, by leaving the spot at once, but she prevented this, by rising from her seat and requesting me to stay.

"I may as well take this opportunity, Bailie," she said, "of performing what my conscience imposes on me as a duty, before you leave this place, and that is to express to you my gratitude and thanks for what you have done for my poor uncle and myself, in so noble, munificent, and disinterested a manner; and which is all the more appreciable, that I am convinced you acted thus, in ignorance that you were benefitting one in particular who, instead of being worthy of your consideration, should have been rather the subject of your ire, if such a sentiment could be a tenant in your breast, as I am certain it can never be!"

"Ah! my dear sir," she continued—whilst I looked sheepish and modest, but yet, in my mind's eye, representing the fox dressed in the lamb's clothing, so great was my consciousness of my own cunning—"you little know what relief and joy you have brought to my worthy and venerated uncle by the disinterested part you have acted, and how much in consequence you have rendered me happy!"

"And when I take into consideration," she went on to say, "as I have often done, the prudish, and the pragmatic—the cold-blooded way, indeed, I may say—with which I have acted towards you, and for which you have so nobly avenged yourself by heaping, as it were, coals of fire on my head, I am at a loss, how I can make atonement. I feel so much,

s 2

indeed, on this point, that the only thing I would ask, is that henceforth, while you forgive me, as I am sure you will, you will forget me for ever!"

I was rather taken by surprise with this speech, and at first, as I must confess, with delight, on hearing her express, as it were, regret for having refused me, and admiration for my conduct towards her uncle and herself; but my new fledged hopes and happiness fell at the hint contained in her peroration, namely, that after forgiving, I should "forget her for ever!" My jealous heart, indeed, construed this into the appearance of a desire for an estrangement that, while gently giving me an honourable discharge as she had done before, would be extremely convenient for herself, in respect that it would leave her free and unfettered, to bestow her hand on any laird, lord, or baronet, that might have fame and name, though not a penny in his pouch, to bestow upon her. I therefore hung down my head, and, having nothing to say, remained silent.

This, perhaps, was the very best thing I could have done, for to have attempted to be my own advocate, under the circumstances, would have certainly resulted in failure. It threw, likewise, the onus of speech on my fair antagonist, seeing that my perplexity could have only been caused by what she had said already, while, at the same time, it committed me to neither approval, nor disapproval of what she had suggested. I was, therefore, not surprised when she resumed the colloquy, which I thus innocently led her into.

"Bailie!" she said, "you appear to be sad, and indeed I might have inferred as much as that, from the deep sigh you heaved, whilst it unconsciously drew another from me, that has led to my being discovered here, not, however, I protest, as an eavesdropper, for I never dreamt you would have deserted the company of my uncle and his guests so soon, and have wandered to this lone spot. Perhaps, therefore, I may be acting wrongly in continuing to intrude upon the quietude you may be seeking, and, therefore, with your permission, will fly to the Keep, particularly as by this time the other gentlemen may have sought the drawing-room, and will be wondering where I am."

"Alas!" I at last found words to say, "you have guessed truly, when you suppose that I am sad—sad, did I say?—

why, I am miserable!—and all the more so, that I have no one to tell my tale of woe to—no one to sympathise with me!"

"Indeed!" replied Miss Gentle, "I am surprised to hear you say so, for you, who have wealth, influence, and power, can surely command such desiderata. It is only poor people like my uncle and myself, who must shift for ourselves in that way, and be glad to get through life without kicks, let alone sympathy and pity!"

"And yet," she continued, while checking herself, "I should be the last person in the world to say so much, after what we have received at your kind hands; but my only apology for so speaking, must be the recency of it, which has scarcely yet given me time to realise the happy fact, to the extent I am sure I yet will. Well, be consoled by this, that even as we have found a friend in our need, and when we least expected him, so may you likewise be lucky, and as, indeed, you far more deserve to be!"

"I duly estimate your kind wishes," I replied, "but I fear I am forbidden to hope for so great a boon. There is no one to pity the wretch that is plunged in love, and yet, at the same time, is distracted with despair!"

"Ah, Bailie!" cried Miss Gentle, while an arch twinkle sparkled in her eye, and a humorous smile played on her features, "is that where the evil lies, and is that, too, the extent of it? Well, I could not have supposed that your philosophy would have permitted you to be enchained, or enthralled to such an extent, by any one, however fair: and if for no other reason than what is contained in our apt Scotch proverb, which says,—'There is as good fish in the sea as ever came out of it!'"

"But this fish," I replied, while with a grim smile I attempted, in despair, to reciprocate what I considered to be, on her part a sort of joke, "is one that does not come to every line, and, at the same time, is so greatly desiderated and appreciated by me, that I cannot think of trying for any other, and therefore must plunge after her, sink or swim as I may!"

"That being the case," answered Miss Gentle, "you must just adopt another proverb, namely, 'faint heart never won fair lady,' and therefore press her more determinately.

Fish, you know, as experience in boating and fishing excursions at Castle-Winsey have taught me, will take the bait, if
not at one time, perhaps at another, and particularly at the
turn of the tide; so what do you say to try a sharper hook
and a new bait, all which you great Glasgow merchants can
command?"

"Ah!" I cried, "if my whole fortune, means, and substance
could form a bait sufficiently acceptable to her whom I adore,
I would lay them joyfully at her feet; but alas! she is not to
be won by such paltry inducements, as already I have found
to my mortification, and indeed as you yourself were a
witness to, one morning in the garden of Castle-Winsey. If,
however, there existed any chance of that fair one—whom I
continue to love as my soul—relenting: if any sacrifice—
any—"

But here I was interrupted by Miss Gentle, who, by this
time, was blushing deeply, while she laid her hand on my
arm, as if to impose silence, and I intuitively acceded to the
implied request, not, however, without shrinking from the
answer I trembled to anticipate.

"Permit me," she said, "before you utter one word more,
to say something that both my conscience and my duty
instruct me I should now, after what I have heard, disburden
myself of, and it is simply this:—When you first honoured
me with your flattering declaration I was taken perfectly
aback—not only so, I was in a position that prevented me
giving any other reply to your proposal than I did then; for,
as I may now tell you, I had to contemplate not only my own,
but my poor uncle's circumstances, and these forbade any other
mode of procedure than what I adopted—indeed what I was
forced to adopt. Now, however, these circumstances are
changed, instead of being an invalid, he is restored to promising health; and instead of being beggars, we are placed in
comparative wealth—thanks to your munificence and liberality. It would, therefore, ill become me, to allow you to
again make a presentation that, under the circumstances, it
would be my duty likewise to refuse. I therefore at once
stop you in your generous proposal, as I feel, instead, that
I should now be the offerer, insignificant and insufficient
though the gift I have to submit for acceptance, may be!"

She paused for a moment, while I was filled with amaze-

ment at what she had said, and anxiety as to what she might
farther say; for in her countenance I now read great pertur-
bation if not painfulness of mind.

"My dear friend," at last she continued, "the offer I have
to make is what is essentially your due—and if it be accepted,
perhaps that acceptance will be more than my due. It is
simply this heart and this hand, and which I freely bestow
upon you for better—for worse—for now—and for ever!"

As she said this she held out her hand to me—that hand
which I esteemed beyond all other treasures in the world—
while I dropped on my knee, and covered it with kisses!

CHAPTER LII.

INTRODUCTORY DOGGERELS.

Unfurl the flag—bedeck the hall—
Shower gifts the bride upon.
Ring marriage bells—shout praises all—
But, oh!—be short Mess John!

The Goosedubbs Poet.

WERE this a fashionable romance, instead of a plain and unpretentious narrative, I might very soon bring it to a conclusion, in the usual gratifying and desirable style, generally adopted in the perorations of such works, and which is so appreciated by the "gentle and benevolent reader," who always delights in happy consummations, and the reconcilement of differences and difficulties, in the shape of a marriage betwixt the hero and heroine of the tale: although their after careers may never be touched upon at all; farther inquiry and interest concerning these circumstances being at an end when matrimony intervenes.

This, however, is a style of conclusion I do not consider myself amenable to, and which, even although I had not the excuse I have alluded to—to enable me to place all normal rules at defiance—I would not choose to adopt. I feel, in the first place, a reluctance to part with old friends in so callous and summary a manner, as would be necessary thereby, and, in the second, I consider it a duty not to leave any thing to the fancy, when there are actually farther facts to deal with, which, on being revealed, may tend to instruction, and perhaps to morality.

I, therefore, go on with my narration as before, in my own plain, unadorned, and, I hope, modest manner, such as becomes a mercantile man, however successful: and above all, a conscience-struck and repentant culprit, who can only appease his mind by an honest and veracious confession regarding every particular of a career, which he is partly ashamed, and partly proud of.

To resume then:—After Miss Gentle's confession—or rather, admission—of her sentiments towards me, and after a proper pledging of troths to each other, and perhaps a few endearing salutations, and protestations of never-fading, and eternal so-and-sos, such as lovers, on occasions of the kind, always indulge in, but which the reader will possibly gladly, so far as concerns my case, excuse me entering into particulars regarding, I returned with her, to Lammerlee Keep, in a very different frame of mind to that in which I had left it: when we found that Lord Strath- arden and his guests had risen from the table, Jackson being in a most mel- lifluous and philanthropic humour: for he was ever shaking hands with his host, and talking maud- lingly, in consequence of of the port he had imbibed: and Lord Stratharden, pleased by seeing his guest happy, although the state of his health had forbidden him from joining the latter in libations, deeper than water coloured with a little wine.

And perhaps it was just as well for me, that Jackson was in that jolly state, for it dispelled the awkwardness that otherwise Miss Gentle and I might have felt—under the new circumstances in which we were placed, as engaged lovers— had the company remained in the same stiff humour to each other, that characterised our meeting before dinner.

We had therefore great fun in witnessing Jackson's antics, —for he actually attempted to dance—and in hearkening to his screaming—he likewise having essayed to sing—the ser- vices of the old spinnet being brought into requisition, on both occasions.

At last the hour of our departure arrived: when Lord

Stratharden and Miss Gentle accompanied us along the
avenue a short way—Jackson and his Lordship leading, and
Miss Gentle and I bringing up the rear—when I had the
pleasure of arranging with her, as to our future correspondence, and likewise as to my communicating suitably with
her uncle in regard to my pretensions to his neice's hand:
the same being still dependent—as had been dutifully
stipulated by Miss Gentle—on his approval and consent.

We then bade adieu to each other, with many kind wishes
and sentiments on our part, and hospitable invitations to
Lamerlee Keep on future occasions, on that of Lord
Stratharden and Miss Gentle, after which I gave Jackson
my arm—he requiring a little steadying—when we pursued
our way towards the village, in the course of which I communicated to him the engagement I had entered into with
Miss Gentle, which so delighted him—as he at last saw in it,
as he confessed, the consummation of his own suit with Miss
M'Chuckie: I now being fairly out of his way as a rival: the
only thing he had continued to dread—that he proposed we
should have a little recreation in the shape of leap-frog, in
order to give vent to any exuberant overflow of spirits,
which otherwise might have burst their bonds, if not relieved
by some such safety valve. Away then we accordingly went,
vaulting over each other's back along the dusty road, and in
the clear moonlight, as though we had been acrobats instead

of staid business-like men; the only circumstance of the
like kind that I had seen before, having been on the part of
a lot of ministers, after a preaching Monday's dinner, on
their way home from a certain hospitable manse, that shall
be nameless.

Some months afterwards, I was united in the holy bands of
matrimony to Miss Gentle, the ceremony being performed in
Lammerlee Keep, by my respected and esteemed friend, the
Reverend Nahum Gust: on which occasion there were
present, in addition to a few neighbouring aristocratic friends
of Lord Stratharden and Miss Gentle, Mr. and Mrs. Tweel,
and Miss M'Chuckie—the latter acting as one of the bride's
maids — Mr. Jackson, of course, and my excellent and
constant friend, Mr. Garnethill, whom, although not mentioned by me of late, I had still kept up my usual happy and
pleasant intimacy with, all along.

The affair, as we quiet men like to call such ceremonies,
was kept within the most unostentatious limits that could
have been observed. Lord Stratharden, with the concur-
rence of his niece and myself, having forbidden anything
like a show of flags, or a firing of guns, or a demonstration,
indeed, of any description whatever, taking place in the
village, but in lieu of this, I distributed, through the
agency and management of Mr. Stapfurrow, the sum of
fifty pounds, to the most deserving and needful poor of the

parish, and which arrangement I learned afterwards, gave more satisfaction, and did more benefit, than ten times the sum, expended in vulgar display, or puffed off in powder could have done.

The only inopportune and regretable thing that did take place, was on the part of Lord Stratharden's antique butler, Adam, and my new-fangled footman, Sam,—now promoted from being merely "buttons," to a regular suit of livery, and all through that gratuitous interference which *will* be indulged in by servants, ancient and modern, on such happy family occasions.

It happened simply from a desire on the part of these officials to do every honour to their respective chiefs, that vulgar fancy could suggest, and was originated by my man Sam bringing along with him—and without my knowledge —in the rumble of my carriage, a flag that he had borrowed from the mate of a ship I owned—then lying at the Broomie-law harbour — and which was in fact a private signal I myself had devised, half in joke, and half in earnest—the device upon it being a locomotive at full puff, with the motto "Pergé," the same being dog Latin for " go-a-head," and which is an expression that I have always had a partiality for!

This flag, which was of new bunting, Sam had arranged with Adam should be hoisted the moment the nuptial knot was tied, on a flag-staff, placed on one of the turrets of Lammer-lee Keep, along with the old banner of the family, which had been rummaged out by the said Adam from an old lumber press, that had not been intruded upon for many a day, and which was duly devoted to a flag-staff on another turret, and therefore my feelings may be judged of, when on looking up to the battlements of the Keep, as we drove off after the ceremony, to behold the bright private-signal, which used to adorn the truck of the Nimble Nancy, as my barque was denominated, waving harmoniously and blendingly with the faded and ragged banner of Stratharden and Invergray, on which was emblazoned a lion *couchant*, with the motto "Fuimus," which being translated, means "We were!"

This trifling circumstance is perhaps not worthy of the notice I have given it, but as it furnished an opportunity to an invidious baronet—a next door neighbour of Lord Stratharden, whose estate I afterwards purchased, and who subsequently became a wine merchant—to perpetrate an offensive joke at our mutual expense, about the blending of what was gone, with what was fresh, I would rather it had not happened, although, let me tell him (the baronet) that he will perhaps find "blending" not to be a bad method with which to treat his own wines.

Be that as it may, the blending of the banners did not interfere with that of Lord Stratharden and his guests, on this happy occasion; for—as Jackson reported to me afterwards—all enjoyed themselves to the fullest extent, and particularly my reverend friend Nahum, who gave his lordship's old port as fair a trial as Jackson himself had done, on a former happy occasion, and, for aught I know, may have again done, on this still happier one, although he did not amplify sufficiently upon it, so as to instruct me to that extent; the probability being, that he rather chose to be moderate in his potations, in consequence of Miss M'Chuckie's presence : he having determined to take advantage of the occasion to bring her to a decision as to his suit, one way or other, and which, I am happy to say, was favourable; for, only six weeks afterwards, the reverend Nahum was again called on to officiate—this time at St. Blythswood Terrace—when Jasper Jackson became the happiest of men, and Matilda M'Chuckie, of course, the happiest of women !

My subsequent commercial, and matrimonial career, up till very lately, embracing, as that does, a space of time amounting to nearly twenty years, has been so placid, comfortable, and unvaried, that I feel scarcely called upon to chronicle particularly, any of the events that took place within it.

With regard to that distinguishing portion of it, however, which I have first named, I may state, that although I retired, on marrying, ostensibly from business, I did not do so from money-making; for, having acquired the considerable capital I had done, I found actually, that control although I did every transaction I entered into, by a moderate expectation of profit, and, consequently, by an accompanying assurance against risk, I could not prevent my riches augmenting. I found, in short, that money made money, and this circumstance, coupled with my good luck, which still continued, and continues to stand by me, has placed me in a position of wealth, far beyond what I ever could have expected, and I may say, almost wished, even in my most romancing days. I had Jackson, likewise, always ready to administer to my profit, in the way of pointing out good and safe investments, and, in addition, a whole host of sycophants, that buzzed about me as I walked up and down the Exchange Room, while suggesting this and that stock, as likely to go up, or go down, and to communicate, as "a profound secret," what was to be the dividend of this or that railway, long before it was declared—so great is the inclination of such people to benefit rich men—catch them doing so to poor ones!—and hence I was enabled to speculate to good purpose, almost without running any risk whatever.

With regard to the other distinguishing portion of my career, namely, the matrimonial one, I found in it every advantage, I may say blessing, I could have desired. My wife brought me a numerous progeny of sons and daughters, while she proved to be a most delightful companion, as well as an amiable instructress, and kind friend at the same time. In her I found, notwithstanding her aristocratic origin, and high and cultivated breeding, one who had no pride—at any rate, no false pride—and of so humble and self-denying a disposition, that it was with difficulty I could get her to sanction an expenditure such as I considered due to her position, and certainly such as was warranted by the ample means at my command.

Of course, it will not be wondered at, if I confess to having practised towards her a certain reticence, in regard to my origin, and in particular, as to the many improprieties and reprehensible actions, I had committed in my former lifetime, and which, in consequence of their having weighed so heavily on my mind—as a penance as it were—I have already made a clean breast of, to the reader. This I was enabled the more easily to do from the absence of any impertinent—though it might have been justifiable—curiosity on her part; for it is nothing but my duty towards her, to state that while she evinced the liveliest interest in, and expressed the highest commendation of the perseverance and struggles, with which—I did not deny—I had fought through life as the "architect of my own fortune"—to use a favourite cant phrase of the snobocracy to which I belong—she never probed me with a question, or assumed an inference as to my antecedents, that could place me in a dilemma, or call a blush to my face.

On the contrary, she seemed to esteem me more and more, as in the course of our married confidence, I went on to reveal a few things—encouraged as I was thereto by the Christian philosophy and charitable consideration she evinced as her great religious characteristics, and which taught her to know that no one was perfect—which I otherwise might have kept to myself.

So much did this charm, on her part, extend its influence over me, that in the course of time I found it relieving to my mind to communicate to her—to a prudent extent—what lay on my conscience, in regard to my conduct towards poor Sissy, and which necessarily caused me to reveal the fearful secret, pent up till then, within my breast, of the catastrophe that had almost led to her ignominious death, and which in fact had led to her ignominious banishment.

As I expected, this confession was received by my wife with the painful interest that might have been anticipated; but still with that resignation and liberality which I had pretty safely calculated would be the case, and indeed without which assurance I would have taken right good care—would I not?—not to have said one single word, regarding!

The confession, if I may so call it—explained as it was to her, in my own *judicious* way—gave me great comfort, for it removed to a considerable extent what had hung over me for many years like a nightmare, and had made me miserable and distracted at times, when I should have been cheerful and joyous—the visitation, if I may call it so, having generally

come upon me when I was in the midst of company, like
" Nebuchadnezzar," &c., &c., as my friend Nahum used to
dwell upon, in the pulpit.

It furnished, too, a theme that both of us could indulge in
conversation about, and that, too, in a way which gave me
real pleasure, inasmuch as it did justice to poor Sissy, of
whose true character my wife at last—in consequence of
what I narrated to her, and in particular from what she read
in the newspaper reports of her case, which I had carefully
preserved—formed the highest possible opinion, notwithstanding the doom to which she had been subjected, as a
felon and an exile, from her native country. So much so,
indeed, was this the case, that I have reason to know my
wife, who was a thorough Christian, and in every sense of
the word, a properly pious person, though most unobtrusive,
as all really religious and good people are, never failed to
remember her in her private devotions.

With regard to my father and mother, I did not say much,
excepting that I had the satisfaction of communicating
one day to her, that I had placed over their remains a
neat granite head-stone, with a Latin inscription, stating
that the one had been a respectable mariner, and the other
his wife—all which, of course, nobody that I cared about,
could translate.

And thus years rolled over our heads, making them gray,
but wiser at the same time, and our family grew up, and the
world prospered with us, while wealth and good connections
afforded us every opportunity of happiness that we could
desire: our time, with an agreeable variety, being spent
partly in the City of the west, where we kept up a splendid
town-house, and partly in the neighbourhood of Lammerlee,
where I had purchased a small property that marched with it,
or rather Invergray: and which, at the death of Lord
Stratharden will, in connection with his estates—that will
then become mine, in fee simple—form a territory of no
small magnitude.

This property has on it an excellent and comfortable mansion, the same having been the residence of the baronet that
sneered at the unfurling of the banners, as has already been
duly mentioned, and being adjacent to Lammerlee Keep,
where Lord Stratharden continued, and still continues to

reside, in excellent health I am happy to say, though now a very old man, we have had every opportunity of enjoying his delightful society: one great advantage along with that being the pleasant circumstance that it has allowed my children to be much with him, and to receive from him instructions and advice, moral and political, which cannot fail to be of service particularly to the male portion thereof, should they turn their attention to public affairs, and which their position and fortunes will well entitle them to do hereafter, should they choose, as public men, to serve the State.

Indeed, had I myself felt any desire to be distinguished in that way, I could have taken advantage of ample opportunities for the purpose. I have had repeated requisitions presented to me to allow myself to be proposed as a candidate, not only for the county in which I have so great a stake, but for my native City. I have, however, as yet resisted these flattering invitations, from a feeling that if I were to enter Parliament for the former, I would be subjected to such envy and malignity, as might disturb the placidity of my domestic happiness; and if for the latter, it would only be to represent a community that returned me entirely on account of my wealth. I, therefore, for the present, prefer not to think of parliamentary honours; but should I pass from that resolution, it will then be to enter St. Steven's as the purchased possessor of some English borough, the free-holders of which can neither bother me with their claims, nor disgust me with their sycophancy.

These, however, are minor matters pertaining to my story; for I have now to enter upon a circumstance of much more importance connected with it, seeing that it is of particular interest to me, and I have no doubt will likewise be so to the reader, when it is told.

Having had occasion about a couple of years ago, to go to
London, accompanied by my wife, in order to place my
daughter at a fashionable boarding school, that had been
recommended to us, by our valued friend the Duchess of
Dumbarton, we took up our residence at one of those
distinguished hotels in Pall-Mall, where we were so fortunate
as to secure appartments, that had been at one time occupied
by one of the crowned heads of Europe, and where we found
ourselves extremely comfortable and well attended to; so
much so, indeed, that but for the extreme expense thereof—
although I did not grudge it—we might have supposed
ourselves to have been in our own house.

At the same time we were to meet our oldest son, then
seventeen years of age, who was attending one of the
Universities, where he had made a most creditable appearance
as a wrangler.

In the same house there were, of course, other guests, but
owing to the excellent arrangements of the establishment,
we seldom came in contact with them, everything being
conducted there, as though it were a private residence, the
only apartments in common being a smoking-saloon and a
billiard-room, but these, of course, alone available for gentlemen.

Into the latter I had strayed one afternoon with no other
purpose, than that of smoking a quiet cigar, and killing
lethargy by practising a few strokes with the marker, more
as a learner than a regular player—for I knew little about
the game—when I found a gentleman present, of a military

appearance, for he wore a considerable moustache, who was amusing himself apparently very much to his own satisfaction, by playing at what the French would call *solitaire:* so I sat down seemingly unnoticed by him, and soon became rather interested in his proceedings, particularly as he handled his cue amazingly, and bagged his balls wonderfully: all which proved him to be a first-rate artist at such work.

After a little, I began to think that his features—notwithstanding the hirsute embellishment on his face—were not unfamiliar to me, and as he went on, this impression became stronger: so that I at last walked up to him, and giving myself no time for farther introduction said:—"Can it be possible that I now see before me, and thus unexpectedly, my old and esteemed friend, Tom Throstle?"

The gentleman paused from his amusement, and staring for a moment in my face, while at the same time he frankly held out his hand, replied, "Indeed you do; while in you I behold one, whom I have been burning with impatience to see, and yet shrinking from the very idea of meeting!"

"You astonish me!" I answered, as I wrung at the same time his hand, "by such a negative compliment, but as I am not aware I have ever done any thing that should make my friends shun me, and particularly so old and so dear a one as you are, I am filled with curiosity to know your reason for thus qualifying the desire you express towards a renewal of our intimacy!"

"My dear fellow!" cried Tom, while he again shook me heartily by the hand, and smiled in a way that brought back the remembrance of his ancient *bonhomie,* "let me explain at once, that my diffidence proceeds, not from any change in my esteem towards you—that is as warm and as kindly as ever—it is entirely from a feeling, on my part, that my position is not such as to warrant me in claiming consideration from you!"

"What you say," I answered, "puzzles me more and more, for I never heard aught to your disadvantage; indeed I have not heard of you at all, since you gave up favouring me with your correspondence some twenty years ago—while the fact of your being an inmate of this house, as well as your appearance, speak at once in proof of your respectability,

T 2

disclosing, as they do, that you have returned to your native land both as a gentleman, and a man of fortune!"

"Well," said Tom, as he took me by the arm, and we both, as if by mutual desire, walked into the adjoining smoking-room, which was vacant, and the door of which he carefully closed against intrusion, "you are so far right in your conclusions, for I have nothing to say against Fortune, which has indeed been very kind to me—though I must confess that I have not been a maker, but an acquirer of her gifts—only there is such a thing, as that along with that, I may have entered into relationships, which my friends may not respect, nor desire to adopt, though they may have no objections to the fortune!"

"About that," I replied, "I feel I have no right to inquire—for what you darkly hint at, may be something or nothing—only I cannot conceive that any one can be justified in looking down upon you, if what you have acquired—or rather, if the means by which you have acquired it—have not compromised your honour and honesty?"

"Ah! it's all right in respect to these," rejoined Tom, while he assumed the careless swagger that used to distinguish him in days of yore, "only it has not been done in such a genteel way, as perhaps my now great friends would like; for I must tell you that I have heard of your exalted position in society, and of your connection with the aristocracy. But the best way," he continued, "will perhaps be to come out with all the facts at once, for Tom Throstle is the old man, and thinks there is nothing like candour, particularly to one whom he knows and can trust: one indeed who will make his friend's secret his own: so if you will lend me your ears for a minute, on that understanding, I will tell you all about that, which has caused me to act the part I have done, since I have returned to this country, in respect to my old friends, amongst whom, I need scarcely say, I esteem you the very first!"

"Know, then," he went on to say—while I nodded acquiescence, in his implied understanding, that what he revealed should be considered "strictly confidential,"—"that the way I acquired the fortune I am now master of, was not by trade or commerce—for to tell you the truth I found it as difficult to get on in that way in Australia, as it could have been in the mother-country—but by marrying the widow of a rich convict: she herself having been a convict, though, in consequence of her good conduct, subsequently a pardoned one!"

"In the colony from which we have come," he continued, "such a circumstance may not have created any surprise, or set a-going any foul-mouthed gossip; but in this country the case is very different, so that in returning to the latter, as has been the object of our desire for years, we have contemplated the act as a risk, and the facing of our former fellow-citizens as an ordeal, that only the extreme of caution, prudence, and modesty on our part, should warrant us in attempting. Here, however, at last we are, and although in possession of something like a quarter of a million sterling, only desirous of living in privacy and unostentatious retirement: towards which end, I have for some time past been in treaty for an estate situated in the south of England, where we expect to be enabled at last to live, unknowing and unknown."

I could not help marvelling at the extreme modesty which this speech indicated on the part of Tom and his wife, although at the same time I saw much philosophy and propriety in the resolution they had come to. I, however, rallied him on the subject, and pointed out to him the folly of being too sensitive, as to what the world might say of him or his wife, even if it came to know the real facts. I likewise represented to him, the probability of the secret never being found out; and ultimately suggested, that after all, if those who were most critical as to their neighbour's faults, and the most severe in animadverting upon them, were themselves to be scrutinised in regard to their morals and conduct, they would perhaps be found more worthy of reprehension, than those they would indulge their venom against.

Tom grinned a grim acquiescence to this suggestion on my part, and seemingly was consoled by it; for he now entered into a long and discursive narrative regarding his career, since I had last parted with him so many years before, down to the period when he was at last so lucky in falling upon his feet, as has been described. This drew from him some details with regard to his wife, whom, notwithstanding the circumstances connected with her antecedents, he represented in so favourable a light, that I became quite interested in, and desirous to be introduced to her.

This, after the expression of some misgivings as to the propriety of his doing so, without giving his wife previous notice of his intention—but which he agreed with me in thinking might possibly be just as well: by its having the appearance of being improvised—he at last agreed to, and accordingly led me to an elegant drawing-room, where we found seated, two ladies, the one elderly, though not old, but blooming with much matronly robustness and becoming *embonpoint*, and the other a comely young woman of fifteen or sixteen years of age, to whom he introduced me as his wife and daughter.

I gazed for a moment on the former, while realising a fact, that had rushed upon me like the flash of an unexpected electrical stroke, and which seemingly was in like manner felt by the lady, as she fell into my extended arms exclaiming, "My brother!" while I, unable to do more, clasped her to my bosom, and breathed into her ear the single, but to me the ever present and eventful word, "Sissy!"

CHAPTER LIII.

INTRODUCTORY DOGGERELS.

The music ends,—the prompter stops,—
    The actors rant no more;
The lights grow dim,—the curtain drops,—
    Adieu!—the play is o'er!

The Goosedubbs Poet.

My task is ended : my self-undertaking has come to a close: my confession concludes!

It is not, however, for me to say, or even to hope that the said confession should be accepted as a propitiation towards the condonement, by the world, of the many grievous sins I have committed, and which no one can be more seriously sensible of, than myself. Of course, my "gentle readers" never committed any such sins. They never aimed at rising in the world without taking along with them their whole kith and kin, and fairly dividing with all, the wealth they acquired. They never, after getting on a bit, were annoyed by their fathers eating their fish with their knives, or their mothers drinking out of their wine coolers. They never received coldly their country cousins. They never cut their *quondam* contemporaries. They always shook hands with their old acquaintances when they met them, and even asked them to dinner—though Mr. Batch still remained a baker, and Mr. Banes a butcher. They never committed such venal offences as saying one thing and meaning another. They never indulged in mental reservations. They never, in a word, did that in their hearts and in their own secrecy, which they shrank from doing before the world. I alone am the exceptional sinner, to be reviled, execrated, blamed, and banned to all time coming!

If I say anything more, therefore, it is simply that I may not part abruptly with the reader, who has followed me thus far, and thus faithfully, with a patience that deserves all the amends I am enabled to make to so esteemed a constituent, be the same, a he, or a she, old or young, plain or beautiful: and this duty I will perhaps best fulfil, by succinctly adding a few explicative lines, giving some slight particulars, without which my narrative possibly would be incomplete.

On communicating to my wife what had taken place, only a few rooms beyond the apartments where she and I had been residing for upwards of a week, in perfect ignorance of the eventful propinquity of those, and particularly of one, with whom we had in common, such peculiar relationship, she was so much affected and impressed, that she could only get 'relief in tears, and better still, by having recourse to sincere and heartfelt prayer; after which she desired to be introduced to her sister-in-law.

That interview was indeed a scene to be ever remembered by Tom Throstle and me—although there was nothing but what was pleasing and delightful connected with it. It was the meeting of extremes, and yet these extremes were so extreme, that they actually came to combine with each other, like the action of physical incongruities, when subjected to those all-powerful laws which no human understanding can fathom, and no human genius can divert from their purposes. On the one hand, there was the highly-reared and artificially-cultivated patrician dame: keen to do justice; and on the other, the basely-neglected, and cruelly-used plebeian outcast: bashful to receive it; and yet they blended together and became natural and harmonious.

It is said that an Ionic capital, having once upon a time, fallen to the sward from its lofty column, was found surrounded by weeds and wildflowers gracefully clustering about

its volutes, and that this suggested, to some great artist of bygone Grecian days, the Corinthian Capital—the most beautiful of architectural designs, and the emblem of everything that is noble and chivalric. Why, then, should there not have been as happy a combination in this case, and with as pleasing a result, though only so in privacy, and secrecy?

And, indeed, such was the case; for, from that day, the sisters-in-law were never separated from each other, more than circumstances, connected with their respective establishments, necessarily prescribed. They became, in short, friends and companions,—confidants and mutual advisers, —attendants on each other in the hour of sickness,— and communers together on more important and sacred occasions.

Let us, therefore, leave these two pure souls together, to the proper indulgence in what is so good and appropriate, and estimable, and I might almost add, holy: while I advert to matters more worldly, that naturally and necessarily were left to Tom Throstle and me.

From him I learned that, after Sissy had arrived in the colony as a convict, she had conducted herself with so much propriety, that she had been appointed to the situation of nurse, and subsequently promoted to that of matron of an hospital, where her good conduct gave so much satisfaction as to induce the Governor to extend to her the privilege of being drafted into private service, and which was subsequently enlarged to a ticket-of-leave, and latterly to entire freedom, on the new system permitting that description of arrangement being introduced into the colony, as a reward to well-behaved convicts.

It so happened, however, that the master she got was an old and extremely wealthy man, who himself had originally come to the colony as a convict, and he being pleased with his servant, had ultimately married her, and, dying shortly afterwards, had left her his entire fortune, amounting to nearly three hundred thousand pounds sterling.*

The valuable prize in the shape of a rich widow without incumbrances, though tinctured with the drawbacks that have been explained, at last fell to the lucky lot of poor Tom Throstle, then a struggling, but still a respected, and respectable merchant. He married her, without any knowledge whatever of her origin, beyond the fact that she was a fellow countrywoman, and on the implicit understanding, or rather covenant, that he should never inquire as to her connections; and farther, that if ever they returned to their own country, they should live in the strictest retirement—for it is a singular fact, that while he was my fellow-chum and lodger, in our youthful days, he never saw, but only heard of her—to enforce which contract she retained in her own possession the entire control of half the aforesaid means, over which she had now the unlimited power.

I farther learned a circumstance, connected with this resolution on her part, and which indeed was only communicated to Tom himself, after the re-union that had taken place betwixt my sister and me, that touched my feelings greatly, and farther added to the great debt of love and gratitude I owed her, namely, that she had been secretly in her own mind, induced to make this reservation, in order to present me with the residue she had retained, if so be, she found that I either required, or wanted to possess it; but which of course I was enabled to decline, in consequence of my own superabundant fortune: not, however, without being duly impressed with a sense of her extreme liberality

* NOTE K.—Rich Convicts. *See Appendix.*

and munificence, as well as affected by her intense sisterly love and devotion to one who had so many misgivings on his conscience, as to his conduct to her—a sentiment which my wife heartily partook of, on learning regarding this very extraordinary instance of proposed generosity and Christian self-denial; but which was all in keeping with her characteristics, even from the time when she was a poor "Goosedubbs bairn."

This sacrifice of acquirement—if so it may be called—however on my part, was compensated by what subsequently occurred in our family intercourse; my oldest son, it so happened, fell in love with Tom and Sissy's only daughter, and they are now engaged to be married when a suitable time arrives, when what has been declined by me, will be settled on the youthful pair, whom I likewise will be enabled to subsidise, to a degree that will ever maintain the honours and titles of Stratharden and Lammerlee, as they should be.

In the meantime Tom, by my advice—assisted, of course, by that of the useful and faithful Jackson, who has now a most extensive and remunerative professional practice in his native City—has purchased an estate, situated not far from ours, and where he and his wife live in comfort, opulence, and happiness, respected by the community at large, and adored by the immediate circle of their own relations and friends, amongst whom I may mention that Lord Stratharden, now a robust nonagenarian, I am happy to say, is one of the warmest and kindest.

Of course, at that nobleman's death, the estates will fall to me in fee simple, while my wife will inherit his titles as a peeress in her own right, and in the course of time and of nature, these will ultimately descend to my son and Sissy's daughter, and their heirs!

Thus shall be read a great moral! What has sprung from the Goosedubbs—what has been vile and contemptible—what has been despised and abandoned—what has been still estimable and good—shall, by the inscrutable decree and mysterious rule of an Omnipotent Providence, be destined to keep flowing, in lusty, legitimate, and refreshed life, the blood of Kings: aye even that of the Plantagenets, the Tudors, and the Stuarts!*

* NOTE L.—Royal Blood. *See Appendix.*

Who then will despise a beggar's benison? Who, above all, will gainsay the truthful distich of my worthy friend, the poet of the Goosedubbs, with which I began, as I will now finish my story:—

> "The germ lies buried in the earth,
>   Neglected and despised;
> But soon 'twill claim from Nature, birth:
>   And be both praised and prized.

> "Yes!—many a paltry, buried thing,—
>   Which e'en the hogs reject,—
> Shall from the world a status wring,
>   And gain fame and respect!"

AND SO ENDS

APPENDIX TO VOL. II.

F.—CITY OF GLASGOW ARMS, p. 36.

The following is an excerpt from M'Ure's History of Glasgow, published in 1636:—

"The arms of the city is an oak tree, with a bird on its top, a salmond, with a ring in its mouth, and a bell, explained in Latin verse as below, by the famous Dr. Main, professor of physick in the university of Glasgow.

'Salmo maris, terræque arbos, avis aeris, urbi
  Promittunt quicquid trina elementa ferunt.
Et campana (frequens celebret quod uuminis aras
  Urbs) superesse polo non peritura docet.
Neve quis indubitet sociari æterna caducis,
  Annulus id, pignus conjugiale notat.'

The above Latin verse Englished thus, [by J. B., 1685].

The salmon which a fish is of the sea,
The oak which springs from earth that loftie tree,
The bird on it which in the air doth flee,
O GLASGOW does presage all things to thee!
To which the sea, or air, or fertile earth
Do either give their nowrishment or birth.
The bell that doth to publick worship call,
Sayes heaven will give most lasting things of all,
The ring, the token of the marriage is,
Of things in heaven and earth both thee to bless."

The motto to the Arms of the City of Glasgow, as described above, is "LET GLASGOW FLOURISH BY THE PREACHING OF THE WORD," but now-a-days the last half thereof is dropped, and the motto is simply—"Let Glasgow Flourish."

G.—THE HERRING-BANE CLUB, p. 173.

Glasgow is so celebrated for its Clubs that the late Dr. John Straug, for many years Chamberlain of the City, found enough of materials connected with twenty-six clubs, to enable him to write a very entertaining book regarding them, consisting of no less than 599 pages. In these, honourable mention is made of the following Clubs:— The Hodge-Podge, My Lord Ross's, the Morning and Evening, the Gaelic, the Accidental, the Face, the Grog, the Camperdown, the Meridian, the Pig, the Beefsteak or Tinkler, the Medical, the What-You-Please, the Cowl, the Gegg, the Banditti, the Packers and Every Night, the Post-Office, the French, the Anderston Social, the Duck, the Waterloo, the Shuna, the Sma' Weft, the Crow, &c.

It may be mentioned that although the "Herring-bane Club" does not figure in the above list under that name, a description of it is nevertheless not absent from the worthy doctor's pages. Like all the other Clubs named, however, it has long ceased to exist, the Forbes M'Kenzie Act having knocked it, in particular, on the head.

H—MERCANTILE FORGED BILLS, p. 201.

The many instances at the present day, recorded in the newspapers, of forgeries being committed by mercantile men of respectable standing, and even of title, may well warrant any one in believing that numerous crimes of the kind have been committed, without being found out. In the olden time, however, when hanging was the punishment for such, it is a singular fact, that bill forgeries were much more frequent than now; and the reason given for this anomaly is, that money lenders discounted such paper—knowing it to be forged—more readily than genuine paper, under the belief that "neck security" was the best of all guarantees for its being paid when due. Many good, and even romantic stories are told connected with such transactions. Indeed, the writer of this remembers an after-dinner conversation, where a worthy and kind-hearted host, to prove a bit of gossip he had been indulging in, regarding a brother merchant, then long dead, arose from the table, and after rummaging in a desk, produced a bill with the names of the said merchant and the host attached to it, respectively as drawer and acceptor—the latter being evidently a very clumsy forgery—while he exclaimed, "there, Sir, I paid that hundred pounds rather than allow the poor devil to be hanged, and his family disgraced and ruined!" And on the query being put to him:—"How did your friend recompense you for so great a boon?" He replied, "Recompense me! why Sir, he never forgave me; but died detesting me, twenty years ago!"

Commercial ethics present an extensive field for study and contemplation!

I.—INORDINATE BANK ACCOMMODATION, p. 238.

The circumstances related in chapters XLVII. and XLVIII. will, of course, be deemed by many as bordering upon, if not exceeding the extreme of possibility, and even of extravagant romance, allowable to any writer of fiction; but this will best be proved by what has appeared from time to time, since the stoppage of the Western Bank in 1857, in various forms, in the several newspapers of the day, published throughout the country.

The following is an excerpt from Lord Kinloch's "note" to his interlocuter of 8th January, 1861, in regard to an action brought against the directors of the Western Bank, when, in noticing the several points, his lordship, *inter alia*, says:—

"The advances brought next into controversy were those set forth in the 45th, 46th, and 47th articles of the condescendence, as advances made to the four firms therein specifically named.

"The substance of the articles, as the Lord Ordinary gathers it, is the following:—The four firms in question were, so far back as 1847, in bad circumstances and doubtful credit. To keep themselves afloat, they commenced and carried on a system of manufacture of accommodation bills, drawn for the most part on acceptors who were worthless; and in the case of two of the firms, on obscure persons, induced to grant their signatures by a small pecuniary consideration. The directors, who were in a position to know the condition of the parties, and the nature of the transactions, lent their aid to these firms by discounting their worthless paper to an enormous extent, the original bills being replaced, as they fell due, by others of the same description. This course of accommodation continued downwards until it exceeded a million in amount. The 46th article expressly says—'The directors and members of committee of management, during their respective tenures of office, knew, or by reasonable inquiry such as they were bound to make, might have readily and certainly known, that the four firms to whom the said advances were made, were, at the date of said advances, in bad and insolvent circumstances, or in such circumstances as to be quite unworthy of credit, and unable to repay the said advances, and that they were only temporarily kept up by the continued advances made to them as aforesaid, and enabled to carry on business and keep up false appearances by reason of the said continued advances, and by the adoption and pursuance of the system above-mentioned, whereby the said advances were continued and increased, and allowed to remain unpaid as aforesaid. The aggregate advances made as aforesaid, to the said four firms, at the period of the stoppage of the bank amounted to £1,212,379 17s. 6d., or thereby, and thus nearly absorbed the whole capital stock of the bank.'"

The following is an extract from the speech of Mr. Braddy, in a debate which took place on the affairs of the Western Bank of Scot-

land in the House of Commons on Friday, the 16th April, 1858, as
reported in the *Times* of next day :—

  "There was one Smith, a merchant in Glasgow, who, being ruined,
sent for a Mr. Monteith and told him he was about to become bankrupt. Monteith proceeded to the Western Bank and told the manager,
who said at once it must not be. He advanced accordingly £6000.
Mr. Monteith likewise availed himself of such facilities, and in a very
short period obtained discounts on bills to the extent of £124,000 from
said Bank. Another firm became bankrupt owing the Bank £383,000.
They had obtained signatures to bills through agents in London,
Liverpool, and Belfast, paying a commission to the parties who lent
their names. The number was 75, including milliners and tailors,
and other small tradesmen, many of them being females."

  The following is a condensed report of the examination in December,
1857, in the Bankruptcy Court, of one of the partners of a celebrated
firm in Glasgow — more celebrated, however, for the extent of its
failure and the inordinate amount of accommodation it received from
the Western Bank, than for anything else :—

  "The bankrupt deponed,—That he and his brothers commenced
business in 1834, with a capital of £1738. That they carried on with
various ups and downs till 1857, when they ended with liabilities
amounting to £423,535 13s. 1d., and assets estimated at £211,274 2s. 3d.,
the deficiency being £212,281 10s. 10d. That they employed in Ireland
30,000 hands; and that they built a warehouse and offices for the
accommodation of their business in Glasgow, which cost upwards of
£90,000.

  "On being further interrogated, the bankrupt deponed :—We first
found it necessary to have recourse to accommodation bills in 1845.
First year, to a limited extent, such as £8000, to £10,000; in 1849 it
had reached £16,000, or thereby; in 1850, £30,000; in 1854, £80,000;
in 1856, £188,000, and at the time of our suspension in October
1857, our total accommodation paper had reached £383,000, of
which the proportion for our own behoof was £359,000; our charge
for discounts in 1857 having amounted to £40,000. The bankrupt
further deponed that, in 1854, the number of parties giving accommodation (that is signing bills), was 10; in 1855, 13; in 1856, 20; and
in 1857, 75; likewise that many of these had no commission, but
the greater part had a commission varying from 1 to 1½ per cent. for
signing said bills.

  "Being further interrogated, the bankrupt depones :—Some of
these parties we did not know at all. About 32 we did not know,
excepting by the names on their bills, and from the information of
those who obtained them for us, who certified they were respectable
people. They had such names as 'Wagstaff,' 'Crow,' 'Popham,'
&c., and several were minors and females—

  *   *   *   *   *   *   *   *

  "It was chiefly at the Western Bank that these accommodation bills were discounted. We experienced no difficulty in getting them discounted until last summer, and then the desire was expressed by the Bank that we should reduce our discount account on the aggregate.

* * * * * * * *

"I am not aware that the Western Bank charged more than its ordinary rate of discount. We never directly nor indirectly gave more than the ordinary rate of interest.

* * * * * * * *

"The immediate cause of our suspending payments arose out of the investigation which the Western Bank set about making into several of their accounts in September last; up to that time, my firm was in its usual good credit.

* * * * * * * *

"Interrogated by Mr. Fleming—How does it happen that the bills granted for accommodation are taken for sums bearing odd shillings and pence, instead of round sums?

I know no particular reason.

Interrogated by Mr. Naismith—How long have you known Johnston and Kempfield?

I have known the firm for about three years, and the partner, Mr. Johnston for a long time.

Interrogated—Do you know if Kempfield is Mrs. Johnston? (laughter).

I am not aware that Kempfield is Mrs. Johnstone. I am, however, only speaking from recollection. The firm is not now solvent.

Were they ever, in your opinion, in a position to justify them in accepting to the amount of £20,000?

Depones—no.

* * * * * * * *

"I have known the firm of Pembarton & Seymour since the beginning of this year. The amount of their acceptances to us is about £18,000.

The only party in that firm that I know is Mr. Pembarton.

Interrogated — Do you know whether Seymour is Pembarton's wife?

Depones—I do not, (laughter). I cannot tell where their place of business is. It is in London.

Interrogated—Does E. Bosquet carry on an independent business; or is she a servant to Mr. Baines?

Depones—I understand her to carry on an independent business.

Depones further:—

I took no steps to ascertain the position of these parties myself, having sufficient confidence in the representations of our agents. I had no doubt they 'existed,' else I would not have offered their names to our bankers.

Interrogated—Out of the 75 acceptors, how many are solvent?

Depones—With the exception of the Belfast agent, and the London agent, all the acceptors have stopped payment."

The following letter, signed " *The Editor of the Belfast Mercantile Journal*," appeared in the city article of the *Times* of 15th December, 1857 :—

" Sir,—Your observations regarding the failures of certain banking establishments in Glasgow meet the general approbation of the mercantile community. Not many years since a certain gentleman became indebted to one of these banks to the extent of several hundred thousand pounds. When he was hauled up, it was found he had 'no assets,' and the bank therefore 'insured his life' to the extent of their debt, upon which they, of course, pay a very heavy annual tax. This gentleman called on the bank some time afterwards, and told one of the managers, ' I am offered a lucrative situation in Sierra Leone, but you know if I go out there, the policy will be vitiated. However, I must go, as I cannot starve.' What then was to be done? The same man is now comfortably living on the Continent, on an annuity granted him by this bank, which annuity, added to the premium of insurance, forms a nice little item in the expenses of the establishment. The amount involved in the above transaction was, I have good grounds for believing, no less than £350,000, and I am also further led to believe that this amount forms part of the assets of the bank."

The following is another condensed report of the examination of the partner of a bankrupt firm, which took place before the Sheriff in February, 1858 :—

"The bankrupt became a partner of the firm in 1844. Was then about twenty-two years of age. Had charge of the financial department. 'Our liabilities amount to £196,400 1s. 4d.; and our assets to £56,678 17s. 1d.; leaving a deficiency upon the abstract statement of £138,732 4s. 3d. Our total amount of accommodation bills is £187,812 1s. 9d. Referring to 22 parties in London who gave the accommodation, I only know 5 of them. Baines accommodated us with paper to the amount of £12,899 : we paid him £200 to £300 for said accommodation. He is now bankrupt. Cowell is in the lace trade. He accommodated us to the amount of £11,761 14s. : we paid him 1¼ per cent. commission for that accommodation. A laceman accommodated us to the extent of £6426; and another in the muslin trade to the extent of £16,205. The Western Bank, which really accommodated us by discounting these bills, put a finisher to us by its failure. The bills were, on an average, turned over every four months for upwards of two years previous to our bankruptcy.'"

K.—RICH CONVICTS, p. 296.

It is well known that many convicts transported to the Colonies, after getting "free pardons" or "tickets-of-leave" have made enormous fortunes in various ways, although the "yellow" of their old "toggery" continued to tinge prejudicially the brightest hues of their subsequent clothing and adornments in the eyes of the free Colonists. One convict is still remembered, who, as a private bill discounter, accumulated a fortune of several hundred thousand pounds, although he could not write, and had to substitute a cross for his name. Another as a publican, amassed, and left nearly a hundred thousand pounds; while fortunes of from fifty to eighty thousand pounds were not considered unusual for *respectable* convicts to acquire.

L.—Royal Blood, p. 297.

The following letter signed "Nemo," appeared in a number of the *Glasgow Herald*, published in 1864, on a discussion that took place regarding the emblazonments that appear in some memorial windows, then recently placed in the Cathedral :—

"Sir,—As a Glasgow man, and interested in all that relates to its local history, I cannot say that I approve of your suggestion that texts of Scripture should be substituted for the names in the windows in Lauder's Crypt. Suppose these names taken collectively do indicate a genealogy, what then? Why should that be objectionable in this obscure crypt which is tolerated and approved in the principal windows of the Cathedral. In one prominent window, a Mr. ——, a Glasgow man, exhibits no less than thirty-two shields, which any one at a glance may see indicates not only a descent from the Royal Family of Scotland, but a descent from three of the Archbishops of Glasgow. Again, in a still more important window, one of our worthy city Members exhibits arms indicating descent from Buchanan of that ilk—which he is justly entitled to do, and has no doubt the sanction of the Lord Lyon for it—while every student of history, and especially of Glasgow history, knows that this family is directly descended from the kings of the Stuart line. I could point to many other instances in the Cathedral where the shields so prominently exhibited necessarily imply a claim to Royal descent. Nor is there anything extraordinary in this to any one acquainted with Scottish history. It is notorious that, of all nations in the world, there is none where so many of the private gentry are descended from the Royal Family as in Scotland, and it is equally well known that, of all the cities in the kingdom, none contains so many families so descended, as Glasgow. Look at Buchanan of Auchmar's History, which contains the genealogy of probably not less than fifty private families of the name of Buchanan, many of them belonging to Glasgow, all traced to King Robert I. Look, again, at that well-known book, "M'Ure's History of Glasgow," where he gives the descent from the Royal Family of Stuart of so many Glasgow families, that to enumerate them would fill half of one of your columns. Let me just name a few, taken at random.

These are the families of Young, Orr, Paton, Bell, Maxwell, Morison, Stark, Hamilton, MacEwan, and MacUre; with Stirlings, Murdochs, Smiths, Cochranes, Cross's, Crawfords, Lukes, Bogles, Knox's, Campbells, and a host of others, all or most of whom have now their representatives living among us. These are all strictly Glasgow families, and M'Ure gives the genealogy of each, link by link, from one or other of the Stuart kings. He does so, as Buchanan does in his work, because he thought it would be interesting to the Glasgow people. To me it is interesting, and if the windows in Lauder's Crypt do, as is said, represent one of these old Glasgow lines of descent, I cannot, I confess, see what objection can be stated to it. To withdraw the names would be to obliterate all trace of the genealogy, and this, I think, would be regretted by many besides myself, who know nothing of Mr. ——, and take no interest in his genealogy, except as a specimen of a class of descents of which our native city contains so many."

One of the principal progenitors of Glasgow families, claiming to have royal blood in their veins, was Archibald Lyon, a younger son of the Earl of Strathmore, who came to Glasgow in the 16th century and married Margaret Dunlop, thereafter settling down as a merchant of the place, trading to France, Poland, and Holland : in which pursuits he acquired a large fortune. The Earl of Strathmore, the father of the said Archibald Lyon, was the direct descendant of the Lord of Glammis, who, in 1374, married Lady Jean, daughter of King Robert II.; and how that marriage was brought about, is thus quaintly narrated in "Crawfurd's Notes on Buchanan":—

"John Lyon, a depender of James, first Earl of Crawfurd, by the Earl's recommendation, became first Secretary to King Robert, and thereafter Chancellour; and having privately begotten the King's daughter with child, the Earl of Crawfurd so brought the matter about, that the King gave him the lady in marriage, and the lands of Glammis in heritage for portion. Thereafter, the Earl being offended with this John Lyon for unthankfulness, killed him near to Forfar."

GLASGOW: PRINTED BY ROBERT ANDERSON, 85 QUEEN STREET.

www.ingramcontent.com/pod-product-compliance
Lightning Source LLC
Chambersburg PA
CBHW021033030726
47496CB00006B/1516